DECLAN C

SILVATICI

1066: The English Resistance

STORYDONKEY

StoryDonkey

The Loft, 2A St Patricks Road, Dalkey,

Co Dublin, A96 HD40, Ireland

Copyright © 2022 Declan Croghan

All rights reserved.

ISBN: 978-1-7396715-0-1

Declan Croghan has asserted his right to be identified
as the author of this Work in accordance with the
Copyright, Designs and Patents Act 1988

All rights reserved. No part of this publication may be
reproduced, stored in a retrieval system,
or transmitted in any form or by any means,
electronic, mechanical, photocopying, recording,
or otherwise, without the prior permission
of both the copyright owner
and the above publisher of this book.

About the Author

Declan Croghan is a playwright and screenwriter known for creating shows such as *The Body Farm* for the BBC, *Life of Crime* for ITV and *Murder Prevention* for Channel 5. He has written multiple episodes of British primetime television for shows such as *Waking the Dead*, *Where the Heart is*, *Ballykissangel*, *Taggart* and *Ripper Street*. He has just completed writing on three seasons of *Vikings: Valhalla* for Netflix. This is his first novel.

For Lulu & Heddie

1

KALLÍN

He awoke to a sharp shock of cold air as his mother stripped away his bedding delivering a quick set of hot stinging smacks, "Kallín-son! Wake up! Up!"

In that moment he knew his recurring nightmare was coming true; the world was ending.

Mother grabbed him by the ears and looked straight into him, "We're going to have to run…"

His mind raced with questions that he didn't want answers to as he set about trying to find his clothing that was strewn about somewhere in the darkness of their tent. Tripping about like a dancing drunk, his lanky teenage limbs outdid each other to be clumsy.

She grabbed and stopped him, "Listen!"

The night filled with horror: roaring monsters and screaming people, his people, the Rohán.

"What's happening, Mother?"

He hoped that she would whisper to him, *go back to sleep, Kallín-son, it's just your bad dream.* Instead, she urged, "Take this," and pushed the handle of a sword into his fist, "It's your time now."

"My battle blade?" He gripped the leather-bound handle. He'd made many an offering of rabbits and fish to Morrigan the Mother God of war, imploring her to let him be presented with it. He was well trained and of age to become a warrior, having lived through sixteen winters. But as much as he had wished to get his battle blade, he didn't want to get it like this. He remembered Old-Mallan's advice: *be careful what you wish for* ... Then he was sure, *It's all my fault!*

Mother pushed him to the flap of the tent.

He protested, "I'm naked and—"

She warned him, "Listen! Don't be stoppin nor lookin backwards! D'ya hear me now? Do ya?"

"Yes, Mother. But—"

She shoved a shield at him, "Take this. Strap it tight. Keep it close. Stay low. Stay fast. Stay—"

"I know. I know all that. But I'm buck naked! "

She slapped him rough-handed into his face, like she would slap anyone, hitting him right across his gob, splitting his lip, "Shut up the slobbering! You're a warrior now. You've a shield and a battle blade! The first of the Rohán fought naked like this! Tis all you need for to fight! And if you go home this night, then you will sit by the fire with our people and you will tell them your warrior's story. Do you understand me?"

He understood. "I love you, Mother."

"I love you too, Kallín-son."

She turned him about-face and pushed him out into the night, "Head for the forest!"

"Can you run?" He looked at her large pregnant belly.

"I can run as well as you. Go!"

He exited the tent into the chaos and saw that the attack on the camp was moving in from the west, from the river, under the cover of the fog. Then in the glare of the sentinel torch-fires, he caught a clear sighting of their attackers.

Norsemen...

Terrified little-ones scurried all around him, running, ducking and weaving. But he was not pulled into the current. His mind cleared away the residue of sleep, and quickly figured that the Norsemen had landed in boats, in great numbers, possibly hundreds of them, and were now attacking fast. But they had not yet penetrated the inner circle of the camp. They didn't know the lay of the Rohán's intricate and deadly defences that were now injuring them and slowing them. A handful of the old-ones formed a defensive firing line, shooting volleys of arrows into the snared Norsemen. But he knew this was not the place to make a stand: They must get to the forest.

From behind him, Mother said, "The east path. Quickly!"

Mother and son took off running between the tents that were laid out in a series of circles, each tent interlocking with criss-crossed-wattle-pickets to create a great concentric maze that bought them valuable minutes to escape to the safety of the forest.

He watched the flaming torches of the Norsemen circumventing the camp defences; he shouted to Mother, "They mean to surround the camp!"

Mother saw another part of their plan, "And they mean to cut us off from the forest!"

Every Rohán, young and old, knew to make for the safety of the forest where they were at their deadliest and most feared, and where no enemy would dare to follow them into its dark interior. As the Norse torches gathered in numbers blocking the path to the forest, Kallín's mind raced faster than he ran. He'd been haunted by his recurring nightmare of monsters coming to kill his people. Many a dark hour of the night had been spent imagining his escape in various different ways. He knew exactly how he was going to get both himself and his mother to the safety of the forest.

There's a badger run through the long grass that'll make a good shortcut.

"This way, Mother."

She followed him off the well-beaten path and took to a small trail only wide enough for one person. She ran tightly behind him.

"This is a good path," she told him as they travelled in the cover of the shoulder-high-reeds that kept them out of the sightlines of the Norsemen. She added, "Good cover, well done, Kallín-son."

He liked her praise; it warmed him up inside. She didn't give him much praise, but admittedly, he didn't normally do all that much that was praiseworthy. He could turn his hand to most things. He was middling at sword work and archery, at setting traps and making fire, but he didn't excel at anything in particular. His teachers said that he had the quality of an 'all-rounder'. In Rohán terms that meant he would be a fair to middling warrior but he would never distinguish himself in battle … and he most certainly would never have a warriors story told about him by the Seanachaí.

I'll try harder, he pledged to no god in particular. *If we live through this, I'll be a better son, and Mother'll be proud of me. I'll join Father in the best of the battle-work, and make plenty of coin. Make a story worth telling by the fire.*

Bursting full of the best of intentions and fortified with an iron resolve, he ran fast, shield to shoulder, blade cocked at the ready, head down, charging like a front-line storm-warrior! Suddenly, a creature as big as a bear slammed into his shield and launched him ... airborne...

For moments, the world spun around him, no up nor down, just swirling black air, until he landed face-first somewhere in the long reeds! Winded. No time to wonder about it. He regained himself and got his bearings.

Be ready.

He readied his blade, hugged his shield, and eased through the reeds ... back to the path.

Mother?

He looked into the night for her, nothing but the dark. A terrible empty void opened up in his heart that threatened to swallow him into the abyss.

Be silent.

He broke that rule and called out into the night, "Mother!"

Immediately a huge dark shape climbed from the ground, forming into a bearskin covered beserker, snarling, cursing, continually growing from the darkness to a height of more than twenty hands high. The eyes of the huge man-beast searched the night, found Kallín, focused on him as the predator on prey, growled, and in a great roar of fury charged at him!

Kallín had imagined facing a beserker warrior many times, and he'd always won his battles with great flair while waving to the cheers of an adoring crowd. His mother was usually somewhere in his victory dream, glowing at him with pride, and bragging about him to other women. But this was not like any of those imagined acts of heroism. The beserker in front of him was beyond any kind of monster he had dared to create in his mind. It looked like four Norsemen moulded into one by some dark magic to make a demon, adorned with two huge arms, each one wider than Kallín's torso, and so long that the huge fists hung past the knees ... But it was the enormous misshapen head that was truly disturbing to look at. It was the size of at least six normal heads, and a great big hang-jaw on him. As for his eyes, they were sunken, small, and beady and put Kallín in mind of two piss-holes in the snow. Whatever kind of creature the beserker's mother was, it was not a human. All of that said, the aspect of the beserker that gave Kallín the most fear was the stench of him that was a heady mix of stale piss, sweat and blood: The reek of battle.

Be brave.

The young Rohán planted his feet wide apart, one foot forward, shield to his shoulder, blade at the ready; he would make his stand here: win or go home.

I am always homeward bound.

Then another option opened up in his mind. One he had not imagined in his countless victories.

Run!

He reasoned, *Mother's got a hiding spot in the reeds. She's safe. Lead the beast away from her. Run to the forest!*

Loosening his grip on his shield strap while spinning himself in a perfect pirouette, he launched the deadly disc at the charging berserker, and keeping a continuous motion, he took off running! A howl came from behind him. His shield had found its target. Sensing an unseen danger in the darkness ahead of him, he threw himself through a gap in the bush, landed flat on his back and skidded down the soft wet ground that banked steeply to the marshland. Plummeting faster and faster out of control, and gaining much too much speed, he dug his heels into the soft ground, popping himself upright into a run keeping up his flat-out-speed into the treacherously boggy marsh water.

But the young Rohán would not be consumed by the quagmire. He knew all the good places to step and hop. He was glad to be bare-skinned-naked now, skipping over the surface like a smooth flat-stone, and travelling without the hinderance of clothing like the first of the Rohán who walked the world looking for a fight. Behind him, the bloodied giant berserker came to an abrupt halt, hip deep in humiliation and spewing futile Norse curses after him.

Reaching the safety of the dry ground on the other side, Kallín fired back a few of his own curses at the bogged-down giant, "Ya dirty gowl of smelly norsedog bastard! May ya get the cursed black bollox rot! May your lying tongue turn fat in your gob and choke ya! May your gunner eyes swell up until they pop out of your big huge ugly head! May you get the scutters so bad that you shite out your beating heart into a bucket!"

It felt good to roar insults into the night and make gestures. The fear left him.

He thought, *Their boats are beached on the bank of the river. They'll not want to be raiding too far inland. The big gowl of a norsedog will not bother to wade his hairy arse through the bog after me.*

Then Kallín learned that he was wrong.

The grunting and cursing continued. Louder. Closer. His pursuer was not giving up on chasing him. The young Rohán had a new problem. Dozens of flaming torches fanned out along the way into the forest: He was cut off.

There are no problems in battle, only solutions. He made a new plan, *I'll get deep into the bramble tunnels. Hide. Wait it out. That big gowl will not fit in after me.*

He quickly crossed the weir, deftly climbing up the bank at its steepest part then running for the safety of the sprawling bramblefield; weighing his chances as he ran, *I've no gold. I'm not worth the chase.*

The balance of probability was in his favour.

But any hope that he fostered of the giant Norseman giving up was snuffed out when he heard his pursuer roar, "Thrall!"

The Norse word for ... *Slave...*

The young Rohán knew in that instant that these Norsemen were not normal vikingrs looking for an easy pillage, they were the most feared kind of vikingrs: Slavers.

Dropping onto his hands and knees, he crawled quickly into the thicket of brambles, scurrying blindly through the narrow tunnels of knotted vines, his naked body paying the toll on the worst of the thorns as he weaved his way deeper into the heart of the dense warren, into its deepest part. When he was too far in for the beserker to follow him, he stopped. His flesh screamed. He offered up the pain in a silent prayer, *Morrigan, Mother God of war, I, Kallín of the Rohán, do give you all this pain in offering and I pledge to you the blood of my first killing in your honour for the favour of making the gowling norsedog that is after me get peeled to the bone if he comes in the bramble. May he also have his eyes taken out please Mother God, and if you have the time to make him suffer some more, may he also get his bollox wrapped in great snares of thorns. Also, Mother God, will you—* His holy thoughts were interrupted by a slight movement in the darkness. Close. He readied his blade, held his breath, listened ... heard breathing ... sharp and afraid, coming and going in gulps.

Not a norsedog...

He ventured a whisper, "Who's there?"

The breathing stopped suddenly. A whisperer answered, "Me."

Hearing a familiar voice filled his belly with warmth and gave him a great wave of comfort throughout his being. He whispered back, "Ríona-girl?"

Ríona moved to him. "Kallín-boy. Some gowling night, huh?"

She immediately made an effort to not show any fear, and he did likewise, becoming almost casual.

"Gowling is right," he said.

They shared the familiar closeness of two pups that roughed and tumbled together, ate together, grew together and trained as warriors together. He was glad it was her. Ríona was a really good fighter. Better than him. He asked her, "What weapons have you got, so?"

"My spear only. They were on us too fast to stand ground. There's maybe a few hundred of the smelly gowlers. How did they get past the gowling sentries? Tell me that, will you?"

"Don't know," he told her. "Any more of the pack in here with you?"

"Maybe," she said, "I saw Foxy and Una goin at them with bows and arrows."

He wasn't ready to hear the names of friends. It caught him a little. But he dug down deeper into himself, and swallowed it.

"Making a stand were they?" He asked.

"I think so." She told him, "Out on the path they were."

"Fools." He was angry with them, "They'll be done out there for sure. We should be all making for the forest where we belong."

"Too gowling right, boy," she agreed, "then some gowling seeing-to the norsedogs would get, huh? D'you think?"

She was feeling him out. How afraid was he? As much as she was?

He just kept on thinking about his battle training, *The fallen have gone, don't get anchored to them, move on, fight forward, find a way to victory.* He told her, "I'd say if we could get a dozen of us into the forest, we'd cut them to shreds and send them away with their tails between their legs for sure."

"Can you imagine if our warriors was here now? Huh?"

He nodded, "I think they knew our warriors are away at battle."

"D'you think?"

He added, "I think these norsedogs were up north fighting in the battle too, and they lost … and now they are sailing home fast, raiding our camp on the way for easy slaves."

She agreed, "That would be the cut of the norsedogs, sure enough, a gowled and ill-bred people that they are. I heard that they make themselves with animals."

He thought that much was true, judging by the great abomination that had chased him here. For that creature could only have been made by offending the natural order of the world. He felt that the beast was thinking about him, about catching him, and thinking about nothing else. He had heard warriors talk about the beserker. It was said that when the beast is set on a man, that it will not stop until it has killed him. It gave him a sick feeling in the pit of his stomach. He tried not to think of it getting its hands on him and tearing his body limb from limb. He wanted to tell Ríona, but he dared not spread his fear. It is a poison. He would tell her the story when this was all over and they were safe again by the fire.

She sensed the fear growing in him and interrupted his thoughts, "But here, Kallín-boy, how did they get past the sentries? Not even in the gowling fog should that happen. Hey? Tell me that."

She was angry again. That was good. He fed off it and subdued the terrible premonition that the beast berserker was going to get him.

"That... I don't know," he told her.

She listened to the night, "Why has it gone so quiet?"

He'd never seen a slave-raid before, but he knew that there were two stages to capturing slaves. First comes the killing of all those who have fight in them, and then comes the rounding up of all those who are compliant and will make slaves. The Norsemen had completed the first part of their raid. There was no more resistance to them. They were most likely taking water now and resting before they rounded up their bounty, from which they would pick the best and fill their boats, and then they would slaughter the rest. Kallín did not share this with Ríona.

"Maybe they're gone," he told her. It was a stupid thing to say. But maybe a false hope was better than no hope at all.

Her spirits lifted right away. She examined him in the darkness, "Are you buck naked there, Kallín-boy?"

There was a jibe in her voice. He liked it. It was nice to step back from the pure fear. He told her, "I'd no time to dress, did I?"

She made a little laugh, "I'm the same way." And she settled into her normal banter, "Don't be gombeen gawkin at me now. Don't want your eyes poppin out of your head!"

He made his best effort to be a foil for her. It felt normal, "I can see nothing. Anyways, even if I could see something, sure I'd not be bothered by anything you have, Ríona-girl," he told her.

She nudged him in the ribs with her elbow, "Go-wan I'm only messin with you, sure. You can look at me if you want to, boy."

For a moment they were forgetting that Norsemen had just destroyed their camp.

"I seen you already," he told her.

"That was in the start of the summer. They've got bigger now ...

Have a feel if you want."

She waited.

He waited.

Whatever was happening between them, it was not meant to happen here.

Not now.

The night was then torn by a long shrill of agony that put an end to any hope they had that the Norsemen had gone.

He said, "It's all goin to shite out there, isn't it?"

She nodded, spat, and told him, "Tis well gowled up." After a moment she went on, "Better to be naked for fighting anyways. Isn't it? The first of the Rohán fought naked, do you know that? Huh?"

Everybody knows that, he thought, but he simply answered, "I know … They fought without armour because they knew no fear."

"That right? No fear. Gowl me. Didn't know that bit of it." She nodded her head in agreement with herself, "That's the truth of it now. They knew no fear. Them was the true warriors, I'm tellin you." Then she asked him, "What way are you fixed for a weapon, so?"

"I have my battle blade."

"Gowl yourself off."

"What…?" he asked her.

Her voice raised in an outraged whisper, "Your battle blade? Already? But you're not a warrior yet."

"My mother gave it to me."

"That doesn't matter, boy. You haven't had your trials, no more than I have, sure."

He argued, "Well, if I wet my blade tonight to kill a norsedog, won't I be a warrior then by Morrigan's rite of battle?"

She thought about that, and agreed, "You will. That's for sure," she added, "And I might use my spear to make a kill of a norsedog myself … and that way we will both be made warriors this night by the Mother God of war. Huh? You think?"

"I think I like that."

More tortured screams drifted in the cold air.

She said, "Hear that?"

"I hear it."

"Did it sound like Foxy or Una to you?"

He was starting to identify the screams too, but he told her, "I don't want to know who it is."

She knew he was right. Every warrior knows that you lose friends in battle. You can't stop the fight and go to them and start crying about it. She needed to think more like him. More like a warrior. She told him, "That won't be me ... Wont. Be. Me. I'll not be sport for the gowling norsedogs."

"They want slaves now," he told her.

She thought about that. They both knew that if they walked out to the Norsemen without carrying arms, and surrendered, that they would probably not be killed, owing to their youth, and they would be taken as slaves. This was the crossroad, this was where the big decision was to be made: slave or warrior?

He said, "I'd rather go home."

She said, "I'm with you. I'll tell you now, boy...I'm surely homeward bound."

Kallín agreed, "We will get away together or we will go home together this night," he took her hand and added, "but we will make our first kill this night, and then go home as warriors."

Her spirits lifted. She squeezed his hand tightly, and sighed, "To go home as a warrior ... that would be wonderful. Wouldn't it? Hey, boy?"

They both imagined all their people waiting to welcome them home like heroes. A great feast would be thrown in their honour and all would gather around the fire to listen to their warrior story of how they killed the Norsemen.

"It surely would be," he agreed.

They entwined their fingers and said the Rohán motto together, "I am always homeward bound."

Kallín heard a new sound that was much quieter than the screaming, "Listen…"

Under the cacophony of screaming, he made out numerous tiny sounds closer to them in the bramble ... barely sounds at all; like a cloud of fluttering moths. As the sound formed in the air, the pair realised that it was the frantic tittawitting of terrified whispers.

She whispered to him, "We are not the only ones to think that the bramble is a good place to be hiding in."

She was right. The bramble was full of young Rohán that, for now, were unknown to the Norsemen. But for how long would they hold their nerve? The answer came quickly. One of the little-ones started crying ... loudly.

As with wolf pups, when one starts howling, it sets off the others.

Kallín pointed out, "Well, them gowling norsedogs is here looking for young slaves. Now that they know of a few dozen hiding in here, they'll swarm around the bramble now."

Ríona suggested, "We can make a run for it to the forest. What d'you think?"

"They're waiting for that."

She agreed, "You're right. What's the plan, so?"

He was surprised, "You're askin me?"

She shrugged, "Your father is Chieftain. So you have some sense passed into you from him … and your mother is said to have been a great warrior. You've got the sense for battle bred into you that way … well, you got more sense than me anyways. Huh? So, hatch a plan there, boy."

He briefly thought about his father leading the fighting in whatever battle they were hired into in the north. But he pushed the thought out of his mind for fear that he would not be able to think of anything else. He said, "We'll wait."

Ríona wasn't impressed, "That's your plan? Wait?"

He reminded her, "Sometimes no plan is the best plan of all."

She shook her head, "Don't start with all that battle-craft shite. It does me gowling head in, so it does. I'm not good for thinking. I'm good for the fighting. You know? Give me a weapon and just tell me where and when…" She smiled at him, "But you're a chieftain's son, sure enough, with your fancy head on your fine shoulders. We'll wait so, boy. C'mon and get close to me for some heat, will you?"

He nudged closer to her and she nudged closer to him. Their bodies touched and immediately a great heat was generated between them. She put an arm around him and pulled him in tighter to her, and told him, "We'll get more heat lying together," and in the same breath she eased herself back, taking him with her. His body was suddenly burning. Everything about her became fascinating to him; she eclipsed the night and everything in it. There was only her soft skin and round curves. She pulled him to her so that he lay upon her, and she wrapped her strong legs around him, locking him there.

She whispered, "I claim you."

He whispered, "I claim you."

"We are coupled," she said, and kissed him hard.

His nature was to be tentative.

Hers was not.

She told him, "Harder."

He abandoned himself.

She consumed him.

They forgot about the Norsemen, about the horror, about the cold, about the pains in their limbs, about all their doubts for the future. They dwelt in that perfect moment like the first two of their kind to walk in the world … until the perfection was cracked by the most ancient of warning sounds that sent a primal shudder through their entire being: the whip-cracks of dry bramble being chewed by a hungry fire.

The Norsemen's plan was a simple one: If they could not enter the bramble then they would burn it.

Panic spread throughout the warren quicker than the fire. Wailing in sorrow turned to screaming in fear. Little-ones took off running blindly into the night in every direction.

Kallín took Ríona by the hand, "Wait…"

He was washed over again by a sudden calm. This is what they were trained for. He reminded himself of his teaching; *do not add to the problem with another problem. Be patient. Allow the enemy to make their mistakes. Let them reveal their plan to you.* He told himself, *The norsedogs will soon have their hands full.*

The crimson inferno flowed towards them, a living creature, inhaling all the cold air from the night, then holding the world in a suffocating limbo, until a moment later, furiously exhaling its rage in screaming tongues of searing flame.

Ríona warned him, "We'll be burned alive for sure, Kallín-boy."

But she did not let go of his hand; she trusted him, she held firm by his side in the face of death.

Only when Kallín feared that they would be swallowed by flame, did he make his move, "For the forest. Run. Now!"

The pair ran hand-in-hand, naked and blind, through the black smoke and thorns, choking, listening to the screams, then adjusting their direction to veer away from the danger. Then — in a moment — they were out of the burning brambles and in the clearing… The open ground between them and the forest shimmered like a mirage of freedom. At the edge of the darkness, flame shadows danced like a battalion of demons rejoicing in the horror of it all, mocking all who burned in the inferno. All around were Norsemen with their hands full of screaming little-ones who had run from the fire and into their clutches. The Norsemen's eyes darted to the new prey breaking from cover. They instantly dropped their little prey and turned their full attention on Kallín and Ríona.

Slaving was the same as all other forms of hunting; some prey are trophies. The two young hand-holding Rohán were a highly valued catch for a Norse slaver who would get a high price for them as a breeding pair.

A sharp tug on Kallín's hair tail almost wrenched him off his feet. He knew it was the monster berserker that had a firm hold of him. In that same moment the young Rohán stopped thinking and let his training take over. He'd been drilled in combat skills since he could walk. The constant mind-numbing repetition of fighting-moves trained his body to act independently, freeing him from the cumbersome task of having to make time-consuming decisions. This instilled muscle memory had the lethal result in combat of enabling him to move quicker than his thoughts through the process of reflex. Every defence and attack move became an unconscious part of his nature, like walking, running or breathing. And so, without a thought, in the same moment that he felt the pull on his hair, he kicked back into the berserker's knee and heard the satisfying crack as it snapped, and joint gave way, bending where it should not, to beserker's roar of pain. In the same fluid movement, as the great beast collapsed, the young Rohán spun around slicing with his battle-blade in a great battlecry!

"Rohán!"

The ferocious arc of the blade sliced opened the beserker's throat, cutting off his fabled Norse battle roar into the wet hiss of his last desperate breath!

The world stopped. The great beast-bred Norse abomination fumbled with his fingers over his gaping wound in a futile effort to stem the violent gushes of hot ejaculating blood.

Kallín wished that his father and mother could see him now, shining red in the victory gleam of his first blood, wetting his blade and making his entry through Morrigan's battle-rite into the ranks of the Rohán Warriors.

Ríona roared, "Rohán!" and she stabbed the half dead man-beast in the heart with her spear, so that she shared the kill, and also made her journey into the warrior ranks.

Kallín shouted to her, "Run!"

The two blood covered Rohán turned and ran to freedom.

The slave hunt changed in its nature. The young Rohán had killed one of the Norsemen's number. Now they were a great prize indeed. A competition ensued. Wagers were shouted. The Norsemen began egging and jeering each other on, fanning out in a circle, preventing the two young Rohán from escaping into the forest.

But Kallín and Ríona were not an easy catch. With skilled footwork, they weaved and dodged like a pair of hares outwitting the hounds, working their way ever closer to the trees, closer to freedom, until in a breath, Kallín knew that they would make it to safety.

Ríona sensed freedom too.

Kallín shared a smiled with his running companion just as an arrow hit her in the leg, and took her down.

"Kallín!" She called out, "Gowl on it! No!"

Kallín stopped, turned and skipped to one side as the sharp breath of an arrow glanced his skin and passed through the space where he had stood a heartbeat ago. He instinctively dropped to the ground beside Ríona, and eyeballed the smiling Norse archer, and thought, *What I wouldn't give to have my bow with me now. You would be doing a jig of death with an arrow in your bollox.* Pulling Ríona to her feet, he helped her to cover, taking the weight off her wounded leg. She cried out! A second arrow penetrated deep into her torso. The Norsemen were no longer trying to wound them; they would rather kill their prey than see it escape. Blood spouted from Ríona's mouth, and they both knew that a vital part of her was hit.

She cried, "I'm done, Kallín-boy."

"You're not," he lied.

She pleaded, "Send me home."

He assured her, "We're going home together."

She grabbed his hair, "No! You run, d'you hear me, Kallín-boy? Kill them later. Run now — Live!"

She kissed him hard on the mouth.

Her blood tasted hot and sweet.

She told him, "Send me home!"

A Rohán cannot go home by their own hand.

He watched the Norsemen coming closer, slowly, leering, laughing and taunting them. He knew what they would do to Ríona if he left her alive. He looked into her eyes and whispered to her, "I am always homeward bound. Go home, Ríona. Go home."

He pushed his blade into her heart as swiftly and cleanly as he could. Her body turned into a lifeless corpse in his arms.

She went home.

He was alone.

Taking up Ríona's spear, he roared furiously into the night, "Archer! Hear me Archer!"

The Norsemen stopped to listen to the roaring coming from the forest …

Kallín roared from the darkness, "Archer! You die by the spear of Ríona! Warrior of the Rohán!"

The Norsemen watched in disbelief as the spear came whistling straight and true from the darkness and skewered the archer through the heart, killing him where he stood.

They did not dare pursue their prey any further into the forest.

Kallín ran into the darkness.

I am always homeward bound.

2

THE ATHELING

In the finest library assembled in Christendom, a twelve-year-old boy, Edgar the Atheling, was being schooled by an old monk.

"Fear your own mistakes over those of your enemy," Brother Matthew quoted in his warbling voice that was worn-out from a lifetime of lecturing to students. He took a long, deep, wheezy breath into his equally worn-out lungs and asked his student, "Who advised that, my lord?"

"Pox on the Greek philosophers," replied the young Prince.

Brother Matthew saw half of the answer in the impish reply, and asked his student, "Pox on any Greek philosopher in particular?"

"Poxy Thucydides," the Prince told the old monk, and qualified his statement on the Greek philosopher of war, "but he is far from the worst of them. I find all the Greeks wearisome with their endless thinking about thinking."

"Very good, my lord," Matthew placated his student, "thinking about thinking can be taxing."

Edgar weighed his wily old tutor and caught a searing glint in his ancient eyes that peered out from under his overgrown eyebrow bushes. "Touché old monk," he told him, "that was well put. I liked the flow and skip of it."

The young Prince then walked away and stood at the great window of the library that looked out onto the bustling Hungarian Royal Court below. He then went into one of his performances, lowering his voice so as to project it from his diaphragm, and to speak like an Actor! He began slowly, "How I long to be out in the world!" He filled the moment with as much melancholy as could be rammed up the arse of a line of poetry. Then he leaned on the window frame in a tragic pose that he had much practiced, holding one hand to his brow and the other up to the heavens; he made a great sigh and declared, "I will jump out of this poxy window, and maybe … I will fly away like a bird." He let his voice sing high for that part, and then lowered it in a great vocal plunge for the next part, finding the most tragic tone he could muster, "Or is it my plight to plummet in first flight?" He dropped to his knees, "Thus…" and leaving a generous beat for emphasis, he continued in a thoughtful but tortured way, "me being a hatchling spat unready from the maw of the unloving nest…" He remained kneeling and carefully picked up the imaginary little dead bird, and with a great contortion of his face to make it even more tragic, he went on, "and there be ended…" For his finalé, he threw both hands out wide in a great gesture of the crucified Christ, "… on the poxy unforgiving ground!"

Margaret, his elder sister by six years, looked up from her book, "Will you stop playing at being a thespian, Edgar, and please find a new curse word."

In the gifts of birth, Margaret had won the double bounty of intelligence and beauty. From the time she was an infant, people who looked upon her were truly surprised by her large dark eyes, delicate features, and radiant skin. As she grew in the safe sanctuary of the inner circle of the Hungarian Royal Court, her visage became a thing to see to such an extent that she could not venture anywhere without people stopping to stare at her. She constantly needed a guard to prevent them from touching her. As she got older, what she wore became the fashion of the Court. If she made up her hair a certain way on Sunday, it would be the way to have it by Monday. While such intense attention might have overwhelmed most young women, Margaret took it in her stride. For like a child who is born cursed with a hump grows accustomed to people staring at her in pity or disgust, so too does one who is born with beauty become accustomed to people looking upon her with pleasure, and as she grows older, desire.

Edgar asked her, "What good curses have you got then, sister?"

Margaret smiled at him, "I will not be baited into profanity, little brother."

Edgar turned his attentions to his tutor-monk and asked him,

"Brother Matthew, there must be some rancid old curses locked away in the monastic vaults?" The boy jumped into a fighting pose, "Let's have a flitting duel!"

Matthew demurred, "Alas, my lord, cursing is a subject that I am not an authority on. Nor do I have any craft for flitting."

Edgar was suddenly filled with faux disappointment, "What is the point of a poxy language if it does not have the verbal weaponry in it to be offensive? Are we to spend our whole time going about the world politely with not one good insult in us to throw at our enemies?"

Margaret called to the old monk, "Brother Matthew, let him go to the barracks and play swords with the soldiers. Tire him out."

"Yes," Edgar agreed, "soldiers have good curses. No craft of the language of course, on account of their low birth and ignorance and so on, but they are blunt, and dirty, and offensive all the same."

Brother Matthew raised his hands in protest, "I would like to do nothing more than that, my lady, but King Solomon himself has instructed me to intensify the young Prince's preparations, and the houseguards have put extra precautions around your brother's person. He is confined to his quarters."

Margaret carefully closed her book. The monk had already given away enough, she asked him, "King Solomon himself, you say?"

"Yes, my lady…"

Margaret read the growing unease in the monk's old body, and asked him, casually, not wanting to send him into flight like a startled pigeon, "My Brother's time approaches?"

Brother Matthew lowered his eyes and looked about the floor as if searching for a lost thought that may have fallen from his head, "I em ... This is not for me to say, my lady. I must go to..."

Margaret implored him politely, "Stay, Brother Matthew." And she looked to Edgar, with a nod for him to be active in the matter.

Edgar joined his sister, "Yes. Stay, Brother Matthew, please," and then he poured out a plea with a dollop of treacle and over-acted sincerity, "I do so much enjoy your tutoring of me, and I do miss your holy sweet presence so when you are not near me."

Margaret gave her brother a sharp look, *don't overdo it.*

Matthew, like a lame old dog, was steadfastly limping on his gout-ridden feet to the door.

Margaret moved like a breeze from her chair and intercepted him softly, "Brother Matthew."

She gently brought him to a halt with her slender hand on his shoulder, and spoke in a soft clean tone, enunciating her words as crisply as frost-covered leaves cracking under foot, so that the old monk would understand that she was serious, "You have been with the House of Wessex since we were exiled from England ... Your first loyalty is surely not to the Hungarian King?"

Matthew stopped and looked in a sudden realisation at the beautiful English Princess whom he had known since her birth, and indeed, had baptised. But it was not until that moment that he realised she was no longer a young precocious girl, but had grown into a politically astute young future queen. He also knew that she was to be his true legacy: that she would be important in the world, and have a great hand in the affairs of England.

He told her, "The King of England is on his deathbed, my lady."

Margaret looked to her brother and told him, "You will soon be King."

3

THE KING

"Are you there, Wulfstan?" The King asked into the darkness.

"I am here, my King." Wulfstan assured him, as he knelt beside his King's deathbed. He'd been there day and night, waiting, watching his King's fading features pale in the light of the candles that were perched around the bed like a ring of sentinel angels.

King Edward's most trusted man was not a noble, nor a bishop, but a landless and untitled soldier, the seven foot tall red-bearded brute who was the Captain of the King's personal guard.

On the nearby table, that was a new addition to the King's bedroom since he had become bedridden with gangrene, sat a pile of death warrants, pardons and various royal decrees which awaited his signature. The reach of his rule was now reduced to an arm's length. Bureaucracy, bribery and corruption were now the weaponry in the war for England's future.

Along the borders of this small realm of the dying, servants flitted about doing battle with the invading legions of flies that were arriving in force to claim the King's decomposing limbs. Beyond that battlefield, in the dark phantom regions where the sentinel candlelight could not penetrate, an audience of nobles watched, and waited. Each one held posies of lavender under their noses so as to fend off the stench of a body that was rotting its way to being a corpse. First and foremost amongst the morbid audience stood Harold Godwinson who was the Earl of Wessex and the most powerful man in England. He constantly shifted his weight from foot to foot, as impatient as an ambitious understudy standing in the wings and waiting for his cue to take to the stage, to enter the bright lights and play his part as the new King Of England. But he must wait…wait until the curtain is lowered on King Edward's final performance.

The old bastard is milking every last drop of life out of it, he thought to himself. Then he said a silent prayer that the old King might hurry up and fucking die.

Beside Harold stood his equally ambitious, and impatient, younger brother, Gyrth Godwinson, Earl of East Anglia and Oxfordshire. He was not one for standing on ceremony, and should his elder brother give him the nod, he would happily walk over to the King's bed and cut his long skinny neck.

Next in the Godwinson line stood the youngest Godwinson brother, Leofwine, Earl of Kent. He would rather have been anywhere else, and drunk, than here. But if he had to be here, he refused to be sober about it, and so he constantly sipped from a goblet of wine to maintain his mental and emotional comfort.

Beside these three Godwinson brothers stood their beautiful sister, Queen Consort Edyth, the long-suffering wife, and soon to be widow, of the King. She had been patiently waiting to be a widow since the King's limbs slowly began to rot more than a year ago. Why he did not end himself was beyond her.

Combined, the three brothers and sister formed the core of the House of Godwin, the most powerful family dynasty that England had ever known. But as great and powerful as their House was, everything that they possessed in the world came from the whim of the King. Many of the older families despised them and relished in the fact that the final act of this tragedy was not yet written. Who among them could say if the infamous Godwins would rise to claim the throne of England, or, as many hoped for, lose everything and fall back into the abyss of obscurity that their father emerged from as a lowly servant?

Edward whispered, "Out all, but for loyal Wulfstan."

Even the hushed word of a King carried absolute authority. While Wulfstan stayed kneeling, the audience was quickly and quietly cleared out without protest. When Edward was satisfied that the darkness around him was empty of ears, he told the man that he trusted with his life, "You will soon be free of your oath to me, good Wulfstan."

Wulfstan made to protest, but Edward put a hand on his shoulder, "You cannot protect the person of the King from this assassin."

Wulfstan did not disagree with him.

"Time is against us now." Edward continued, "The winter of my reign has come. God has not seen fit to grant me an heir…All that I am will vanish without a trace from the earth." Edward then came to the main burden of his worry, "We cannot know the mind of God. But one thing is for sure…When I die, the wolves will come to devour England."

Wulfstan reminded him, "England is no lamb, my King."

Edward smiled, "Indeed, she is not." He took Wulfstan's hand, "I have a final task for you."

Wulfstan waited.

Edward said, "It is time for a tactical retreat. This battle is lost, but the war for England goes on and can yet be won. You and I, Wulfstan, we will outwit them…Harold Godwinson will surely make a grab for the Crown, but he is too much hated by the old families. He and his brothers have pillaged too many titles and lands from them. He will not have the support of the Witan to defend the realm." Edward took him by the hand and told him, "It is time to bring the true blood of The House of Wessex back to England."

Wulfstan was confused, "My King, is Harold Godwinson not the Earl of Wessex?"

Edward became animated as he explained, "He is Wessex in name only, not by blood. He is not legitimate. It is a curse upon my bloodline that I have not ridded the land of all Godwinsons. My sin of marrying into them was a cursed act, and it must be amended before I face God. How can I look at my maker and tell him that I have lost his England that our blessed Alfred made? The first of Wessex… We must make restitution, Wulfstan, else I will be for an eternity in purgatory."

Wulfstan urged his King, "Tell me what I must do, my lord."

Edward shuddered as a wave of pain hit him like a battering ram hitting the portcullis. It sent a great wave of agony through him, gripping his heart momentarily in death's fist. He knew that eventually one such assault would breech his defences, and he would be conquered. He got his breath back and explained, "The true Earl of Wessex is alive, and he is of my own bloodline. King Ironside's grandson, Edgar, is the legitimate Atheling to the crown of England." The King then made a heavy sigh, "Yet, Edgar is only a boy…and I dare not take him from his safe place."

Wulfstan encouraged him, "Many a boy king has ruled well into his manhood, my King. And he will be well-served by loyal men."

22

Edward asked his Huscarl, "Will he be served by you, as you have served me?"

Wulfstan told him, "My life oath to you is my oath to him. I renew it now before God."

Edward smiled, "We might do it yet, loyal Wulfstan...God willing. If we are to save England from being carved up like spoil, we must get the Atheling here and have him crowned. I need you to bring him to his throne."

"It will be done, my King."

4

THE GODWINSONS

Harold Godwinson swept into his private chambers where his two brothers and sister waited for him. His tallness and long facial features gave him the appearance of a lurking vulture that put the fear of the Devil into the servants.

He bellowed, "Clears me out like a fucking servant and keeps his fucking Irish hound in there with him ... I am the fucking Earl of Wessex! Damn him! I am within my rights to be offended, am I not?" He paced and rounded, "Do you agree with me, Sister?"

Queen Edyth draped herself across a couch, sipping her wine through thin red-painted lips. At the sound of Harold's voice she slowly closed her eyes and pretended that he was not there. Then she took a hefty swallow of her wine that she imbibed from the moment she woke in the morning, never getting drunk but avoiding being sober, dwelling in a carefully balanced limbo.

Leofwine, her young brother, sat beside her coiled up in a great fur that was made from the coats of five great bears. He also had the habit of drinking cupfuls of wine, but without the finesse of his sister. He gulped it from early in the morning, taking the shortest route possible through the day to oblivion in the evening, and ending every night in unconsciousness. He was about halfway on his journey when his brother Harold returned from visiting the deathbed of their brother-in-law, the King. Leofwine took his sister's hand and shared a private nudge. Then he told his hotheaded brother Harold, "Will you stop prancing about like a rutting beast? You'll break into a horse sweat and the air will stink up like a stable. And please lower the boom of your voice. My head is in a fragile condition."

Edyth gave a snigger and slinked under the furs with Leofwine. The pair snuggled in to one another like a pair of conspiratory cats.

Harold spat back, "I'm to be ridiculed by two maids hiding under a fur?"

Leofwine smiled at him and took no insult at being called a maid. He was often mistaken for one of the ladies-in-waiting; especially when he went about the halls of the court dressed in his sister's fine gowns.

Edyth playfully pouted and scolded her older brother, "Harold, don't be cruel to Leo."

Leofwine very gently kissed her impish nose that twitched when his lips landed on it, fixed her hair behind her ear, which was part of his habit to constantly pamper her, and whispered, "Thank you, Edee. You are my guardian angel." He then told Harold, "I do agree with you, big brother. I too wonder what on God's green earth the King would have to say to the red hound … that is not for your ears?"

They watched their brother brew on that for a moment.

Leofwine nudged Edyth and went on, "You know, I did hear, from a very good source, that the red hound's mother was actually a wild Irish donkey!"

Edyth giggled and wrinkled her toes.

Leofwine went on, "Strike me dead if I do tell a lie! Popped right out of a donkey's arse! I was told it by the farrier who saw it all. For does the Irish monster not have a head on him that puts you in mind of a great red donkey?"

Edyth pulled in closer to her little brother, "Leo … you funny goose." And she kissed him on the cheek and then put her head on his shoulder.

Not far away, in the corner where the food was piled upon a serving table, stood the ever-hungry beast that was Gyrth Godwinson, the brother next after Harold. He stopped stuffing his face with a soft-boiled suckling piglet, and thought he could better his younger brother's wit. He stood awkwardly wide-legged in a silence for far too long, adjusting himself and wiping the grease from his beard before announcing in a put-on commoner's voice from no part of the world that anyone could identify, "Maybe Dee King's going to send his Huscarl hound to hell to make a deeeeel with the divil."

He was met with blank faces. He fumbled his thoughts into order. Fixed his crotch again, and went on to explain his supposed joke, "I mean, for to make a kind of contract, if you will, with the Devil for more time in the world of the living, more time here in the world. If you see? But the Irish hound would say 'deeeel' and 'divil' and the like." Then he forced out a constipated laugh for himself, "Ha! Ha! Funny or what?"

Leofwine shared a look of derision with Edyth. They had secretly decided many years ago that Gyrth was a bastard baby conceived by their mother in some drunken rampage with a horny swine herder. For like all Danes, their mother turned savage when she drank and she would fuck or fight anyone when she was in the cups. But they also knew that they needed Gyrth. He was their protector.

Leofwine told him, "That was well put, Brother."

Gyrth lapped up the praise, smiled and explained, "Perhaps I could have structured it more sturdily … I had no time for composition. It was very much off the cuff, as they say."

"Not at all," Leofwine told him, "it was sturdily put as a marching order."

Edyth agreed, "Here, here. You should write a play, Brother."

Gyrth blushed easily when his sister praised him, and he would just as easily kill anyone who offended her.

Of all of the Godwinsons, Gyrth was the most suited to being a soldier. He possessed the stout frame and wide stance necessary for infantrymen to stand their ground and hold the line. He earned his title as the protector of the family at the age of ten when he beat Harold's tutor to death with his bare fists. The tutor had taken a stick to Harold to chastise him. It was the last time anyone raised a hand to any of the Godwinson children. His berserk temper was inherited from his mother's blood. When Harold set Gyrth on someone, they rarely survived the attack.

Harold knew well that he would need his brother's violent loyalty in the battles to come, and supported his effort at being funny with a roar of a hoax laughter, "Good one, brother! That surely is a good one! A deeeel with the Divil. Fucking Irish Donkey!"

Gyrth let out his customary big snorting laugh that made him sound like a rutting pig, and was the main reason why Edyth and Leofwine suspected his paternal line was linked to a swine herder.

Harold added, "It is surely for hell that he is bound, the decrepit old grave dodger."

Edyth then reminded her brothers, "It is of my husband, the King, that you speak."

Harold cruelly reminded her, "And had you produced an heir from that arrangement, we would not be wading through this moat of shit."

Leofwine defended his sister, "That is uncalled for, Brother. Matters of that nature are with God. And none of us can afford to offend the heavens."

Harold felt the threat of God's wrath in his little brother's warning, he relented, "I am much sorry, Sister. I am hot. Forgive me. I will light a candle and say a prayer for my sin against you."

She made an unforgiving grin, "I hold no grudge, Brother. It is my privilege to have been prostituted this past twenty years for the sake of the family's fortunes." She raised her goblet to him, "To your good fortune, Brother."

Harold smiled to her and reminded her, "I think if you check your treasury and land holdings, you will find that your own fortunes have grown substantially … Dare I say, that you are the richest woman in England."

Edyth told him, "Dare I say, I've earned it."

Leofwine took his sister's delicate pale hand in his own equally delicate and paler hand and encouraged her, "You care not for all that land and wealth … I know that, Edee."

She fought off a smile. He was teasing her.

He went on, "You should be at your husband's bedside, Edee. It is your place as Queen. And that monk that you have employed to write the magnificent Vita Edwardi Regis … have your holy biographer come in and observe, so that he may write a touching first hand account of you, the devoted Queen, sitting at the bedside of her dying King."

She read him. She knew her little brother was the shrewdest man in England, "Are you teasing me still, Leo?"

He petted her shoulder softly, "No my dear, Edee. When Edward departs the world … regardless of who takes his place on the throne, you will need the good favour of the Witan in order to keep what is yours, what was given to you by your dead King husband."

She weighed that. He was right. She had a lot to win or lose with the death of her husband. And if her brother Harold should not secure the crown … then what?

Leo lightened the mood and waved his hand in the air as if swatting at flies, "Just march in and command the red hound out of the room and back to his barracks. Better still, send him back to that fucking wilderness of Ireland with his pension purse up his big hairy arse."

Edyth agreed and told Harold, "That should be your first task as King, Brother. Pension out the red giant. Give him some land near Wales or Scotland where he might be murdered."

Harold sneered, "A pension purse? The gallows more like."

Edyth advised him, "You need the Huscarls, Brother… You cannot kill their favourite captain."

Harold swallowed more drink. He knew she was right. He moaned, "Fucking Huscarls."

Leofwine squeezed her hand again, and leaned into her, "Go to him, Edee."

Harold poured another drink, "And still he lives! Like a disease, he plots against me as he rots. Will he not die?" He drank deeply, "Damn him."

Edyth reassured him, "He has sworn to leave you the throne."

Harold paced again, "Sworn it to whom? You and me? To his horse? Why not swear it to our Uncle Bishop? Why not call the Witan to assemble around his festering deathbed and swear it to them? No ... He waits and he plots..."

Gyrth drew his dagger, and told Harold, "It matters not who the rotting King swears the crown to or does not swear it to. When he dies we will make you King and there is none in England to stop us..."

Harold stopped pacing, and realised, "You're right, Brother. There are none."

Leofwine smiled and raised his goblet, "A toast then... To Harold... The soon to be King of England."

They raised their goblets and drank.

At the same time, a gentle but persistent tapping came to the door. It was a tapping that Gyrth could identify, "Enter, Rat."

A small thin man who looked very like a rodent, entered and spoke in a hoarse rasping voice, "Me lords… Me Queen…" The man seemed unsure about speaking his news and stood licking his lips.

Gyrth ordered him, "Out with it, man!"

The man relieved himself of the burning information, "I have word on the whereabouts of the red bearded Huscarl, me lord "

5

WARRIORS

Kallín waited out the night tucked into the hollowed trunk of a dead tree. The black sky turned grey, green, blue, then suddenly violet before gushing plumes of blood-red clouds over the horizon in a dawn that was heralded by euphoric birdsong, rejoicing in the birth of a new day.

It was the first sunrise that the young Rohán had seen with truly opened eyes. Now he understood why the sunburst was the ensign of the Rohán's battle banner; there was no sunrise as beautiful as the one seen by a warrior who survives a battle. The newly fought-for day of life day is full of promise, and great possibilities. Truly, it was the first day of the rest of his life.

The heat penetrated the forest and found him, filled him with warmth, and thawed the numbness of death out of his limbs. The pain of the flesh returned to him, so too did the pain of the heart.

The instant he thought of his Mother and Ríona he felt he would be swept away in madness. He put the pain away from him, vowing to them that he would not forget them and that he would avenge them.

Slowly, the drowning tide of pain receded just enough so that he could breathe again.

It's time to move now, he told himself. He knew that if he lay in the dead tree any longer that he would simply give up and die in it.

Like an insect birthing from its pupae state, he crawled naked stiff and sore out of his cocoon, listening for predators, watching for danger, blade at the ready …Carefully, he moved his limbs in sequence, testing his joints for damage. Upon finding that his body was able, he straightened up and walked, retracing his steps back to the camp.

Mother.

He had not seen her body, and until he did, she was alive to him. He must find her dead or alive.

At the forest edge the singing of full-bellied crows filled the air like a tavern of drunks. He knew all the crow songs. This one was a song about eating fresh corpses, and it told him that the Norsemen had left.

In the clearing, the various parts of Riona's corpse were strewn about, hacked in rage. He stood motionless until his heart bled out all of his love for her. Then the empty place where Ríona's love had lived in his heart was filled with a burning hunger for revenge.

He walked on.

Ríona's mutilated remains were left where they lay because the Rohán do not make an elaborate burial ceremony over the corpses of their dead. Fallen warriors are left on the battlefield. The bodies of those that die outside of battle are brought to an open place where the animals can feast upon their remains.

What our body has taken from the earth in our life is returned to the earth in our death.

But the dead are not forgotten. Their memory is kept alive in the annals of the great Story Of The Rohán that is recited by the Seanchaí at the gathering of the Clans. All Rohán warriors carry their own story that begins with their first kill.

He stopped and looked at the blood-soaked patch where he'd slain the berserker and thought, *My warrior story began here.* The sodden blood-muck oozed between his toes … It felt good to stand in the blood-patch of his kill.

The Norsemen had taken the bodies of their dead with them. With the whisper of pride, he walked on, passing the smouldering bramble patch that was burned to black now. The trees that stood witness to the terrible act were scorched. But nothing was dead here. In the forest nothing is ever really dead. The roots of the vines still lived in the earth, and in the spring, green shoots will grow anew, stronger.

Mother…

He must find her.

He came to the last place that he saw Mother on the track of the badger run. He scoured the ground, carefully reading the story of their chase in the broken soil.

This is where I ran into the norsedog.

Working his way back, he saw only his own tracks.

Mother did not come this way after me.

Further back on the badger run he found her tracks deeply bitten into the soil, made from the sharp turns of a fighting stance, and then … blood.

Mother is not here, neither is her corpse.

Then in the bushes, a great impression of where a body had fallen … and looking closer at the amount of muck-blood … bled out.

A heavy body. Too big for Mother. A norsedog.

Mother's tracks turned back … in the opposite direction from his tracks. Three sets of norseman tracks chasing her.

He realised, *She lead the norsedogs away from me.*

He followed her run back to their camp where her tracks mingled into oblivion with the muck-blood of a prolonged and hard-fought mêlée.

Everywhere there were Rohán dead. Crows had already come to the feast. Soon, foxes and wolves would come for their portion of the spoil. But it would be the flies that would win the ground in a day, for once their larvae bloom on the battlefield, no living creature can withstand being in their ferocious black cloud. The great fly swarm will leave only bones for the earth to swallow.

Moving on, he found a circle of corpses in the centre of the camp where the Rohán had made their last stand. Their fighting force was comprised of mothers who were not away at battle, the old and the young. He could tell that they were formidable from the amount of Norse blood churned into the ankle-deep moat of muck-blood that circled the battle site. But they would have been outnumbered at least ten-to-one by heavily armed and battle seasoned Norsemen. The Rohán corpses had been mutilated and their weapons plundered as trophies. He examined the ground and read the story of the fight. The Rohán rallied in a circle three ranks deep. The first rank was shields and half spears, second rank was long spears to attack over the shoulders of the first rank, third rank was swords for close combat on any attacker who should push through the first two ranks. Inside this triple ranked circle the ground was full of small footprints where the little-ones had been gathered. All of the first rank of the frontline defenders had been cleaved with long axes. The Norsemen had no appetite for close combat with these battle-hardened and wily old retired warriors. The second spear-line of mothers held out long and hard; all of their bodies bore many defensive wounds from sword and axe attack. The Norsemen were in close combat here. But the Norse numbers were great and they wore away the valiant Rohán defence, cut by cut in a bloody battle of attrition. The last line was the short blade that surrounded the little ones. They defended them hand-to-hand to the last. Some of the little-ones must have picked up weapons and fought too. They were then killed in strange slow ways for the sport of the Norsemen. Kallín understood that killing was a necessary part of battle but he could not fathom the Norse appetite for torture — especially the torture of children.

No Rohán could ever harm a child. He took comfort in the fact that the Norse and the Rohán were different species.

Kallín took some more moments to set the battle to his memory, for it was now his job to carry this part of the Rohán's story and keep it alive. When he had fully committed their last stand to story, he moved on and told himself, *Mother is not here, neither is her corpse.*

Returning to his tent he found a bloody hand print on the centre post. He knew it was Mother's hand. Then, on the ground, her bloody spear ... broken. He read the story in the earth; great arching swoops of a violent struggle.

This is where Mother was taken.

He picked up her fur, lay down on his bed, buried his face in it and quietly wept. Having lost love, he was now losing what he needed the most: hope.

He lay motionless and empty. Maybe he was there for some hours ... until he heard a voice, soft and low, whisper, "Kallín-boy."

Kallín looked to the flap of his tent, "Brun-boy?"

The tall figure of Brun carefully entered the tent. The tall slender youth was a few winters older than Kallín, but he'd failed at his trials to be a warrior more than twice.

Brun told him, "She killed one a them here, so she did."

Kallín asked him, "And what occurred then?"

"They took her with the others then ... in the boats."

A young pregnant slave is worth coin. Mother lives...

Brun asked him, "What do we do now so?"

There was a Rohán ritual to be followed after a battle. Kallín told him, "We wash, and we fresh braid our hair now, as is the way of the warrior."

Rohán warriors are taught to groom themselves before battle so as to prepare themselves to go home. If they survive the battle, they are to wash and groom so as not to carry the reek of battle on them.

The two young Rohán stood naked by the wash barrel in the corner of the tent and washed in silence the way warriors do. Kallín washed away the Norseman's blood from his hands and feet. Lavender water purified his skin and purged the reek from his flesh. There was not a part of him that did not have a stinging cut from the thorns, or a bruise that gave off a dull throb. Before he became a warrior, any one of these wounds would have given him cause to seek comfort from Mother, but now he was consuming the pain in its various forms as he would a bitter fruit; it was the acquired taste of a warrior; each morsel a little taste of a death, an exotic spice that makes life taste all the sweeter.

Brun washed Kallín's back. Kallín felt that there was something different in Brun's touch. It was not rough-handed like a mother's hand, nor strong like a father's, nor was it hungry for him like Ríona's hand. It was gentle and careful, a hand that wanted to neither give nor take from him. The hand of a friend.

Kallín reciprocated in the bathing. While washing Brun's naked back, he noticed long thin scars, and some that were still weals. These were not fighting scars. He felt anger rising in him and asked Brun, "Who whipped you that way?"

"My father."

"Why?"

"For failing my warrior trials. I've to take them again after the season is out. I'll not pass … I know it."

"What did you fail by?"

"Combat … I don't have the skill for fighting." Brun looked to the floor in shame, "Sure, I hid from the whole fight last night."

Kallín smiled, "We all hid, Brun-boy."

"I was afraid…"

Kallín told him, "Anyone who says they were not afraid is telling a lie."

Brun met his eye, "I was under the bed here when they took your mother … I stayed hidden."

Kallín thought for a moment and then assured him, "That is what she would have wanted you to do."

"You think so?"

"I know so." Kallín told him, "I'll make your braid for you."

Brun turned his back to him. Kallín began to comb out Brun's long black hair that went all the way down his scarred back. He asked him, "Is your mother away fighting then?"

"She is ... and my father."

"That's good so," Kallín told him, "She'll be back for you then."

Brun brightened, "She will surely, Kallín-boy."

Kallín's fingers worked deftly braiding the thick weave and entwining the green ribbon into it. He asked Brun, "Do you know of the battle rite of Morrigan?"

"To be made warrior through battle?"

"That's that one. Did you fight last night?"

"I told you ... I hid."

Kallín said, "I think I saw you kill a norsedog with a spear ... In fact, I'd stand over the fact as a witness to it in front of the council, if I had to. I'm sure it was you ... and by Morrigan's rite you are now a warrior ... and cannot be whipped again by any hand."

Brun went quiet for a moment, then asked him, "If you say you saw it then..."

Kallín said, "It was on the small track of the badger run. The blood of it and the story is there in the bush for proof." He turned Brun to look at him, "You know the spot?"

"I know it."

Brun reached behind and took his braid in his hand and examined it, "You've weaved in the green ribbon..."

Kallín told him, "As I said... you are a warrior now. You wear the green ribbon."

Then Brun held out his hand, "Can I make your braid for you now, so?"

"You can." Kallín handed Brun his ribbon of green, and turned his back to him.

Brun began his work, separating the long black mane into three tails that reached all the way down Kallín's back.

"It's good thick hair that you have," Brun told him.

"Mother complains that it gets too wild."

"No," Brun told him, "I like it."

Brun's delicate hands worked fast to make the braid and weave in the green ribbon. When his work was done, he stood back and admired it, "It's a good lookin braid there. You are handsome with it..."

Kallín made a smile. "We should dress..." He walked to his clothes and dressed himself in a shirt woven from hemp, sturdy trussers made of deer hide and boots made from the same deer pelt and tied lengths of leather chord around each leg in a criss-cross pattern.

Brun dressed much the same but felt he had to let Kallín know, "I'm not the same as you, Kallín-boy."

Kallín read him and smiled, "No two trees are purely alike."

Outside, a twig snapped under a careless foot.

Kallín whispered, "Stay here."

Brun picked up the half of the broken spear, and whispered back, "I'm with you now. If we're going home now, then so be it."

Kallín knew that Brun was not going to go back into hiding, he whispered to him, "Stay behind me…"

Brun nodded in earnest.

Kallín pushed slowly through the flap, blade at the ready.

Outside the tent, two dozen little-ones stood in silence … waiting.

At the centre of them stood a girl who was taller than the rest and coming into the age of a warrior. She spoke, "Kallín-boy."

"Aífe-girl."

Brun interrupted, "It's Kallín-man now. He became warrior through battle."

Aífe smiled, "I'm happy for that." And she asked Brun, "And you?"

Kallín answered first, "He is Brun-man, I seen his kill."

Aífe's smile grew wider, "'Tis good to have two warriors with us now then."

The rest of the little-ones smiled too.

Aífe then asked him, "Did you see my sister, Ríona-girl?"

"She's gone home," Kallín told her.

Aífe looked to the ground.

Kallín added, "But she's gone home as a warrior. She's called Ríona-woman now, and before she went we paired. She is my wife."

Aífe looked up at him, "Warrior-woman and wife. So … you are my brother now?"

"I am."

"How did her story end then?"

Kallín was about to tell them Ríona's story, but he noticed the frightened faces of all the little-ones. He said, "It is such a great story … So first, let us all set a new camp in the forest, get washed, and make our braids fresh, and then I'll tell you Ríona's warrior story from beginning to end, as we eat a feast in her honour."

They got busy moving provisions into the safety of the forest, and moving the little-one away from their dead. When a suitable place in the forest was found they made camp, then set to washing their faces and braiding their hair. The relocation and the small piece of ritual brought with it a seed of comfort, a small promise that the world would be made right again.

When all were washed clean and freshly braided, they gathered in a tight circle around the fire, eating strips of cured meat, dried berries, and drinking jugs of creamy goat milk in great hungry gulps. Kallín told them the story of how he and Ríona became warriors by the rite of battle. He garnished it well with valiant fighting and he gave Ríona the first stab at the great berserker, and when it came to the part of her death, he gave that to the cruel arrow of the Norse archer. So, all in all, it was a story of how Ríona had saved his life. She was an instant hero. Her story would be retold many, many times, growing in its proportions, as all good warrior stories should. When Kallín was finished, he told them, "You will all wait here in the forest for the warriors to return. They will be returned here soon."

Aífe asked him, "How can you know?"

He told her, "Because Brun here is going north to find them and tell them."

Brun stopped eating mid-bite, "I will do it surely."

Aífe looked at Kallín, reading him, "And what of you?"

Kallín told her, "I am going south through the forest."

"Why?"

He explained, "The Norsemen will follow the river. But they will stop again to sell their slaves in the market at Grim Haven. I can get there before them. I can save mother, and the others too."

"I can help you, Kallín-man," Aífe told him.

"You will surely help me," he told her, "for you will keep these little-ones safe until the warriors return. And then you will tell them where I have gone to, so that they can come and help me."

Aífe told him, "And when the warriors come to you in Grim Haven … I will be with them, and I will wet my sword to become a warrior too."

He smiled at that and told her, "That's a battle I want to be in."

He loaded up his water-skin, tucked a few fistfuls of dried meat, berries and nuts into his scout sack, and Brun did the same. Then one young Rohán warrior went north and the other south.

6

THE LONER WOLF

Kallín ran all through the day and well into the night that wrapped its black cloak around him. When he thought of stopping to rest, he only needed to think of her, *'Mother…'* and he was freshly filled with a renewed determination to track down the Norse slavers, and rescue her.

He worked his way over the unfamiliar ground in a tired blind jog. His water ran out. Suddenly all the light of the moon was lost. A moment after, he was blinded as the night sky was ripped in a great searing flash. The earth shuddered under the shock of a deafening thunder boom … followed by a pristine silence. The smell of scorched air filled the night. The forest waited with bated breath. Every creature, great and small, took shelter. Then came the perfect pit-pat of the first few fat drops of rain hitting the crisp leaves, the tidy rhythm then gave way to a deafening deluge.

The downpour brought a great wind with it and quickly built itself into a strong storm, blowing debris through the gaps in the trees like spears and arrows. There was no cover, and no hope of moving forward in it.

Rest up… He thought, *The storm will make high seas. They'll not sail blind in the night, in the bad weather. They'll stopover in Grim Haven, and wait it out there for sure. Rest up.*

By a stroke of great fortune, he found a cave, a safe place to rest out of the storm.

Rest here. And I'll set off at the first light. I'll make good goin in the light...

He entered the cave, protected from the elements in a muffled shroud of darkness.

A good spot .

His senses adjusted to the darkness and the quietness. Then his sixth sense told him that he was not alone. He froze. Gripped his blade. Every part of him reached into the darkness. A low sound grew and formed into a growl. He recognised it, the unmistakable snarl...

Wolf!

In his next breath the beast was on him faster than he could pull his blade from its scabbard. Sinking its teeth into his shoulder, its fangs finding enough grip there to get a deep hold on him, it threw him to the ground. Again and again, the huge beast shook and flung him, dragging and tossing him, tearing at his arms and face. He screamed to no avail. There was no pity in the beast. No pity in the gods. He was food. His cries were lost in the howls of the raging storm raging outside. He was being swallowed by the all-consuming agony. Then in the deepest region of his pain, in a place where pain becomes everything, a place where he no longer existed, a place where he was simply a memory of himself, he knew what he must do in order to give that distant memory of life a chance to survive.

Leave here, he thought, *get out of the world of pain, go away from it ... go home ... go home.*

It was not too difficult for him to leave the torn body. His ragged flesh wanted to die, wanted to be over, wanted to be out of the pain. He surely had enough of the world and its endless hardship. He wanted to be with his ancient kinfolk. All he needed to do was allow his spirit to become unanchored from the body and drift homeward. He let go, stopped screaming, stopped wriggling, let his body be lifeless. Almost.

The wolf, thinking its killing was done, stopped to rest itself before devouring its fresh meat.

Kallín listened to the panting of the beast getting its breath back...

Blade ... where are you?

His fingers crept along the floor, searching blind. Fumbling.

I need you ... Blade.

Then he and his blade found each other. Slowly, he gripped the hilt and felt its leather covering, soaked with his hot blood. It made the blade slide easily from the scabbard.

Thank you...

With the blade ready, he stayed still, floating in the sea of agony, trying not to sink.

Come on you gowling wolf, come and eat me now ... come now and say a halloo to my battle blade.

The wolf cocked its snout and took in the smell of the fresh blood, then it licked the air with relish and came closer to begin its victory meal.

Kallín felt the wolf's tongue run along his torn face, it was almost soothing.

You smell as bad as a stinking norsedog ... Come closer to me ... come.

With all the young Rohán had left in him, he plunged his blade into the wolf's chest, right to the hilt, right into the heart.

How d'you like me now?

The wolf cried out in a great long howl of surprised agony.

Gowlyah! Gowlyah! Gowlyah!

He stabbed the wolf again and again.

Gowlyah! Gowl...

The wolf pulled away. Howling.

Now who is the meat? Who?

The wolf's howling turned to crying as it withdrew further into the darkness where it lay whimpering ... and dying.

Kallín could not move. He was dying too. But he wanted desperately to outlive the wolf at least. He thought, *not yet ... do not go home, not yet. My warrior story must outlive the wolf so that I will have something to say for myself when I meet Ríona. To have killed two Norseman and a wolf, a huge wolf. That is something at least. That is worthy of a story...*

He clung on to his sliver of life and listened to the wolf's panting becoming broken and then suddenly, mid-pant, it stopped...

The wonderful silence of victory filled the cave, and for a moment there was nothing but Kallín and his life.

He told himself, *I won!*

The world outside raged on in a storm. Nothing of any consequence had occurred in this dark cave; one creature killed another is all. Such acts happen multiple times every moment of every day and every night.

What will eat my body now? He wondered, *worms and birds?* He told himself, *I'm going home.*

He was somehow out of the pain now, skimming on the surface of it, like an insect pond-strider marching homeward. He consoled himself with all the infinite possibilities that home had waiting for him, taking comfort from seeing Ríona and all of his kinfolk. He realised that the rain had stopped and the morning had broken outside. The night had passed. The birds sang; he took pleasure in listening to them.

I am always homeward bound.

7

LUNA

Luna stood naked in front of the wash-bucket, tied up her great unwieldy mop of fire-red hair, cupped her hands, and scooping the cold water, splashed it between her legs, then under her arms and around her neck and face. She briefly looked at her body. It seemed to change every night now. Her breasts would get bigger or smaller, she would notice more hair between her legs and under her arms, and sometimes she would fall into floods of tears for no reason. Other times she would be plunged suddenly into a murderous rage, and she would need to walk in the forest for fear that she would commit a murder. Nana told her she was turning from a girl into a woman now and all of that turmoil was natural. Some nights she'd lie awake, missing an imaginary boy that she was in love with. Sometimes she caught a glimpse of him in her dreams, his lips, or his eyes… She never saw his entire face but she knew that she would know when she found him, and she knew that she would find him soon.

Dipping the washrag in the bowl of lavender-perfumed water, she squeezed out the excess she didn't need from it, and began to wash herself. Last night was one of those sleepless night. She'd been awake with the longing for her unknown boy while she was listening to the storm. Normally, she took great joy from being in the safety of the cave, wrapped up in her bed of warm pelts, safe and dry while the thunder raged outside and pounded the world above them. But the storm last night was different. There was more than rain and thunder in it, something in it that called her out of bed and to the mouth of the cave. She watched the lightening cutting the black sky the way she would slice a howler. The thunder made the ground shudder. But in between all of that, in the slices of silence, she listened for him. She felt that he was out there in the night. She even thought that she heard him crying out to her. But she could not be sure that it was not a cunning wolf.

She asked Rosy, who was maybe a year younger and who joined her at the wash bucket, "Did you hear them howls in the wind all the night? It sounded to me like the Loner Wolf caught a man. Do you think so, young Rosy?"

Rosy didn't like being called 'young' and she didn't like the way that Luna was getting breasts and thinking that she was the boss. Of course, Luna saw right into Rosy, and made sure that she rubbed salt into the jealous wound every chance she got.

Rosy went on the defensive, "I was in a tight sleep all the night, so I was…" and she threw a look to Old-Nana who was snoring in stops and starts in her chair.

Rosy knew Nana didn't like to hear talk of sleeplessness. In Nana's opinion, and her opinion was the only one that mattered here, restlessness was a symptom of a hungry heart. She often warned the girls about the lonesome hunger that takes a girl away on long rambles into the forest, until eventually, they ramble into the clutches of a wolf … and they do not come back.

Rosy secretly hoped that Luna would go for a good ramble and not come back, and then she could have Nana and Dina all to herself. But she kept all those devious jealous thoughts to herself for fear of unleashing Luna's terrible temper on her. She went about her business of washing herself, and egging her way into being Nana's favourite, saying loud enough to be overheard, "Be best for us all to be getting good and tight into our sleeps in the bed, I think, and not be with the hungry heart all the time in the night."

Luna smiled to herself and thought, *there are no flies on you, young Rosy.*

She could well have commented on Rosy's own strange nocturnal habits of eating hidden food when she thinks all are asleep. But Luna knew Rosy would turn it into a storm of an argument, and put herself in the middle of it as the weeping innocent.

The girls had been found wandering in the forest by Nana when they were very small. Folk from villages and farms sometimes abandoned their unwanted children to the forest. Other times, little-ones just wandered into the trees of their own accord. Other times, they were chased in by raiders. Whatever the reasons that brought them to the dark interior of the hinterland, most would quickly perish from thirst or cold, or simply be eaten by the wolves. But sometimes they made it to Nana's patch. Nana only took the girls. She fed the boys to the wolves. As for the girls that she took in, most of them died. Of those that lived past being children, all were eventually compelled by the force that drives all creatures to leave the nest. It had been some years now since a little-one had made it onto her patch. She knew that the world beyond the forest was changing. Of late, she had noticed more and more men making deep incursions into parts of the forest where normally no man would come.

Rosy was most likely abandoned because of her clubbed foot, but it did not hamper her in any way and she moved around the forest and the caves as quick-footed as a young wild piglet.

As for Luna's offence at birth, Nana could not say what it was for sure. The girl did not carry any physical deformity on her body. In fact the opposite was true. When Nana found her as a little-one she was feeding on the leftovers from kill made by the wolfpack. The wolves lay in a circle, full bellied and amused by the little creature with the great head of flame red hair. Now, she'd grown into a sturdily framed and well-proportioned young woman with strong arms, a sure foot, and power in her hips. Nana suspected that it might be a perceived curse in Luna's blood that was the cause of offence that saw her abandoned. She had a wild look in her green eyes that made Nana think that she was the product of a Celt raider. It was most likely that her mother could not keep her on account of the big flaming shock of wild red hair on her. Add to that her terrible temper and appetite for violence, and there was more than enough proof that she was the bastard of a Celt.

The third of Nana's girls, Dina, joined the other two at the wash bucket. Dina had come into the forest when she was about five years old after her family were attacked and taken as slaves by Norse raiders. She was left unharmed at the forest edge by the raiders when they discovered she was blind. The Norse were known to be careful with cripples and the blind, and they did not kill them for fear of offending their gods, some of whom were blind and crippled. Dina had been deprived of the power of sight, but her blindness had given her the skill to explore the vast labyrinth of the cave system deep into its most impenetrable parts. In the great subterranean wilderness, she found all manner of nameless things that grew and lived there. She cultivated strange black fungi, white flowers, blind fish, glowing snakes, transparent frogs, one-eyed toads and pink newts; turning their blood, sap, flesh, and venom from deadly poisons into medicines. There was no end to the healing potions that she was able to make with various effects; some took away infection from wounds, or soothed rashes and burns. Others made you happy or warm or sleepy or energetic or thoughtful. But it was her cudu that was most enjoyed by the girls: a chewing cud, kept in the side of the mouth so that its effects would be released slowly or quickly as desired. Nana had discovered that she could put the cudu in her pipe and smoke it.

Dina said, "I heard the strange sound too," and added, "it sounded much like a howler being eaten by the Loner Wolf in his lair."

Luna asked her, "Do you think it was a Norseman? Maybe there is more of them."

Dina smiled, "If there is more of them, then they will be in your traps and food for the wolfpack."

Nana roused with a growl from her sleep.

Luna suspected that the old woman had been half awake for a good while already, earwigging the conversation, and coming back into the world slowly.

Nana cleared her throat with a great croak and spat the produce into the darkness that surrounded their oasis of candlelight in the cavern, then she grumbled, "What's that talk now about a howler and the Loner Wolf?"

Touching a long thin length of spill-grass to the candle flame, she ignited it in a tiny flash. Then her gnarly hand cradled the little spit of flame, protecting it from the draft as she carefully brought it to the bowl of her smoking pipe. In a dozen short-rapid-continuous puffs on the long stem, she drafted the air into the chamber, pulling it along the shank and bore, so that it created a current that fanned the flame in the bowl, making it burn into the black ball of cudo and ignite it, giving it life ... Then with long slow drawn sucks, she drew in the cudo flames deeper into the draught hole until the entire contents glowed bright and forced the Cudo to give up its treasure in a cloud of pungent smoke. Her puffing stopped for a heartbeat as she savoured a mouthful of the deliciously bitter vapours before inhaling them deeply into her hungry lungs. Immediately, she felt the miraculous effect working on her old crippling bone aches and joint pains.

The girls waited until Nana had sucked down at least a half dozen good lungfuls, for they knew well that the old woman could not face the day until she had made herself comfortably numb.

After that waiting time, Luna spoke, "Sounded like the Loner Wolf got a howler up there in his cave. Woke me right up, so it did."

Nana didn't like that one bit, "One man on his own, doesn't sound right to me."

She thought for a moment, then offered up a judgement on the matter in a cloud of wise cudu smoke, "I'm thinking that we stay out of that matter unless the trouble comes onto our patch."

Rosy eagerly nodded in agreement, "Yes, Nana. I didn't hear any howlers in the traps. Do you remember that one howler that I killed, Nana?"

Luna grinned at Rosy, forever weaving and embroidering her little lie about killing a howler.

The truth was that Luna built the traps to kill men instantly, but sometimes they accidentally caught one that didn't get killed immediately, and he would be left howling in the trap. It was Luna's task to find the howler, and finish the job, strip the corpse of valuables and leave it easy for the wolfpack to eat it. Then she would repair and reset the traps. It was because of this arrangement of supplying meat to the wolves that they lived alongside the wolfpack in a mutually beneficial way, the wolves giving an extra layer of protection to them in return for the manmeat.

Rosy had wanted to help out with the traps one morning, as she approached a corpse, it kicked its leg out at her. Luna assured her that the corpse was dead. But nothing would convince Rosy, and she took it into her head to stab the corpse multiple times with a spear. And so, the story of 'how Rosy killed a howler' was born. In one version the corpse actually got out of the trap and chased her. Luna let Rosy run with her story. Luna herself had killed and disposed of more howlers than she could count, and she knew that something in Rosy needed that story.

Nana nodded, "I remember, Rosy. Good girl."

Nana had no time for spoofing, but she had a great soft spot for the plump, club-footed, young Rosy who always seemed desperate for her love. Nana added, "We'll stay out of the matter with the Loner Wolf until we know what way the wind is blowing with it."

Luna felt her face fill with hot blood. She knew that she should just go for a walk in the forest to cool her head, but she heard herself talking, "Strange howling it was," she said back to Nana with a twist of defiance, "a sweetness in it. Didn't sound all the way like a man."

Nana raised an eyebrow at her, "Man or boy, we want nothing to do with it if it has a cock on it."

Rosy sniggered as loudly as she could, "Luna wants a cock, I think. Maybe that is what she is hungry for in the night."

Luna felt her chest beat faster, but she ignored Rosy and answered Nana, "I don't see why we can't keep a boy if we find one that's to our liking. What's so bad about a cock anyway?"

Nana simply said, flat, "Boys become men. And men get to sticking their cock into a woman, and then they get to thinking that they own the woman." She sucked deep on her pipe and asked the girls, "Do you want to be cock-owned, is that it?"

Luna felt her temper running now in her veins, but at the same time she felt Dina's hand touching her arm to calm her.

Rosy jumped in, "I'll never be a man's thing and let him stick his cock in me like a billy goat, so I won't."

Nana blew a cloud and spat out a glob of black smoke spit. Then she said in a tone of final resolution, "Let that be an end to it now." She punctuated it with a grunt of finality.

We'll see about that, Luna thought to herself as she dried her face, "You're right, Nana. As you always are."

Nana examined her through the swirling grey cloud that she had just exhaled. There was not an ounce of sincerity in the girl's voice, and she could hear the impudence ringing in it.

Luna finished dressing, pulled a strap tight around her tidy waist and shoved an axe handle into it as if she had been raised for making murder and plunder. She slipped on her boots, swirled her green-hooded cloak around her, and travelled to the tunnel, momentarily stopping to look back at Nana and spill out a mouthful of ripe lies in the most agreeable tone she could muster, "I'll be off then to check them rabbit snares for the good fresh meat." Then she threw a look to Rosy and added, "I'm sure you'd love to make Nana's morning hot sup of brew for her." Away into the darkness she skipped like a gust of wind before she could be cross-interrogated by the old woman.

Rosy jumped on the opportunity, "Will I follow her, Nana?"

Dina grabbed Rosy's pudgy arm and pinched it hard, making Rosy squeal like a little pig.

Nana, despite herself, broke into a fit of laughing that turned to dangerous coughing. The two girls tended to her, getting her phlegm settled down again for fear she would choke on it.

Luna made her way through the trees, checking her traps as she went; each one was empty. When she came to the clearing in the hollow that marks the edge of their patch and the beginning of the wolf's territory, she saw that someone had run through the soft waterlogged earth. Examining the ground closer, she thought, *Them's deep tired tracks, so they are ... He's back deep in the heel and running crooked. On his last legs.*

She followed the tired desperate tracks...

And he's gone running into the Loner Wolf's cave...

Nearing the cave entrance she heard the happy humming of the flesh flies feasting on a corpse. She'd often sat and listened to their song for a whole day, watching them devour the flesh from the bones of a body caught in one of her traps. She wondered at how the creatures found the corpse so quickly after death, and how the arrival of one fly quickly turned into a swarming cloud of a countless hoard. But it was their incessant hard work that she most admired. To her, they were no less splendid than the wolf ... or the man.

She looked and listened carefully. There was no sound or sign of the Loner Wolf, and her curiosity was devouring her. She entered the cave. Slowly.

Inside, as her eyes adjusted to the half-light, she saw that the flies were feasting on the carcass of the huge Loner Wolf. Further into the darkness, she made out a ragged pile. On closer inspection, she saw it was the remains of a boy. He was all torn to pieces, and he was dead.

How did a boy kill the Loner Wolf?

She moved back to the dead beast, looking for clues, and saw the jewelled handle protruding from its chest. She carefully withdrew it, examining its strangely curved blade that was decorated in endless intricate patterns. Its metal seemed to shimmer like water as the light moved over it. The green gem of the pommel danced in the light and momentarily hypnotised her.

Then something else puzzled her ... *Why are the flies not feasting on the corpse of the boy?*

She moved to the dead boy and looked him over. No blood pumped from his wounds. His pale white flesh was as cold as the skin of a river-stone to touch.

Putting her ear close to his mouth, she heard a short sharp rasp of a desperate breath. Then silence.

She waited. Nothing more. *Was I mistaken? Maybe it was the wind I heard?*

He snatched another gasp of life.

He lives…

She examined closer the exposed wounds where the wolf had torn the flesh. She was certain that he would soon be suitable carrion for the flies. She took her axe from her belt, *It would be a mercy to him to send him on his way, for what kind of horrendous ugly creature would he be if he lived?* She thought again, *if he lived?* Something stirred in her. *Is this him?* Parts of her dreams flashed in and out of her mind. And in a moment she knew, *It is you. I found you. I love you.*

She put her axe back into her belt.

8

THREE BROTHERS

Harold Godwinson drank deeply from his jug, "I fear the red hound is making for the Court of Hungary to bring home the cunting little fucking Atheling."

"Of course he is," Gyrth agreed, "the hound acts as the hand of the King."

Harold struggled with the reasoning, "Why would Edward swear loyalty to my face and bugger me from the rear?"

Leofwine held out his goblet as if it contained the answer, "The cunting King was swearing the crown to you when he was still able to plough the furrow of our sister and thought he might get an heir out of her. If she produced the issue, you would be no more than King Regent, keeping the throne warm for his son. Now that God has cursed him heirless, and he's on his way to hell, he's protecting the last spit of his bloodline … the exiled Atheling."

The plot swirled around the air between the brothers, forming, taking life, each waiting for the other to be the first to speak of the deadly solution to their problem.

Gyrth rolled his drink thoughtfully in the goblet, and quietly said, "It's a dangerous road from Hungary … bandits and what have you. No place for a little prince."

Leofwine smiled, and agreed, "And with no more protection than three guards?"

Harold simply said, "Well, Brothers, let us hope that something terrible does not befall the Atheling."

Leofwine honed the idea, "And should anything happen to the precious one, let it be by the hands of Flemish mercenaries so that all minds of the Witan will think to blame the Bastard of Normandy."

Harold liked that. William of Normandy was a real threat to him and his ambitions for the throne. He added, "They might even conclude that the Bastard Duke may have roped in the help of our conniving back-stabbing little brother, Tostig, who is presently in Normandy bollock-licking the Bastard like a runt hound."

Gyrth drank to that, "Oh, to see the sword go into the bastard Norman and our bollock-licking runt of a brother. Both done down in one fell swoop."

They laughed, drank and fell silent in agreement. The plotting was done. The plan to kill the Atheling was set in motion.

9

INCOGNITUS

Wulfstan immediately set about carrying out the King's order to bring the Atheling home to England. Choosing two of his best Huscarls, he brought them into his private chamber that was situated at the end of the barracks and told them, "You'll join me on a mission. We will be only three in number."

His first pick was Peter, a young Londoner, born and bred, who was, without any doubt, the best man amongst them with a sword. He'd landed himself in prison for killing three Flemish mercenaries in a tavern fight. Wulfstan, knowing how good the Flemish mercenaries were at their trade, thought a lad who can kill three of them was too good to waste on the gallows. He recommended to the King that Peter's sentence be commuted to service of the Crown. The King agreed with his Captain and took the condemned man into the Huscarls.

Peter knew that if he was coming along then Wulfstan was expecting to see action. "Goin on a bloody one, are we?"

Wulfstan simply told him, "We're about the King's business."

The second man was a swarthy black-eyed Iberian called Javier who attracted women to him like a flower attracts bees. He assumed, "We'll be crossing foreign soil…"

Javier's own area of skill was orientation and the safe navigation over terrain that was often inhospitable and hostile. He had come to England as a Saracen Guide, bringing pilgrims to and from the Holy

Land. When the pious King Edward the Confessor made the pilgrimage, he used the services of the Saracen. On the successful conclusion of his great journey, the King made Javier an offer that he could not refuse.

Wulfstan began to remove his Captain's cape and breastplate, while informing his two handpicked men, "We three Huscarls will never be on a greater mission than this... We're travelling incognito."

Incognitus for the Huscarl meant working in a form of battledress used for discreet missions such as carrying out kidnappings or assassinations.

The three men quickly got out of their armour that identified them as Huscarls and replaced it with a discreet chainmail vest that was worn under the shirt. They then doubled up on small weapons, putting two seax blades into underarm scabbards. On their hips they placed two swords made from the finest cauldron steel and a half dozen throwing knives. Finally, they covered all of the weaponry in a full-length hooded black leather cloak. They then set off for the London docks, avoiding the main road by cutting through the shanty town of Cheapside, an endless labyrinth of narrow dangerous alleyways that sprawled around the outer city wall.

Wulfstan was surprised when he was met by the Earl of Wessex, Harold Godwinson, and six of his very well dressed cronies, including his brother Gyrth, acting as a bodyguard.

The windows and doors on either side of the narrow street filled with curious eyes waiting with great anticipation to see the imminent slaughter of the fancy men. Who knows what valuable trinkets might be had from their sweet-smelling corpses?

Harold began with telling Wulfstan, "You are out of your royal colours, Huscarl."

Wulfstan knew, if this gaggle of fancy Earls had intercepted him here, that he was being spied upon. A quick scan of the surrounds revealed a familiar rat-faced wretch peering around a corner. Wulfstan nodded to Peter who immediately slipped away from the parley. He then turned his attention back to Harold, "It's not often one sees men of your fine calibre in these parts. Are you lost, my lords?"

Those in earshot, behind walls and doors, laughed.

Harold didn't like being ridiculed. He mustered up as much threat as he could, "I will ask the questions. You have been with the King this morning?"

Wulfstan did not answer him. He simply looked down upon him as if he had noticed a rodent and was deciding how to kill it.

Harold felt the unadulterated threat oozing from the Huscarl. Despite his best efforts, fear percolated in the pit of his guts. He reminded Wulfstan, "I am the Earl of Wessex."

Wulfstan reminded him, calmly, as if he was talking to a simpleton, "And I am a Huscarl, my lord. I serve only the King … as his sword…"

Gyrth stepped in, "Indeed you do, my good man, and what business are you about for the King now? And incognitus?"

Wulfstan was growing impatient. He had already given this spawn of a court-crawler more time than he had to give, "That business is the King's business." And with a smile that he might give a gentle young maid, and speaking in a soft tone that would not trouble a baby, he said, "Now. Step aside … like good lords."

Terrible screams were heard coming from a nearby alley; someone was being mutilated.

Wulfstan told Gyrth, "That will be your rat … making his last squeals." He then pushed through on his way.

Harold and his crew of cronies moved to the side of the narrow alley and stood ankle deep in the shit-clogged gully.

Harold looked on in disgust as Gyrth's rat-faced spy came staggering around the corner, howling, his eyes gouged out and his tongue cut from his mouth.

Harold told Gyrth, "Put the poor bastard out of his misery."

Gyrth drew his blade and cut the throat of his spy, leaving him to fall dead into the shit, and that was an end to it.

Harold watched the three Huscarls walk away and told his cohort, "The red Irish hound will rue this day that he showed impudence to the future King of England."

10

MARGARET

In Edgar's quarters a half dozen candelabras were positioned along the floor, illuminating him in a sweeping theatrical light as he rehearsed his King's speech. He made great efforts to swirl his cloak in wide turns, stopping suddenly to synchronise his movements with his punctuation. He perfected his commanding finger pointing, his surprised eyebrow raising, his angry frowning, and the touching of his forehead and chin with his clenched fist for added serious effect, as he had observed the thespians do.

Margaret watched him with amusement and reminded him, "We have not yet left Hungary. It might be premature to be practicing your speech to the people of England."

He was momentarily put off his stride, and asked her, "Do you doubt that I will be King?"

She smiled and assured him, "I do not doubt it. But there is much work to be done between now and then."

"What nature of work?" he asked her.

"The Witan?"

He threw his arms up, "A collection of grubby nobles with begging bowls in hand."

She reminded him, "Who must elect you before you can be crowned."

He walked away from her, "I don't want to think about all of that now. The people will love me. I will bring them great flitting contests. I will assemble the sharpest wits from the corners of the realm and build a great stage whereupon they will fight it out." Then he stood upon a chair and announced, as if he were addressing an audience, "My lords, and my ladies, and plebs!"

Margaret advised them, "Perhaps 'plebs' is not a good term."

Edgar was at a loss, "What term should I use for plebs?"

She offered, "Common folk?"

He repeated it, "Common folk… Yes. I like it. And maybe an encouraging compliment such as 'hard-working'. Hmm? Yes. And honest. Good. " He returned to his performance, "My lords, my ladies, and my hard-working honest common folk! We shall set to flitting! A great roasting of one another with the best insults ever uttered! May the best wit win! To the winner, I give a golden goblet and the title of Wit Laureate to the King. To the losers, buckets of shit!"

Margaret eventually smiled at his antics and reminded her young brother, "There may be more important matters to the 'hard-working honest common folk' than flitting."

Edgar replied, "I disagree, Sister. The hard-working honest common folk will grow to enjoy the flitting and be even inspired to raise their minds from the mundane tasks of… whatever it is that they do all day."

She smiled, "They spend their time being honest and hard-working."

"Mock me. But I will have you know that a sharp wit is more effective at cutting down an enemy than a fine edged sword. I shall bring my laureate with me to battle."

Margaret laughed.

Edgar immediately raised to it, "You mock me too much now."

Margaret covered her mouth, "No. Sorry. It was a sneeze!"

"I think you laughed at me. No … snorted."

"Laughed or snorted? No, brother, a catch in my breath from a sneeze was all. Tis the cold air."

He nodded, "Good for you then. I would not wish to know what befalls a young maid who has the audacity to laugh or snort at her King."

"Em? Pardon me, my King?"

Edgar asked her, "Am I not your King?"

Margaret told him, "No… At least, not yet." And she reminded him, "You are still the Atheling."

Edgar shrugged it off and walked to the silver polished plate that showed his reflection in a favourable visage, and told her, "Well, when I am King, you would do well to be more respectful toward me."

"I see."

He went on, "I will be a fair King, but I will not tolerate sniggering, or snorting."

She was curious, "Dare I ask why sniggering and snorting is to be outlawed?"

He thought, and told her, "If you are to laugh, then laugh, full and hearty. Let your laughter be the music of your soul. But sniggering and snorting, I do not like, one is the thin broth of an unspoken snide remark, and the other is an involuntary mouth fart. All of my soldiers will laugh loudly from their belly at our enemies."

She was trying to keep up, "Your soldiers?"

"Yes, for it is among them that I intend to spend most of my time … training them."

Once again, her brother had lost her, "Dare I ask, what you will be training them in?"

He looked at her in disbelief, "Have you not been paying attention? I will train them in the art of verbal combat, of course! The sharpening of their wits is as important as the sharpening of their swords!"

She was now in disbelief, "You will train your soldiers in the art of wielding deadly insults?"

"Yes. Like a magnificent choir … thousands of men issuing clever and insulting rhymes and chants at the enemy."

"Such as?"

Edmund thought then shouted out, "Who are you? Who are you?" He then explained to her, "That would be reserved for an army or an enemy that might have too high of an opinion of themselves."

"Well…"

Then the young Prince pulled some parchment from his pocket, "I composed this one. 'Your sister is your mother. Your father is your brother. You are the ill gotten corruption of a bastard!' That one is dedicated to William the Bastard Duke of Normandy."

Margaret put her hands up, "I am wrong. You have won the argument."

But he would not be sated now, "You don't understand war-craft, Sister." And he went on to explain, "The art of the well crafted insult will be as good a tool on the battlefield as any other. The ability to shout a well-written and creatively imagined pre-battle insults over the field — to emotionally wound your enemy — will be devastating."

She played along with him, "Indeed. And perhaps, that insult could be of such a high art that the enemy would simply cry and wave the flag to your superior wit."

He lifted his chin, "If they have any sense, they will," he told her while he preened himself in the reflection.

She got up from her reading chair, "I pity the fool who faces you on the battlefield, brother. For surely, they will have no idea of what class of King it is that they have come to fight with."

"I know you mock me," he told her, "You think you're disguising your jeering with compliments, but you are simply no better than a servant behind a curtain whispering your insults to the moths. Pitta witta pitta witta."

"Brother, please, I would not attempt to cross swords with you. Wait! Did I say swords? Pardon me, I forgot that we will have no swords at our battles for England." She declared in a stout voice like a war captain, "Come with your biggest books and your best words you mighty armies of Normandy!"

Edgar turned to her, his face was suddenly filled with worry, "Don't say that." And he thought about it, "Do you think Normandy will invade?"

She came closer to him, "Of course they will. And you, Brother, you will turn your appetite for insult into a hunger for true warcraft, and you will find endlessly clever ways to kill your enemies."

Edgar thought about that, "Yes I will..." He asked her, "Tell me one of the ways."

Margaret came close to him, "You have been taught in war history, of the bravery of the Spartans, the discipline of the Romans, the audacity of Alexander, haven't you?"

"Yes, I have," he told her, "but it would please me greatly to hear you describe one of my great victories to come."

"Sit," she told him.

He sat next to her and suggested, "A Spartan victory perhaps. They are my favourite warriors."

She began, "The Norman Bastard Duke landed on the shores of Wessex with ten thousand men."

"So many?" Edgar asked.

"I'm afraid so," she told him and continued, "England was at his mercy. Before him was the brave King Edgar of England!"

"Yes!" He got to his feet.

She continued, "A true son of Wessex. A true Saxon warrior. And with only three hundred brave men."

"So few?" Edgar asked.

"I'm afraid so," she told him and continued, "the Bastard Duke could not believe his advantage. But the young King had no fear in him."

"Come forward!" Edgar shouted, "Come forward to battle with your great misshapen bastard's head on you! Bring your illegitimate claim, come sideways on your ugly wide-arsed carthorse!"

Margaret smiled and went on, "The Bastard Duke was much insulted by the young King but he did not have the wit to respond. He simply growled like a dumb beast of the field and took the hump from it."

Edgar added, "And he cried?"

Margaret smiled, "Cried?"

"Like a little humpy bastard whelp," Edgar told her.

"Well and good," She said, "but he has ten thousand men."

Edgar wondered, "Are you sure this is a battle I win?"

"Of course," she told him, "because you remember how to turn his advantage of numbers in your favour."

"Yes... I do. Remind me..."

Margaret continued, "The young English King made a retreat!"

Edgar wasn't sure that he liked that, "A retreat?"

"A feigned retreat," she assured him.

"Of course," Edgar said, "I know that."

She continued, "The bastard Duke, seeing the young King run before him, sent his best cavalry unit in pursuit to cut them down. However ... King Edgar had laid his plan well. His men, on foot, ran through a boggy field ... Wherein they had laid hidden paths of stepping stones so as they would not sink into the mire."

Edgar was seeing his plan emerge, "Boggy ground is unsuitable for horses."

"And this bog field had a particular shape to it," She stopped and waited for Edgar to remember his lessons.

It came to him, "It was surrounded on three sides by high cliff face..."

She continued, "Cut into that cliff face was a narrow gully..."

Edward began to see it all, "A gully wide enough to stand thirty men shoulder to shoulder. Like the Spartans at the battle of Thermopylae... "

She joined him, looking at the same imagined battle, "Like King Leonidas, King Edgar formed up his three hundred in the ranks of thirty, ten deep and they waited."

"Singing poems of insults on the invaders!" Edgar shouted.

"Yes!" She agreed, and continued, "The Norman horses floundered in the thick bog and their heavy soldiers were forced to dismount and approach England's position on foot and in full heavy armour. Many Normans simply sank out of sight in their metal, the bog consuming them. Others peeled off their chest plates and helmets and struggled on to the English line. The English bowmen made easy meat of them. Those Normans that made it to the frontline were tired from the slog on boggy foreign soil and they were in turn cut down by the fresh eager Englishmen defending their Motherland."

"How many have I killed?"

Margaret told him, "Five hundred."

"So few?"

"I'm afraid so," she said and continued, "the furious Norman bastard duke sent everything he had in a great wave. But the ranks of Normans were funnelled into the gully, so that they could only meet the English line in equal numbers, in lines of thirty. And Edgar, like a Roman commander..."

Edgar thought hard and recalled his lessons, it came to him, "Cohort Rotatio!"

She continued, "As the English frontline tired, on the command of the whistle, they fell back through the ranks of nine lines to the rear, to rest. So that the Norman frontline, weary and fading, were met constantly by fresh eager Englishmen looking to draw their share of the invader's blood."

Edgar saw it before him, "The Norman bodies piled high."

She told him, "So high that they formed a barricade of corpses ... So that the Norman's then had to climb over the bodies of their fallen brothers only to be met at the top of the corpse hill…"

Edgar shouted, "By fresh English swords and spears."

They let that settle ... Then Edgar asked, "Do I win?"

"You don't have to win."

He examined that, confused.

She explained, "You need only to stand and hold your ground … and wait for your opponent to lose heart. He is the attacker. Let him spend his men on your defences. Lack of progress against a steady defence will sap his soldiers of their resolve and they will lose their appetite for the battle. Then … Find times in the battle where you stand aloft and issue rousing words to your men."

Edgar stood upon a chair, "Foolish Normans, you have followed the misbegotten Duke on his malfeasant crusade that is an offence against God! For the Duke himself is a corruption in the flesh! A shat out of the arse of a blacksmith after a stable buggering! And does not Aristotle warn us of hubris?" He broke from his oration and asked her, "What do you think? Does Aristotle make the argument?"

She advised him, "Maybe speak in more base terms."

"Base?"

She explained, "Many of your men will be simple men from the land. They will not have read Aristotle..."

"I see..."

She encouraged him, "Speak about why they are fighting."

"Because they love me?"

"No brother, do not give them speeches about kings and poets. They are fighting for their families, for their acre of England, for the roof they live under, for the man standing next to them in the battle."

Edgar sat down and put his head in his hands, "This rousing the men will need some thought. I'd be best prepared with some words on parchment..."

"Never read to them," she warned him, and sat beside him, advising him, "If you cannot speak to them from the heart, then say nothing at all."

"And stand silent?"

She assured him, "As long as you stand with them in battle, they will stand with you."

"Why?"

"Because you are their King."

A knock came to the door.

Margaret said aloud, "Enter."

Brother Matthew came into the room accompanied by a huge red-bearded brute. He told them, "This is Wulfstan."

11

ROHÁN

Nana could tell by the skippy gait of Luna as she entered the cave that she had found more than a rabbit out in the forest. She asked her, "Is he alive then?"

Luna slowed and answered, "He's mostly dead," and she continued to the sewing box.

Rosy looked on, not daring to speak.

Nana asked, "What has him that way then? Is he in a trap?"

"No," Luna told her, "he's in the Loner Wolf's cave."

Nana was confused, "And how is he alive in there. And how did you go in to it?"

Luna left a moment to read Nana's face before she then told her, "The boy killed the big old beast, so he did."

Nana weighed that up, "A boy has never killed the old loner?"

"He did so. With this." Luna handed Nana the blade.

Nana looked it over and asked her, "A boy only? You're sure?"

"A boy," Luna assured her, "my own age about," and added, "not a man yet."

Nana held the knife up to the candlelight, and looked at the blade's inscriptions, "Tis an ancient spell it has written in it ... Not any kind of markings that I can read. Tis a very fine warriors blade of some kind. Rohán, if I had to make a guess at it. And he only a boy, you say?"

"Yes."

Rosy asked, "And have you put an end to him the way you would a howler?"

Luna turned on Rosy, "I have not. He's not a howler, is he?"

Rosy put her hands up, "Don't beat me! I was only askin."

Luna stopped short of hitting her but held her in a glare.

Rosy couldn't resist another stab, "Tis Nana who says there are to be no boys or men!"

At that Luna lashed out quicker than the blink of an eye and caught Rosy with a fist full in the face that sent her spinning onto the floor with a bloody mouth.

Nana barked, "Luna!"

Luna came to a halt.

Dina came up from the tunnel that goes into the bowels of the cave, and she warned Rosy, "You'll not live to be a woman if you don't mind that mouth of yours."

None of them were in any doubt that Luna would kill Rosy if she pushed her far enough.

Nana began to think that maybe letting Luna have a mate might not be a bad thing.

Maybe we could do with a boy, she thought, *one that can fight ... if the boy can be tamed.* Nana said, "A boy with a warrior blade the like of this ... I'm thinking he's one of the Rohán for sure."

Luna forgot about killing Rosy and turned to Nana, "You think?"

Rosy, even with a bloody mouth and under the threat of murder, got her bit in, "I heard the Rohán would kill you soon as look at you."

Luna turned back to her, "Do I have to murder you? Is that it?"

Rosy started crying, "I know you all hate me!"

Nana sighed and told Rosy, "If she murders you it will be your own fault. To be honest, I'd be happy with the bit of peace and quiet."

Rosy's crying came to an abrupt halt. This was not the response that Nana usually made. Nana warned her, "Now stop biting off what you can't chew. Shut up."

Then Nana looked back to Luna and explained, "The Rohán do often make camp in the summer on the north edge of the forest, in the wide meadow by the river, while their men are away doing battle for coin up in Umbria." She thought and sucked her pipe, and guessed, "Maybe that meadowland wasn't the safe place that they thought it to be."

Luna watched the old woman's face change, lighten, as she came to a decision.

Nana went on, "The Rohán are the natural folk of the land and good to be good to." And then she asked, "What way is he from the fight?"

"All torn asunder," Luna answered.

Nana weighed it, "Torn asunder and still he lives."

Luna added, "Just about."

Nana finally decided, "We'll have a go at keeping him in the world so."

Luna was delighted, "That's good so."

Nana pulled herself up out of the chair. The three girls knew well not to offer help to her unless she asked for it. They waited as her bones creaked in protest like an old tree swaying in the wind. She sucked hard on her pipe and got to her feet, "There now. There." And she steadied herself. "Get me my stick."

Rosy rushed to get the long walking staff, "Here you are, Nana, I have it for you."

The old woman gripped it in her gnarly fist, "Good girl." All was forgiven. "Let us go to him."

She moved out of the cave, leaving little puffs of the intoxicating smoke behind her as she went.

Nana and Dina got busy on the boy. Luna dragged the wolf's carcass out to the forest. The flies were not pleased about the relocation of their feast from the safe environs of the cave to the outdoors, where they in turn became a feast for the birds.

Rosy sat some distance away on a rock with her lip out watching Luna make quick work of skinning the wolf.

Luna shouted at her, "Get off your lazy arse and dig a hole to bury the carcass in."

Rosy went to her usual excuse, "My foot is paining me something awful, so it is."

Nana shouted from the cave, "My foot will be up your arse if you don't help!"

Rosy moved quickly off her rock and set to digging the hole.

Luna disembowelled the carcass and took the great loops of intestines to the river to clean them. The rest of the wolf was buried by Rosy, putting it beyond the of reach of the flies who gave up their campaign of harassment and went in search of new plunder.

Back in the cave Dina and Nana set to cleaning the boy's wounds with warm water that was infused with one of Dina's healing potions. Luna joined them.

"He's been a lucky lad," Nana said.

He didn't look very lucky to Luna, and she asked, "How is that, Nana?"

Nana explained, "His flesh is torn but inside of his body is intact. If the Loner Wolf had gotten into him, into his innards, he'd be food for the flies now."

Luna thought, *Any small bit of luck is better than no luck at all.*

When the wounds were sufficiently cleaned, Nana said, "Time for the gut."

Luna opened the wet pelt that held the clean wolf-gut that she had washed and cut into long sewing strips. The three sets of skilled hands strung their fine wishbone needles made from the bones of a rabbit's ribcage, using the cured wolf-gut as thread, they set about their task of sewing the boy back together.

"There's not a jug a blood left in him," Nana said.

"But he's not dead," Luna reminded her.

Nana nodded, "And that in itself is already a kind of dark magic, for he is no more than a corpse that is still taking breath. He's most likely already half way across the river."

Nana was from the old Jute people who believed that the dead crossed a river that flowed between the worlds of the living and the dead. The girls often enjoyed her stories about the world of the dead. She had no end of knowledge about it, and Luna often wondered if the old woman had been over on the other side of that river and come back again.

Nana went on, "He might not thank us for pulling him back to the land of the living. We could be making a vengeful monster here in this cave, if he lives."

But Nana didn't stop sewing.

Luna and Dina kept up their sewing on him too.

The hours went by like that, humming and sewing.

Luna took the task of mending the long opening gash that ran the length of his face. As she made her most delicate stitches along his jaw, she thought, *He musta been surely handsome before the wolf did get at him.*

Nana noticed her girl daydreaming over the boy and told her, "Don't bother being fancy," she added, "he's not going to be handsome again no matter how fine your needlework. Be quick. Speed is the better medicine for him now. Get him closed up."

Luna began working for speed rather than beauty. But she fancied that even with the scar on his face that he would be still handsome. *For scars are surely things to be proud of when they have been earned in a fight, especially a fight that you have won.*

Nana sat back and cracked her back, "That's him all closed up. Now get the poultice on him to keep the puss out."

They laid him naked on a bed of pelts and covered him completely in the thick paste that Dina made from ingredients known only to herself. The cave was immediately infused with a crisp clean aroma. The healing began.

12

JAVIER

The servants quickly packed Edgar's great travel trunks for his journey to England. He went about the room from wardrobe to wardrobe instructing them, "I do not care for anything in this one, but I want everything from here, also, the cloaks from there."

Wulfstan entered the young Prince's quarters and looked on the scene with amusement.

Edgar was happy to see him, "Wulfstan. They say that you are the best of all the Huscarls, is that so?"

Wulfstan answered, "I wouldn't say that, my lord, there are better men than me. But I am their Captain."

Edgar weighed that, "Indeed. Well, we will not be long now. We can get this loaded."

Wulfstan put it as best he could, and told him, "My lord, we will not be bringing luggage."

Edgar was at a loss. "Why not?"

Wulfstan explained, "We will be travelling incognitus."

Edgar was at even more of a loss, "Why would I travel so?"

"For your safety, my lord."

"But I have you for that, and your cavalry of Huscarls."

Wulfstan smiled, "We are a small cohort of three men only."

"Three…?" Edgar was stunned, "There are powerful men who wish me dead. How will three men meet our requirements?"

Wulfstan explained, "For what we need to do, three is better than three hundred."

Edgar became perplexed and asked, "And what is it that we need to do?"

Wulfstan answered, "We need to avoid all contact with your enemies."

This seemed absurd to the young Prince, "Avoid them? But the Huscarls are the best soldiers in all of Christendom. Why would you hide from a fight?"

Wulfstan carefully burst the Prince's bubble of ignorance, "My lord, even Huscarls can be defeated in battle. The only battle that is guaranteed to leave you unharmed, is the one that you avoid. We cannot risk your person."

Margaret entered and picked up enough of the tail-end of the discussion to know its contents. She told her brother, "Listen to Wulfstan. He knows his trade better than you or I."

Wulfstan told Edgar, "We will be on horseback, and we will need you disguised. You cannot travel as royalty."

Edgar was slightly intrigued by that. He'd never been anyone apart from himself, the Atheling. He wondered, "Disguised as what? A soldier perhaps?"

Wulfstan shook his head, "No, my lord. We need a disguise that might continue to give you safe passage even if you lose your bodyguard."

Edgar thought about that. He was hitting a blank.

Margaret cracked it, "A monk?"

Wulfstan confirmed it, "Yes, my lady."

The young Prince immediately saw the flaw in their chosen disguise, "But a monk will not work. For apart from the robes, and what have you, he must be tonsured."

Wulfstan and Margaret did not respond to that and simply waited for the pebble to hit the bottom of the well. When it finally plonked, Edgar protested, "No!"

He strode about the room flinging clothes in the air, "I am most certainly not being tonsured!" He protested.

Wulfstan and Margaret made no effort to persuade him or stop his ranting.

Edgar broke into his supply of curses, "Poxy, shit, bollox, scab and arse-boil and..." He called to Wulfstan, "Give me a good curse word!"

Wulfstan told him, "I like to use 'Putain' my lord."

Edgar stopped in his tracks, "I like that word. 'Pu-tain'. What does it mean?"

Wulfstan shrugged, "I know not. It is a Norman curse, my lord."

"Normans..." Edgar darkened a little, "They would have the very lowest of curses at their disposal in their filthy tongue." He closed his eyes, "I will commit it to memory. Pu...tain. It rolls beautifully.

Margaret warned him, "Be careful, brother, all these curses you collect will have to be unpacked before God at your judgement."

Edgar kept his eyes closed tightly as he repeated the word over and over in his mind, *Putain, Putain, Putain,* and told her, "God will not mind my booty of curses. Why else would he have put them in the world if he did not want us to find them and use them?"

Brother Matthew entered, tearful, with a black Benedictine robe in one hand and a fine shaving blade in the other.

Edgar looked at him, and he knew why he had come, "So ... The balding of my noggin was premeditated by a secret pact. The conspirators now gather about my person..."

Matthew filled with guilt and explained, "There was no ill meant by it my precious Prince."

Edgar flopped into a chair and sighed, "Do what you will to me. Putain..."

Soon after, Edgar felt the bald patch of his tonsure that had been expertly shaved into the top of his skull. The material of the black habit scrapped his skin at the neck and cuffs. "This feels like sackcloth," he complained.

Matthew confirmed, "It is not unlike sackcloth, my lord. It is intended to be uncomfortable."

Edgar was at a loss, "Bloomin monks. Why would you want your garments to be uncomfortable?"

Matthew explained, "For the sins of the flesh, my lord."

Wulfstan added, "There will be other uncomfortable elements to your attire."

Edgar asked, "Am I to be flogged along the way like Jesus?"

Matthew blessed himself.

Wulfstan buried his smile, and told the young Prince, "You must wear a chainmail under your habit."

Edgar perked up at that, "That's good. Like a soldier. Are you wearing such a piece of armour?"

"I am, my lord."

Edgar liked that, "And perhaps a fine sword for me too?"

"No, my lord."

Edgar's mood swung, "No Sword? And why not? I am trained in the art of it."

Wulfstan explained, "My lord, if you should find yourself needing to wield a sword, then we can assume that three of the best Huscarls in Christendom are lying dead at your feet. I will have failed you."

Edgar paced, as was his nature, "And I should be slaughtered, unarmed, like meat?"

"No, my lord. There is every chance that you are worth more alive than you are dead."

Edgar stopped, "I see your reasoning. It is sound."

Wulfstan added, "But should that not be the case..." Wulfstan produced a pouch, "I would like to instruct both you and your sister in the use of these weapons."

Edgar moved quickly to him, "Let me see..."

Wulfstan unwrapped the pouch and produced two hand sized crucifixes.

Edgar stopped, annoyed, "Do you play with me?"

"I do not, sire," Wulfstan told him, and he took the head of the crucifix and pulled it so that it split in half and produced a short thin spike-blade, and he explained, "It is used, thus, into the throat, or the eyes, or the temple of the skull."

Edgar smiled, "It is very clever, is it not?"

Wulfstan continued, "I would very much like to take some time, before we leave, to instruct you and drill you on its use."

Edgar picked the weapon up in his hand, it was heavier than he expected, "What is there to learn on it. You have shown me."

Wulfstan explained, "My lord, when we are in the heat of battle, we do not want to think about which moves our sword arm or our shield arm are to perform. We want these moves to happen unthinkingly. And for that, we train the body, in drill, in repetition. So that should you ever need to use this knife, you will do so without needing to think about it. Without hesitation."

Edgar nodded, "I understand." And he asked Wulfstan, "You will drill me?"

Wulfstan told him, "No, my lord."

Edgar was at a loss, "Why not you?"

Wulfstan admitted, "Because I am not the best teacher in this skill. You will be instructed by Javier."

The tall dark Iberian came to the door of the room, put his hand on his heart and bowed his head, "As-salamu alaikum, I am at your service, my Prince."

Edgar's eyes lit up like diamonds, he whispered, "You are a Saracen..."

Javier smiled and replied, "My lord," Then he looked across the room, "My lady."

Margaret turned away and looked out of the window. She had never seen such a specimen of a man before. She feared that he would see the turmoil that he was creating in her. She would simply avoid making eye contact with him.

A solid leather ball the size of a man's head was fixed to a pillar and crudely painted with two eyes that were her targets.

"Again," Javier calmly told Margaret, again…

Margaret was intrigued by the Iberian, the sound of his voice, his patience. Edgar had long since fallen to sleep, worn out like an excited pup who had chased too many hares. Regardless of his bravado, he did not really have an appetite or the physical aptitude for physical violence.

Javier instructed her, over and over. The night went on, the same way, same tone, same speed, time after time, every time. He said, "On guard." She stood at the ready, gripping the crucifix that hung around her neck. He said, "Draw." She pulled the crucifix apart to release the blade. He said, "Ready." She put one foot in front of the other in a strong stance and gripped the handle of the blade in her hand. He said, "Aim". She cocked her elbow back. He said, "Attack ." She punched the blade into the left eye. He said again, "Attack." She punched the blade into the right eye. Then just as she thought that her effort was enough to satisfy him, he said, "We will go again."

Her arm gave up. She had reached a point where she could do no more, "Enough," she told him.

Javier simply nodded, "If that is your wish. But you will not be ready to use the weapon, should you need to."

She became annoyed, "I have done it countless times. I am not stupid."

He smiled, "We are not teaching your mind, my lady. We are teaching your body … to act without your mind. The mind, especially a clever one, picks up and learns easily with curiosity. But the body has no such hunger to learn. The body is a stubborn beast. The only way to teach it is to break it by repetition, until the moves becomes a memory in the muscles of the body. You are close, my lady."

"I cannot. My arm is locked in pain."

He smiled, "It is a cramp, my lady. Please… allow me." He lead her to her chair, "Sit, please."

She sat.

He gently took her slender arm in his hand and told her, "This will hurt … at first. But it will then feel better." He gripped the entirety of her shoulder in his fist and then kneaded as he would a ball of bread dough…

She was glad that she was sitting, for the sensation that went through her body would have taken her legs away from under her.

"Let your head rest forward, my lady"

One hand pressed its fingers deep into her shoulder, and she made an involuntary moan. It was the most beautiful pain. His other hand worked down her arm, kneading it. She was filled with the most intoxicating cocktail of pain and pleasure. Time stopped for her. She drifted away. At some point she opened her eyes to see that he was kneading her hand and then each finger. She watched his hand working. Whatever willpower she had was long gone from her. This man could simply have done whatever he pleased with her, and she would not have protested.

He stopped, looked at her, "Better?"

She gathered her thoughts enough to say, "Yes."

He smiled, "Again?"

She smiled.

He stood up and went by the leather ball.

"On Guard."

This time when she attacked the ball, her arm was free and fast, and her aim was deadly. He was silent. She had reached the point where she was carrying out the series of movements without a thought. Fast.

She was still managing not to look him in the eyes, for too long … and replied with as much indifference as she could muster, "Thank you."

Javier then spoke to her in a private tone, and told her, "You must stay close to your brother at all times. He does not have the resolve for fighting that you possess. In the end, it may well come to it that you are his only protection."

Margaret, examining her weapon to no particular end, nodded and replied, "Do not fear … I will give my life for my brother. And for England."

Margaret had read more than a few epic romance tales on the

momentous encounters that consume the protagonists in a blaze of love, triggering cataclysmic events that created new worlds as Antony and Cleopatra, or brought destruction as with Paris and Helen. Up to now, she had viewed all such tales as nonsense. She did not believe that intelligent people could become slaves to their emotions. But now she realised that she was wrong. It was entirely possible. She was truly fearful of this previously unknown weakness.

She told herself, *I can never afford to lose control of myself and give my will over to be... What? Consumed by a man? It would be no better than me stepping upon the pyre to be willingly burned at the stake. But worse than that, it would be a dangerous liability for the safety of Edgar, and a threat to the integrity of the realm.*

She took in the dark handsome face of Javier, and thought, *Whatever dark seductive powers you possess, and I am in no doubt that you could seduce any woman that you set your eyes upon, I must be sure in my ability to defend myself from you. My first love must always be England. I must make sure I cannot be put under your spell, or the spell of any other man. I must learn from you.*

She steeled herself, purposefully making strong direct eye contact with him and held it. Her heart raced. She kept a calm exterior, making sure that her voice did not tremble, and give away her rising anxiety. She asked him, purposefully hitting the bawdy double entendre on the nose, "Is there anything else you wish to teach me?"

Javier smiled, "At this time I think that you know all that you need to, my lady."

She did not release him from her gaze.

Edgar stirred, and moaned, "Show her how to use the garrotte, I've always imagined it to be her weapon of choice."

Margaret looked away from Javier and smiled, the first tasting of him was over. She had nibbled enough. For now.

In the dead of night the horses were made ready. They were travelling as a cohort of five, comprising the three Huscarls dressed as common journeymen, a young monk and a young nun, with a packhorse in tow carrying a tent, extra clothing, furs, food, and water. As they mounted their horses in the stables, Edgar stopped and did the accounting. They were, by his reckoning, one horse short. He asked, "Where is Brother Matthew's horse?"

The old gout-ridden monk had come to see them off. He explained to his young student, "My Prince, I would not make the journey of a hundred yards."

Edgar wrestled with the sudden wave of unexpected emotions that flooded him. Until this moment, he had no understanding of his depth of love for the old monk. In fact, had someone asked the young Prince yesterday if he cared for his old teacher, he would have told them he did not. Now it was plain that the opposite was true.

Edgar told him, "I want you to come with me to England."

Matthew was also struggling with great emotion, for he knew that this would be the last time that he would see his young Prince. But he did not bring that knowledge into their discussion. Instead, he asked the Prince, "Perhaps I could follow later in a cart? I cannot mount a horse ... And then, God willing, I would arrive to you in England some time after you have been crowned King."

Edgar thought on that. The idea of the old monk arriving into the great palace and seeing him on the throne pleased him. "Yes. I like that idea," he told Matthew, "you must have a cart prepared for you with plenty of soft hay for you to lie upon. You must follow us at first light tomorrow."

Matthew smiled, "As you wish, my lord."

Edgar happily mounted onto his horse.

Margaret came to the old monk and unexpectedly hugged him. Matthew was so unprepared for it that he almost broke and made tears.

She told him, "Thank you for all you have done," and whispered in his ear, "I will never forget you in my prayers."

Matthew whispered to her, "Take care of him for me."

She smiled, "You will soon be able to do your service to us from Heaven."

Matthew nodded, "I hope so, my lady."

She kissed him on the forehead.

Edgar complained, "Come on. Don't make a theatrical Greek scene out of it. We will see the old moaner soon enough."

Margaret smiled, and went to her horse and mounted it.

Mathew stood at the stable doors and watched the cohort go until they were swallowed into the night. He slowly made his way back to his quarters. In his monastic cell that was void of any comforts apart from his bed, he knelt and said his prayers. Then he climbed into his blankets. His life's work was done. He had educated a future king and a future queen, and unknowingly, a future saint. He was tired now. It had been a long life. He went into a well-deserved sleep and slept so soundly that he never woke up again.

Margaret watched her brother sleeping under a pile of furs. He was not built for the road, but he was holding up better than she expected. At the beginning of their journey the nightly discussions around the fire were polite and practical. But after the third week of travelling, the boundaries of the discussions were worn away to the point where they no longer existed. Edgar much enjoyed hearing the Huscarls tell their tall tales of soldiering and expanding his knowledge of curse words. Margaret was genuinely in awe of these men who entered in and out of deadly situations without a second thought. Each of them had almost lost their lives more than a dozen times, and yet here they were, hardy and full of optimism, ready to laugh and sing at a moment's opportunity. But it was Javier who interested her more than the others because he held a bounty of vital secrets.

She stood up from the fire, "I feel the need for a walk and to take in the night air."

The men got to their feet out of politeness, and Wulfstan made ready to escort her.

She then offered, "Javier, perhaps you could be my guard?"

"Of course, my lady."

She turned and walked away from the light of the fire into the darkness. Javier looked to Wulfstan. Neither of them needed to exchange words on the matter. Javier knew that was a line he dare not cross as he followed Margaret into the night.

In the darkness some distance from the campfire, Margaret watched the moon and listened for Javier approaching behind her. She spoke without looking at him, "You must find me very bold."

Javier kept at least twelve big footsteps away from her, "Not at all, my lady," he lied.

She looked at him, "Do not fear me, Javier."

He took a step back.

She assured him, "I have no improper intentions toward you."

He made a small sigh of relief, said nothing, and still kept his distance.

She went on, "But I do require intimacy with you."

At this he started to make his defence, "My lady, I would be boiled and flayed and…"

She raised her hand, "I would not see you harmed … You misunderstand my intentions. Let me explain, better." She sat on a nearby fallen tree, "When I first laid eyes on you, you took my breath away and infused yourself into my thoughts and dreams the way a spice works into meat. It occurred to me that you, and men like you, are a kind of opium to a woman's heart. I'm sure you know what I talk of. You see how I look at you. There is no need to be coy with me."

Javier could see no way out other than being honest, "I understand, my lady."

She asked him, "Tell me honestly. Did you see the weakness in me? When I looked at you?"

Javier told her, "Yes."

She lowered her eyes, "I am like a lamb to the slaughter."

Javier tried to explain his thoughts, "No, my lady. Such thoughts … feelings even, these are all normal in women … and in men too."

She looked at him and smiled, "You are not so naive are you? A man and a woman are not the same. For a man, such things are trivial. He might bed as many women as he likes, and fall in and out of love as easily as he would climb on and off his horse. All that will come his way for being a rogue are hearty congratulations from other men. If you do not know that already, then you should know it now. It is not so for a woman … We are marshalled by different laws … And yet, our appetites are just as full and lusty as those of a man."

"I apologise, my lady." Javier faltered a little, "I did not … know that."

She asked, "What part of it were you ignorant of?"

He was uncomfortable now, speaking too much, "The em… appetite part." And he admitted, "I am much out of knowledge, my lady."

She smiled, "So quickly into the deep waters? Are you blushing?"

"Probably. Definitely. "

"My. My. Tell me, and tell me honestly, how many women have you bedded?"

"Bedded?"

"Yes."

"My lady…"

"Tell me."

"I em…" he searched his mind, and asked her, "This season?"

She raised an eyebrow, "This season? Fine. How many this season?"

Javier did a quick round up, "Baker's dozen … perhaps."

She thought about that, "And are there Ladies among your conquests?"

"Two ladies, my lady."

"And the others?"

"Lady's maids, mostly, my lady."

She thought about that and then asked him, "And are your devices of seduction the same for the lady as for the maid?"

He was unsure, "Devices, my lady?"

She asked him, "Do you treat one different from the other?"

"No, my lady, I treat them all the same."

"And how is that then?" She asked.

"As a queen," he told her.

Now it was her turn to blush. She sighed, "I fear you are too good at this."

He told her honestly, "My lady, as God is my witness, I have no idea what this is. I do not play it as a game. I do not set out with a plan. Women happen upon me and I… I truly feel that I love them. But it is… "

"Fleeting?"

"Yes," he agreed, "That is a good word for it. Fleeting."

She laughed softly. "I am retaining you to train me in the finer skills of combat."

He was instantly relieved, "Of course."

She added, "But not with the sword."

He was at a sudden loss. Again.

She explained, "You will train me in the fine skills of seduction."

He backed away, "My lady…"

She rose to her feet, "If you do not… I fear that I will one day fall prey to a seducer who is not as honest and as loyal as you are. Such a fall for the wrong man, would be, for me … fatal."

"My lady… It is you who are the seductress."

She was not sure what he meant, "Continue."

He gathered his thoughts and presented it in a better way, "I mean to say, I have travelled all of Christendom from Constantinople to Rome and to London … I do not wish to be a braggart, so forgive me when I say, I have known the intimate company of every kind of beautiful woman that God has made and put on this earth, from maids to queens and even an empress. But you are, by far, the most beautiful woman that I have ever seen in my life…"

After a moment, she told him, "You flatter me, I think."

He got down on his knees, "I swear it. It was I who was struck deeply by you … like I have never been struck … I have loved you from that moment to this … and I will do so, happily unrequited, until the end of my days." And he gestured back to the fire, "And it is so with the men in my company. You have the greatest beauty any of us have seen." And he smiled, "That is a power … a power that is greater than an army."

She smiled, "Then … if it is true … you must show me how to use my power. Will you do that, Javier?"

He lowered his head, "It will be … my honour, my lady."

Wulfstan arrived, watching the darkness, and asked Javier, "What are you praying about now?"

Javier got to his feet, "There is always something to pray for."

She asked Wulfstan, "What is the problem?"

He told her, "Peter has come back from a recognisance. We're being tracked."

Javier's mood changed. He became alert and ready for violence.

"How many," she asked.

Wulfstan answered flat with no emotion, "Maybe a dozen or so."

She didn't like those odds, "A dozen? We are less than half that number."

He smiled, "We could safely deal with double that number."

She then smiled too, "I believe you could."

He took that as the compliment that it was meant to be, "Thank you, my lady."

She asked him, "What's to be done?"

Back at the fire, Margaret watched Wulfstan draw a map into the ground with the tip of his dagger. Javier and Peter gathered around as he explained, "The assassins won't make their move within the borders of the Holy Roman Empire. Our Prince has a handful of competitors for the crown, and none of them can afford to offend the greatest power in Christendom by committing regicide within its borders."

Peter advised, "They'll wait until we are at the coast. Try to kill us quietly there and put us in the water to go undiscovered."

Javier had other ideas, "We can enter their camp tonight and put an end to them."

Wulfstan normally liked suggestions that involved daring acts of sudden violence, but he didn't like it this time, "We risk too much. We are all that stands between danger and our Prince."

Javier added, "And our Princess."

Margaret quickly weighed the problem and came to a solution, "We will make for Fécamp."

Wulfstan reminded her, "Our plans are to make for Hamburg. There is a boat waiting for us, my lady."

She quietly told him, "Our plans have changed. We will make for the Benedictine Abbey at Fécamp."

The men shared a look. But it was left to Wulfstan to tell her, "Fécamp is on the Normandy coast ... my lady."

She smiled, "I have studied my geography, Wulfstan, and my history. Many of the monks in the Abbey there are English monks. They once had a fine abbey in Wessex that our grandfather, King Ironside, built for them. But our grandfather was betrayed and murdered by King Canute. Our family, The House of Wessex, was forced into exile and our lands and title were given to the man who betrayed our grandfather — Godwin. Godwin then usurped the title of The Earl of Wessex. The monks refused to recognise him as their Earl. Godwin then exiled the monks and seized their lands. I have studied my enemies. Those mercenaries that follow us are either in the hire of Godwin's son, Harold Godwinson or William the Bastard Duke of Normandy. So, weigh that."

Wulfstan and his men thought about it, but nothing came to them.

Edgar had been following the conversation from the warmth of his furs. He joined them at the fire, informing them, "My sister is the cleverest of us all. When we enter the Abbey at Fécamp, the monks will be obliged to immediately inform their Duke, William. But the monk's first loyalty is to Rome. They will also inform the Pope. If it is the Bastard Duke who has put these assassins on us, his plan is out of the shadows and Rome will have an eye on matters. For William to prove his innocence, he must now give us safe passage to England. If the assassins are in the pay of the charlatan Harold Godwinson, then William will still be obliged to protect us, and give us safe passage to England. If all of that should fail us, there are monks there who are loyal to the true House of Wessex and they will see us safely to England. Either way..."

Wulfstan smiled, "We have safe passage from Normandy to England."

"Scotland," Margaret corrected them.

Edgar was also at a loss now, "Sister?"

"We are for Scotland. London is not safe for us until you are crowned. We will travel by sea journey to Edinburgh."

Edgar asked, "Why would we go to the Scots?"

She explained, "I have a pledge of protection made to me on my baptism from King Malcolm. He will honour it. We will wait in his protection until King Edward dies. Then you can be crowned in York and proceed to London as King."

Wulfstan shook his head. He was truly out of his league. "I'm glad I am a simple soldier. We will do as my lady says. We will make for Fécamp."

13

LOVERS

Luna looked at the scarred swollen face protruding from the cocoon of furs.

She thought, *He looks like a giant's babby, so he does.*

She observed that his lips were cracked, and his skin was drying out like a hide. He would not last long if she could not make him drink. She had an idea. Hoping that he had the reflex of a newborn to suckle, she fashioned a tit from the bollox bag and cock skin of the wolf and filled it with water. Then holding the long wet flute of cock skin to his lips and letting it drip slowly, the liquid found its way into his parched mouth. Easing the cock-nipple gently between his lips, she urged him, "Come on now. Come on. Suck." To her delight, he suddenly latched on and sucked heavily like a hungry baby goat. He emptied the bollox bag in no time. She filled it again. Once more, he went at it like a starving suckling. After a few minutes, she decided that he was running the risk of taking too much too quickly. She pulled the teat from his mouth with a pop. A faint pitiful whimper came from him. Then he simply lay there in a silent quiver.

She rubbed his head, "Hush now."

His breathing settled.

More than a week came and went like that. She dared not move him. All that was needed for him to heal, she brought to the cave. She never left his side. Each morning she peeled the pelts away, cleaned his wounds, covered him in the poultice, and fed him with the wolf bollox tit. His water was fortified with a thin gruel and Dina's potion. One morning while cleaning him she noticed that he was coming back closer to life. His cock was attempting to rise. When she touched it. It responded by getting larger. She held it, and when she squeezed it she felt his heartbeat in it. She rubbed her fingers through his hair.

In the quiet hours of the night, Luna lay naked on the warm pelts next to the boy, giving him her heat, examining his body and tracing his healing scars with her finger. His skin was hot to the touch, and when she put his hand between her legs, he moaned. It filled her with a hungry feeling. She lit the cudu in the pipe, inhaled it, held it, and when he inhaled, she exhaled the sweet smoke into his face so that he consumed it. Immediately his breathing calmed, deepened, slowed. His body relaxed.

She lay her head on his shoulder and held his cock. She liked the feel of it pulsing in her hand. She whispered, "You and me will stay together, maybe. I do like your cock. It's a nice thing to hold. And I don't mind that your face is all scarred. I like that too. And you won't mind me with the rad hair on me and how I am with the bad temper that I have, neither. And even if I do lose my temper, I will try really hard not to kill you."

His eyes opened.

She looked into them. "And lovely eyes you have." After some time of looking into his vacant eyes, she asked him, "Do you have any sense left in your head at all?"

Slowly something stirred in his eyes. Thoughts coming to life. Then a question forming. He made a hoarse sound.

"That's nothing. Tis only a grunt you're making. Do you have words at all?"

His grunting moan then turned into a word, "What...?"

She told him, "The wolf got you."

It came back to him. After a moment he starting croaking again, "My Mother... I have to..." He tried to move, and everything hurt.

"You can't move."

Then the pain of the flesh came to him, and he moaned like a howler in a trap.

She took out a small ball of cudu and held it at his mouth, "Open"

He moaned and opened his mouth like a hungry hatchling in a nest.

She popped the ball of cudu into his gob, "Swallow this for the pain."

He swallowed.

She watched his eyes. Slowly she saw him come out of the world of pain and into the soft lovely place that the cudu takes you to. Some moments later, he smiled, and looked back at her, into her eyes, as if he were seeing her for the first time.

She looked right back into him. She saw him then. Then she held his cock, again, tight, "Do you like that?"

"I do."

She put his hand between her legs, again, "Do you like that?"

"I do."

She smiled, "Tis good that we like the same things so. We make a good pair, I'm thinking."

They stayed like that and said nothing for the longest time. Eventually she worked up the courage to have a go at kissing him. He moved his lips with hers. She eased her tongue into his mouth. He tasted salty and sweet. She became hungry for him and forced her tongue further in. He responded in kind. They were equally hungry.

She said, "Rub it."

He rubbed between her legs, as she often did in the nights. She held his cock and worked it.

Then she stopped him, "I'm going to get up on you now. Don't move."

She carefully straddled him. Then she eased herself down onto his cock, so that it went into her. Slowly, carefully, she moved down, feeling it entering her further, "Easy now" she advised herself, "Don't kill him." Down she went on it, until his cock was fully inside of her. She stayed like that for a time, panting, feeling him throbbing in her. She had come to the end of her knowledge, imagination and creativity.

She asked him, "Do you know the rest of it?"

He placed his hands on her hips and slowly rocked her back and forth. She followed the instruction of his hands, riding him, slow steps, as if taking a horse walking. Then he urged her on, pushing her hips. She felt that great madness rising in her, and she feared it. "Easy…" she whispered to him,… "easy now." She grew afraid that she might lose herself and go out of control. "Not hard," she warned him, "I will kill you." She removed his hands from her hips and took control, continually reminding herself, "Easy. Easy. Don't kill him." Keeping to a slow gentle canter.

He asked her, "Who are you?"

"Luna."

He whispered it, "Luna…" Then he said, "I am called Kallín."

She said it, "Kallín"

She liked the sound of it. Then without warning her insides ignited in a flash of tremendous heat. Her body was suddenly engulfed in a burning fire, and it consumed them both in its beautiful death.

14

FÉCAMP

The bed was an unforgiving solid straw pallet, but Margaret was happy to lie upon it. The long weeks of journey on horseback had made her sore in places that she did not know existed. But she was glad of the hardship. *My life in the court,* she thought, *has made me soft and precious like a summer flower.*

She knew that she would need to be tough for the coming trials.

When she closed her eyes and thought of setting foot on English soil, her heart sang. She'd spent her whole life in preparation, learning the history and geography of a home that she'd never seen. In her dreams she found herself walking over the rolling hills of her family home in Wessex. It was a dream she often composed before going to sleep. But on this night, a new thought continually forced its way through all of her prayers and good intentions to have pure dreams: Javier. She scolded herself and knew that she must find a way to steel herself from the attraction. But for now … she did not fight it. For now … it was a comfort to her to indulge in … thinking of his dark eyes. She knew that he was camped outside of her door keeping guard. That was how she slept. Safe. Her dreams were not saintly.

Outside of Margaret's door, Javier sat in a chair. At the next door along, Wulfstan sat outside of the Prince's room. Peter patrolled the grounds. The night passed without incident.

Sometime just after daybreak, a heavy cavalry arrived under royal banners.

Margaret woke to a knock on her door.

"Who is it?" she asked.

"Javier, my lady."

"One moment." She rose from her bed and made herself presentable. Then composing herself, she told him, "Enter."

Javier opened the door but did not take a step inside the small cell, he told her, "He has come here, my lady."

Margaret was at a loss. "Of whom do you speak?"

"The Duke of Normandy," he told her.

Her heart and her mind began to race with possibilities. Had she got it wrong by bringing them into the wolf's lair?

Javier eased her mind, "Your reasoning still holds strong, my lady. The Duke can do no harm to you or your brother while you are within his borders. You are now under the eye of Rome."

"What do you imagine that his reason is for coming here?" she asked him.

Javier smiled, "Maybe he just wants to see if the rumours are true."

"Rumours?" she asked him, "What rumours?"

"Of your beauty," he replied.

She turned away, "Then I shall make myself as dull as a nun."

"My lady, if I might advise you?"

She told him, "You may. I would like that."

Javier told her, "It is most likely that the Duke is here to gauge the size of the problem he will soon have facing him in war, should he invade England. He will be trying to assay your metal, and that of your brother."

"I see."

"My advice to you would be to hide from him."

She grew perplexed again, "Do you suggest that I climb under my bed?"

"Not at all, my lady. I should have said, disguise yourself from him."

She was now intrigued, "What manner of disguise?"

Javier went on, "I would suggest that you meet him, but show him a version of yourself that is closer to what he hopes to see."

She asked him, "What does he hope to see?"

He told her, "A young naive princess, who is indeed the most beautiful of all, and maybe is … in awe of him?"

She was at a loss, "And why would I want to present that?"

Javier explained, "So that he will have no idea who he is to meet in battle." And he grew serious, "Be in no doubt, my lady, he will invade England, and we will meet him in war. We must do everything to conceal our strengths from him, until battle comes."

She smiled at that, "You think I will be a strength in a battle?"

Javier told her, "I have no doubt that you will one day be a great queen and lead armies into battle."

She thought for a moment, "Awed princess it is then."

A short time later, there was a great commotion in the halls as Edgar joined his sister. He entered her room, stopped, and looked at her in surprise, "Why are you done like that?"

"Like what," she smiled and batted her eyes.

"What the…? Are you for the theatre? Your hair? Your … face."

"Brother, I am indeed for the theatre, but I am playing a part and you must do the same."

Edgar was suddenly intrigued, and asked her, "Are we really to have a play?"

"Of sorts," she told him, "we are to put on a performance for the Duke of Normandy."

Edgar was stumped, "You jest."

"I do not."

He was insulted, "Why would we entertain the ugly Bastard? I've heard he has no love for the arts and doesn't even speak Latin."

She agreed, "All that is true, but," she explained, "our war with the illegitimate begins here and now," she went on, "what he sees here today is what he will expect to meet when he invades England."

Edgar made a fist, "Then let us put the fear of God into him!"

She smiled, "Brave Brother, have you forgotten your battle craft? When you are weak, appear strong. When you are strong…

"Appear weak," he added.

She explained, "We will be a lethal enemy to face in battle."

"We will," he agreed.

She told him, "So we must play at being our opposite to him. We must leave him thinking that we are as harmless to him as the beasts of the field." But she could see he was not taking to the idea, and so she worked him again, in a different way, rubbing up his pride, "Of course, you are the more talented thespian of the two of us, so I will be relying on your theatrical skills to carry the greater weight of the performance."

Edgar responded to that, "It is true that I am a gifted thespian, I grant you that." He began a small circling walk with his finger on his chin, "I will use my finest dramatist skills to create a whole new character, Prince Chin-Chinertin, yes! I must rehearse myself privately. The Bastard will think me completely gormless. Wait and see!" And then he excitedly blew out of the room to some private place to create his masterpiece.

She wanted to tell him to not to ham it up, as is his usual fault in playing theatrical parts, but this time she did not give him direction because she herself would need direction for the part she was about to play. Thankfully, she knew where to find advice in the matter, she called out, "Javier, please come in."

Javier entered and was stopped by her smile, "My lady?"

She asked him, "Tutor me in how to perform seduction," and she blinked.

Javier understood the workings of this play. He'd seen it performed many times in the various Royal Courts where he stood as a silent witness in the role of a discreet bodyguard at the doors to private chambers.

He began, "The Duke will be, on his first sight of you, hungry to look upon you. But he is also a married Duke and working hard to stay in the favour of Rome, so that he might invade England with Papal approval. He will work at being pious in front of his ever-present monks. In the first instance, keep your eyes to the floor. This invites him to gaze upon your visage without challenge."

"As if I were no more than a beautiful statue?"

"Yes, my lady."

"So … He desires obedience in a woman?"

Javier wrestled to find the correct interpretation, "Yes … but with a certain amount of resistance, so to show chastity and make his … conquest … worthy."

"I see," said Margaret, and asked him, "Are all men so inclined?"

"No … Not all, my lady."

"Good. For I would never marry with such a man."

"Of course not, but this is not a meeting with a suitor. He is already married. It is a kind of duel of wits, you must remember. In this matter, you will hold the blade to his throat."

"Yes," she agreed and composed herself, "So … I look down thus?" she asked and looked down.

Javier took a step back, "Yes … Thus is … captivating. Truly."

She looked up at him.

He told her, "And when you do look at him, do it like that, and he will be as a hungry bird eating out of your hand."

She smiled and asked, "As you are?"

Javier looked to the floor.

"I am sorry, Javier. I have made you feel uncomfortable."

He shook his head and smiled, "It is not uncomfortable that you have made me, my lady." He smiled to himself and swept the stupid thoughts out of his head, and got back to his teaching, "Just remember, my lady, at all times, the trick of keeping a bird feeding from your hand is to not feed it too much. It is the same trick that is vital in the art of seduction, and in the art of war; keep your enemy marching to the beat of your drum, less is more."

He smiled at her, unguarded, and in a moment, it was Margaret who was the bird ready to eat from his hand…

She told him, "I understand now."

He advised her, "Give away the attention of your eyes in very small portions as a lure. And when he is hooked, play him as you would a fish."

She told him, "I have never fished."

He smiled, "Well, some day I will take you fishing, my lady." He bowed his head, "Now, if you will excuse me." And he left.

She took a deep breath and recited to herself, *less is more. Less is more.*

The handful of displaced Benedictines from Wessex who were living with their brothers in Fécamp, heard that the Prince and Princess of their much loved House of Wessex was meeting with William. They set about decorating the chapel of the Fécamp Abbey with banners and flags, and filled it with as much pomp and circumstance as the they could muster to create a suitable venue for the Duke of Normandy to receive the future King of England. William assumed all of the pomp was on his account, and no one told him any differently. He sat himself on a raised throne in front of the altar, the height facilitated him to look down his long nose upon the English Royals when they arrived. He wore his favourite great regal cloak which had been brought to Normandy from Constantinople. There was not another cloak like it in all of Europe, made of the exclusive fine purple silk reserved solely for the Byzantine Imperial Bloodline. Of course, William the Bastard was not a part of that bloodline. Once he was comfortably arranged he quickly grew impatient.

"Where are they?" he growled at his monk, Brother Tomas.

Tomas informed him, "I am told they are on their way, my lord, apparently the young Prince has an affliction that inhibits him from making normal speed."

William's curiosity was suddenly piqued, he wondered aloud, "An affliction?"

In the great hallway of the Abbey, Edgar and Margaret came to the impressive oak doors of the chapel.

Edgar whispered to her, "Hold my hand."

Margaret was not privy to the full details of Edgar's intended character portrayal, he did not want to spoil the surprise for her, but she had no doubt that his performance would be entertaining and memorable. She immediately took his hand, whereupon he turned his feet inward, so that he walked like a bandy-footed pigeon. He then stuck out his chin to make his head extend on the full length of his neck and protrude at least a foot ahead of his feet.

Margaret felt the rise of a stage corpse in her chest. She thought terrible thoughts to subdue it.

The great doors swung open!

The royal pair began their long regal entrance up the grand central isle, where Edgar proceeded to make his pigeon toed walk, flapping down his feet as if he were a duck, so that his steps echoed around the great vaulted ceiling.

William's eyes widened, he looked to his shrewd monk who stood some distance away from him. Brother Tomas simply raised his shoulders in a shrug and whispered to William, "I fear the Prince has been too much inbred, my lord."

William watched Edgar with a growing curiosity. But as the pair got closer to him, his eyes were drawn away from the clown act and onto Margaret who kept her eyes to the floor. He whispered at his monk, "She is … angelic … is she not?"

Brother Tomas, himself a veteran of the Royal Courts of Europe, knew he was looking at a potentially dangerous young queen in the making, agreed, but with less surety, "Yes, my lord. Angelic she seems."

Margaret kept her eyes lowered and made a seductive curtsey, slow, poetic. She felt William's eyes on her, as Javier had predicted, devouring her visage. She waited for a moment, fully curtsied to him, and then begun to slowly rise back to her full height. As she rose back up, she briefly raised her eye-line so as to catch William fully unprepared, sitting like a hungry dog gawping at meat. Then a moment later, she looked down again.

Brother Tomas whispered privately to his Duke, "My lord, your mouth hangs open."

William closed his mouth and went so far as to keep his finger under his chin so that his jaw would not hang loose on its hinges again.

Edgar then went into the next part of his performance, bowed overly long and slow and low … until his head almost tipped the floor and everyone waited, holding their breath to see if the imbecile would fall over. He then sprang erect and apologised in appalling French, "Purdon muwah. I am practice-ing my bow-wing."

Brother Tomas spoke to the royal visitors in English, "Welcome dear Atheling Edgar and Princess Margaret. I am Brother Tomas. I present to you, William, Duke of Normandy. The Duke is most glad that you came to us for safe passage when you suspected danger. And, how clever of you to disguise the young Prince…" he smiled knowingly to Margaret, and continued, "as a monk."

Margaret sensed that the wily monk could see through their performance. But she had confidence in her abilities. She looked at him wide eyed and brightly open faced, ready to smile at any moment, as a child might look at a father, and spoke to him in perfect Latin, "The disguise was a necessary precaution suggested to us by our own beloved holy monk, Brother Matthew. It was not meant as an insult or a mockery to your holy order, Brother Tomas."

Now it was Tomas's turn to be impressed by her. "Who educated you in Latin, my lady?"

"Our own beloved Brother Matthew," she answered, and went on, "He had me studying in preparation from the time I could first walk, Brother."

Tomas smiled, "He taught you well. What perfect Latin you have. And so … beautifully spoken." And then he asked, "Studying in preparation for what, exactly?"

Brother Tomas suspected that her extensive education in Latin was for use in the Royal Courts of Europe, where Latin is the language for official business. She was being groomed to be a queen.

Keeping her open bare face of a child, she told him, "My teaching was in preparation to join the holy orders, Brother."

Tomas was suddenly stung with a stab of shame at having been so wrong with his assumption.

William growled to his monk, "What is this Latin babbling about?"

Tomas explained, "We are speaking of her preparations for holy orders, my lord."

William growled again, "Speak French."

"Yes, my lord." Tomas went on to explain, "I will translate for our Duke William, he does not speak … English."

Margaret thought with a soft angelic smile, *Nor does the ignorant mongrel speak Latin.*

Edgar, with his chin firmly out, shouted loudly to Tomas, "I spweek Fwench, minsure!"

William sniggered and caught the snarl of his laugh somewhere in his throat with a cough to smother it.

Tomas too almost broke. Even though he suspected that the young Prince was clown acting, it somehow just made it more absurdly funny to him. For if there was a joke being played, then it was hitting the mark. The Duke was swallowing the performance as a gullible fish swallows the bait: hook, line and sinker.

Edgar, sensing the ripeness in his audience to laugh, went on harder in the most deplorable French, "Gwait Noble Duck, we fill yew wit the luv!"

William's stern face quivered and a tear escaped his eye. He could only nod.

Tomas pinched himself under his robe and told Edgar, "The Duke intends to see you safely on your way. You will travel under his…" Tomas was distracted by a long dribble coming from Edgar's mouth and landing on the floor in a puddle. Edgar kept on looking at him, not batting an eye. Tomas went on, "Safety. Under his safety."

Edgar built his performance, loudly, "When weee get to Engaland I am getting a dawg!"

He watched William struggle to keep a straight face.

Then the thespian Prince delivered his punchline that was guaranteed to crack his audience, and he started clapping his hands in frenzied delight, "And a new pony! Yippppeee!"

William broke, rose quickly to his feet and walked out in a hurry.

Tomas was left hanging, tearful, "Well. It seems that my lord is…"

A great howl of painful laughter came from the sacristy!

Tomas explained, "Indisposed."

Later, Margaret sat alone in the privacy of her room, analysing the meeting with the bastard duke. Recalling that every contact with your enemy is an opportunity to learn about him. In this first contact with William, she noted some important details of his character. His clothes were overly grandiose, and he dressed himself in shining Byzantine silk cloth. Also, it was coloured imperial purple. Yet this Duke was not even a king, never mind an emperor. It could be argued that his gaudy presentation of self-importance was the laughable portrait of the vanity of a jumped up bastard. She would have agreed with that interpretation if it were not for his eyes. For when she looked briefly into those dark orbs that gazed upon her, she saw that they were vacant of any humanity, they were the eyes of a predatory beast. She knew that if a man is ambitious enough and ruthless enough, that he may conquer the world as Alexander did. She knew in her heart, as surely as if it were whispered into her ear by the divine voice of God, that the Norman's hunger would consume England.

But there was one more important observation from her meeting with the Norman that worried her above the others. Amongst all the pompous banners of support from the various dukes of Flanders and war magnates from surrounding fiefdoms, a Papal banner hung over William's head in pride of place. She now knew that William the Bastard had the backing of Rome to make his conquest of England.

Edgar kept up his clown act for the whole of the day and into the next day until they finally boarded the boat that William had supplied. There wasn't a soul in Normandy who did not believe that the Atheling was touched by angels. Margaret suspected that Brother Tomas saw through the ruse, but, importantly, he did not share his insight with his Duke. If anything, Margaret surmised, the monk seemed to take pleasure from the Duke being led by the nose. Or maybe, she hoped, the monk knew he was serving a man who had no soul.

As Margaret approached the dock with Edgar and Wulfstan, Javier and Peter — she noticed a dozen monks waiting at the boat.

Wulfstan became cautious, "What is this?"

Margaret smiled, "I know what it is."

One of the monks, a large older man, came forward, "Princess Margaret, Prince Edgar, I am Brother Bernard from the old Abbey at Hastings. It was my pleasure and a blessing to have met your grandfather when I was a youth. We have come to renew our holy pledge to you. We will pray night and day for the Crown of England to be placed on Edgar's rightful head."

The monks kneeled. Bernard went on in Latin, making the pledge of his holy order to the House of Wessex.

Margaret spotted William watching from a distance, "We should set sail."

They received the blessing from the monks and boarded the boat, setting off on their voyage while the monks gathered on the end of the pier and began their prayers for the safe journey.

William watched them sail away, and spoke privately to Tomas, "The idiot Prince will not be a problem. The Witan will never vote him over Harold Godwinson to be King of England … Will they?"

Tomas then broached a problem he could see, "But … should they end up in the hands of the Scot King, Malcolm, then they would be perfect puppets. Especially the Atheling … and if Malcolm were to wed the Princess Margaret and make her Queen? And as you can see, the Church adores her."

William carefully considered the danger of that. A war with a fractured England and the unpopular Harold Godwinson as King, he can win. But if King Malcolm of Scotland came to England's aid with the Atheling crowned King and his sister made Queen of Scotland, and with the support of the church — it would be too much to conquer. He told Tomas, "See to it that the Atheling comes into danger, and that we then in turn come to his rescue so that we are obliged to take him into our protective custody … Whereupon I will be King of England until he comes of age … if God wills him to live that long."

Tomas asked, "And if a rescue cannot be arranged?"

William told him, "If that is the case … Then see to it that no one will have the Atheling as a puppet King."

Brother Tomas asked, "And as for the Princess?"

William paused at that decision and then told him, "I cannot think ill of her."

Tomas agreed, "I am of the same mind, my lord. Perhaps she could join our own order of Nuns here … in Fécamp? Where you could keep a watchful eye on her."

William warmed to that idea and agreed, "That would be to my liking."

Brother Tomas bowed, and replied, "As you wish, my lord."

15

TIED

Nana watched Luna hover about the fire making a soup for her foundling. "He's awoken then?"

"He has indeed," Luna replied with way too much music in her tone. She might as well have sung a love poem about him to the old woman.

Nana asked her, "And does he speak?"

Luna looked at the old woman and could not keep the smile from her face when she said, "He speaks with a lovely voice so he does. His name is Kallín."

Dina made a smile, it was plain that Luna was taken by her foundling.

Nana watched her piling meat into the bowl and asked her, "He's off the broth then, and eating meat now?"

Luna slowed a little, "Yes. He likes his meat."

Nana gave a little laugh, "I'd say he does now," and asked her, "did he say how he came to be here?"

"He did not," Luna answered, already getting defensive. "I didn't want to wear him out with talk."

Rosy let out a big snigger, "Don't wear him out."

Luna turned on her, "What?"

Rosy didn't back down, "We can hear the howls of yis. The whole feckin forest can hear yis like a pair of wolves up in the cave!"

Luna made to go for her but Dina got between them, and told Luna,

"She's only saying what we all heard."

Luna backed down. She would not lay a hand on blind Dina.

When the air had settled, Nana warned Luna, "He may well wish to return to where he came from, to his own people."

Luna turned and looked fiercely at the old woman, as if she had thrown a curse at her, and in that same moment she realised that she was being foolish. Nana was not saying anything that she was not already thinking herself.

Nana nodded her head and said in a soft voice, "But I would think that if he has any sense then he will stay here with you."

Dina smiled at that.

Luna smiled at it too.

Kallín knew that the young Rohán who ran into the cave to get out of the storm some months past, was dead. An idiot creature who was that careless had no business being in the world, and he was at a loss as to how his former-self had made it so far in life. He'd been coddled by his mother and protected from the real dangers of the world, living in the safety of the clan. That life was gone now. When he opened his eyes from his long sleep in limbo, he was surprised to find himself, not only alive, but somehow sewn back together again. The girl with the flaming hair brought him thin gruel and spoon-fed him as a mother would feed a weaning infant. When the pain came to consume him, she gave him a medicine that she called 'cudu'. At first it was bitter, but then as he chewed it — the pain left him. He grew to love the taste of it. As the weeks past, cudu became his most loved thing in the world, for not only did it numb his body from pain, it took his mind on great voyages, long journeys to exotic places that were not of this world; it freed him. It was on one of his cudo trips that he understood that the gods care not for the Rohán, or for him; but by the same measure, they cared not what he did or did not do. There was no requirement for worship, rituals, rules or obedience. But more than that, when he thought about his mother, and Ríona … it was as if they were someone else's memories, someone else's pain.

Luna asked him as she tended to his wounds, "Will you want to be going back to your people, once you've healed all the way?"

"I have no people," he told her.

She contained her joy at his answer. "You are like me so," she told him as she dwelt on the scar that ran down his face, and gently traced it with her finger. She looked at him in a way that let him know that she wanted him; and without any ceremony, they coupled. They were well matched.

The heavy snow began to fall — covering the forest. Those birds that could migrate to warmer climates, did so. Those animals that could dig in and hibernate, did so. All of the other creatures in the forest moved very carefully because this was the season in which the wolves got fat.

Weeks passed in a routine of Luna coming to the cave to feed him, checking his healing wounds, and coupling with him. She brought him his blade and his mended clothes. But she warned him, "Don't go a wandering around outside. I have many traps set up. It was slim luck that you didn't run into them before the loner-wolf got you." Then she showed him her gift for him, "I made you a cloak of the beast." And she handed him the pelt of the loner-wolf, and smiled, "The head is made into a hood ... put it on you."

When he cloaked the great pelt around him, he was filled with a sickly feeling; he had not realised that the wolf was so large. It was truly slim luck that he was still in the world. But then, he felt his life running hot in veins, he felt the pleasure of victory.

"Thank you," he asked her, "how can I ... give you what you have given to me?"

She smiled, "I don't give a thing to get a thing back."

"That's good so ... because you have saved me from death and given me a new life. That is more than I can ever give back to you."

One morning he left the confines of the cave. Outside, he picked up Luna's tracks in the snow and followed them down the slope into the thicker part of the forest where he heard her voice calling out, "Stop!"

Luna came towards him, adding, "Don't move."

He asked her, "What is it?"

Luna warned him, "Careful. They are false tracks..." And she lifted a snow covered wattle hatch and showed him, "Look. I have this for anyone who might try to track me back to our cave..."

He peered into the hole in the ground to see sharp stakes that would have impaled him had he stepped on the wattle covering and fallen through it. He noticed the stakes were dark, "They are stained with blood."

She smiled, "I've caught a few howlers it."

He asked her, "Howlers?"

"Norsemen and the like," She told him.

His heart filled with joy. For while much of the Rohán in him was dead now, the blood hatred of Norsemen still burned hot in his veins.

She added, "I've made many traps. All different kinds. I'll show them all to you later. Come. Meet Nana now. She's curious about you."

Kallín appeared at the entrance to Nana's cavern.

Luna waited to see what Nana would say.

Nana liked that he didn't step over the threshold without being invited, and when he stepped in he said with good manners, "All good tidings on this dwelling and all good wishes to those who dwell in it."

Nana asked him, "Are you Rohán then?"

"I was," he told her. A sadness filled him the moment he said it.

"Was?" She shook her head, "Right so … then what are you now?"

He shrugged, "I don't know. Something that was dead and put back together in the cave."

Nana sucked on her pipe, "No … you're more than that. I don't know what it is that you are … maybe that's what you have to find out."

Nana watched the light between the two young lovers, and asked him, "Now that you are up. Where will you go?"

Kallín told Nana, "I want to stay here," he told Luna, "with you."

Nana cleared her spit and explained, "All well and good you want to stay, and I'm thinking Luna here would be a good match for you. It's no secret to me that the two of you already have been coupling. And there might already be a baby started." She took a sup of her brew and nodded, then continued, "If you are staying, you will get tied with Luna."

Luna was about to protest but in the same beat of her heart it made sense to her, and it was her heart's desire. And if it was that Kallín did not agree, then it was better to know it now, rather than later.

Kallín smiled. "That is my wish too."

They would be tied.

16

NEWS

Gyrth arrived back to London in the blizzard and made his way directly to Harold's quarters, entering quickly, beating the snow from his cape.

Harold greeted him, "Tell me the little cunting Prince is indeed dead."

Gyrth poured himself a full goblet of warm mulled wine and put a mouthful of it down him before he answered, "Good as."

Harold was not impressed, "What does that mean?"

Gyrth sat with a great flop into the chair, "It means, we tracked him and his Huscarls from Hungary and through the Holy fucking Empire, then suddenly they changed direction and cut off into fucking Normandy."

Harold rose from his seat, "Damn it. Did they meet with the bastard?"

"Fear not!" Gyrth assured him, "They were not long in the abbey at Fécamp."

"Did they meet with the bastard or not?"

"They did, but, I'm told it was a short event. Apparently the Atheling is a bandy-legged or some such."

"A bandy-legged? That does not sound accurate."

Gyrth went on, "It's what I was told from a reliable source. The bastard could not wait to be rid of them. He put them in a boat the next day."

"I'm sure he was glad to see the back of them. So then what?"

"They set for London … But devious little cunt that the Prince is, they kept on up the coast … making for Scotland."

Harold paced hard, "This story better end abruptly before they reach fucking Malcolm."

Gyrth smiled, "Fear not … it's a good ending. They sailed into the night. And then, a storm from the east swallowed them. All lost at sea." He raised his goblet, "Cheers."

Harold felt a wave of happiness come over him. "Yes … Lost at sea. Perfect. I can mourn the little cunt and gain the support of those who might have favoured him over me."

Gyrth asked, "How goes the corpse King, any closer to death?"

Harold nodded, "Ever closer, inching to the grave every day, but not yet dead enough to put him his tomb. Our sister has grown devoted."

Gyrth asked, "She is by his side now?"

"Always," Harold sneered.

Gyrth smiled, "Maybe someone should give him the bad news that his Atheling has perished? You know he's holding out to hear of his return."

17

EDYTH

Queen Consort Edyth sat at the bedside of her dying husband. His skin had now turned a bright yellow with spotted boils, his eyes blood-red and blind, his lips blue and speechless, and his tongue black and puss-oozing so that his whole head seemed to be a putrid rotting orb, but somehow, his mind was still his. In the last few weeks of his illness she had become devoted to him. She had no idea why, it was beyond her. There was something so tragic about him that she could not hold out against him.

Leofwine joined her from the darkness that surrounded the bed. He sat next to her, "Will you not take rest?"

She took his hand in hers, "Dear brother, I fear that should I take my eyes from him that he will pass away while my back is turned."

"Would his passing not be a blessing to him?" he asked her, "Why does he hold on?"

She told him, "He waits for word of the Atheling, I think."

Leofwine looked away from her and she saw it, "Tell me."

"The Atheling was lost at sea."

Edward stirred.

She soothed him, "Easy, Husband."

The question was issued in a sliver of a whisper from the King's lips, "The Atheling?"

She did not feel that she could lie to him now, "He is lost,

Husband."

The King sighed, "Then England is lost."

In that same breath his life left him, and he was gone.

A snow-covered London woke to church bells pealing the news that the King was dead. The Nobles of the land were called to the great Witan, so that they might choose their new King.

There was only one contender for the Crown: Harold Godwinson.

18

STORM

Margaret watched the sinking sun turn to fire and ignite the infinite horizon of the North Sea in a great inferno of colour. Then the sky blew a kiss. The sail suddenly filled and threatened to blow them over. The keel bit deeply into the water. Javier heaved the tiller, and cut a perfect balancing act between the forces of the wind and the water. They made speed and glided through the waves. The young Princess had never experienced anything so exhilarating as sailing. Fingers of rough wind ran through her hair, tossing it and freeing it from its tied-tidiness, the sea spray caressed her face: her lips tasted the tangy salty kiss. She was free in it. She called to Edgar, "Isn't it exhilarating?"

Prince Edgar hung his head over the side of the boat, his face pea-green-pale as the sea, "I will not live to see land," he moaned.

Peter passed him a hefty water skin, "Keep drinking, my Prince."

Edgar explained, "It will not stay in me, Peter. No sooner have I swallowed, and I spout it back out like some absurd water fountain ornament."

Peter persisted, "You can go a long time without food, lord, but without water inside of you, you will not last the journey. Drink. In small sips. Please."

Edgar relented, took the water-skin, and miserably sucked from it.

Up on the bow, Margaret was joined by Wulfstan, "It is wondrous, is it not, my lady?"

She agreed, "It is indeed. It's hard to imagine that the scourge of the

Norsemen came out of something so beautiful."

"It is, my lady."

She looked to the sky, "Shouldn't we be making for land? Night will fall soon."

Wulfstan replied, "If it is not too much for the young Prince, I thought it better that we would press on."

Margaret was at a loss, "Sail in the night?"

"Yes."

"Is it possible?"

Wulfstan explained, "Javier has the Moor's skill of navigating by the stars," and added, "I suspect that the assassins are sailing that boat that we can see in the distance behind us."

Margaret looked to the stern and saw, some distance back, a mark that could just be made out scraping along the horizon, "Is that a sail?" she asked.

"It is," he told her, "and it is a big one. Faster than we are … They will follow us to land."

Javier smiled, "But will they follow us into the night?"

The men smiled.

Wulfstan added, "Not unless they have a Saracen onboard to pilot them."

She watched Javier reading the darkening skies, he was in his natural element of danger.

They pushed on as the coastline of England burned red under the last of the setting sun and then vanished into darkness; all around them was black but for the sky above them that shimmered with vast clouds of stars. To sail by day was wondrous, but to sail by night was the most magical of all experiences. Javier navigated them through the darkness, the sea had fallen to calm, but the sail was catching enough of the soft wind to propel them. They rested to the sounds of the lapping water along the hull and the rhythmic creak of the mast.

Edgar's sea sickness abated. He lay on his back in the boat watching the canopy twinkle above him. "I feel that we are sailing in the firmament," he told his sister.

Margaret lay beside her brother, enjoying the rocking and swaying over the world of water. Edgar was talking to her, but she was too far on her path to slumber. She watched Javier's strong hand on the tiller, how it gripped gently but firmly, and pulled, then pushed, and with each movement of his powerful arm the craft gave itself to his will and swayed this way and that, and she gave way to it too, letting go of all her will, for she had no control over the great forces that carried her along. Javier was in control; she gave all of herself over to his strong and careful hands. She slept.

Javier was not happy, he privately advised Wulfstan, "This calm is not good."

Wulfstan weighed it up, "How long before the storm?"

Javier looked to the eastern sky, "The stars are disappearing ... It will hit soon. We will not make Edinburgh."

Wulfstan came to a decision, "There is a safe place called Grim Haven in the mouth of the Humber."

"I know it," Javier told him.

"Make for it." He told Peter, "Tent-cover the Prince and Princess."

Peter pulled a tarp over the sleeping brother and sister to protect them from the coming elements.

Margaret woke to a great thud of a wave hitting them that threw her some inches into the air. A moment later she searched for her bearings and fixed her eyes on the inside of a tent. A roof of sorts had been made over her head. But outside of this impromptu protection, all hell was breaking loose. She made her way out of the cover, looking out onto the heaving deck and was met by a blinding white-out. All around her the snow and ice attacked them, violent and cutting.

Wulfstan shouted, "Stay under cover, my lady, it's an ice storm!"

The great clouds of hail raged and accumulated so quickly and heavily onboard that it was all Peter and Wulfstan could do to bail it out of the craft and chop away the fast-forming ice on the gunwales and mast. Javier fought with the tiller to keep the boat on a course west, to land, running hard away on the leading edge of the storm that was charging around them and growing stronger in great waves.

Javier warned Wulfstan, "When we hit land, we will hit it hard! The Prince and Princess should be secured!"

Wulfstan worked, fighting to keep his balance while he tied a rope around Margaret and Edgar, telling them, "Stay under your furs in the cover. I will come for you when it is safe!"

They both believed him and followed his order, staying tied and secured in the makeshift tent.

There'd been many a time that Margaret and her brother had hidden like this under covers while great storms raged in Hungary, but it had always been in the safety of strong walls and a solid roof in a warm bedroom. Oftentimes she'd imagined the racket in the heavens into a great adventure. It struck her now that more than once she had placed them in a boat in the middle of a great storm.

Edgar clung to her in the muffled darkness, "Are you afraid?"

She comforted him, "We are in God's hands. We will soon know if he means for you to be King of England."

"I am not afraid," he lied.

19

TOSTIG

In Normandy both pieces of information regarding the Atheling being lost at sea and the death of King Edward reached William. He ordered Brother Tomas, "Bring him in"

In the hallway waited the exiled Tostig Godwinson, former Duke of York who had been banished from England three months ago by his brother Harold. He'd been travelling for some weeks as an emissary between Normandy and Norway. Wrapped in his heavy furs, he looked more like a Norseman than an Englishman. Brother Tomas opened the door and silently indicated for him to enter. It was ordered that at no time during Tostig's visits between Norway and Normandy should his name ever be mentioned. The only written word of his visits were in sealed letters to Rome.

Tostig came right up to the fire, desperate for heat.

"Drink. Eat. Get warmed," William told him, and he gestured to the ever-present full table of food and wine.

Tostig went to it, "Thank you, my lord, I bring an offer from King Harald Hardrada."

"Let us hear it."

Tostig looked unsure and then looked to Brother Tomas.

William assured him, "Whatever it is that you have to tell me, you can also tell Brother Tomas, for indeed, this whole arrangement was his plan." William drank and smiled, "Though I suspect the plan came from a higher power, am I right, Brother Tomas?"

Tomas bowed his head, "I could not say, my lord, but suffice to say, I am but a humble servant of the Holy Father in all matters."

William smiled at that, "Answer enough for me, clever monk," he turned to Tostig, "Now, to your purpose."

Tostig began, "Hardrada offers to take his share of the old Daneland and Mercia and make his seat in York, in tandem with your invasion of the south."

William weighed that, and asked, "And what has been offered you for your efforts and loyalty?"

Tostig drank and answered him, "I am to be returned to my rightful place as the Earl of Northumbria. I profit nothing from the war to come that is not mine by right."

"That's admirable," William told him, "and are you asking for heads?"

"Only two, My lord, I've asked that I might spike the heads of Earls Morcar and Edwin."

William liked that, "Good. Revenge will often fuel the fight long after love has paled into insignificance. Rest the night and return to Norway in the morning. Tell Hardrada we have an agreement. We will divide the English forces, I will defeat Godwinson and extend my claim to York and no further, and I will set my throne as King of England in London."

Tostig got to his feet, "I will travel back to Norway now, my lord."

William placed a hand on his shoulder, "You will rest now. And you will travel in the morning. Time is on our side in this matter. We must give your brothers the opportunity to wangle the Witan. Hey?" He laughed, "Let's make sure they choose the right man." Then William examined Tostig's eyes closer, "Are you ready to kill your own brothers?"

Tostig answered without a glimmer, "With my own hands." He then added, "Of course, there is one brother that I would not harm … might I see him?"

William nodded, "And when our fight is won you may have him in your care. Go to him now."

"Thank you, my lord, and if I might take him some food?"

"Of course."

Tostig grabbed an assortment of meats and cake from the table and left the room.

When Tostig left, William asked Brother Tomas, "Who brought us the news of the Atheling's death?"

"Our own agent in Grim Haven, my lord."

"Remind me of Grim Haven."

Tomas explained, "A trading town on the mouth of the great Humber River."

William thought and asked, "And what of the Atheling's corpse...? Or those of any of his crew, or his sister, Margaret, have they washed ashore?"

"Not that we know of."

William darkened, "So actually, what we should have been told is that the Atheling is missing at sea. Not lost."

Tomas agreed, "Our agent may have been too eager to send you good news. But should they have survived the storm, they will wash up in Grim Haven."

William ordered, "Send word to be on the watch for a simpleton boy monk travelling with guards. And send the word by three pigeons so it is sure to arrive."

"Yes, my lord. And if the Atheling is found to be alive?"

William weighed it, "King Edward is dead ... Godwinson is on the Throne. Everything suits our plan. Keep to the plan of the kidnap ... I would sooner keep Rome happy and have the Atheling alive in my safe custody. Kill all in his party."

"All...?"

"Yes. We cannot have the Princess marrying into Scotland."

20

WULFNOTH

In a reasonably comfortable cell in the dungeon of William's castle, was kept Wulfnoth Godwinson, the youngest of the Godwinson brothers who had been given as a hostage in negotiations with King Edward and the Normans some years ago. However, William, for reasons that no one could understand, still kept him, even though the negotiations with Edward had long since concluded.

"Brother…" Wulfnoth was delighted to see Tostig, and asked, "Am I to be freed?"

Tostig was disturbed by the sight of his brother, but he hid that from him, "Soon, Brother. Soon."

"Harold has sent you? He's not forsaken me?"

Tostig did not have the heart to tell him that his eldest brother had banned all mention of his name and thought of him as dead. He smiled and lied, "You are in all our prayers. It will not be long until you are with me in my castle in York."

"That is wonderful. Wonderful. I will soon be free."

"You will. Look," Tostig opened his parcel, "I have brought us a feast."

21

GRIM HAVEN

Outside of their fur cocoon the boat bucked and swayed in ways that no boat was meant to, but its keel clung on to the sea and it fought. The men worked to prevent it going top-heavy and keeling over.

Suddenly they were lifted on a great wave.

"Land ahead!" Javier called out. Though he could not see it, he knew that the sea had met the coast, and as a consequence of this great unstoppable force meeting the immovable earth, great waves were generated, waves that would grow to be the size of mountains, mountains that would break with unimaginable force when they made landfall. "Brace yourselves!" The roar of the crashing waves became so loud that no one could hear anything else. They became flotsam in the crest of a great wave and surfed, until they came to a violent crushing stop and were thrown like jetsam in all directions. But each of them had tied a mooring rope from their waist to the mast that prevented them being flung overboard.

They had hit land. Thankfully, it was a beach.

But the ordeal was not over.

"Hold fast!" Javier roared as another breaking wave came crashing behind them, picking them up again and throwing them further onto the beach. They rode it out. A set of two more big rollers hit them and pushed beyond the reach of the break. Their eventual resting place was not a grave.

Wulfstan shouted an order over the racket of the elements, "Dig in!"

Margaret and Edgar watched as the men heaved the boat some distance further onto the shore then lowered the mast and capsized the craft so that the hull became a roof over them. A survival space was made, they all piled in under the cover. It did not take long for their combined body heat to make it cosy. The storm roared with even more anger outside. Edgar imagined that it was throwing a temper tantrum at having been outwitted by them, but the young Atheling's fear was salved when Peter began to sing a sea shanty about being a sailor stuck in an upturned boat on beach in a storm as it blew, "Halloo! Halloo!"

Javier pulled out a bottle of spirit, slugged on it and passed it around. They all joined in the singing and Halloooing as the storm raged.

Wulfstan passed the bottle of spirit to Margaret, "Take a swig, it will revive you and drive the cold from you."

Margaret lifted the bottle to her mouth and carefully swigged. The liquid fire burned a path down her gullet and turned her belly into a furnace. "It is indeed hot!" She exclaimed.

The men laughed and sang as Edgar took his go at the drink. He spluttered his first attempt, caught out by the fact that a liquid that was cold to the touch of the hands could burn to the touch of the tongue. But he was determined not to be outdone, and on his second swallow he got a belly full of it down him. They cheered, and the singing lifted to new heights.

As the simple verses repeated, Edgar learned them and joined in the shanty. He particularly loved the rude parts about 'frigging in the rigging' and the deaf Captain with the peg leg that got stuck in the shit house. It seemed that God did indeed want Edgar to be the King of England, for no matter how loud the elements howled, they did not breach the happy sanctuary of their halloooing beached boat. In fact, Edgar felt so happy that he was sure that this was going to be the happiest moment of his entire life ... And he drank and sang some more in the good company until he passed out.

Edgar opened his eyes. The drinking and the singing had sent him into the deepest of sleeps he'd ever had, but as he began to rise from his bed he felt a sudden pain like he had been kicked in the head by a donkey, "What on God's earth is that pain?" He sat up slowly. He was alone. Outside of the tented boat he could hear murmuring. The side of the boat had been raised and covered in the sail so that it made a flap that opened ... through the gap came a heavenly smell. He stuck his head out into the world, "What is that scent?"

Wulfstan handed him a plate, "We call it smokey rasher, my lord."

"Smokey rasher?" Edgar took up a strip of the thin meat; it was hot and crispy. He bit it ... He chewed in silence for some moments, closed his eyes and whispered, "This is the most delicious food I have ever tasted. I want to eat nothing else but smokey rasher from now on." He asked Wulfstan, "How do you make it?"

Wulfstan smiled, "It is simple soldier rations. Marching food. We cure the pig meat in a smoke and then dry it out so that it keeps. You can eat it cold or heat it up on a fire."

Edgar closed his eyes again and chewed more.

Wulfstan added, "It's a good cure for morning head."

"Morning head?" Edgar asked.

"When you've been hard on the drink the night before," Wulfstan explained with a knowing grin.

Edgar smiled and chewed with more vigour. He liked the company of soldiers. He liked how they sang in the storm, drank too much and then got a little sad and sang about their dead mates or lost sweethearts before falling asleep. But most of all he liked how they made smokey rasher in the morning. He told Wulfstan, "I fancy that if I was not set for being a King that I could live a very happy life as a soldier."

Wulfstan nodded his head, "You would make a good soldier, my lord. But you will make a great King."

"Will I truly be a great King?"

"Yes."

"Will you stick by me?"

"I'll live or die by you," he told the boy.

"Really?"

"I have sworn it to our King Edward."

"Why?"

"Because I used to be a slave, and he made me free. Now I am a soldier, and there is no greater honour for me than to serve the King of England."

The ice storm had passed. Margaret watched the spent waves rolling to shore, slowly and lazily churning on one another before flopping exhausted onto the beach. They surrendered themselves to the frozen ground, their body-mass vanishing as they changed from water to ice. Hip-deep pristine snow carpeted the beach for as far as the eye could see. Further inland, the rivers and lakes froze solid too, and here and there on the flat open ground of the midlands, hands of the storm-winds had crafted great towering monuments of snowdrifts big enough to swallow a castle. All was quiet. The forests were shrouded in white silence and the sky was void of birds or clouds — a perfect blue dome covered the world. The low winter sun climbed to its noon zenith … but it gave no heat.

Winter had come to England.

Wulfstan joined her and asked, "We may have been outdone by the sea."

She asked him, "Do you know where we are?"

"A day or so from the Humber," he told her.

"Do you think the assassins made it after us?"

He smiled, "If they entered into the storm after us, they did not come out of it."

She smiled and said, "That is good. Perhaps this early winter snow is a godsend."

"Perhaps," he agreed, "We are surely in God's hands now."

She smiled at that. "If we are somewhere near the mouth of the Humber, then on the south side of the estuary is a port village, is there not?"

"There is, my lady," impressed by her knowledge, he told her, "it is called Grim by the Sea, but most folk call it Grim Haven. It's not much of a place to be in once the weather clears. Full of slavers and rogues and pirates."

She asked, "But surely nothing that would trouble a Huscarl?"

He flushed a little with pride and told her, "Nothing at all to trouble us, my lady."

"Then we should go there to secure horses and provisions and make our way to York."

"York?"

"Yes. We can hold safely there in the abbey. I will send word to King Malcolm."

"You trust York, my lady?"

She told him, "I trust that Morcar, the Earl of Northumbria who displaced Tostig Godwinson, and hates the Godwinsons, will support my brother in his rightful claim to be King of England."

He smiled, "You are well informed, my lady."

"Perhaps," she said, "but I fear that there is much going on with plots between Rome and Normandy that I do not know of…" She brushed the snow from her cloak, "I'm not sure that we can entirely trust our church."

Wulfstan shrugged, "Never trusted them to begin with."

They shared a smile.

Soon after eating a hot meal of smokey rashers and blood sausage, the Huscarls fashioned a skid-sled from ship's wood and put their royal cargo on it. They made lats of wood and fixed them to their feet, and, with the use of long poles to push them along, they set off sliding their feet and pulled the sled behind them as if they were a team of dogs.

Edgar was curious, "What is this that you are doing?"

Peter explained, "It is called skidda, my lord. It is how Norsemen travel through the snow."

Edgar fancied it, "Skidda? I think I can master that!"

Wulfstan warned him, "It takes an amount of training, my lord."

"Nonsense," Edgar told him, "I will do it."

Margaret warned her young brother, "Edgar, you are not in the least bit athletically inclined," but her words fell upon deaf ears.

Edgar was strapped into a pair of skidda and insisted, "Stand aside. I will know what to do." He began to move slowly along the gentle slope, smiling to his sister, "What did I tell you?" But his smile faded as he picked up speed, "How do I stop?" But it was too late for that, he was off down the hill at a great speed. Peter and Javier raced after him. Thankfully, the Prince was consumed by a snow drift that swallowed him whole. He quickly regretted his hubris as he was unceremoniously recovered and placed back onto the sled where he was content to stay put for the rest of the trip.

Grim Haven was much bigger than Margaret had been expecting, and much busier too. All along the bank jetties reached out like great branches into the Humber River. Then joined by walkways, they gave the appearance of a great spider's web. All along the shore buildings jostled for position. Further in, a great warren of ramshackle buildings spread out in no particular order. But the thing that struck her most about Grim Haven was the smell of shit. It would be safe to say that it hit her like a slap in the face. She did not let that deter her.

Wulfstan pointed out, "The storm has driven in a lot of boats."

As they got closer, Margaret became particularly interested in the dockside that was heaving with busy trade. Gold and silver changed hands, and cargo moved from boat to dock and dock to boat. Her eye was drawn to a cage of miserables. Edgar joined her. They looked upon the hopeless faces of people who had been taken from a life somewhere and who were now no longer considered people. The practice of slaving was abhorrent to her.

"Be careful," Peter warned her, "Desperate people can be dangerous."

Margaret examined the eyes of one particular young boy who was Edgar's age and stared out at her. Wulfstan put a gentle hand on her shoulder, "My lady Margaret, you can do nothing for these wretches."

Margaret accepted that he was right. For now at least.

As they made their way further into the town, Margaret told Edgar, "When you are King you must end slavery in England."

Edgar promised her, "I will, sister. It will be the first thing that I do. I swear it to you."

The cohort weaved their way through the narrow heaving streets, moving further into the heart of the town that got busier and fuller until the Huscarls were moving people out of their way as they would cattle. Nobody put up any kind of protest.

"This is what we're after," Wulfstan nodded to a double-storey building that stood pride of place looming over the other buildings, its walls pulsated with a great cacophony of babble.

"What is it?" Edgar asked Wulfstan.

"A tavern"

Edgar grew eager, "I have heard of such places. 'Dens of iniquity,' Brother Matthew called them. Full of all the vices of man: gambling, drunkenness, fornication ... I must go in!"

Margaret was not so keen on it, "Perhaps I will wait here and admire the interesting views."

Javier added, "I shall stay with my lady."

Edgar was already making a line for the tavern, "Wulfstan, why is there a picture of a wolf's head on the wall?"

Wulfstan walked with him, "It is what the tavern is called, my lord."

Edgar beamed, "The Wolf's Head ... What a perfect name for such a perfectly scruffy kip. And the smell of it! You can already get it from here. Pure filth. Excellent."

Wulfstan slowed his young Prince, "My lord, I would ask you to be silent in the tavern and let me do all of the talking. Keep up your guise of a young monk."

Edgar didn't slow his pace, "Of course, as you wish. I can portray a monk in my sleep. But I must see a pirate. Preferably one with a peg leg and missing an eye. And I want to hear some new curse words."

Wulfstan assured him, "Not to worry, my lord, there will be plenty of that sort in there and I have no doubt your ears will be filled with fresh curses."

Margaret watched her brother excitedly enter the tavern with Wulfstan and Peter. In so many ways he was still a boy, excited at childish things. She wondered how he would lead men into bloody battle, for battles would surely follow his crowning.

"You look worried, my lady," Javier said.

She smiled, "You are too observant."

He nodded, "It is a fault of mine." And then as if he could read her thoughts, "Your brother will make a great King."

She blushed a little. If he could read her mind that easily, what else he could see in her thoughts? "Thank you."

"And you… are destined to be a queen."

She stiffened at that, "I think not."

"You do not wish this?" he asked her.

"No. I do not wish it."

He was at a loss, "I supposed that all princesses wished to be a queen."

She smiled, "Not this one."

"Why not?"

She told him, "I do not wish to be made property."

He nodded, "But there are times when the King is the property of the Queen, is there not?"

She smiled, "That cannot happen for me."

"Why not?"

"Because such arrangements are made when the Princess is the only option for heir to the crown. I have a brother, he will be King. I would not wish for it to be any other way."

Javier apologised, "I understand. Forgive my ignorance in the matter. I should know better."

She smiled at him, and liked how he looked when he was wrong-footed, "You must not be sorry for talking honestly to me. I enjoy it … and I need someone honest close by me."

Javier looked her in the eyes and promised her, "I am your man in all matters."

Margaret then became aware of a group of children who had gathered around and were staring up at her in adoration. After a moment she smiled and said, "Good day?"

The children immediately lit up and pushed one of their number to the front who then plucked up the courage to speak and asked her, "Are you a Princess?"

It was in the same moment that Javier noticed that adults too were looking at Margaret.

Margaret asked the child, "What would make you think that?"

The child answered, "You are so beautiful."

The word "Princess" rippled around the crowd and Javier instinctively put his hand on the hilt of his sword, but Margaret stayed his hand and told him, "I am not in danger…" She turned her attention back to the children, and asked the first one, "What is your name?"

Inside the Wolf's Head, Edgar found more than he could have imagined by way of criminality and skulduggery with a full cast of wonderful villains swimming in a heady sewage of flowing beer, foul language and stale piss.

"It truly stinks with the most peculiar stench, does it not, Peter?"

Peter agreed, "It does…" and he was careful not to call Edgar by name or title, "young monk."

Edgar was delighted with it all and took it all in as Wulfstan did his business at the bar with a horse trader. Edgar pointed out to Peter, "Look at that one, do you think he was born that ugly or grew that way from foul deeds?"

Peter explained, "I think that fellow has had the pox. It leaves the face cratered."

Edgar was amazed, "And look how that woman comes to sit on his lap, and he the ugliest fellow in the tavern."

Peter steered around the subject, "Perhaps she has bad eyes."

Edgar burst out in laughter, "Good one!" Then Edgar came closer to Peter's ear in a confidential manner, and asked him, "Tell me, Peter, why does the woman on his lap have her breasts exposed so? Is it a custom of some sort?"

"Well," explained Peter, "if you had a stall on the street to sell, say hot bread, you would put the bread out where the customers can see it."

Edgar thought about that, and after a moment of watching the woman wrestling about and laughing on a man's lap, it dawned on him, "Of course. Yes. And look how his hand is going up between her legs … How much does it cost?"

Peter was already off his path, "I've … no idea, young monk. Not the sort of trade a King's Huscarl gets involved with."

Edgar was terribly disappointed, "Really?"

Peter was unable to keep his face straight and smiled, "But I would suppose that the cost is dependent on the … quality of the bread."

Edgar figured it out, "So this is a financial transaction?"

"It is," Peter told him.

"She will lie with him for coin."

"She will."

Edgar was sad for her, "I hope she makes a lot of coin from him, for he is ugly and I can smell the stink of him from here."

Peter stayed silent on that one.

Edgar lit up again and asked him, "Have you done intercourse, Peter? I only ask because I am thinking that I might do it myself, and I need some instruction in the matter … in the process of the act."

Wulfstan was busy negotiating for a team of horses.

The horse trader's eye continuously drifted to Edgar, and he commented, "That young monk must be an important cargo for you..." He looked at Peter, and commented, "Two bodyguards."

Wulfstan was impatient at the best of times. Normally on incognitus missions, they would simply commandeer what they needed and leave the horse trader dead if that was required. He made one more attempt at being reasonable and told the trader, "We are leaving here with the horses we need. That can be either good fortune for you, or bad."

Edgar eagerly watched the development of a transaction of another sort happening at the table between the sailor and the prostitute, but the sailor grew uncomfortable under the boy's glare and shouted to him, "Hey monk, why don't you go mind your own fucking business? Do your fucking prayers. You cunt."

Edgar was not sure if the sailor was talking to him and asked, "Are you addressing me, my man?"

Those in earshot laughed at the sailor, as did the woman on his lap, she mocked him, "Excuse me! I do beg your pardon! My man!"

The sailor's pockmarked face glowed a violent red with embarrassment. He pushed the woman away, stood up from his seat and walked to Edgar, threatening, "I'll give you fucking..." A sword met his neck in a whisper and hovered there a whisker from cutting his throat. Peter advised the sailor, "Don't lose your head now … My man."

The Sailor froze on the spot, "I meant nuttin by it. I meant no'arm to the young monk. Eh?"

The chatter dropped, the room scanned the two black cloaked men and their young monk.

Peter smiled, "No harm done then," and lowered his sword.

Wulfstan told the horse trader, "We need to get our business done now, one way or the other."

The horse trader felt the threat of death that hung in the air around these men. He nodded, "I have what you need. This way."

Wulfstan made to follow the horse trader but noticed that Edgar was fixed on the spot staring at the sailor. Peter came close to Edgar and quietly said, "We should go..."

"We will not," Edgar told him loudly and continued to stare at the sailor. He then took a step closer to the confused sailor. All eyes in the hushed tavern were on them. Edgar told him, "I don't believe you meant no harm to me, my man … I think you meant to do me harm, much harm."

The sailor bore into him with a threatening look, became ready to make his move, and warned, "Young monk ... be careful now."

On that, a half-dozen other men, who were the sailor's shipmates, rose up from their table and stood wide-footed at the ready.

The sailor felt the support behind him and took courage from it, and he warned Edgar, "Now go on your way..."

But Edgar did not budge, "You dare to tell me what to do?"

The sailor looked to his shipmates, and at the same time he put his hand upon the hilt of his blade that was in its scabbard on his hip. Before the sailor looked back to Edgar, Peter cut the sailor's head from his shoulders.

Edgar watched the headless corpse stand for a moment gushing blood into the empty space that the head had once occupied, and then topple like a felled tree onto the floor.

Silence filled the Wolf's Head Tavern.

Wulfstan joined Peter. They threw back their cloaks at the ready, revealing their weaponry. Even the untrained eye could see that these men were professional fighters and no match for anything that this crowd of drinkers had to offer. Even in a large number, they would simply be weeds to cut down. The other sailors sat back down. Men closer to the scene turned their attention back to their jugs of ale. Edgar went to the dead sailor, knelt by him, and felt along his belt, found his purse, tugged it free, and weighed it in his hand, "Hefty enough." He then went to the prostitute who had been on the sailor's lap, "For you, madam, in compensation for the loss of your earnings."

She took the purse with a great happy surprise, "Thank you!" Then she slipped her hand up his habit and felt between legs and offered, "Let me show you how grateful I am." And she smiled, "Plenty of life there!"

Wulfstan reached in and pulled his charge away from her, "Now, we must go."

Edgar asked him, "Is there not time for the lady to show her gratitude?"

Wulfstan kept him moving, "At some point you and I need to have a talk. Right now, we need to go."

Edgar suggested, "We will tell my sister nothing of this. I would not have her worry."

Wulfstan fought off a smile as he watched the young Prince make his way out of the tavern and thought, *He is as a young fucking King of England should be.*

At the back of the tavern, a tall lean man with a clean-shaven face and a tonsured head under his hood, got to his feet and quietly left through the back door. He went directly to a cabin where a dozen Flemish mercenaries rested out of sight, waiting. He told them, "He is here," he added, "they are buying horses and provisions for travel. They will make for York. Let us get out ahead of them and set the trap."

The twelve men moved quickly in silence and got on under way in minutes.

The horse trader made a good deal on account of the fact that Wulfstan did not wish to kill him and draw any more attention to their progress through Grim Haven.

Soon after, they were ready for the off.

Wulfstan outlined the journey ahead as they set off on their horses, "We can make good time along the frozen River Humber and then follow the Ouse to avoid the forest. The river will bring us all the way to York. We will need to stop a night on the way."

Margaret remembered, "There is a monastery that way, is there not? One that keeps the Heart Of Saint Cuthbert."

"There is, My lady." Again, Wulfstan was quietly impressed by her knowledge of the land.

"Then let us rest up there tonight," she said.

The great frozen Humber went out before them, flat white and perfect, their hoof marks the only blemish upon it, so that it seemed to her that they were the first people in the world to travel it. But that solitary perfection did not last as they ventured further inland. "What are these marks here in the snow?" she asked.

A long set of parallel lines ran out into the distance.

Edgar offered, "They look like skidda tracks."

Wulfstan agreed, "You are right, my lord. They are the tracks of skidda."

Edgar added, "One man."

Javier looked closer at them, "No … a number of men travelling in single file so as to hide their number," he looked to Wulfstan, "trained men."

Wulfstan knew then that they had trouble ahead, but going back was not an option. He said, "When the tracks stop, we will be ready." And he turned to Peter, "Set out ahead of us, keep point."

Peter set off to patrol the way ahead.

Margaret asked Wulfstan, "Are we in danger?"

Wulfstan gave her a smile, "We are always in danger, my lady."

She returned the smile, "Then my grandfather's saying stands true, 'We are always at war, never more so than when we are at peace.'"

Wulfstan agreed, "King Ironside was a truly great King. We'll know the outcome of this attempt on your person by nightfall."

22

SKIDDERS

Rosy came at speed into the cave, "Norsemen is comin up river now!" she shouted, her round face glowing red and snotty-nosed from her hard running.

Luna, Dina, Nana and Kallín looked up from their soup. They all thought that maybe Rosy had been doing too much cudu again.

"The river is frozen," Luna told her.

"I know that it is." Rosy replied defensively.

Luna asked her, "And then how is it possible that the Norsemen is sailing up it, so?"

Rosy stood her ground, "They're not sailing up river, are they? They're skidding on it."

Luna wondered aloud, "Sure, the raiding season is over," and she added, "why are the Norsemen here?"

Dina added, "If they're skidding, they're not raiding. They're not slaving. They're on some other kind of business."

Nana advised them, "And their business is not our business. Skidding Norsemen is a bad sign. Leave them out-of-season devils to their own doings."

But Kallín had his own mind, and his belly ignited in a fire at the very mention of Norsemen. At the same time his mind filled with memories of the slaughter of his clan and his mother. He was suddenly filled with a huge appetite to cut as many Norse throats as he could. He told them, "I will go and see."

He put on his wolf cloak, its great head making a perfect hood over his head, and the rest of it was long and wide enough to wrap around him and to be tied in the middle with a strap. Into the strap he fixed his battle-blade. With his feet and legs also covered in hide, he looked like a wolf-man as he went out of the cave without another word.

Luna understood that all the life of the world was set by the seasons. Winter was the time for the forest to be sleeping away the long dark nights, waiting for the Spring to arrive and wake the earth. Spring is the start of the Norsemen's raiding season. Norsemen coming into the winter-land troubled her. It was an event that was out of harmony with the seasons. In a sudden pang of her heart, she knew that she must not let Kallín out of her sight. She told Dina and Rosy, "Stay to care for Nana." And then she called after Kallín, "I'm coming with you."

After wrapping herself in a cloak of winter-thick pelts made from deer hide, she armed herself with her axe and bow, a full quiver of arrows and a pouch of dried berries and nuts. Then she ran to catch up with him. Nana sucked hard on her pipe, watching the pair of them go; she did not present any argument for them to stay. She knew that there was no stopping them now. These young chicks had grown their flight feathers. Natural needs and urges that control the world and all the creatures that live in it were at play in their affairs now. That's how lives began and ended.

The wolf and the deer made fast ground to the bank of the frozen river. They found a shared running rhythm and ran as one. Here and there they fleetingly glanced to each other and passed unspoken thoughts back and forth between them. The snow did not accumulate very high on the forest floor owing to the thickness of the canopy. But it was necessary to always listen carefully for the telltale crack of a snow-ladened branch that was about to break overhead. Such branches were killers.

Luna knew the point on the river where Rosy saw the Norsemen. Guessing at their rate of travel, she worked out where they could intercept them. The river made great bends as it searched its way through the forest looking for the path of least resistance to the sea. Hence, the advantage of travelling by the river route was the skidders could stay out of the danger of the forest. But the disadvantage was that the river did not run straight. Its endless twists and turns were time consuming; for while the skidders travelled fast, they did not travel far.

Luna and Kallín could travel quickly as the crow flies straight through the dense interior of the forest. They set off fast, avoiding Luna's numerous traps, and other naturally dangerous parts of hidden pitfalls and dangerously hanging older trees. The pair kept up their speed until they reached a vantage point on a risen bank that looked out over the vast snow-covered river, the snow perfectly untouched, the river's roar smothered under the thick ice.

"This is a good place for us to eye them up," Luna explained, "they must come by this way."

The unmarked snow was clear proof to the pair that the skidders had not yet come by.

Kallín advised her, "It's hard cold here in the wind."

They were out of the cover of the trees that protected them from the deadly ice-wind that travelled on a ruthless course straight down the river from the north, freezing everything that it touched. They would not survive for long being motionless in the open.

He pushed his blade against the crust of the snow, and felt that it was still dry and soft underneath its crisp top layer, "We should dig in to hide ourselves from the freeze."

Luna nodded in agreement. They quickly dug out a hole in the snowbank, and concealed themselves in it, huddled close together for warmth. She liked being like this with him, so close that she could feel his heartbeat next to her. His breath smelled of the sweet dry berries that they had eaten on the run. She watched their breath-clouds coming and going in a fog that mingled them and lingered in the cold air.

She studied his full lips for a moment and then she kissed him.

It seemed to her that when they were kissing, they both went to another place, a place where they were unconcerned about the world; it was a place that she liked to dwell in for as long as she could.

It was not too much longer before they were interrupted by the calls of the old winter crows, flying high and excited. These winter crows were the old crows that did not have it in them to fly away with the rest for the winter. They were the oldest and the wiliest of all the creatures of the forest. It was said that they were over forty winters old. They had the skills to find food where there was none. The winter crows follow warriors because they know they kill men, and dead men make delicious carrion.

The crow song was then followed by the cold swish of the skidda gliding on the snow. The wolf and the deer stopped kissing and watched the party of skidders emerge around a bend, coming in to view in a line like a giant eel, a dozen of them on their long flat skids, making their tracks along the snow, following the course of the river.

Luna studied them. She'd seen a good number of Norsemen come up and down the river over the years, and more than a few of them ended up caught in her traps. She was familiar with how they travelled, and how they should look. Something with these skidders was not right. It was clear from their clothing that they were different. She had not seen their kind before. They were lightly armed and didn't have shields. They wore heavy wool cloth in place of furs. But most strangely, they did not have beards. They travelled fast on their skidda, gliding effortlessly over the snow.

"They are not Norsemen," she whispered to Kallín.

"What are they then?" He whispered back to her.

"I don't know…"

He asked her, "How can you know that they are not Norse?"

She told him, "Because I have seen every kind of man from here caught in the traps … I've never seen the like of them," she added, "and they don't know the lay of the land. Look. They have a pathfinder."

One of their number was skidding along ahead of the pack, leading them, they followed in his tracks precisely to a man.

Kallín could tell from the discipline of their movement, "They are trained men. But not the pathfinder … He's much too slight and slender for battle work. But the others … they are warriors."

He felt a grip of curiosity on his mind; he knew it would pull him to track them. But, also, he didn't want it to pull Luna from the safety of the forest, so he offered, "I will track them alone."

She looked at him and instantly felt a deep pang of pain that was sharp as a knife going into her heart, and in that same moment she knew that she could not bear to live for any time without him. She would simply die, "No." She added, "Where you go, I go. We will track them together, and wherever that track leads us, we will be there together, for good or bad. That is how we should be when we are tied." She kissed him and whispered to him, "I'd rather be dead with you than be alive without you."

He took both of her hands in his, "It is the same for me. Alive or dead then, we are to be tied together always."

The deer and the wolf easily tracked the party of skidders as they journeyed along the frozen river that ambled through the forest.

Eventually Luna and Kallín came to the edge of their domain, to the edge of forest. Before them lay the vast open ground of the north moorlands that afforded no cover to hunt or hide as it was now covered in its winter blanket, making it barren and inhospitable.

They watched the line of skidders follow their pathfinder who left the river and travelled over the open ground further north.

Luna said, "If we are to follow them, we'll have to be moving out of the cover. Is it worth it, do you think?"

Kallín wrestled with it. The danger was there to see in plain view.

What of the unseen? What of the unknown rewards?

The snare of curiosity tightened on his mind, he looked at her and answered, "The half dozen winter crows are still following them. And them old crows know a thing or two that we don't…"

She smiled, and said, "We'll stay back from them out of sight and follow their tracks in the snow, keepin a safe distance. The crows will tell us the rest."

He kissed her.

After the kiss, he looked north, "The wind is in our face, so we'll smell them if we get too close."

They shared a smile about that.

The wolf and the deer moved from the safety of the forest into the danger of the open ground.

23

FROZEN

Margaret urged her horse on slightly so that it caught up to Javier's. She could just about see out of her furs, "I meant to thank you for your excellent advice in the matter of dealing with the Bastard Duke."

He nodded and told her, "There is no thanks required, my lady. It was a deceptions that I much enjoyed watching, and I shall never forget. I hope that when your brother becomes King that you will allow us to tell the story."

She told him, "I hope it is one of many stories worth telling about our journey. I meant to ask, how did you know that the storm would drive us onto a flat beach and not rocks of destruction?"

"I didn't, my lady."

"Really?"

"Sometimes, no matter how good you are, you still need luck."

"Or the hand of God," she added.

"Indeed, The hand of God is always welcome, when it is acting in your favour."

She was still curious, "Do you pray to God?"

He shrugged, "I am not worthy. I would not expect him to listen to me and I have no ambitions in the next life. That is why a man like me needs to be lucky."

"And what is a man like you?"

"A soldier, no more, no less, I live by the sword and I will no doubt die by it too."

She smiled, "I think men like you make their own luck." She looked around the pristine landscape, "Isn't beautiful?"

"If you are warm," he joked, "but if you are cold ... or trying to hide, it is not beautiful ... but, yes, there is beauty in all things."

"Even dangerous things?"

His black eyes darkened, "Especially in dangerous things, my lady."

She asked him, "What of the men who made these tracks that are running ahead of us?" she asked him.

He smiled, "They have underestimated us, and that is the greatest mistake that an enemy can make."

"What are you two discussing?" Edgar joined them.

Margaret told him, "Beautiful things."

Edgar rolled his eyes, "Save me. Javier, tell me honestly, how many men have you killed?"

"One," Javier told him.

Edgar was visibly disappointed, "Only One?"

"Is one not enough?" Javier asked him.

"Well ... it seems a paltry body count for a seasoned warrior such as yourself."

Javier agreed with a nod, "It is... but I should explain, that for me, every man I kill is the same man."

Edgar weighed that, "He ... is a ghoul who continuously comes back to life?"

Javier shook his head, "No ... I mean, he is my enemy."

"Ah. I understand. But why do you not keep count?"

Javier went on, "If I was to remember them all individually there would be no room in my mind. It is easier to remember one faceless enemy. That would be my advice to you when you begin to kill men."

"I have already seen a man killed."

Margaret cut across, "Brother, do not tell lies. You have never killed a man."

Edgar was slighted, "I have too! We killed that sailor in the tavern!"

Margaret stopped her horse, "I beg your pardon?"

Edgar realised he had dropped himself in it, "He was attacking me, and well ... We defended my person."

She looked to Wulfstan, "I am not a military expert, but it occurs to me that the point of travelling incognito is so that we may go unnoticed, is it not?"

Wulfstan told her, "It is, my lady."

Margaret was growing livid, "Then explain to me how killing men in taverns is going unnoticed?"

Wulfstan went on to explain, "It was my fault, my lady, I…"

Edgar raised his hand, "Wulfstan! Stop. Do not explain yourself. You were doing your duty." He turned to Margaret, "Sister, do not reprimand my men."

"Your men?" she asked him.

"Well, whose men do you supposed they are?"

Margaret pointed out to him, "They are the King's men."

"Yes," he agreed, "and I am to be King."

"You are not yet King," she turned to Wulfstan, "I have no doubt that the action in the tavern was how we were revealed and now have assassins travelling ahead of us to lay a trap." She urged her horse and moved on.

Edgar stuck his chin in the air and announced, "I apologise for my sister's behaviour…" and he whispered to Wulfstan, "She must never know that I caused the incident with the sailor. She will hold it over me for all time."

Wulfstan nodded, "I will take it to my grave, my lord."

They moved on.

Peter had stopped ahead of them, examining new tracks. He reported to Wulfstan, "We are not the only ones now tracking the skidda, see." He indicated to two sets of footprints that were also travelling in the same direction.

Wulfstan was at a bit of a loss, "They are both light built…" He read the source of the tracks, "They came out of the forest." He wondered aloud, "Why would two Silvatici come out of their cover to track soldiers?"

"What are Silvatici?" Edgar asked him.

"The wild people of the forest," Wulfstan told him.

Edgar looked into the darkness of the trees.

Peter added, "They probably have eyes on us now."

Edgar suggested, "We should best stay out of there."

Wulfstan agreed, "That is the common thought on it, my lord."

Javier came forward, "I should go on ahead with Peter. We have no idea what is before us."

Wulfstan nodded, "Agreed."

Peter and Javier went forward ahead of the cohort.

Margaret wanted to call after Javier to be careful, but she stopped herself. She dare not show her feelings for him.

24

PROMISES

Harold Godwinson's pages fussed around him, adjusting his cloak, making sure that everything was perfect. Gyrth waited at the door and said, "The Witan is assembled and awaits your presence…"

Harold asked, "All of them?"

Gyrth smiled, "All whom matter."

Harold weighed that and asked his brother, "You've been assured?"

Gyrth unconsciously gripped the hilt of his sword, "They are your men."

A tall black-robed Bishop entered the chambers and advised, "Each Noble has his hand out further than the next. You'll be bankrupt if you buy them all."

Harold responded dryly, "Uncle Bishop, what a surprise to see you … unannounced."

Gyrth added, "We have the coffers … and if we run short, we'll raise taxes on them in the north who is not here for the Witan."

Bishop Alwyn was less impressed by his nephew Gyrth than he was with Harold. He told them, "Tis easy to make yourself more hated. I would imagine that we might have learned from the mistakes of your brother Tostig who tried to tax the north too much and now finds himself banished."

Harold spat, "I will not have the traitor's name mentioned in these walls."

Alwyn was curious, "He is made a traitor, how?"

Harold was in disbelief that his uncle did not know 'how', and explained, "He is known to be in the company of the Bastard Duke of Normandy, who all fucking know, has designs to invade England."

Alwyn smiled, "Dear nephew, that is not making him a traitor. You are not yet King, and Tostig has sworn no oath to you, or the Crown of England. In fact, many would think that he is in his right, considering you did not lift a finger to prevent his banishment."

Harold threw his hands in the air, "What do I care? Why are you here?"

Alwyn reminded him, "You cannot become King without two acts … the first being the Witan to vote you King. And the second, for God to make you King … wherein a bishop will place the crown upon your head and bless your reign."

"Of course … but why are you here now, at this moment…?"

Alwyn told him, "You have bigger problems than an empty treasury and a reluctant Witan."

Harold waited…

Alwyn continued, "The Atheling in on English soil."

Gyrth protested, "He died at sea!"

Alwyn raised his hand, "He landed at Grim Haven with his sister. One of his Huscarl's killed some drunkard who caused an offence to the young Prince, else we would not know of their presence. They are making for York."

Harold ordered Gyrth, "Get to York and end it."

Alwyn waved at Gyrth, "Do not."

Harold was furious, "You speak over your King!"

Alwyn turned on him, "Mark your tongue, sire! And mark your vanity to boot! You are not yet King, and you would do well to learn how to take council when you are King … or you will not be King for very long…"

Harold, uncharacteristically, backed down, "Forgive me, Uncle, I am much bothered this morning by events."

Alwyn went on in a calm voice, "All that said, I am the same way. The Atheling must not be harmed, nor his sister. When the nobles of the north learn he is alive they will rally to him."

Harold was at a loss, "I am to do nothing?"

"You will do everything," Alwyn told him, "everything to protect him … keep him safe … in your care."

Harold smiled, "Of course. Gyrth go and…"

"Not Gyrth," Alwyn told him, "wait until you have the authority of

King and then send your Huscarls. This act must be the act of a king… Do it in full banner. Bring him to your safety."

Gyrth added, "But there is no need to take the red hound into your care."

Alwyn smiled, "On that point, we do agree. The three Huscarls who travel with him must not return.

An hour later Harold sat on the throne and addressed one of the nobles, "Lord Lincoln … you supported my claim to be King."

"Yes, my King."

"And you have not asked me for coin."

Lincoln replied, "I have no need of coin, my King."

"Indeed," Harold agreed, "you've been abroad making coin at soldiering?"

"I have, my King, with the Byzantines. They have many enemies in many of the lands they hold. Running an empire is a bloody business and … expensive."

Harold smiled, "And running a meagre kingdom, not so much, aye? So, you need not coin. What of title?"

Lincoln told him, "I have no need for title, my King. I have my father's good name and hold one of the oldest titles in England being the Earl of Lincoln. I have my house. I have my land. I am a contented man."

"Indeed you are," Harold was immediately on the defensive, "many of the older families say that I am not the true Earl of Wessex, what say you to that?"

"They do not say it to me, my King. But I will say this on the matter. Before there was an Earl of Wessex, or an Earl of Sussex, or any earls at all … there were kings here who ruled this land before the Romans came. Everything that we have, we have taken from them. It is ours by battle. Won in blood. No man is entitled to anything that he cannot protect."

Harold nodded, "I like that answer very much." Then Harold remembered something, "My father told me once that the man who says he wants nothing, usually wants everything. So I will ask you again, what do you want?"

"If there was one gift from the crown that I could ask for, I would ask for the hand of your widowed sister."

Harold thought for a moment, "She's barren. And requires more pampering than a racing mare with a temper to drive God out of the church."

"You asked me what I wished for."

Harold nodded, "Good. You shall have her... after some period of mourning, of course. And in return you will take command of the Huscarls."

Lincoln asked, "What of Wulfstan?"

"You will kill him," Harold told him, "and the two that travel with him."

Lincoln advised him, "You may wish to offer Javier freedom to return to his people."

"Why?

Lincoln explained, "His father is a Khalif."

Harold laughed to himself, "What is that to me?"

"A Khalif who controls the gate to the Holy Land, my King. To kill his son could see the gates of Jerusalem closed to England."

Harold darkened, "You are well informed … so be it. Offer him his leave out of England."

A female voice spoke from the darkness, "Offer the three of them their leave." Edyth stepped from the shadows, dressed in black and holding a goblet of wine.

Harold scolded her, "You enter the King's presence without permission?"

"Forgive me, brother. The presence that you occupy was mine not a day passed. I forget myself." She looked to Lincoln, "So, young Lord Lincoln, we are to be wed?"

Lincoln got down on one knee, "If you will have me, my Queen."

She smiled at him. He was handsome in a carefree soldier's way that she liked. "And why would a young buck with an ancient name and a big reputation want to marry a middling aged widow woman?"

Lincoln told her, "Ever since you made your promise to me when I danced with you, I have been jealous of your King husband Edward."

"Danced with me? No…"

He explained, "I was your page… at your wedding. You danced with me and you promised me that…"

She remembered, "You were a child."

"I was seven, my lady. Old enough to have my heart branded. When I heard your husband was sickly, I returned to England … in the hope."

Harold held his hand up, "Do I have to hear this. He is besotted with you. You are ... well, you are what you are. Let it be done and get on with it."

Edyth smiled. "Let it be done then. I am nothing if not a woman who keeps my promises. And no period of mourning."

25

ROSY

Fat and sticky wet snow started falling heavily and piled up fast in the forest canopy. Rosy carefully made her way along the forest floor to check on the traps and snares. She didn't like this kind of snow. She liked the kind that was light as fluff, the kind that she could blow off the palm of her hand as if it were powder. This kind was the wet snow that accumulated on the branches and would eventually snap them without warning. If you were not quick enough, it would easily bury you, and you would not be found until spring when the thaw comes. She often thought of how it would be to die buried in the snow, to freeze solid in the deadly grip of it. Then sometimes she imagined what it would be like to die in one of Luna's terrible mantraps. She often enjoyed making her spoof story about her killing a howler, but the truth was that she didn't like the task of checking the mantraps. She knew that she wouldn't be able to kill a howler if she found one caught there alive.

Sometimes she imagined that she was a small creature like a rabbit, and she tried to think about what their lives must be like for them. Everything in the forest wants to eat them. She loved to eat them. But as much as she loved to eat them, she could not bear to kill them. Sometimes they would be trapped only by the foot, and she would let them free again. But the thing she disliked most about the snow was the silence that it made. It seemed to suck the sound of life out of the air. She would often tap her ears to make sure that she hadn't gone suddenly deaf. The slightest creak of a tree branch would echo with a loud crack and put the heart across her thinking it was all going to come down on top of her. She stepped as lightly as she could, but she could not stop the snow from crunching and squeaking underfoot. Suddenly, She felt that she was being watched. She stopped moving and drew her knife, "I'm no soft meal like a rabbit."

She waited.

Then a girl's voice spoke, "We mean no harm to you."

Rosy's heart beat so loudly that she was sure it was making a thumping racket like a great drum in the soundless white air.

She warned them, "Be careful where you step."

The girl's voice told her, "We've seen your traps. Good ones too. We're looking for a boy."

Rosy asked, "A Rohán boy?"

"That's right."

"Kallín?"

"That's right."

From the white blanket, faces began to appear. Little faces. Dozens of them.

Rosy began to weep, "Tis only babbies that you all are ... What happened to you all?"

A girl of about Rosy's own age stepped out of the white, "I am called Aífe of the Rohán."

"And I am called Rosy ... Just Rosy."

The little ones looked up at her, the snow gathering in cones on their hoods. She offered, "Will you come in by the fire and have hot soup?"

All the faces smiled.

Nana rubbed her eyes, and then rubbed them again for she thought she was dreaming, or maybe she had smoked the wrong cudu. She asked, "Is what I'm looking at real?"

A dozen little-ones stood staring at her in silence.

Another twenty or so bigger ones were spread around the cave in silence. Rosy was at the fire stirring a pot. "You'll all need to pass the same bowl, taking a sip at a time."

One of the little-ones spoke, "She's a Nana..."

That was immediately followed by the collective sigh.

Nana looked closely at the one who spoke, "How did you come to be here?"

"I brought them in," Rosy told her.

Nana raised both of her eyebrows, "Well, we better put out a lot more traps if we are to feed them through this winter."

Aífe spoke from the darkness, "We can feed ourselves. We'll not be leaning on no one."

Nana nodded her head, "Rohán" Then she let out a deep sigh and asked them, "Tell me what has happened to you all."

All the little-ones immediately began to spill out their stories in a great babble. Nana nodded at each of them as if she could understand every word that each of them was saying, "I hear you…" She told them, "I hear you. That's terrible," she assured them. They went on like that … emptying out their tragedy and Nana nodding and soothing them. After a time, Nana held up her hand and said, "Let me tell you a story."

Silence fell and the little-ones immediately sat and watched Nana sucking on her pipe and loading up for her story.

Nana began, "When I was a young girl … no bigger than you … a spell was cast on me that turned me into a deer…"

Little eyes widened, they all pulled closer…

In the night the older ones sat around the fire while all the little-ones slept in a great pile on the pelts like wolf pups.

Brun smiled, "They feel safe in here."

Dina told him, "They need to rest. Little-ones don't last long in the fear."

Aífe had other things on her mind, "How long has Kallín been gone?"

"Three days," Dina told her, "four tomorrow."

Aífe looked at the others, "I'm going to find him in the first light. None of you are to come if you don't want to."

Brun held up his finger, "I am coming with you."

Aífe looked to the others. They all had a finger in the air. "We are two dozen then." She asked Dina, "Can we leave the little-ones with you until we return?"

Before Dina answered, Rosy told them, "I will take care of them."

Aífe simply smiled to her. She knew Rosy would care for them well.

In the morning, the little-ones tearfully watched the older-ones check their arrow quills and blade edges and set off from the cave without a sound into the white forest. After the Rohán had vanished,

Rosy felt herself being surrounded by a dozen small bodies.

Nana watched and smiled to herself. Rosy, the girl who was always desperately hungry for her love, would be hungry for love no more. She was surrounded by more love now than any one person could ever consume.

Rosy looked down at her flock and told them, "All them braids need doing up fresh."

26

GOD OF GOLD

Kallín and Luna stayed low, not cresting the hill until the skidders had dropped down over the other side. That's how it went on, up and down, until evening crept in and brought the cold snap with it. The dying sun raged red against the coming of the dark. The snow shimmered. The skidders came to a sudden a halt on the crest of a hill, laying themselves flat along the ridge, spying on something on the other side. The crows circled.

Kallín said, "We should move to the west of them, use the sun-glare for cover."

They moved quickly and quietly under the cover and found a safe vantage point from where they could see what the skidders were spying on.

Luna asked him, "What is that place?"

At the bottom of the hill sat a high stone-walled fortification. At its centre stood a large building that boasted a bell tower which was adorned with a great cross on top of it.

"Listen," he whispered.

Drifting in the air came a chorus of many voices, high, low and middling, all in harmonised singing of Latin words.

Kallín whispered to her, "It's a holy place for monks."

"What are monks?"

He explained as much as he knew, "Holy men who sing to their god."

She worried, "What does their god do for them?"

Kallín shrugged.

She worried a bit more, "Is their god in there, do you think?"

Kallín shrugged again; he did not know about the god of the monks, he knew only one thing about monks, "It's said that they collect gold for their god and store it up in great piles for worship."

"Stores of gold...? In great piles?" Luna's heart began to beat faster.

He guessed, "It must be what the skidders have come for, I'm thinking."

Luna could hardly imagine what they might find in there once the skidders had done stealing and killing. But then she also worried, "Look at them walls and the strong gate there, as well. There's only a dozen of them skidders. Sure they'll not get in there, will they?"

Kallín knew she was right, and told her, "Maybe they are just a scout party for an army who will come this way. I'd say that much."

Luna's heart sank a few feet into the cold earth, and she said, "There's no killing made by scouts." She looked up to the cloud of circling hungry crows, "Even the old winter crows was fooled by them."

Kallín watched the skidders, adding, "I might be wrong. It might be that they are not just come here for a look at the monks. Watch them there. They are up to something."

The pair watched the pathfinder pull his hood down and reveal his tonsured head, then he removed his outer travel garment to reveal a monk's black habit under it. The rest of the group of skidders put one of their number on their shoulders and carried him, as they would carry a corpse. The pathfinder went out in front, crying out prayers in Latin and waving a cross, and in that way, they proceeded to the closed gates of the monastery.

At the gate, the pathfinder monk implored the monks inside to give his dead brother a Christian burial.

The monks opened the gate. But no sooner had they done so, and the skidders began cutting them down. There were no war hollers, just silent, well-practiced, efficient killing.

Luna's heart lifted, "They have come for looting, so they have."

Kallín agreed, "They have, surely."

Luna admired their work, "They are very skilled at the slaughtering, aren't they?"

Kallín agreed, "They are."

Then Luna worried, "But will the monk's god protect them and kill the raiders, do you think?"

Kallín worried about that too, "That, I don't know…"

The skidders disappeared from view into the interior of the monastery, closed the gates behind them. The great chorus of singing turned to screaming.

After some time of listening to the carnage, Luna said, "I don't think the monk's god is a war god. Do you?"

Kallín agreed, "I think their god cares for gold and singing, and not much else."

The screams of the monks went up to the darkening heavens, calling for their god, louder and louder. Luna watched as the sky grew colder and darker. The monk's god remained indifferent to their suffering.

Luna shook her head, "Who would want a god the like of that?"

Kallín began to dig a hollow in the snow, "Who would want any kind of a god at all? From what I've seen so far in the world, all the gods are of no use to us."

Luna wasn't sure if she wanted to agree with that, "Let's not get on the wrong side of all of the gods … There's probably gods that we have not yet heard of … maybe one or two of them are good for something."

"Maybe."

She helped him to scoop out a hollow, "Enough about gods anyway."

He nodded to her in agreement and said, "Them raiders will not dwell for too long in there."

The pair of them got comfortable and settled into the hollow to wait for the skidders to finish their raid.

She agreed, "Raiders do like to get in, get the loot, and get out."

But as the hours passed into the darkness and all went silent, it became obvious to them that the raiders were not in their usual efficient hurry.

Luna wondered, "Why would they close the gates? They should be making away with their spoil by now, surely?"

Kallín had been thinking about that too, "They did not come all this way just to make sport. I'm thinking that they're looking for something very valuable in there that the monks will not give up."

Again, Luna's heart beat fast as she wondered, "What could be so valuable that these monks would suffer such torture and death to keep it from them?"

They both held each other close for the heat and shared their thoughts about what the most valuable object in the world might be.

The full moon came up on the white world and painted everything in a silver glow, making it almost as bright as day.

Kallín, sensed someone behind him, he turned to see two men.

Javier warned him, "Do not make a mistake now, Silvatici."

Luna thought about going for her bow, but Peter was already taking it from her.

"Don't be foolish," he smiled, "there is no need for you to die here."

Wulfstan came to a halt. Margaret pulled her horse up beside him, and Edgar came to the other side. They watched Peter and Javier return with their two finds.

Edgar was curious, "Are they the Silvatici?"

Wulfstan warned, "Be careful not to get too close. They are wild and will bite like dogs." Then he turned his attention back to the two creatures, and asked them, "Why are you tracking the skidders?" He waited. After a moment, he warned them, "If you have nothing to tell me, then you are of no use to me. But I'm not letting you walk away unless I know what your business is."

Kallín knew these men would kill them in the blink of an eye, he admitted to the red bearded giant, "We were going to make spoil from them."

Wulfstan fought off a smile. He asked him, "How did you come by that fine wolf pelt?"

Kallín answered without bragging, "I killed the wolf for it."

"And what about those scars on your face?"

"That's what the wolf took for payment."

Wulfstan looked closer at him, "That green ribbon in your hair … you're Rohán?"

"I am."

He looked to Luna, "What about you, little red Celt?"

She just looked at Wulfstan with a stare that actually gave him a chill. Wulfstan asked her again, "I asked you a question."

Kallín knew that Luna would not give in. He thought fast and told him, "She's mute."

Luna now turned her deadly stare on Kallín.

Wulfstan nodded, "Probably a blessing."

Javier and Peter laughed.

Margaret came forward, "Do not taunt them." Then she looked at the pair, "What can you tell me of the men you followed?"

Kallín had never imagined that a creature could look so beautiful as the one that was looking at him. For a moment he forgot who he was and where he was. But a deadly glare from Luna brought him back to his senses. He quickly began, "First I thought they were raiders … but now I don't think so."

"Why so?" Margaret asked him.

"Well … they entered the gates by playing at being monks, and then they set to killing, and they've not come out." He looked at Edgar and then back to Margaret, it was clear to him that they were valuable. He added, "Maybe it's a trap."

Margaret nodded her head, "I think you're right." She turned to Wulfstan, "What do we do?"

Wulfstan examined Kallín, "You're Rohán, you say?"

"I am."

"Are you for hire as a fighter?"

Kallín filled with pride, "I am."

"What about her?" Wulfstan asked.

Luna told him, "I am also for hire as a fighter."

Wulfstan smiled.

27

SNARE

The pathfinder watched from the monastery walls as the cohort of five horse-backed travellers made their way along the path to the gates. He could clearly make out the three well-built Huscarls and the two smaller riders that they escorted. It would be twelve skilled men against three, and they would take the two young royals hostage without any problems. The pathfinder reminded his twelve mercenaries, "Do not harm the Atheling or the Princess."

Wulfstan stopped in front of the gates and called out to the walls, "I travel under the King's warrant. Open the gates."

The gates opened.

The cohort entered.

The twelve Flemish mercenaries waited in a horseshoe formation in the open ground of the bailey. It was an overly-confident position to take up. The three Huscarls came through the gate first, and at the same time, they each threw their pair of knives, fast from the darkness, wounding six of the twelve raiders. In the same movement, the Huscarls dismounted and attacked the unwounded six with their long and short swords.

Kallín jumped from his horse, as did Luna, and they set about their part of the attack, as instructed, to quickly move in on the first six wounded men and kill them as quickly as they could. Kallín was truly surprised at the speed and efficiency that Luna set to killing. He had only sent two wounded mercenaries on their way with the axe, and in the same time Luna had dispatched four. Then she threw her axe to lodge it in the head of a mercenary who was doubling up in an attack on Peter. The slaughter of the mercenaries was quick, and it was over as fast as it started.

Margaret and Edgar waited outside of the monastery. Edgar complained, "I should be in there — in the thick of it."

"No, you should not," Margaret scolded him.

Edgar wasn't letting it go, "I am a good swordsman. I could earn my place in the fight."

She told him, "There is a long way between sword-playing and sword-fighting."

Edgar was offended, "Do you think that I don't have it in me?"

She looked to him, sitting in the snow, waiting, being covered in fresh snowfall, and she told him, "I have no doubt that you have it in you."

He seemed placated by that.

Wulfstan came to the gate and waved for them to enter.

The pair walked down the short distance to the silent monastery.

As Margaret reached Wulfstan, he told her privately, "Brace yourself, my lady, there is much slaughter."

Margaret took a deep breath and moved through the gates.

Inside, torchlight illuminated the horror of mutilated corpses strewn about the place. Margaret's mind momentarily raced into a swirl of confusion trying to place actions into the void, until she told herself that she was trying to find reason in madness. The dead are beyond such rational, and she need not understand how each one fell.

Edgar was moving in his stride, in boyish awe, as if he was watching a play upon the stage, "What a great bloody fight. When I am King, I will give you two Silvatici your weight in gold."

Luna and Kallín shared a look, *when I am King?*

Margaret watched her brother looking closer at the dead and reminded him, "Brother, stay close to Wulfstan."

Edgar asked, "What does it matter? They are all dead."

"Not all of them," Kallín added.

The Huscarls moved close to Edgar and Margaret.

Wulfstan growled to Kallín, "Speak."

"They were thirteen in number. One of their number is not among them here."

Wulfstan looked at the twelve dead mercenaries, "You are sure?"

Kallín told him, "The thirteenth man was a pathfinder. He had his head balded like a monk and spoke to the monks in their language."

"Latin," Margaret said, and then she called out into the empty walls in Latin, "Come out of your hiding now, and confess your part in the plot here, and on my word, you will not be harmed."

Along the bottom of the wall, amongst a pile of dead monks that the raiders had killed, a corpse rose to its feet.

"That is him," Kallín said.

Wulfstan cocked his axe to throw it and kill him, but Margaret told him, "He is not to be harmed." She called to the pathfinder, "Come."

The slender pathfinder made his way to them, carefully stepping over the dead, showing his empty hands.

"That's far enough," Javier stopped him and searched him.

The pathfinder went straight into his defence, "I was a hostage, my lady."

She heard his heavy foreign accent and weighed it, "Which monastery do you belong to?"

He answered, "I was travelling to York when I was set upon in Grim Haven, my lady."

He was avoiding her question. She sharpened her tone with him, "Travelling from where?"

"London, my lady."

Luna stepped out from the darkness, and began to examine the pathfinder, sniffing the air around him, and said, "He lies."

Margaret was curious, "How can you know?"

"I can smell it."

Margaret shook her head, "We'll not plunge into nonsense ... One cannot smell lies."

Luna told her, "He should be killed."

Margaret told her, firmly, "I gave him my word that he would not be harmed."

In the blink of an eye, Luna cut his throat. The pathfinder fell to the ground and bled out. Luna looked back to Margaret and told her, "Your word is not my word."

Javier bristled and moved towards Luna.

A young girl's voice called from the darkness, "Unless you can move quicker than an arrow ... Don't move at all."

Kallín knew the voice, "Aífe-girl?"

A circle of young Rohán moved into the light, their two dozen bows trained on the three Huscarls.

Wulfstan ordered his men, "Don't move against them."

Edgar was amazed by them, "How did they move on us like shadows? What an excellent skill. And they are only children..."

Aífe warned him, "There are no children here, fancy-boy."

Edgar was insulted by that but he did not go into an argument over it.

Then Brun stepped out and told them, "We mean none of you any harm. We've come for our own only."

Kallín was confused to see Brun, and asked him, "Where is my father?"

Brun told him, "He is gone home."

For a moment all was silent. The only sound was the lick of the torch flames against the cold night air, and the whisper of the vapour rising from the hot blood that still oozed from the fresh corpses.

Kallín absorbed the fact that his father was gone home.

Brun added, "All of the Rohán who went north ... are gone home with him."

Aífe told Kallín, "You are our Chieftain now."

Kallín quietly told them, "Lower your bows."

Wulfstan breathed a sigh of relief as the bows were eased, and the arrows pointed away from them. He didn't know much about the forest dwellers, but he could tell right away that these little-ones had seen plenty of killing, and they knew how to use their bows.

Aífe then put the palm of her hand under the snow so as to feel the earth, she warned them, "We should go..." And she explained, "Horses... Lots of horses riding hard this way."

They all looked to Kallín now.

He agreed with her, "To the forest."

The Rohán moved back into the darkness.

Kallín told Margaret, "I think these dead raiders meant to do harm to you. And I think the others coming on horses mean the same. You should come with us..."

Margaret examined the scarred face of this wild youth, but his eyes were not so wild as the rest of him. They looked straight and true at her. Unflinching. She turned to Wulfstan, "What do you think?"

Wulfstan nodded, "He is right."

Margaret approached Kallín, "Thank you. We'll come with you."

Luna advised, "There'll be no place for your horses in the forest. And we need to be travelling fast over the ground." Then she walked to Margaret, "You'll not make much speed in that fancy dress you wear."

Wulfstan joined Margaret, "She's right, my lady. If I might suggest a solution?"

A few minutes later, the Rohán were running across the open ground to the forest. With them ran three big Huscarls. And on Wulfstan's back rode Margaret. On Javier's back rode Edgar.

As they entered into the cover of the dense trees, Edgar watched in amazement as the two dozen Rohán disappeared up the tree trunks and into the branches.

Kallín told them, "This is good." He looked back from the forest to the open ground that glistened in the moonlight. Their tracks plain to see in it.

Luna told him, "We'll not be hard to track."

Kallín nodded and told her, "We can take them from here." He turned to Edgar and asked him, "Can you climb a tree?"

Edgar looked to the great sprawl of branches over their heads and saw the Rohán crawling among them with ease, and taking up firing positions with their bows. He told Kallín, "I can try."

Kallín nodded, "Good."

Javier hoisted the young Prince up into the branches. Hands reached out from the darkness and pulled him up to a safe spot. Margaret began to explain, "I will stay on the ground and..." But Wulfstan was already heaving her into the branches, and telling her, "These little-ones know what they are about, my lady."

She was soon perched like a bird on a branch. Part of her felt ridiculous. Part of her was more excited than she had ever been.

Moments later the ground began to vibrate as the cavalry of thirty followed their tracks to the edge of the forest.

Javier couldn't believe his eyes, "Kingsmen?" He made to move forward, but Wulfstan put a hand on his shoulder and stopped him, "Wait."

Lincoln stopped his cavalry of Kingsmen fifty yards from the tree-line and called out from his horse into the silent white wilderness, "Know this, Wulfstan! We mean the Atheling no harm. He is under the protection of King Harold of England."

Edgar could not believe his ears. He asked Margaret, "How can this be?"

Margaret placed a hand on her brother's shoulder and whispered to him, "Do not give yourself away, Brother."

Wulfstan filled with sadness. He had failed his King.

Lincoln went on, shouting into the forest, "King Harold has offered to pension out you three Huscarls that travel with the Atheling. There is no ill will against you. Prince Edgar, know that your sister will be treated as a princess. What say you, young Prince?"

Edgar shouted from the trees, "I say, damn you. I say, damn you, and damn that illegitimate Godwinson to hell!"

Lincoln waited a moment and then added, "Know this, young Prince, that should you not come with us of your own free will, I am warranted to take you into our custody by force. For your own protection."

Edgar thought about that, he looked to Kallín, and told him, "I do not wish to see any of you harmed."

Kallín assured him, "We could cut them down before they even make it to the trees."

Edgar grew excited by the thoughts of a battle, "What do you say, Sister?"

Margaret looked at the two dozen grim forest fighters, perched in the trees, bows at the ready, "I think it would be a foolish soldier who would take on these Silvatici."

Edgar shouted back out from the forest, "Come then. Execute your warrant!"

The Kingsmen dismounted and walked forward. Kallín drew his bow and measured the first one of them to come into range and fired. The luckless soldier was immediately killed with an arrow in the eye.

Lincoln called out, "Charge!"

The Kingsmen came forward at a run, but they were cut down in a wave of arrows and then another wave, so that by the time they made it to the trees there was only a half doze of them left, and this portion of Kingsmen were put to death by the three Huscarls.

Lincoln looked on from a safe distance, beyond the range of the arrows. He shouted into the trees, "So be it young Prince, you are putting yourself beyond the protection of the King." Then he turned and galloped away.

An hour later, Edgar and Margaret gathered with Wulfstan to work a plan. Kallín and Luna stayed near.

Edgar asked Margaret, "What are we to do?"

Margaret thought it out, "If we can get to York, then we can make for the safety of Scotland."

Wulfstan told her, "They will have patrols on every road." Then Wulfstan turned to Kallín, "I am told that your people have secret ways to travel the land from the time before the Romans built the roads?"

Kallín told him, "It is true. We still know all the old ways across the moorlands and through the forests."

Margaret asked him, "Is there an old way to York?"

Kallín answered, "We have a way. It is not easy going. You would have no horses."

Margaret insisted, "We can go on foot as well as the next."

Kallín came to a decision, "I will take you there then."

Luna shook her head at him, "Why?"

Kallín looked to the faces of what was left of his clan, watching him. He explained, "I want to know what happened to our Rohán warriors in York. And I want revenge. That is why."

Luna saw the rage in his eyes. He was not for turning.

He addressed his clan, "You will all return to the caves with Luna. She speaks for me in all matters. Do as she tells you."

Brun stood up, "I'm coming with you so."

Kallín smiled at him, "I would have you with the clan. You are more needed there than with me."

Brun made to protest.

Kallín cut him off, "It's what I wish, Brun."

Luna smiled to herself, and told Margaret, "You will not make it through the forest dressed like that." She drew her blade and knelt in front of her, "I'll have to ruin your fine dress."

Margaret replied, "There's nothing fine about it."

Luna shrugged and then ran her blade between Margaret's legs, cutting her dress and making two long strips that she then trussed tightly around each of Margaret's legs. She then admired her good work, "Now, you are trussered properly."

Margaret was warming to the savage girl, "Thank you."

Luna was bluntly honest with her, "I'm not doing this for you. If you cannot travel well, then you will slow them down. If you slow them down, you make them easy prey. I know what Kallín is made of. He will not leave you to die. He will die with you."

Margaret promised her, "I won't let that happen."

28

YORK

The dense trees offered some cover from the worst of the ruthless ice-storm that came in relentless waves of easterly wind. The constant howling through the branches made it almost impossible to hear, or to be heard.

Kallín moved close to his cabal of night-trekkers and warned them, "Walk gently, find your footing with each step, for a trip could set off a snow fall from the trees above us and we'd be buried for sure."

Edgar looked out from under his hood. He could see nothing, and in the same moment, ice particles quickly punished his face in a stinging punch. The young Prince stepped as carefully as he could, but owing to the fact that his limbs were numb, he had no idea if his feet were firmly on the ground. He simply held the tail of Wulfstan's cloak and was brought along blindly.

Margaret was not doing so well either. The hours of persistent effort in the freezing snow and constant pain had drained her. She stopped, frozen, snow-blind, and called out, "I fear I might collapse."

In the same moment, she felt arms around, and she was lifted like a child by Javier, who apologised, "Forgive me, my lady, think of me as a horse."

She didn't argue with him. He carried her along in his arms. She pulled her hood around her face, and rested her head on his shoulder. The safe, cradling sway of his gait sent her instantly into a deep sleep. Somewhere further along their trail, Edgar also succumbed to the elements and climbed onto Wulfstan's back.

That was how the party went on its way, slowly, carefully, following some invisible path through the dense trees: a path known only to the Rohán.

As the dawn broke, the storm from the east was outdone by a new storm from the north. The northern snow was wetter and heavier than the icy snow from the east. It also had the added curse of sticking, so that it quickly piled up on man and beast alike. Soon everything and everyone in it became encased.

The ground underfoot turned from crisp ice to bog-slush. Kallín brought them to the north end of the forest and looked out over the open ground that was a sea of driving snow drifting in great mounds higher than a man.

"We are here," Kallín told Wulfstan, "the walls of York are ahead of us. Through that."

Wulfstan could not see York's walls through the whiteout, but he trusted that his young Silvatici guide was right.

Edmund looked out from under his snow-matted hood, "Are we there yet?"

Wulfstan answered, "We are close, but still far, my lord. We must cover that open ground. If our enemies are going to pounce, they will be somewhere out there … between us and the safety of York … waiting for us." He drew his sword and Peter did the same. Javier would carry the sleeping Princess until he could not.

Edgar came to the front, "I need a sword too."

Wulfstan shook his head, "No, my lord, you must keep to your disguise of being a simple monk; if you are captured, then, and only then, declare your true identity."

It was not going to turn into a debate. They moved out of the protection of the forest and into the open ground, beginning their struggle, hip-deep, through the all-consuming snow.

They were no more than fifty steps out of the cover of the trees, when they heard the galloping of horses coming at them.

There was no time to make it back to the cover of the forest. Kallín drew his bow. They readied for the fight.

A voice called to them, "Hold your arrows!"

Wulfstan signalled for Kallín to hold his shot. The horses came to a halt and circled them, and at the same time their leader dismounted.

152

Wulfstan recognised the man, "My Lord Morcar."

Morcar came to them, "I heard the news of your journey. I prayed you would make for York. We found a cavalry of Harold's Kingsmen waiting to ambush you and dealt with them." He looked to Edgar, "My lord, you are in danger and..." Morcar stopped as he caught sight of Margaret who emerged from behind Javier, "Princess Margaret?"

Margaret held herself as well as her numb body could manage, and answered, "Earl of Northumbria, I presume," and she even managed a smile.

Morcar bowed his head, and quickly said, "Please, let us get you all into the warm."

The last leg of their journey to York was completed on horseback.

Once inside the outer walls of the city, they felt the benefit of the protection from the full force of the weather. In a silent procession they made their way through the empty streets lined by great buildings of stone that loomed all around them.

The cohort entered a great inner courtyard that was circled with large fire pits that gave life saving heat to the wall-guards perched like living statues, keeping their vigil for unknown dangers.

"Come this way." A houseguard instructed Kallín and directed him away from the others. Kallín snatched a look at back at the young Prince and Princess, but they were already hurrying inside another building with the Earl of Northumbria.

Inside the great Minster, Margaret and Edgar were greeted by Bishop Ealdred, a tall thin man who kept the Saxon tradition of a long beard. Age had given him a naturally tonsured head from a retreating boundary of white hair. "Welcome. Please. Come into the fire. My Prince. My Princess."

Ealdred gently clapped his slender hands and a flurry of young black-clad tonsured monks came from the darkness like a flock of pigeons and joined the visitors who stood shivering in the small island of light. The flock of young monks set to attending to them, taking their wet travel cloaks away and replacing them with warmed blankets.

"This way, please," Ealdred went on, "you must be frozen to the bone."

He brought them on through the grand entrance and into the supper room that was already sending out great heat from its generous fire and mouth-watering smells of meat steaming on the plates.

A great pot of beef and turnip soup simmered somewhere.

Margaret was the first to follow in, "We are most grateful my Lord Bishop."

"I am Ealdred," he replied, "I am the—"

"Bishop of York," she finished his sentence for him and added, "Our own monk, blessed brother Matthew, told us to seek you out if we fell into danger."

"Dear Matthew," The Bishop smiled.

"You crowned Harold King?"

"I did," he told her.

She sounded him out on the matter, "You must be happy that the country has a new King so soon on the death of the old one."

"Happy? No. Relieved? Yes."

"Why relieved, Lord Bishop?"

He explained, "The integrity of England is more important to me than any one king. I am here as God's servant in his holy realm, my lady, and I will always do what is best for England."

She smiled, "I believe you will."

The fire loomed ahead of them, and a number of chairs were set out it in a horseshoe around the hearth to corral the heat escaping from it.

Bishop Ealdred gestured to Margaret, "My lady, sit, please, while we prepare your rooms and a supper."

She gratefully took her intended seat in the pool of heat. Ealdred went on ushering; next, he turned to Edgar, "My dear Prince Edgar."

Edgar had no appetite for niceties. He walked passed the Bishop and took up a stance with his back as close to the fire as he dared without setting himself alight, and he tried to make his teeth stop their chattering.

Wulfstan moved away to stand guard at the door.

"What a grace it is that has kept you alive, my lord" Ealdred told Edgar.

"Really?" Edgar asked him, "What idiot minds took me from the comfort of the Hungarian Court and put me on this fools journey in the first instance?"

The Bishop lowered his head, "Alas, our wise dead King had hoped to hold on to life until you arrived. But still, regardless of your trials and tribulations, we must thank God for your safe arrival."

Margaret told them, "I think that when you fully examine the events, that you will find we are still in the world of the living because of the brave actions of a young Silvatici who defended us from Lincoln's men and showed us safely here through the forest."

"Indeed. God sends the help we need." The Bishop was not about to step away from his doctrine and place the affairs of man into the hands of man.

Margaret did not disagree with him, "And where is God's blessed helper now? I noticed he was ushered away by Lord Morcar's men."

Ealdred answered, "I assure you that no harm will come to him."

Edgar bit like a hound, "I should hope not. I am in his debt and I intend to reward him well ... when I am King."

"Of course, my lord." Ealdred nodded to some servant that was hidden in the darkness beyond the candlelight. The unseen servant then flitted away to change the course of Kallín's journey. In almost the same moment, Morcar entered the room, and spoke with the ease that he would in his own home, "I think we can openly admit that our prayers have been answered."

Margaret was quick with him, "We would have to know first what those prayers were asking God for, would we not?"

Morcar smiled, "Our prayer was for the safe return to England of our rightful King." And he bowed his head to Edgar, "I am forever your servant, my lord."

Edgar felt uneasy with Morcar. But then he reminded himself that this is how the world is to a king, even one who is not, as yet, crowned. He replied to Morcar, "Your pledge is well received Morcar and I know well of you and your brother, that you are both loyal to the true House of Wessex." He then asked the Bishop, "And how did it come to pass that Harold Godwinson, the usurper of my family's title, is on the throne?"

Ealdred explained, "When our dear King Edward died, supporters in the Witan for Harold Godwinson, men who stood to gain from prearranged agreements, argued that with Normandy laying a claim to the English throne, war was surely coming. It was an opportunity for them to argue that a young boy could not lead an army, or take the realm into a war."

Edgar quickly responded, "I am no coward."

Ealdred smiled and said, "That would be a kind of impossibility, my lord, given that you have the blood of the great King Ironside in your veins."

Edgar cut him off, "Are you telling me that you do not support Godwinson's claim to be King?"

Without hesitation, Ealdred answered, "That is precisely what I am telling you, my lord."

Edgar tested that, "Then why did you place the crown on his head?"

Ealdred explained, "Because we did not know if you lived. There was a rumour put into the air that you had perished in the sea."

Margaret asked, "And what of our situation now?"

Ealdred replied, "You survived the storm, but you are now in a dangerous place. The Kingsmen hunt you. No matter how much Harold claims that his efforts are in your interest, in order to take you into his protection, you are a threat to his crown."

"What of Rome's position?"

The Bishop was unsure of his answer to her, "Rome, my lady?"

Margaret went on, "When I met with the Duke of Normandy in the Abbey of Fécamp, he boasted a Papal banner hanging from the rafters for all to see."

Ealdred nodded in agreement, "Yes … I heard that he had been awarded the banner. It's possible that the Pope may favour William over Harold. But … he would never favour any claim to the throne of England over Edgar's claim. The rightful Atheling is God's choice for King."

Margaret weighed that, "Then in the event of a war with England and Normandy, if Harold should lose, the Pope will see Edward prevail in his right to the throne?"

Ealdred looked into the flames of the fire, "One can never presume to know what Rome will do. But William of Normandy will make war. If we can keep our Prince safe until that war is concluded, who can say?" Then the old bishop brightened and added, "But there is a higher power than Rome. How portentous is it that a Silvatici saved the life of our precious Prince and brought him to our safety … I believe that is the defining message on the matter from God."

Margaret, for the first time, felt the burden of destiny, "I pray you are correct, Lord Bishop."

"I pray so too."

Margaret stood, "We will get my brother to Scotland and keep him safe there under the protection of King Malcolm."

Ealdred smiled, "Well, we shall all sleep on it and come up with a plan to get our Prince safely to Scotland. But now, enough of this world of troubles. You must have your supper, and then make your prayers, give up our troubles to God until the morning, and sleep." He clapped his hands smartly and triggered a fresh flurry of young monks from the shadows, "The brothers will show you to your quarters. I bid you all a good night. And God bless you."

29

BISHOP EALDRED

Kallín followed the grim houseguard through the dark corridors that descended into the bowels of the minster's underbelly. The only sound was the rhythmic scrape of chainmail and armour. The further in they went, the darker and quieter it grew. They went on like that, wrapped against the darkness in a small ball of light from the lamp in the houseguard's hand until the twisting and turning passageway spat them out suddenly at great doors big enough for a giant to walk through.

The great doors were pushed open without a sound by two more houseguards. A pure white light came from within.

An armoured hand gestured to the light beyond.

This was as far as the houseguards would go…

What horrors wait for me on the other side?

He moved into the light.

On entering, he was blinded, his eyes smarted and winced with pain.

Slowly his vision adjusted to the glare, and he saw that it emanated from an island of candles, some tall as a man and thick as an arm, others wasted away to a mound of wax. To his left and right, protruding from the shadows, stood statues of finely-robed men and women. The young Rohán knew this was a place of the dead. It was absurd to him that people would make such a worship of corpses. Nothing moved. In the silent presence of the dead kings and queens, he waited, thawing out under his heavy leather cloak, dripping a pool onto the black slate floor, but warming himself nicely. After some time of waiting in the silent peace, a torpor crept into him and tugged on him like an incessant child seeking his attention. He gave in to its demands and sat on the floor. Moments later, he tasted the creamy sleep-soup of fatigue; the bone tiredness set into him. He got warmer in it, until the unstoppable tide washed over him, body and mind, and he was pulled down into the undertow. The breath was sucked out of him until he was no longer in the world of the living but dwelling in some place near the sleeping dead. He may well have met all those dead in that sleep, and he may well have got to know something of them. Somewhere in the corners of that dead sleep he became aware of a voice of the living telling him to wake up. He did not want to return to the world of the living. He liked sleeping with the dead who are beyond pain and hardship. But the call of the living would not give up on him. It called a number of times to his reluctant senses, "Wake up, boy." He opened his eye to see a red-robed and grey bearded ghost looking down upon him.

"You are back among the living," Ealdred informed him in kind warm voice.

The scruffy Rohán climbed back to his feet, his joints and muscles crying with reluctance. The great oak doors glided in silence on well-greased hinges. Then the tidy click of the metal mechanism from the hidden lock sealed him in, tomb-like, with the softly spoken red-robed man. Suddenly, he felt trapped, like one of Luna's howlers, doomed to a painful death. A primal urge to run filled him from the feet up, screaming at him to take off blindly into the dark like a bat. He fought that urge and subdued it, absorbing the fear in his veins as he would the cold shock of jumping into an icy river. Every part of him tingled. The Bishop came quietly into the light. Over his arm he carried a carefully folded fat warm blanket.

Ealdred spoke again, with the same warmth, "Take off that soldier's cloak and wrap up in this," and he handed the blanket to him.

Kallín peeled off the heavy wet cloak and carefully took the soft blanket and felt the heat emanating from it. It had been warmed by a fire the way that a mother warms a swaddle for her baby. He wrapped himself in the soft blanket, and it immediately gave him a great warm hug, inducing a lucid memory of his mother holding him in her arms. It was a recall of such force that he smelled her next to him, and for a moment his heart shuddered with the pain of her loss. It seemed in this strange place of the tombs that parts of himself he thought to be dead were brought back to life.

"I am Bishop Ealdred." He looked over the fretful wild boy with a curious eye and asked, "You are called Kallín?"

Kallín felt the warmth coming back into him. If these people meant him harm, he would have had the pain served out to him already. "Yes."

"I am told you are a Rohán?"

"I am."

Ealdred nodded, "An ancient people. And not many of you left now. What gods do you worship?"

"None."

The Bishop took a moment to weigh that, then asked him, "Surely you have gods?"

"Our gods abandoned us."

"What makes you say that?"

"They let the Norsemen kill us."

"I see. But the Norsemen did not kill you."

Kallín shrugged. "No..."

"Why is that?"

For a long time Kallín searched for an answer. But he could not find one.

The Bishop eventually said, "Your gods may well have abandoned your people, but a boy who survives such an attack by Norsemen, and then survives an attack of a great wolf, and then rescues a king, that boy is not abandoned. I would think that boy is very much favoured God ... and God may well have chosen him ... may well have a plan for him."

30

MORCAR

The next morning Kallín woke in a bed that he did not remember getting into. In fact, he remembered very little of the night before. He may even have slept for a week. He had no way of knowing. He washed in the basin of scented water provided there in his room, freshly braided his hair and went to dress himself only to find his clothing gone … and the black habit of the monk left out for him.

A voice spoke from behind him, "The wolf pelt was infested with fleas," a young monk explained, "the rest of your clothes also needed … burning." Then the young monk pointed to a pair of boots. "These should be a good fit for you."

For a moment Kallín could not believe that they had burned his wolf cloak. It was hard to believe that it was gone, and it felt that a part of him was gone with it. What that part was, he did not know, but he also felt strangely unburdened. He dressed in the habit. It was something soft. He felt the fabric between his fingers and asked the young monk, "Of what beast is this made from?"

The young monk smiled and told him, "Sheep."

"Sheep… I have never seen such a beast."

The monk explained, "It is the hair of the beast. It is called wool."

Kallín rubbed his hand along the smooth fabric. He never imagined that anything could be so soft … "Wool."

It is no wonder that they can all be slaughtered so handily.

Shortly after his breakfast, Kallín was brought to a great room that housed countless scrolls and books and a great table.

Bishop Ealdred entered from some discreet doorway hidden amongst the bookshelves, "How did you sleep?"

"Goodly."

The Bishop smiled. He noted the boy's inquisitive eyes taking in every detail, and explained to him, "This room is called a library. A place where we keep scrolls and books." He picked up a scroll, "This is a scroll." He opened it out, "And this is writing..."

Kallín looked at the marks on the parchment, "What is it for?"

The Bishop explained, "It tells a story. These markings are words. Some words are the words of kings, and they record for all the important laws that the King makes. This one is an account of a great battle. Look here."

The Bishop walked to the huge table. Kallín followed him to see that spread out upon it was a massive parchment. Ealdred told him, "This is a map."

Kallín looked over it.

Ealdred watched the boy absorb it and explained, "This is our island... Up here is Scotland in the north, down here is Wales and all this ... This is England." Then he tested the boy, "Can you find where we are ... On this map?"

Kallín looked for a few moment. He began to understand that this is how a great bird would see if it flew high. That he was looking down on the land. He asked, "Is this water?"

"Yes"

There was one body of water that he knew intimately, "This is the great Umber?"

"Well done..." The Bishop smiled. He was about to move on but he saw Kallín's finger travel...

The boy went on, "We tracked the skidders along the winding Ouse and stopped for their attack here. I then brought us through the marshlands and high forest to here. We are here."

The Bishop was truly amazed. "Yes ... The place you have your finger on is called York."

"York ... My people call it Eoforwic, the place of the great boar." Then his eyes searched the map south of York and found a place marked with a small drawing of a sword, "What is this marking?"

"That marking," Ealdred explained, "is the site of a great battle."

Kallín looked closer at the spot, and a hunch entered his thoughts, the way he might know the end of a joke, "Is it an important place to me?"

Ealdred nodded to him, "It is the place that your father died."

Kallín took a moment and asked, "Do you have the story of the battle?"

Ealdred told him, "There is one better able to tell it, and he comes now."

The doors opened and Morcar entered, "Ah, good morning, the young miraculous Rohán."

Kallín asked him, "You know my clan?"

"I knew your father," Morcar told him. "He and his men were the finest warriors in the field."

"He was in your hire?"

"He was." Morcar went on, "You no doubt would like to know what occurred."

"Yes I would."

Morcar moved to the map table and uncoiled a new map, "This is my battle map. I went against Tostig Godwinson. Do you know who he is?"

"I do not."

Morcar explained, "He was the Earl of Northumbria, and he is the Brother of Harold Godwinson who is now King of England. My army was mainly made up of men from the surrounding lands of Northumbria. It was not difficult to recruit them. Tostig was a cruel Earl and much hated. But I hired one hundred skilled Rohán to break the shield wall. Tostig's army was all Norse mercenaries. He took the high ground," Morcar pointed to a hill on the map, "here, and held it until the Rohán punched a hole through the shield wall and my men poured through the breach. Tostig was dislodged, and we put the two thousand Norse mercenaries into a retreat. We then pursued Tostig and his army to here, the river. He was trapped. I called for a parley, and he made a surrender. Tostig agreed to leave England with his mercenaries. Peace was made. I sent my men back to their homes. The fighting was done. But Tostig and his Norsemen had been humiliated in battle by the Rohán, and as they withdrew, their entire army of two thousand Norse attacked the Rohán camp and slaughtered the one hundred warriors there. I am told that the army of Norsemen then went down river to attack the safe camp where the families of the Rohán waited. Is this true?"

"It is true. Where is this Tostig now?"

"We have reports of him being in Normandy with William the

Bastard, plotting against England."

Bishop Ealdred came closer to them and spoke to Kallín, "It would seem now that you have a name for your revenge."

"He is left England..." Kallín was seething.

"But he will return," Morcar told him.

Kallín saw hope, "Return?"

Morcar explained, "He too desires the English crown and will kill his own brother to get it. He cannot take the crown without coming to England. Can he?"

Kallín thought and then asked, "How can I be in the battle?"

The Bishop smiled, "Not all of the war is fought with the sword. We must first get our Prince to safety, and you can help us greatly to bring that about."

Some hours later, having made an agreement with the Bishop, Kallín sat on a stool having his head tonsured so that he would look like a young monk and be able to act as a decoy for the Prince who was also travelling under the disguise of a monk.

Javier and Peter joined him and looked him over.

Javier smiled, "You look good when you are cleaned."

Kallín said, "I want my blade returned to me."

Javier explained, "If you fall into the enemy's hands you are to tell them you are a monk. A monk would not carry such a weapon. It will remain safely with the Bishop, in his keeping, until we return." He looked to Peter, "It is time."

Javier, Peter and Kallín went to the stables to acquire a horse. "I want your best horse," Javier told the horse dealer.

The dealer was delighted to hear this and brought out a fine looking stallion.

Javier turned to Kallín and asked him, "What do you think of this beast, my lord Prince."

The dealer took a double look at the young monk.

"I like it well," Kallín responded as instructed, and then performed the next part of his play, "See to it that it is fitted comfortably for me. If I am to ride all the way to Winchester on the beast."

A short time after that, Kallín was on the back of the fine black beast. Peter and Javier were either side of him. The horse trader watched them leave before he scurried away to sell his information in the tavern. There were men who would pay a good price to know that the

Prince was travelling south to Winchester.

When Wulfstan saw the horse trader disappear, he called Edgar and Margaret out of hiding and they set off north.

As they made their way along the road, Margaret asked Wulfstan, "Now that we have set loose the word that the Prince is travelling south as a monk, surely they will be captured by the Kingsmen?"

"They will," Wulfstan agreed, "but by the time that they discover our ruse, we will be safely in Scotland."

"I understand that. But what becomes of the decoy ... and those who are guarding him?"

Wulfstan read her and told her, "Those who are guarding him are doing their work according to their own conscience."

Margaret raised an eyebrow, "That is a little too cryptic of an answer."

Wulfstan nodded in agreement, "I am sorry, my lady. I meant to say that they chose to carry out the mission. Their fate is unknown."

Margaret said no more on the matter. But she felt haunted by it. She knew her heart would not be at peace until she knew the outcome of their mission, one way or the other.

31

TAKEN

Kallín swam in total darkness, lost in the abyss, fumbling for a grip, stumbling for a foothold, gasping for a breath, floating, rising, coming to consciousness. He realised that his hands and feet were tied, and he was blindfolded. He listened hard to the muffled air. He guessed that he was most likely in a sack. He was being swayed. His senses searched for more clues: a hard floor, the moaning churn of axles, the rumble of wheels on the rutted road, the heaving breath of horses, the dull rhythmic thump of hooves on the damp earth. He completed the picture of his situation in his mind. He was hogtied in a sack on the back of a wagon.

The kidnapping had taken place so quickly that he did not see or hear any of it. His only true memory of the violent event was the sensation of the air moving behind him before he was struck on the head and sent plummeting into unconsciousness. All that took place after that moment was unknown to him. The wagon creaked and rocked and slowed until it came to a stuttering stop.

He set his plan, watching the coming events play out in his mind.

I'll play feeble like the Prince ... when they cut me free, I'll grab the first sword I see and have at them. It will be quick. Maybe I will get one or even two of them.

But he had to dampen the heat of that plan because it was contrary to what he had made a pact to do with the Bishop. To honour his part of the deal, Kallín must keep to his part in this ruse for as long as possible. He must buy as much time as he could for the Prince to get safely to Scotland. Then, when his decoy deception is discovered, he was to keep his story set to being a monk. That way he would live. And he must live so that he could get to Tostig Godwinson and have revenge on him for the betrayal of the Rohán.

All around him he heard the muffled low chatter of foreign tongues. His ears trained in on movement, footsteps, coming close to him. Suddenly, he was heaved out of the wagon and carried in the sack for a short distance before being dropped roughly on a wooden floor … another floor that moved … but not a wagon.

He began to make out other sounds now: the creaking of wooden joints, the lapping of water along the flanks, the strained whimper of wooden oars bending under the pull, the timed heave of the collective grunts like a choir making a hymn of man versus water.

After a time, he felt a presence near him, a clear sense that someone was staring closely at the sack. The presence knelt close. He smelt stale beer, and the rank breath formed words, "Young Prince, d'you hear me?" it asked him in the voice of a heavy foreign accent, "You must behave. Yes? Behave and you will live. Yes?"

Kallín had been schooled on how to keep his part of the ruse. He meekly answered, "Yes."

"Good. You will not make me be cruel to you. I will take you out of this sacking."

The ropes of the sack were removed and Kallín's tonsured head was uncovered. His eyes immediately adjusted to the moonlight, quickly taking in his surroundings. They were far out on the water with no shore-lights in sight. Twelve rowers pulled them along at speed through the dead calm. Then he heard a gasp of breath and looked to see a monk looking at him in disbelief.

"It is not possible…" Brother Tomas cried.

The ruse was discovered. Kallín waited like a hog for slaughter.

The monk shouted and then turned to speaking in his own tongue to the mercenaries, who ignored him and kept on rowing. When Tomas tired of shouting, he sat on a pile of rope. Kallín examined him. He looked worn out. He threw his hands to either side of him and asked Kallín, "Who are you?"

Kallín answered with the rehearsed lie, "Brother Osbald."

This name, as intended, caught Tomas's interest, "Osbald? Who gave you that name?"

Kallín told him, "Bishop Ealdred christened me that when I came into his care. He is the Bishop of York who did crown King Harold."

Tomas scowled, "I know who he is and who he did crown." Tomas thought it out. Ealdred had outwitted them and sacrificed this young novice in the process.

Tomas came closer to him, and asked him, "Why have you been so foolish?"

Kallín gave the answer he was told to give, "I am under the instructions of my Abbot, so I am in the service of God, am I not?"

32

MOINE DES LOUPS

William the Duke of Normandy listened to Brother Tomas explain why the plan to kidnap the Atheling had failed. The Duke scoffed at the monk's assertions that the young monk was an innocent in all of this.

William scorned him, "I am once more thwarted by Benedictines."

Tomas replied, respectfully, "The order of Fécamp and of York are of the same holy Saint Benedict that is a blessing to you, my lord."

William scowled, "Don't play me for a fool. I will see to this little rat monk myself."

Tomas, with a slight amount of steel in his tone, reminded William, "That is your prerogative as Duke. But I would not be fulfilling my duty to you, as ordered by the Holy Father to advise you, that if it is your intention to stay in the good favour of the Holy Father, then you should not harm the flesh of one of his monks, my lord."

William examined Tomas, "The clever clerics always plotting."

"Plotting for your benefit, my lord," Tomas was quick to remind him.

"We will see," William said and then ordered, "let me look upon the decoy."

Tomas nodded and Kallín was brought in, a guard holding him by each shoulder.

"Bring him closer to me," William seemed suddenly fascinated by him.

Kallín did not understand any of the Norman words that were being spoken around him. He expected this was where he would die. But he was not afraid of going home.

William looked closer at him, "The scars..."

Tomas asked Kallín in English, "How did you come by the scars on your face?"

"A wolf."

"Un loup," Tomas told William.

William's eyes widened, and he ordered, "Let me see the rest of him."

The guards immediately tore Kallín's rope away from him, and he stood naked before William who was wide-eyed at his scars, "Magnificent. Are they not?" he asked Tomas.

Tomas saw an opportunity to help the young monk, "They are indeed..."

William asked, "How could he survive so...?"

Tomas added, "It is miraculous ... is it not, my lord?"

William stopped his thoughts, "Miraculous." He looked back to Kallín, "What of the wolf? Ask him that."

Tomas asked, "Tell us how it occurred."

The Rohán are naturally gifted to tell good stories, and are especially skilled in telling stories of battle. It is how they pass their nights around the campfire, recalling warriors who have gone home and the great events of their warrior's story. Kallín set to tell William of Normandy his own warrior story, explaining. "I was but a runt of a boy, wild in the great forest, one of the people that the English call Silvatici. A name given to us first by the great Roman called Caesar when he brought his army to our shores."

"Silvatici..."

Kallín saw the recognition of the word in William's eyes, and even in the eyes of the guards who seemed to have edged in to listen better.

He then went on, "I was hunting in the night. Alone. I felt the eyes upon me ... then I smelled the stench of the great beast ... his breath ... I looked behind me to see him there ... big as a horse, teeth as long as your fingers, red eyes that burned like hot coals..." The young Rohán felt all the ears of the room trained tightly on him as he went into the details of the fight and Tomas translated. They were like birds eating out of his hand. He was enjoying his place here as a seanchaí. He continued to change and mould his story to suit his needs, sensing the parts they liked and teasing those details out the way he would lure a fish. Mostly, he was careful not to give himself away as a Rohán with a death-wish for Tostig Godwinson, "I was torn ragged and more dead than alive, but I was found by the holy brother monks and put back together, healed, and baptised, and made Christian. I gave my life to God and became, as you see me now, a novice monk."

When William heard the story translated to him, one word stuck with him, "Silvatici."

Tomas explained further to William, "The Silvatici were said to be savages who lived in the dark forests and were descended from the Iceni who were the first people of Britain." He went on to explain, "Bishop Ealdred no doubt named the young monk after the Iceni King Osbald who was favoured by the Romans. Caesar believed that the Silvatici were somehow charmed in battle ... For they fought without any armour ... naked." Tomas then made his move to save the young monk, "Perhaps we could keep him with us in our monastery at Fécamp?"

William weighed that, "Not yet. Let us see if he is truly loved by God. Place him in the oubliette to see how God treats him."

Tomas made an effort to sway the Duke, "My lord, he is but a boy and ... the oubliette is a harsh place for one who has committed no crime."

William reminded him, "He is a Silvatici who killed a wolf ... Only God could make such a miracle. We will see if it is true. If God wants him to live, he will live. Our Holy Father need not worry, the boy's skin will not be broken. He will stay there until I am convinced or until God decides he should die."

Kallín was lead out, naked, and at the same time, a man entered and laughed at him, "What is this?" He spoke in an English accent.

Tomas answered him, "Lord Tostig, how nice to see you. This is one of your countrymen."

Tostig? Kallín's heart raced. His eyes searched the guards for weapons. Two swords within his reach, but would he get close enough? The guards that were holding him sensed the rise in him and instinctively held him tighter.

Don't look at him. He told himself, Don't let him look into your eyes. Don't show yourself or your intentions.

Kallín knew that he could not hide his murderous rage from close inspection and should Tostig see it in him, he would never get his chance to kill him.

Tostig stopped walking, "This is the creature who was the decoy?"

Tomas read Tostig now as did William.

William told Tostig, "He is a monk."

Tostig looked at the scars, "And what was he before he was a monk?"

William told him, "Silvatici."

Tostig paled a little, his eyes fixed on Kallín as he instinctively gripped the handle of his sword.

William and Tomas watched carefully, noticing this unsettling change in Tostig.

Tomas asked Tostig, "You have had dealings with the Silvatici?"

Tostig just nodded. Then he said, "Look at me, boy."

Kallín dug as deeply into himself as he could, and he tried hard not to think about his mother and his father and his people. He tried hard not to think that this was the man who had betrayed his father and who was responsible for all that had occurred to the Rohán.

Tostig shouted, "Look at me!"

Kallín took a breath and reminded himself that he must live so that he can kill this man. He buried his anger and looked at Tostig.

Tostig looked briefly into his eyes and took a step back and looked to William, "Kill him."

William smiled, "You are the Duke now?"

Tostig explained, "I meant to say, my lord, I would advise that you kill him."

Tomas reminded Tostig, "You cannot kill a monk."

Tostig was quick to say, "He is not a monk." Then he looked to William, "You are being duped twice, my lord."

William suddenly roared, "I will not be told instructions by you!"

Tostig immediately lowered his head, "Forgive me, my lord."

William spoke to Tomas, "Tell him to pray."

When Kallín was instructed to pray by Tomas, he understood why the Bishop had gone to such lengths to baptise him and teach him the Pater Noster. He'd also instructed him on how to bless himself and kneel, which Kallín did, before he began to recite the words that he had said over a hundred times in one night until he knew them without thinking, "Pater noster, qui es in coelis, sanctificetur nomen tuum. Adveniat regnum tuum, fiat voluntas tua..."

Brother Tomas was so struck by the image of the naked and scarred boy kneeling and praying, that he knelt and prayed too. At that, the twenty other monks who were in various places knelt and prayed. William felt the great dangerous fervour that the monks carry, and they were showing their power now around this young monk. Eyes fell upon him. He felt compelled to kneel. His soldiers and courtiers knelt. Tostig felt that he had met his reaper. Everything about this boy monk smelled of death. But he was, for the moment, powerless to act. He too knelt.

All was black in the cold windowless oubliette cell where prisoners are put to be forgotten. The prisoner would be brought from the world above as a 'sous le capot' under a black leather hood so that he would have no sense of time, no sense of place. All he would know is the dark abyss. He would not see or speak to another living soul. He would not be fed or watered.

Kallín's universe was now twelve heel-to-toe steps by six heel-to-toe steps. He could not fathom how high the ceiling went up into the darkness. As he blindly explored the walls with his fingers, he found a trickle of water that was surprisingly sweet, and then along the corners where the water pooled, he discovered moss that grew in abundance. He licked the sweet water from the wall when he was thirsty.

After some time, when his hunger set in, he began to eat the moss. It tasted of stone, but stone tasted as good to him as anything else. Soon, he lost any sense of up and down, he could not tell if he was upright or lying down, and all sense of balance was lost so that when he moved he crawled.

He found comfort in the upright iron bars that made up one side of his world. He held on there. Sometimes it felt like the bars were below him and other times it seemed that they were above him and he was hanging on for his life. He tried for a time to have one place in the dark to piss. He did not have the need to shit since he was not eating anything of substance. It soon became a pointless exercise, he barely had a trickle when he pissed and it burned him to try. Time passed. He felt the hair grow on his tonsured bald spot. He had no idea how long it took.

Then somewhere in the timeless darkness he saw light ... it grew stronger and hurt his eyes, the wet walls came into focus and then the bars of the gate. He scurried on his belly into the farthest corner from it and covered his eyes. The great blinding light came to the bars of the gate. A voice whispered from the light, "I found you ... Moine des Loup."

Silence fell again for some time and then the voice spoke again, "Do not fear me, young monk."

As Kallín's eyes settled to the light, he saw that the source of the great orb was a candle flame and that the man holding it was dressed in a white gown, and he wore a crown on his head.

"Are you the monk's Father God?" Kallín asked him. The words scorched his throat, and his voice was no more than rasping air that grated out of his mouth.

The man smiled, "I am Wulfnoth. I am King of this underworld..."

"King Wulfnoth..." Kallín repeated.

King Wulfnoth sat on the floor and waited for whatever time it took for Kallín to crawl over to him. Then they spoke in gentle whispers no louder than the rustling of dry autumn leaves, yet their words filled the silence, and their companionship brought heat and vigour into Kallín's corps-like body.

Wulfnoth told him, "Moine des Loups ... I heard the guards talking about you. I've been searching all over my realm of the underworld for you. I am very curious, you see ... It is a fault of mine, like the curiosity of my creature of a cat called Homer who is drawn by some irresistible force to the sounds of scratching. I gave him his name of Homer on account of the fact that he became blind. You see, he had been born down here in the bowels of the underworld, and so he had no need for sight. But he curiously wandered up into the world of light. Had I not found him, well, his adventures would have come to an abrupt ending in the belly of a hungry dog, no doubt. He is an extremely clever little beast ... and yet ... no matter how bright his little mind, he is so easily teased in that way with simple scratching or the drumming of fingers. He brings me many hours of pleasure to watch him search for the mouse that is not there. Hundreds of times I play him with the trick, and hundreds of times he cannot resist. Surely he must know by now that my scratching fingernails are no mouse. But he cannot help himself, you see? All creatures are made from nature, and their nature is what controls them. But I beg your pardon. I ramble too much. I am too much in my own company and get into long debates that I am at a loss as to where they begin or where they end. I seem to be always debating something or other of no significance at all. I did once fancy myself becoming a master of rhetoric where I could be a wise King for England and use my powers of persuasion to sway friends and foe alike, to replace war and brutality with words, replace conflict with consolation and compromise. What a world would that be? To solve all troubles through debate. A world without war ... That is the world of civilised men. But yet there is always that part of our nature that is always savage. But look! I have cake for you ... Come to me now ... Come. Eat."

Kallín took a closer look at the babbling King and saw now that he was feeble, and thin, and saw too that the gold crown upon his head was made of painted wood. He was a mad fool King.

King Wulfnoth held out a cloth parcel the size of a fist through the bars, "For you. So that you will not die."

Kallín took it, and immediately on unwrapping it, he was hit with the wonderful scent of honey. He looked at the lump in his fist and took a small careful bite, instantly, he was struck by the intense sweet taste, and he let out an involuntary, "hummm."

Wulfnoth smiled at him, "Good, yes?"

"Yes."

The forgotten forest came back to him and for a moment, he heard the bees busy in the meadow, and the distant laughter of children running in and out of the full-berried bramble patch at play. In the same moment that the memory came to him from the deep keep of his senses, it went back into its safe hiding place again. But the taste of honey remained.

Kallín asked King Wulfnoth, "What does 'Moine des Loup' mean?"

"Monk of the Wolves."

Kallín smiled at that. It was not such a bad thing to be called.

Wulfnoth told him, "You are a curiosity to the Normans now."

"Why?"

"Up there — they know you are alive still — down here."

"How do they know that? No one comes here... "

"Oh, There is one who comes. I call him Crepitus. He is silent as the air apart from his creaking knees. He creeps and creaks about the labyrinth of this underworld and listens with his great big ears for breathing or the humming of flies. He sniffs with his long wet snout seeking out the rotting corpses and he keeps the tally of those that the world has forgotten. He reports to Duke William about you. You should be long dead, but yet you live..."

"What time of the year is it, King Wulfnoth?"

"Spring it is. Buds are popping soon and flowers will then bloom."

Kallín thought aloud, "So much time has passed then."

"Time does not really exist down here," Wulfnoth told him.

Kallín was already at ease with his rambling mad King and enjoyed the cake and the candlelight, and the sound of his voice, no matter what he was whispering about.

Wulfnoth went on, "Up there, we have named months, and weeks and days and nights and hours and even little pieces of time called minutes — but time is just an idea ... Is it not? You cannot hold it. You cannot own it. And the days and nights do not know that you count them as they come and go. Whatever the world above us is made of, and the moon and the sun, it does not know of us any more than it knows of the animals and plants that live and die on it. I have a secret for you..."

Kallín kept eating, and after a few moments of silence, he asked Wulfnoth, "What is the secret?"

Wulfnoth shook his head, "Not yet." He smiled and told him, "I must go now to visit my other subjects."

"Stay," the word came out of Kallín without any thought.

Wulfnoth smiled, "Fear not. I will come again and bring you some more cake."

Kallín thought, and asked him, "May I touch you, King?"

Wulfnoth thought about it for a moment. It seemed like a perfectly reasonable request. "You may. What part of me do you wish to touch?"

"Your fine beard."

Wulfnoth put his face to the gap in the bars.

Kallín reached out carefully and touched his beard.

"It is a very fine beard," Kallín told him.

"Thank you. I do comb through it at regular times in the day."

"I would like to have a fine beard the like of it."

"You will. One day."

"Will I?"

"Yes. Your beard will come in and you will be a full man. And…" Wulfnoth examined him in the light, "You will do great things."

"Thank you..."

Wulfnoth went on, "Do not be silent in the darkness. Use your voice. Speak."

Kallín said, "But there is no one to speak to in the darkness."

Wulfnoth told him, "Talk to the darkness. Become its friend. It will show you things. It will reveal great secrets to you."

Then King Wulfnoth of the Underworld and his candlelight disappeared, and Kallín was plunged back into the darkness wherein he slowly and carefully enjoyed every last crumb of his honey cake. And when he had finished every last morsel, he thought for some time, and then he asked the darkness, "Do you hear me?"

There was no measurement of time, other than the visits from King

Wulfnoth, and Kallín could not tell if he came at regular intervals or not. But he discovered that the darkness was a welcoming companion and it showed him how to see in it. He no longer feared being consumed by it. He could look into the blackest part of it, and it would show him anything that he asked of it. He watched Luna and the little-ones going about the forest and playing. He watched his mother alive but working as a slave. And he made plans of how he would find her and free her. Then his father appeared to him, and they talked at length about how he was going to kill Tostig and avenge the betrayal of the Rohán.

Kallín asked King Wulfnoth, "How are you here, and you a King, and an Englishman?"

Wulfnoth smiled, "I am no king. I am ... a fool."

Kallín told him, "You are no fool. You are a good man."

"Am I?"

"Yes."

"I wouldn't know," Wulfnoth told him, "for I have no deeds to measure myself by."

"You saved my life," Kallín told him, "that is a good deed, is it not?"

"Is it?" Wulfnoth asked and seemed bewildered, he went on, "I don't know. In truth, I saved you because I was curious, like my cat Homer. And when I found you to be English, I returned so that we might converse, like we are now. It was not a selfless act on my part."

Kallín assured him, "Well it was a good deed, all the same, no matter the reason for it."

Wulfnoth nodded, "Well ... Maybe in the end ... our good actions count for more than our bad thoughts."

Kallín asked, "How are you here then?"

"I am a hostage to the Duke William."

"Hostage ... Why?"

Wulfnoth looked into the dark distance to some horizon unseen by normal eyes, and after a few moments of thought he answered, "I'm not sure ... Let me see..." He looked further into the dark, examining his past life, "As a boy I was hostaged by my father to King Edward, for reasons I'm vague on. Father died. Then King Edward, for reasons I am also not clear on, gave me as hostage to William ... I em..." He came to a place in his mind where the darkness was too dense to penetrate, "You know, years run together and the boy grows into a man. And here we are, you and I."

Kallín was moved by his story, "You have been hostage since

boyhood?"

"Yes."

"And what of your family?"

"They have not forgotten me. I am soon to be freed ... My brother is now King of England."

Kallín took a moment to figure that out. "Your brother is Harold Godwinson?"

"Yes. Do you know of him?"

Kallín's head began to swim a little, "Yes ... and you also have a brother called Tostig?"

"Yes." Wulfnoth brightened up, "Tostig has been to see me."

"I see."

"He brings me the honey cake."

Kallín stopped eating.

Wulfnoth read him, "I have disturbed you somehow."

Kallín became suspicious of him, "How is that you have free run of the dungeons?"

Wulfnoth relished some fact in his mind, "I like this conversation. It is full of secrets. I have disturbed you and you have knowledge of my family ... Yes. Secrets are ... Irresistible. We must proceed quid pro quo."

"Quid...?"

Wulfnoth explained, "It is a Roman term meaning we give each other equal amounts. Secret for a secret ... But I think I have given you much more than you have given me. Tell me how you know of my Brother Tostig ... while you eat his honey cake."

Kallín thought about his answer. This is how the mad King gets his information about the world above. Kallín knew he would be an expert at smelling out a lie. So he decided to be truthful, in a limited way, "I am a warrior of the Rohán."

"Ha!" Wulfnoth placed his hands on his head in delight, "What a fantastic secret! Oh My! Oh My! Oh My!" He looked at Kallín wide-eyed, "The Moine des Loup is a bloomin Rohán. " Then Wulfnoth froze in thought, "What is the connection then? Between you and my brother Tostig?"

Kallín reminded him, "Quid pro quo."

Wulfnoth clasped his hands in delight, "You have me on a string as I often have poor tormented Homer. Oh, you are clever. You're outwitting me, are you not? Let me see, you require a morsel of a secret..." He searched his mind, then, "I have it here for you. They will free you soon." Wulfnoth read Kallín's face and saw the glow in it,

"Aha! Now it is I who have you on the string. You glow bright with curiosity before my eyes."

Kallín got to it, "I know of your brother because he betrayed my father in battle to the Norsemen and..."

Wulfnoth held up his hands, "Stop! Easy now. Do not spill your secrets like slop from the bucket. This is no way to converse."

Kallín pressed him, "How do you know I will be freed?"

Wulfnoth explained, "People have heard of the 'Moine des Loups' in the dungeon who bears the miracle scars and will not die... They gather at the gates to pray for you. The monks have petitioned Rome. The tide comes in to float your boat." Then in a flat tone he added, "How was your father betrayed by my brother?"

Kallín thought for a moment, "After the treaty with Morcar..."

"Morcar!" Wulfnoth spat out his name, "Morcar is a hound!" Wulfnoth stood and clenched his thin fists, "Rage. Rage. Rage." He looked at his fists in amazement, "I have not been enraged since ... father died. Look at me. I still have it in me. Look! Do you see the rage in me?"

"Yes. I see it," Kallín assured him.

Then Wulfnoth ran out of steam, "Oh ... What a curse. What a base nature that I have under all of my learning I am still an angry savage, am I not?" He looked at Kallín, sadly, "I will miss you when you go. I so much enjoy you."

Kallín asked him, "Why not escape?"

Wulfnoth explained, "I am a hostage."

"But..." Kallín struggled to make his point to him, "You could slip away in the night, get a boat on the coast..."

"No," Wulfnoth interrupted him, "you do not understand. It is a matter of honour."

"Honour? How?"

"My father gave me as his word. My father is dead. I will not break my father's word. I will remain hostage until the agreement is honoured."

"What agreement?"

Wulfnoth shrugged, then put his head in his hands, "I do not know ... I do not ... Know. But there must be one." He looked at Kallín, "Surely? There is one. Or how else am I to be negotiated out into the world?"

Kallín instantly pitied this poor creature, "Well yes. That makes sense now. Your brother, the King, will soon have you home to

England. I am sure..."

Wulfnoth's eyes filled with tears, "England. It is real... Isn't it? I've not imagined it in the darkness."

Kallín knew that this poor unfortunate was just as forgotten now as he was, and that he would never be released from being a hostage; he had lived from boy to man in captivity and he would grow old and die down here.

"England is real," Kallín assured him.

After that, Kallín didn't quiz Wulfnoth anymore. He didn't speak about matters of importance. He encouraged Wulfnoth to tell him about the Greeks and the Romans that he had spent his lifetime of captivity reading about. He was simply glad of his visits, and he ate the honey cake regardless of the fact that it came from Tostig. He hoped that the monks would gain enough weight to have him freed. All he could do was to stay alive, and that was a much easier task now that he had hope. In a place as desolate at the oubliette, even a small amount of hope brought more light into his heart than the summer sun.

One day it felt warm, and there was a hint of freshness making its way in the stale subterranean air. Kallín asked Wulfnoth, "It grows warm. Are the flowers in bloom?"

"Summer comes," Wulfnoth told him, "They say that we will soon be at war ... But I am confused about some of the details."

"What details?"

Wulfnoth went on, "Tostig tells me that William will soon be King of England. But Harold is King ... Do you think that my brothers mean to fight one another?"

"Sounds like it to me."

Wulfnoth shook his head, "But this is not what Father would want..."

Kallín tested him for news closer to his heart, "What do you hear of the prayers for my release?"

Wulfnoth told him, "They continue ... But I fear the Duke is fearful of giving you your freedom as much as he fears giving me mine. Of course, I cannot complain. I am kept in a comfortable place with my books and Homer and..." He looked at Kallín and told him, "You are gone thin. I don't think that my cake will keep you alive much longer. I am sorry."

Kallín smiled. It was not news to him that he was near death. He felt the weakness in him. Sometimes in the dark he felt that he would simply stop breathing and it would be all over. He would go home.

What was holding him in this world? He had no idea. Sometimes it was Luna. Sometimes it was revenge. Sometimes it was fear that he would not find his way home from this place because he did not know where he was.

33

DINA

"This is the problem," Luna explained to Dina, Rosy and Aífe. "We don't have a big enough patch to hunt. There's not enough to feed all the mouths. Now we are in the easy time of the summer with the fat fruit bushes and easy fat rabbit and deer. But we're storing up nothing for the winter, and come the end of the good season, we'll starve in the cold." She unconsciously rubbed her hand over her growing round belly bump, aware that there would be at least one more mouth to feed in four moons of time.

Rosy, more than most, liked her food and liked it being plentiful. Going hungry was not an option for her. She grew grim and asked, "Why can't we go further and hunt?"

Luna told her, "Because then we push into the wolves' patch."

Rosy replied, "I know the wolves won't like it, but there is more of us than there is of them. Maybe we just take the turf."

Luna felt her temper stir, her fists tightened into knots, and the urge to beat Rosy senseless filled her, but she once more rubbed her baby belly, and the presence of her little one there eased down her anger. She coldly told Rosy, "That's a fight we'd lose ... and we'd also lose the protection they give us from the south-end of the forest."

Rosy filled with hurt and swallowed any more suggestions she was about to make, for she knew that when Luna turned cold and spiteful that she was at the limit of her temper.

Dina, who had also been listening to the growing problem, raised her hand, "There is another way..."

Everyone loved Dina, and everyone benefitted from her various forms of cudu that worked all manner of wonders. The whole pack gathered quietly when she spoke, watching and listening as she blindly drew with her fingers in the loose soil of the cave floor, and explained, "There are many tunnels in the underworld. In these places, here and here," she indicated to parts of her map that she had drawn in the soil, "I have felt fresh air, these tunnels lead out to other parts of the world above. I do not know what is beyond them, but someone who has eyes could come with me and look to see."

Luna looked at the great spiderweb that Dina had created in the ground. "I will go with you," she told Dina, and then she rubbed away Dina's work from the dirt. She understood the great value and the great danger of such knowledge of the underworld.

A short time later Luna was blindly holding the end of a rope while Dina took her deep into the bowels of the earth, explaining, "It is better for you to not bring the candle and to learn the ways of the cave blind."

"Is true enough," Luna agreed, but she would have dearly loved to light a candle all the same.

"Slowly," Dina whispered, "try to stop looking into the dark. Try to be at ease with it. The way of being blind will come to you. Lower your head here."

"Ouch!"

Luna, with one hand above her head to feel the cave ceiling that dipped low and then rose to vanish out of reach, she carefully stepped barefoot on the smooth rock that also twisted and turned, and was not level in any one place. For a while, her eyes fought against the darkness, desperately trying to see. It was putting her to the limits of her tolerance to be so completely deprived of one of her senses, and she was growing awkward with the baby bump that was more and more getting in the way of simple physical tasks. But after some time of travelling blind, her eyes accepted their redundancy and her other senses took up the extra work. Mostly it was her sense of touch that became heightened. While her fingers lightly brushed over the cave wall, she imagined she could feel the earth breathing, its skin smooth as water in some places and jagged like teeth in others, wet and dry here and there. It was alive and in a state of constant motion.

"Feel here," Dina told her, and placed Luna's hand on the surface of a round smooth orb of a slick rock.

Luna carefully ran her fingers over the rock's skin and felt scars, "What is it?"

"It is the way-mark for this tunnel. See it."

Luna was at a loss, "See it? How?"

Dina explained, "With your fingers. Gently. Slowly."

Luna followed Dina's instructions and carefully placed her fingers onto the smooth rock, slowly she gently tracing her fingertips along the scars. She was reminded of Kallín's body and the endless happy hours of admiring her fine needle work while exploring him.

Dina sensed her absence and whispered, "Luna?"

Luna felt her face grow hot with a blush.

Dina knew where her companion's mind had drifted, and she assured her with a kind whisper, "He will return to you."

Luna didn't try to hide from Dina's insight into her heart. It seemed to her that in this complete darkness there was no place to hide. She could be as she was, simply present, open to all of her thoughts and feelings. It was her heart's wish to see Kallín again, to love him again, and for him to see his child. She asked Dina, "How can you know that I will see him again?"

Dina assured her, "I have seen it in a vision."

Luna felt that Dina was smiling, but she wanted to be sure, "Was the vision good?"

Dina explained, "You were embraced in a love knot and your child lay between you. Does that sound good enough for you?"

Luna smiled. That vision felt perfect to her and filled her with joy.

Dina nudged her, "Back to the reading."

Luna cleared her mind from the fog of love and returned her attention to the cold reality of being deep in the underworld. She placed her fingers back to the task of deciphering the rock scars. At first she could make nothing of them, they were simply a cluster of violent gashes, but then her mind formed a picture for her. She asked Dina, "An arrow?"

"Yes. And what else?" Dina asked her with encouragement.

Carefully, and slowly, Luna's fingertips explored the crevices, examining and discovering nuances in the ravines there, not violent gashes at all, but carefully inscribed lines with delicate twists. She spoke what her fingers were telling her, "Two lines down and one across … all meeting in a swirl."

Luna heard the smile in Dina's voice, "Yes."

Dina took Luna's hand, opened it, and placing a finger over her palm, she gently traced out the rock carving of the swirl there, "This is the mark for water."

She took Luna's finger and brought it to the rock carving again.

Luna ran her finger over the marking again, "Water."

Dina added, "I will teach the reading of it to you, so that you can travel here without me."

A sudden chill ran though Luna at the thought of being down here without Dina, alone. She could not think of anything worse.

They moved along their way.

It was not long before Luna's fingers found another mark in the wall. She stopped at it and asked Dina, "What is this one?"

Dina stopped too and told her, "I don't understand these ones yet."

Luna was at a loss, "You did not make the carvings?"

Dina told her, "No … I simply found them. I have learned the meaning of a good number of them. But some … are still beyond me."

Luna realised that there was something worse than being down here alone, and that was being down here in the presence of the unknown creatures who made these markings … She gripped her knife handle in her belt.

Dina sensed the fear in Luna and assured her, "I think they were made by the first people. They are long gone from here."

Luna's fear was not eased by that, "How can you know that they are gone?"

Dina explained, "I have rambled in all directions along these ways many times, and I have never found them."

Luna pointed out, "Just because you cannot see something does not mean that it is not there. The rabbit does not see the wolf until it is time to die."

Dina answered her, "Well, if I was a rabbit I would have been long eaten, would I not?"

Luna could not argue with that.

Dina went on, "I would surely have found the people of the underworld long before they found me."

Luna asked, "How can you know that you would have found them?"

Dina told her, "Because I have found their vast village here in the underworld. And I found the place where they died too. In one part there is great piles of old dry bones, some even turning to dust at my touch. The place where they laid out the remains of their dead. Many,

many skulls… big and small. But some of them…"

Dina suddenly stopped.

"Tell me." Luna urged her on. There was nothing worse than stopping a story in the middle, apart from stopping it near the end, which was worse still.

Dina didn't hold out for long and she went on, "Some of the skulls, in the part of the skull where the holes should be for the eyes … there was no holes."

Luna imagined a tribe of people with no eyes. She was filled with a mixture of fear and revulsion but at the same time consumed with a huge curiosity. She wondered, "What brought them to live blind and deep in the underworld?"

Luna did not expect Dina to have an answer to that but she did, "They were searching for something."

"Searching?" Luna's head swam with dizzying possibilities. "For what?"

Dina went on, "They cut a long mine shaft down deep into the earth. It is still there … and it is alive."

"Alive?"

"It breaths hot air."

Luna found herself simply repeating what Dina was telling her in an effort to make her mind grasp it, "Breathes hot air…"

Dina went on unwrapping her secrets with speed, "At the mouth of the shaft are many writings on the wall. I have not yet understood them."

Luna leaned into the darkness and rested herself against the unseen wall there. She felt her thinking muscles twitch in her skull, and her mind ravenously picked over the spoils of what she had just heard; discarding some parts of it and keeping other choice cuts, until she came to the rarest piece of the story, "What did they find at the end of that shaft?"

Dina heard a determined tone in Luna's voice that unsettled her. She felt the curiosity in Luna, and she worried that Luna would set off down into the ancient shaft. She pulled her back to their task at hand, "For that, I have no answer. But I'm sure that their digging was deep and deadly, for if you drop a stone down into it you will not hear it hit the bottom. I sat there a whole day one time waiting to hear the end of it and there was nothing … just the waves of heat that come up out of if like great breathes … and then sometimes a groan."

"A beast?" Luna asked.

"Maybe … I would not venture down it. We should keep on our course. We are close to where we need to be. Come along."

Luna moved along in the dark, her fingers working to find the way along the wall, but her mind was not in the darkness, or on her task. It was instead consumed by the great secret of this underworld and those ancient people who spent many lifetimes digging, but digging to find what?

After some more distance travelling in the pure black, Luna's eyes began to find rock formations taking on hues of grey as the nightlight from the world above them ebbed its way below ground from an unseen ingress. The cave walls began to slightly tremble under her finger tips, and her ears picked out a distant dull moan that she was familiar with: the Umber.

Dina said, "When we hear the great river above us, we climb up then."

The jagged walls of the tunnel gave plenty of options for grips, so even with Luna having to negotiate the way with the encumbrance of her bump, it was an easy enough climb for the two of them to make. It was not long until Luna saw the stars in the night sky appear above her through an opening in the earth.

As soon as she looked up out of the cave tunnel, her heart broke into a fast galloping beat.

"Go to the top," Dina urged her on, with no idea of the peril that she was shoving her up into. For Dina had never seen the sky in the day or in the night, and so she was in no jeopardy from the wonder that was now in it.

Luna climbed out of the hole, once more looking up. She was brought to her knees. She began to silently cry.

Dina scrambled to her, "What is it?"

"The sky…" Luna began, "has a new creature in it."

Dina asked her, "Tell me what you see."

Luna grappled with what she was looking at and explained, "A new light in the sky… bigger than all the rest like a great flaming torch … with a great burning hair-tail streaming long behind it. Like a horse in full gallop, but it does not move…"

Dina took Luna's hand, and with her finger, she drew, and asked, "Is this the image of it?"

Luna was dumbfounded. How could Dina have such a clear picture of something that she could not see? "That is it. How do you know it?"

"I have seen it before," Dina told her, "it is carved into the wall of the cave at the living shaft."

34

FREEDOM

Once more the light came to Kallín's cell. When he looked to the gates it was not Wulfnoth, but two prison guards. Without a word, they began the procedure of opening his gate. With every tiny mechanical click of the lock's mechanism, and the turn of the key, he felt as if they were opening up his heart. His entire being soared with a euphoria known only to those who have been in prison: the pure unadulterated exhilaration of *freedom*.

He wanted to jump with joy, but he could not stand. The gates opened, and the two large black-leather-cloaked and hooded dungeon-guards muttered to him in their tongue. Though he could not understand the words they spoke, he knew by their tone that the words were encouraging him. They took him by the arms and brought him carefully upright. It took him a dozen hobbled steps to get his back straight, and even then, his spine was not entirely straight but curved like that of an old man who had somehow escaped the reaper, grown old beyond his years and was in the process of creeping to his grave. They proceeded with him like that, one set of strong hands on either arm, and walked him along the dank passageway. Its uneven walls and jagged edges gave testament to the fact that this dark underworld had been hewn by unfortunate mine-slaves who created a deep keep wherein they could distil absolute human misery into an absolute purity of hopelessness. When a person was made a prisoner, a truth was revealed to him; the weak must suffer the will of the strong.

Up they went, one excruciating step after another, until after what seemed like a pilgrimage, Kallín was above ground and making his way past the more luxurious cells where sunlight forced its way through the narrow slit-windows in sharp grey sword-blades that cut his eyes when he passed before them. In the dark corners, along the walls, he caught sight of the miserable naked wretches in chains, waiting for their prayers to be answered. Here in the pit of misery, he heard the whispers, 'Moine des Loups'... And as he came close to the bars of the cells, those inside of them struggled, reaching out their hands to him, and one called out in a loud cry, "Moine des Loups-bénissez-moi!" Then a sudden chorus of wailing, "Bénissez-moi!" A bramble tunnel of dirty desperate hands reached out on either side of him. He instinctively held his hands out to either side, touching them all as he went. It was in his nature, as Wulfnoth would say. He had learned the power of hope. The guards dared not hurry him along.

Fresh air flowed over him like the snow-melt-water of a spring river as he emerged blinking from the prison building into the open yard. The smooth cobblestones felt comforting under his bare feet. Above him, a great grey canopy of heavy clouds saved his eyes from the full glare of the sun. The alien Norman world came into focus. He took in the great bailey of the castle: a larger open cobblestone courtyard, surrounded on all sides by incredibly high walls that made his head swim when he looked up at them, and along these dizzying walls ran a great allure where heavily armoured cone-helmeted soldiers patrolled and stood their watch over the parapet. It occurred to him that this world of stone was a prison, within a prison, within a prison — and not one soul within its high walls was free, not the people, not the soldiers, not even the Duke William himself. It was no wonder that he coveted England.

All eyes were on the young miracle monk as he was helped by his guards to the inner wall of the chemise, and there he was met at the gate by Brother Tomas.

"You poor wretch." Tomas whispered to him.

Kallín did not disagree with him.

Tomas went on, "You are blessed indeed. The Holy Father heard of your plight and has denied my Lord William the right to have you forgotten."

Again, Kallín had nothing to add.

Tomas went on, "You will now live with us at the Abbey. But first you must be deloused. Follow me."

"I cannot walk unaided," Kallín told him.

Tomas came close to him, "Lean on me, Brother."

And that is how he went through the door.

On the other side of the chemise wall, Kallín was met with the most terrifying site he'd ever seen: the keep.

The great dark tower stood like a mountain of dread, oozing evil from its granite walls. His body filled with revulsion as he was lead by the monk trough the great iron doors, past the cone-helmeted-guards with the dead eyes of men who have forgotten themselves entirely, and given their will completely over to the mundane brutality of a soldier's life, simply waiting for the order to kill.

The emaciated young monk entered the long barrack room, its walls adorned with clusters of weapons, some of which he could identify, most of which he could not fathom their use. In the centre of the floor he saw a perfectly square hole, large enough to accommodate a horse. On closer inspection he saw that it was covered in highly ornate tiles depicting naked men and women in various sexual acts. It was filled with water.

"What is it?" Kallín asked.

Tomas smiled, "It is called a bath." He admired it, "A gift left behind to us from the ancient Romans who once occupied these barracks."

"A bath..." Kallín repeated the word as two naked soldiers made their way to him and began to peel away his rags without any explanation or ceremony. He was deftly stripped, then painted in a paste made from garlic and lime to kill the lice that infested his body, and then lifted into the bath, whereupon the soldiers proceeded to scrub him and completely shave his entire head and his entire body. He felt that his skin would come away under the scrubbing but thankfully they were as gentle as they were expertly efficient. The ordeal was over as quickly as they could do it. Much revived and clean, he climbed from the bath under his own effort to stand upright naked and red raw. He felt the eyes of the Norman soldiers on him, and he knew they were staring at his scars.

One of them murmured to the other, "Moine des Loups."

He was surprised to see admiration in their eyes.

A clean black Benedictine habit and a pair of sandals were then produced.

Kallín dressed and followed Tomas.

For the next three days Kallín ate and slept in the barracks with the soldiers. On the fourth morning Tomas decided that his young monk was solid enough to make the journey to the Abbey. He collected him from breakfast and brought him to the stables where two fine looking horses awaited them.

Kallín examined his saddle, and was curious about two iron loops hanging on either side, and asked, "What are these?"

"Stirrups," Tomas explained, "to put your feet into. We will teach you how to ride a horse like a Norman."

Kallín grew defensive, "I know how to right a horse, Brother."

"No, you do not," Tomas told him, "you know how to sit on the back of a horse and go along on it like a sack of turnips. That is not riding. Mount him from the left side, your left foot in the stirrup and push yourself up into the saddle."

Kallín tentatively put his foot into the stirrup and followed the instructions. He eased into the saddle and slipped his feet carefully into the stirrups and … he immediately felt the added security.

"You see?" Tomas smiled, "Very simple but very effective. Let us make our way."

The young Rohán had seen some of the world and the fine buildings of York, but he had never imagined that a building could be beautiful. As he entered through the gate into the courtyard of the Abbey of Fécamp and took in the sight of the high spired cathedral within, he was lost in wonder at it. It was the most beautiful thing he had ever seen.

Tomas observed him and smiled, "It is something to see, is it not?"

"Yes. Was it built by God?"

"No." Tomas smiled, "It was built by men … for God."

As they dismounted, Tomas advised him, "Dismount on the left side, the same as you mounted. It is how the horse is trained."

"Trained?" Kallín asked.

Tomas smiled, "Our horses know more than their riders, I assure you of that. And Trojan is a particularly clever beast."

"Trojan?" Kallín asked.

"That is his name."

Kallín repeated the name, "Trojan." Then remembered, "Wulfnoth told me the story of the Trojan Horse."

Tomas looked saddened, "You met Wulfnoth?"

"Yes." Kallín asked him, "Will he ever be free?"

Tomas nodded, "Maybe. Come. Let's get you settled."

As they brought their horses to the stables, they were met by an elderly monk.

Tomas called out, "Ah, Brother Quentin. Meet Brother Osbald."

Quentin smiled. He had a wide open honest face that Kallín liked because it was easy to read, and though Quentin was well on in his years, his face appeared childish, innocent. His brown eyes held not a trace of malice in them. And when he spoke it was with an English accent, "Welcome, Brother Osbald."

Kallín kept his questions to himself and answered, "Thank you, Brother Quentin."

Tomas informed them, "Well, I must away back to our Duke." And he suddenly hugged Kallín, catching him off guard, but in the moment he hugged the boy he felt him break and so he held him all the tighter for fear that he would collapse, "There. Easy now, boy."

Kallín did not know what had struck him, or what it was that was consuming him, or how or why it was taking his legs away. He clung on to Tomas and felt the monk holding him up while something deep inside of him gave way, like an ice dam breaking in the great River Humber. He cried. Tomas simply held him all the tighter. And then Kallín sobbed like a child.

Tomas spoke softly, "This is good."

They simply waited until the young monk was empty of crying.

Kallín then took his own weight again and looked into the kind eyes of Tomas and told him, "Thank you, Brother."

Tomas smiled, "Do not thank me. I am but a servant. Give your thanks to God. It was he who has kept you alive..."

"Why has God kept me alive?"

Tomas told him, "He has a plan for you ... And what that plan is will be revealed to you in time. But right now, you must rest, recover, and put some fat back on those bones."

35

KOMETES

Luna looked at the vision in the sky and she felt her mind being pulled away, far, far away, to a place of wonder so deep that no mind could ever come back from it. She was as helpless as a stick floating in the river's current until Dina sensed Luna was being pulled too far away, and she took her by the wrist, squeezed it hard and said, "Stay."

Luna closed her eyes. Trying.

Dina rummaged into her belt and took out a ball of rich black oily cudu, brought it to Luna's lips and popped it into her mouth.

Luna tasted the bitter tang of the cudu and her mouth quickly numbed as the ingredients went to work. In the next few beats of her heart, the numbness was in her head, making it into a great empty orb that was big enough to hold the world and everything in it … everything in the sky above it… everything that was in the underworld below it.

Dina then took a good dose of cudu herself and journeyed out of her head with her friend.

The two girls lay down on the ground in the night, listening to the run of the river, the rustle of the full trees and the foraging of the night creatures. It did not matter now if the air was hot or cold, or if the ground under them was hard or soft.

The night was washed away by the morning sun. The two girls lay under a full bush, knotted together in a sleeping hug. Dina woke first to the contented trilling of the finches. She cautiously sniffed the air for wolves … In the soupy perfume of fresh morning grass dew, sweet flowers, and the rich nutty sap of sweating oaks, she picked out a slender offensive strand of stink, a reek that was made of ripe ale, stale piss, runny shit and unwashed sweat. She nudged Luna awake, "I smell soldiers."

Luna sat up looking around like an alert rabbit popping its head out of a burrow. She examined the dense woodland that surrounded them, but she saw no soldiers. However, she did now realise that the sound of the river was on the other side. They had crossed under the great river to a patch that they had never been to before.

She told Dina, "I see no soldiers?"

Dina explained, "They are a distance off. Maybe a morning's walk." And she pointed east of their position, "That way."

"A morning away?" Luna measured that, and asked, "And you can smell them from here?"

Dina agreed it was a long way off, but she knew the reason that their stink could make it over such a distance, "There is a great number of them."

"An army…" Luna guessed, and she knew two things about armies. They bring death, but they also make a lot of corpses for spoiling. "We should stalk them."

Dina didn't rise to her idea, "Why?"

"Spoil," Luna told her, with an amount of surprise at having to explain the obvious.

But it was not obvious to Dina, and she asked again, "Why do we need spoil?"

Luna felt a quick involuntary twist of irritation in her gut, but she quickly pinched it out the way she would extinguish the flame of a candle. She understood that Dina did not understand the reason for the spoiling and hoarding of gold and jewels. And that sat fine with her. Luna was honest enough to admit, at least to herself, that the truth of the matter was that Luna did not know why she was driven to hoard wealth. But she was. And she was driven to have it and hoard it with such a hungry ferocity that there was simply no ground to be made by trying to stop her doing it. She had long since stopped trying to stop herself. She knew in her heart that she would quickly and happily kill for gold.

She simply told Dina, "You can go back to the cave."

She was not going to force Dina to come with her.

But as Luna turned to set off on her tracking east, she heard the footsteps of Dina following her.

Dina held out her hand, "This time you can lead me."

Luna took her warm soft hand with a smile and a firm grip, and that is how they went into the woods.

They tracked the strands of stench that hung in the air throughout the morning. All the time the reek got thicker until by noon they came to the edge of the forest and saw in the distance the source of the foul odour. A swarm of hundreds of men loitered in malevolent boredom, sharpening weapons, joking, wrestling or lying about: an army camp.

On the banks of the river, beached boats awaited the soldiers while they in turn awaited their marching orders. Beyond the army, some half day's walk, was the busy port town of Grim Haven.

Dina asked her, "Are they making ready for battle?"

When Luna saw the waiting boats she knew, "Their battle will not be here."

Dina was relieved to hear that, but she also detected the hint of disappointment in Luna's voice. Luna took in all the new ground around them, "This will be hunted bare from the army foraging. We should search deeper into the forest back on our side of the river."

This was music to Dina's ears. This side of the river seemed cursed to her. But her good mood at returning to the caves was quickly dampened when Luna told her, "I want to go to this living mine shaft you found."

36

OMEN

Kallín looked at the four bare walls of the small square cell. A shaft of sunlight came through a portal high up in the domed ceiling. He imagined he was inside an egg … that was cracked.

On either side of the slate floor stood two sturdy beds, each one big enough to accommodate a well-fed monk.

Brother Quentin gestured to the bed on the left as he entered and explained in a soft quiet voice that could sneak up on a rabbit, "This is where you will sleep, Brother Osbald."

"Who sleeps in the other bed?" Kallín asked.

"I do," Quentin smiled, fixing his shining silver hair that was perfectly groomed around his tonsured bald patch. His wide mouth rested in a youthful honest smile. If the silver monk were not an old man, Kallín would have said that his soft pale face was that of a pampered old queen. Quentin, looking to the floor, continued, "You and I are paired. It is my obligation to teach you the ways of our Abbey here."

Kallín asked the question that he'd been holding on to since he heard Quentin speak, "How is it that you are English?"

Quentin smiled, instantly happy to enter into a discussion on a subject that he was comfortable with, and he explained, "I am from our Abbey in Wessex. Originally, that is."

"Wessex. Why are you here then?"

Quentin frowned, "You do not know? Really? Well, I suppose that is entirely possible. Why would you know, after all?"

Kallín didn't like hunting on unfamiliar ground. He knew he was on dangerous turf, deep in a world that he knew very little of, a world that, regardless of its piety and praying, was just as deadly as the wolves' patch of the forest. He became defensive, "Would I be asking you the question if I knew the answer already?"

Quentin saw the temper rise in him, like the hackles on a hound. He immediately broke eye contact, nodding apologetically. He'd heard stories about the Silvatici, and how they have quick tempers and turn easily to murdering. "Forgive me," he said, "I just assumed that you had been told. My fault. Entirely." Quentin went on to explain, "Our Abbey in Hastings was seized by Godwin when King Canute made him Earl of Wessex, and so we were exiled and then mercifully taken in by our kind brothers here in Fécamp."

The name sounded half familiar to Kallín, "Godwin?"

Quentin filled in the gaps, "It is Godwin's son, Harold Godwinson, who is now sitting on the throne of England."

Kallín's head suddenly began to swim with fatigue. The euphoria of freedom was   spent. He was empty, "I must lie down or I will fall asleep where I stand."

"Of course. Forgive me. I will leave you to your rest." Quentin moved to the door. He told his new cellmate, "Sleep well, Brother Osbald. Sleep fast." But Quentin could not leave the cell just yet. There were very important articles of information that he was obliged to pass on. So, he pushed on talking against the tide, fixing his hair, again, "When you wake, you will wish to make your ablutions..." He gestured to a bucket in the corner, "This is the wash-bucket. Your first duty of the morning is to wash your face and your ears." Then he gestured to a bucket in the opposing corner, "This is the piss-bucket. Each day at noon, while we are at prayers, the tanner comes to empty the bucket."

Kallín was sure that he had already slipped into the realm of dreams as he listened to Quentin's prayerful tone droning on like a monastic chant…

The old silver monk went on in his practiced smooth lawyer's tone, "If you need to make a merde, pardon the French, you must go out to the garderobe at the end of the hall." Quentin felt relieved to have gotten the important portions of information unpacked and clearly stated. His legal obligations fulfilled, he smiled, and continued in an advisory capacity, "Don't confuse the buckets. It's sometimes easily done. I've seen it happen. A first mistake warrants a caution from the Abbot, but repeated mistakes are seen as offences of negligence, and the loss to the tanner must be paid. Such costs are normally paid by assisting the tanner in his work. I'm told that one would be better off in hell than in the tannery. Now you know. It's best that I told you. Ignorance of the law is no defence … which seems absurd, for how can one break a law if they do not know said law exists … But there you go. I ramble on. My apologies."

Kallín could hold out no longer. Whatever buckets were which buckets for whatever purpose, or whatever the various laws were about pissing, he did not care. He lay down, the bed took him, caressing his entire being in the comforting hug of the soft sackcloth. He surrendered, letting go of the world, releasing his grip on life, and sailing away, fast, into the realm of sleeping souls.

Quentin covered his unconscious cellmate with a fat and heavy woollen blanket, and whispered, "Sleep well, Moine des loups … may you dream beautiful dreams."

The silver monk woke before daybreak as the call to prayer rang out. He examined his cellmate who'd not moved. The young monk's body lay so still that Quentin feared it had turned into a corpse. He put his ear close to the mouth and listened for breath. It was there, just, as faint as the flapping of butterfly wings. Quentin had a binding duty to wake up his cellmate for prayer … but how? It was forbidden for monks to lay hands on each other in the privacy of their cells. It was deemed to be 'peccata venialia': a gateway sin to the greater 'peccata mortalia' of carnal knowledge. He produced a loud staged cough in an attempt to wake him, but the slumbering soul responded no more or no less than the walls. He then tried another tactic and banged the wash bucket loudly on the floor … but there was still no movement from the corpus in the sack. Finally, Quentin broke the rule and committed the venial sin of putting his hand on Kallín's shoulder and giving him a good shove. The silver monk might as well have been trying to wake the dead from the grave. Nothing stirred. If anything, the young monk seemed to sink further down into the sack.

Quentin suddenly filled with a familiar fear that had haunted him for as long as he could remember. His earliest memory of it was when he was a boy soprano. He had woken naked and bloody in the crypts with no memory of how he had gotten there to find that he had been made a 'castrato'.

He couldn't name his demon. It had no face nor no name that he could call it by. In his attempts to quantify it, to make sense of its purpose, he had concluded that had only one terrible desire: to abuse him.

He knew the ritual of the abuse by heart. The demon would continue to fill him with fear and then suddenly smother him, and eventually, he would faint, wherein the abyss of unconsciousness, unspeakable sins would take place upon his body. He did not have much time before his mind failed him. He got himself out of the suffocating cell.

Pale and panting, the silver monk walked quickly along the fast-flowing floor of the long hall that twisted and turned under his feet, unbalancing him as he desperately made his way to the kitchen to find the safe haven of Brother Bernard.

Brother Bernard was a great happy heap of a man who stood over eighteen hands high and was three arm-lengths of a hug around his girth. As well as being in charge of the kitchens, he was also the physician and the unofficial Abbot of the Wessex monks. His age was undisclosed, but it was widely believed that he had more than fifty winters under his substantial belt.

Quentin found him stirring a large cauldron of unknown, and experimental, soupy contents.

Bernard knew straight away that Quentin was having one of his turns.

Quentin quickly declared, "I have the fear demon in me, Brother."

Bernard smiled, "You do, my lovely," while calmly ushering him to a chair, "Sit down," he instructed him and grabbed a flagon of the Irish monks' Uisce Beatha, "Get a good swallow of that into you," he advised.

Quentin took a swift swig of the uisce and immediately felt the glow of it down his gullet as it made its way in to his being, driving the fear demon out of him. He then experienced the wonderful sensation of his empty morning belly being filled full of a holy heat that caressed the core of him entirely body and soul. The swallow of holy uisce early in the morning was truly a great Godly way to start the day. It was no wonder that the Irish monks called it 'the water of life'. His constitution immediately started to return him, and he sucked again on the neck of the jug for a second deep swig, taking it hungrily like a suckling calf latching on to the mother's tit.

Bernard watched him gulp three times and then he eased the flagon away from him with a soft cautionary instruction, "Enough now."

When Bernard rescued the flagon, he took a little slug of it himself, and as uisce went down into him, he licked the traces of it from his lips, "You need to be mindful of how you consume it. For it's true that the uisce beatha is a powerful holy elixir for driving demons out of the body, but it is a form of demon itself. You have to be careful not to replace one manner of demon in you for another, my lovely."

Bernard placed the flagon back on the shelf, "All things in moderation." Bernard then asked Quentin in a caring tone, "What has brought the fear demon into you now, my lovely?"

"I touched him," Quentin confessed.

"Easy now. Put aside that burden." Bernard put his hand on Quentin's shoulder, "Look. There is nothing ill here in a touch. One brother comforts another. Is that not why we are here?" Then he ran his hand over Quentin's smooth silver head, "Easy. Be easy, brother. Now tell me, why did you touch him?"

Quentin explained in a quivering voice, "I feared that the Moine des Loups would not ever wake again, brother," He became tearful, "I feared that I had been negligent in my duties and let him die in his sack."

Brother Bernard wrinkled his brow. He didn't like to see brothers bearing crosses, especially crosses that did not need to be borne. He grew serious and told his long-time friend, "Firstly, Brother Quentin, your cell brother's name is not 'Moine des Loups'. That is a slanderous title given to him by empty minds and redundant mouths that would be better filled with prayers. He is called 'Osbald': a name given to him by the Bishop of York, no less. He is not to be referred to by any other name. Secondly, those who need to sleep in such a deep sleep, where they are near to their death, they are best left undisturbed. So my instruction to you is, my lovely, let him alone until God decides to wake him or take him."

Bernard then looked to the ceiling as if he were receiving a message from the heavens, his eyes popping wider as the new thought entered his head, "Make sure to place a jug of water next to his bed, for if he does wake, he'll have a parched gullet."

Quentin worried, "What if he doesn't wake, Brother?"

Bernard patted him on the shoulder and comforted him, "That is for God to decide. And should God take him, then he will be in a better place than here. Will he not?"

"He will," Quentin agreed. But the silver monk had no proof that heaven was a better place than here, and he did not see how anyone with an understanding of the law could accept the existence of 'heaven' or even a 'God' for that matter. All the evidence that he had seen to date was circumstantial and anecdotal. There was not a single shred of factual evidence. However, all such misgivings and doubts were kept safely and secretly to himself. He knew enough about the world outside of the walls to know that he didn't want to be excommunicated and cast out of the holy orders for heresy.

Brother Bernard kissed him on his bald tonsure, "Bless you, Brother Quentin."

Quentin closed his eyes, and began his confession, and thought, *Who knows? If there is a God, then it is safer to abide by him in our doubt.* "Forgive me, brother, for I have sinned."

Bernard nodded, "Go on, brother."

"I have had impure thoughts…"

"I know…" Brother Bernard patted Quentin on the head, "I know…"

Kallín slept the sleep of the dead all through the day, then all through the night.

Quentin awoke to the pre-dawn call to prayer. He'd slept surprisingly well having not been visited upon in the night by the demon, and that, in and of itself, was a blessing. He couldn't help wonder if his young cell brother had a holy protective presence about him. He deftly got out of his warm sack into the pinch of the cold air, and quickly and quietly pissed, washed and dressed. Not a sound came from his sleeping cell brother. When the silver monk had completed his ablutions, and combed his hair too much, he stood at the end the young sleeping monks' bed … watching him sleep, wondering, *If the 'Moine des Loups' was, as rumoured, favoured by God; that act of favouritism might be a form of evidence. For if one cannot see the presence of a man, but one can see his footprints, then that is physical evidence of his existence. And if one was to argue the case logically and rationally, then the physical evidence would be enough to establish a prima facia case until such a time as we could perform our legal obligation of habeas corpus. If God is leaving evidence of himself on this young monk, then I am going to find it, and record it, even though seeking empirical evidence of God's existence is an offence that could see me tied to the stake and burned.*

After some time of quiet observation, maybe hours, Quentin was joined by Brother Bernard, who entered the small cell flapping the hems of his habit to encourage the cool air to travel up into his nether regions. The big man was not built for walking. He put his hand up under the blanket and felt Kallín's testicles, thought for a moment and then announced, "There's plenty of life in him."

Quentin didn't question that prognosis, nor did he interrogate Bernard as to how he could make a prognosis by simply fondling a man's genitals. Of course, such intimate contact could bring down the full weight of Canon Law, were it not for the fact that Bernard was their physician. But even so, Quentin worried that Bernard was, yet again, crossing the fine line. He very much hoped that he would not have to defend the old monk in a court before the Bishops.

Bernard weighed something in his mind, and asked, "How long is he in his sleep now?"

Quentin told him, "He's going into this third day…" And he knew, "A man cannot go longer than three days without water — can he?"

Bernard agreed with him, "No he cannot. And yet … Our Lord Jesus was dead for three days in the cave, was he not?"

"He was, Brother. Indeed he was. Dead. And risen." Quentin was at a loss as to what point Bernard was making. The lawyer monk was always cautious of getting too deeply into ecclesiastical conversations with Bernard, especially when he could smell the 'Irish water' on his breath.

Bernard pushed on into trouble, "And yet, Jesus was risen from the dead. Our world is full of miracles ... If we know where to look for them."

Quentin really didn't want to be part of this conversation for fear that other monks would overhear them and report them to the Abbot for being a pair of heretics. He told Bernard, "I should get back to my duties, Brother."

"I often wonder…" Bernard began with the inhalation of a large breath, his big belly rising and filling like a great bellows, and at the same time opening his hands in an expansive gesture like that of a market stall seller displaying his irresistible wares, "Is it a coincidence that three days is also the length of time that a man can survive without water?"

Quentin heard the burst of tetchy sharp whispering from the eavesdroppers out in the hallway, eating up their tales to tell the Fécamp Abbot, stuffing their maws with morsels of gossip like ravenous rats. He edged away from Bernard, and the dangerous conversation.

Bernard raised a finger, "Here's the theological nub: where did Our Saviour go for those three days and nights?"

"I will get the..." Quentin made for the door.

Bernard grabbed him by the cuff of his sleeve and held him close like a fellow conspirator in a murder, whispering to him, deeply but loudly, "Some say that Our Lord dwelled in hell! Yes, and he preached to all the lost souls who had died before having had the blessing of hearing his words…" Brother Bernard then stared hard into Quentin's eyes, and asked him, "But how could there have been a hell? How could a soul be guilty of sin if he doesn't know of sin?"

Quentin watched in fear as Bernard's eyes filled with the look of a demented soul. He pressed Quentin, "What were men like before Moses received the commandments? What is your legal opinion of that?"

The cold sweat broke out on Quentin's waxing face. The fear demon was once more consuming him. He shook his head and desperately pulled his sleeve free of Bernard's meaty grip, turning fast, and proceeding directly away to the chapel to make his prayers.

Bernard watched Quentin scamper away. He sat on the bed next to the sleeping young monk and wondered, "Why did God make us all sinners?"

On noon of the third day when the Angelus bell began pealing the call to prayer, Kallín awoke on fire, kicking the burning blanket off him and leaping from the bed, stripping off his flaming habit, and running to the wash-bucket where he poured the entire contents over his head. He then stood with his arms outstretched so as to let the comforting cold air sooth his scorched naked skin. His nightmare of being consumed in the burning bramble faded and disappeared.

Quentin looked on in fear for his eternal soul at the young naked monk standing scarred and Christlike with a fully erect penis and a fine hairy bollox hanging between his legs.

A moment later Kallín was entirely consumed by two opposing urges; his parched throat screamed for water while his bladder was bursting. He grabbed the water-jug with one hand and his penis with the other and ran to the piss-bucket, stood over it and aimed his unruly piss-horn, unleashing his urgent gallon while chugging down fresh cold water. A great surge of relief washed over him:

simultaneously soothing his gullet and his bladder. The wild torrent of piss began filling the bucket with the great roar of a newly sprung geyser whose gush echoed out of the cell and filled the mute corridors.

Quentin advised him, "Perhaps you should aim your spout to the side of the bucket so that the racket is not too loud … and prideful."

Kallín liked the sound that his piss made in the bucket and was very proud of it. He ignored Quentin and kept his flow aimed right in the bullseye of the bucket where it would make the most noise.

Anyone who doesn't like it can grow a hump!

Quentin had never heard a piss so long and so loud. It was longer and louder even than a horse-piss on the cobblestones of the stable-yard. But he'd heard rumours that this 'Moine des Loups' had been a Silvatici of the forest before he was found by the monks and brought to God. No doubt, there was still a lot of wildman left in the newly minted monk.

Kallín came to the end of his piss and gave his penis a good shaking to fling out the last drops that might linger … only to dribble out of the spout and down his leg.

Quentin watched. Such energetic shaking of the penis was frowned upon as it might encourage the peccata venialia of masturbation. Ecclesiastical Law had very clearly set out the pathway for that particular sin that begins with impure thoughts that plant the seeds of sinful thoughts, which then, in turn, grow into the sinful act of masturbation. It was safe to say that the peccata venialia of masturbation was the bread butter and jam of the confessional. However, there were other options for confession that one could choose from. Gluttony, jealousy, envy and pride also made regular appearances. The only truly dangerous sin to confess in the confessional was to confess that you had no sins to confess.

For reasons that Quentin could not fathom, impure thoughts seemed to float in the air like the scent of flowers; and as one smells the scent of a rose, one cannot but imagine its beautiful bloom. He had no knowledge as to the provenance of impure thoughts, but he could swear that they did not originate inside of him. As he looked over Kallín's naked body, he was having an impure thought, but it was also a beautiful thought. The scarred creature before him was perfect. The story of his suffering was written into his flesh, and Quentin imagined his wounds to be those of Christ after he endured the flagellum.

Of course, legally, impure thoughts are peccata venialia and only become peccata mortalia when they are acted upon, hence, one's soul can survive them with regular penance. Apostle John wrote that Christ said to his brothers, 'As I have loved you, love one another. By this everyone will know that you are my disciples.'

Quentin spent many nights trying to fathom what love is made of. Is it part desire? Part curiosity? Part hunger? Part need? Part lust? If it is made from all of these parts, then in what quantity is each part poured in?

God, for reasons known only to himself, has created men in a great turmoil of temptation. Jesus loved easily. But why did he receive the flagellum and the crucifixion? Legally, under Roman Law, a man could not receive both punishments. It is recorded that Pontius Pilate, the Governor of Judaea, had first ordered Jesus to be freed, but the crowd chanted for Barabbas. Then Pilate ordered that Jesus be flogged and released. But after the flogging, the crowd chanted for crucifixion. Quentin often wondered about that chanting crowd, and why did they hate Jesus? And why, when the law was broken and his son was being tortured, did God not make a divine intervention? Quentin suspected that God let Jesus suffer on the cross in order to punish him for the love he had for his brothers. That is the price of his love...

As the silver monk watched the naked young 'Moine de Loups' washing in the bucket, he let his desires burn freely in him. If he was bound for hell, then so be it. One thing was for sure, he would not be alone there.

Kallín stood in the cobblestoned courtyard, his mind suspended between wonder and fear. His eyes fixed on the omen hovering in the sky while ranks of the monks prayed on their knees, pleading forgiveness for untold sins. All the time encouraging the rapture by imploring various saintly monks of the order to intercede on their behalves, and ask God to spare them from the terrible tortures of the apocalypse, and to ascend them straight into heaven.

Brother Quentin joined him and measured the inquisitive young monk with the practiced eye of a lawyer who had a lifetime of reading men in their various roles as the accused, the accuser, or the witness. He admired how unafraid he was, and thought that he would make for a good client. He told him, "It is called a 'kometes.'"

"Kometes," Kallín repeated. The word made a strange shape in his mouth. He asked the silver monk, "What does it mean?"

"It's a Greek word," Quentin told him, "It means 'head with the long hair.'"

It's what it looks like.

Kallín briefly remembered when he himself had a head with long hair. But that memory of his former self was a painful one, so he quickly put it away again.

Quentin remembered why he had ventured out to the stable-yard, "Brother Bernard requires your help in the kitchen. You should go to him directly."

But before Kallín went to Brother Bernard, he had one more question for Brother Quentin, "Is it as the others say, the End Times?"

Quentin smiled, "It is said that the Kometes is an omen that heralds great change. It may well be the end for some, but for others ... it will be the beginning."

Kallín entered the hot fragrant clouds of the kitchen to find Brother Bernard fussing over trays of various steaming meats. The large hot monk looked up from his work, took a moment to focus on the young monk as if he were an apparition and proclaimed in surprise, "There you are!" Then he asked, as if he hadn't seen him in years, "Where have you been?"

"Looking at the—"

"Matters not now" Bernard scolded him. "You're here now. But don't speak. There's too much to be done. Everyone out there on their knees and we have the most important of guests. Let me think a moment." He then turned his attention back to the food, "Now that's the boiled kidneys and that plate of the fried liver and onions ... All laid out on our best silver..." He turned back to Kallín again with a panicked look in his eyes, "But how am I to know what they desire to eat at this peculiar hour of the day? It is neither breakfast time or luncheon time — is it?"

Kallín was not aware of the arrival of the special guests. "Who is it for?"

Bernard wiped his greasy hand-towel across the rivulets of sweat flowing down his brow, but new beads sprouted from his pores almost as quickly as he wiped them away. He explained, as if it was his last breath before death, "The Duke William and his party arrived without notice in the dead of night. They now require food. That's all I know. I've put a little of every morning food out. I know the Duke's favourite dish is the roasted horse heart stuffed with sage and onion, but I dare not put it out for him before noon. No one would eat heart in the morning, would they? Kidneys and tripe are the morning dish, maybe some blood sausage and liver, do you agree?"

Kallín shrugged. As far as he knew, you could eat what you wanted when you wanted to eat it. This custom of having different kinds of food for different times of the day was a mystery to him. He simply smiled and agreed for fear that the flustered monk might drop down dead, "I think you have chosen suitable dishes, Brother."

Bernard immediately relaxed, but only for a breath, then sucking in a fresh bellyful of anxiety, he announced, "First, the omen in the sky. Now this. What next?" He waited for a moment for an answer that he knew would not come, then he slapped his hands on his wide belly and proclaimed, "Let's get a move on! Come on then! Food won't move itself into the buttery!"

Kallín took up one of the ornate trays of piled meats and followed the old monk who walked in an increasingly lame gait, like an old horse on his way to the knacker's yard.

They proceeded along the hall from the kitchen to the buttery that was adjacent to the Bishop's dining hall.

Kallín, through his duties of serving dinners to the Bishop's table, was, by now, intimately familiar with the buttery. He knew where all of the various treasures were tucked away neatly in their drawers: ornate spoons, knives, goblets and serving jugs of silver and gold. Items that had to be placed in particular ways on the great table and then meticulously cleaned and polished after every meal. The buttery itself was divided from the dining hall by a heavy large red curtain that spanned the full width of the hall itself.

Bernard came to an abrupt halt in the buttery and plopped his tray down with a sigh, urging his young helper, "Please serve. I don't have the legs under me for it."

Kallín looked to the drawers full of cutlery, "What about the settings?"

"They have no need of table settings, I am informed ... they will see to themselves. Whatever that means. Eating with their fingers? Who knows?"

Kallín was more than happy to be the runner of the last leg of the journey to serve the table. It was the most interesting part of the service as he would get to see the finely dressed dignitaries that had come to dine with the Bishop of Normandy, and he might even overhear some gossip from the outside world.

He entered the great dining hall with the first of the large trays of food to find that the hall was empty. The great dining table that ran the length of the floor was not available to place the tray upon because it was full of maps.

Peeping in from behind the heavy red curtain, Brother Bernard whispered, "Use the side tables," and pointed a finger to one of the tables that lined the walls.

These rougher and smaller tables were normally used by the lesser guests who would accompany the dignitaries. As Kallín carried the trays to the side tables, he took in an eyeful of the great map laid out on the dining table. He had seen that map before … he recalled that he had seen it in Bishop Ealdred's library in York. It was a map of England.

He slowed almost to a stop so as to examine the objects placed on the map: tiny replicas of boats at the south coast, and replicas of soldiers and men on horses, also an array of arrows pointing in various directions…

Suddenly the doors swung open and Duke William entered, his impressive purple cloak billowing around him. He was then followed by his generals and ... Tostig Godwinson.

Kallín quickly looked away.

The cohort comprised of twelve battle-eager magnates from Brittany, Flanders, Burgundy and Aquitaine, all having one thing in common: being highborn sons that came into the world too far down the line of succession to inherit title or lands from their fathers. And so, they all equally needed to embark on a war of fortune and secure themselves a piece of the expanding Norman empire in England. They paid no heed to the monk. They were hungry and on a war footing. The only civility they displayed was to form up on either side of the main dining table and wait for the Duke to speak.

William did not look up to greet anyone. He growled at Kallín, "Va!"

Kallín quickly slipped away between the folds of the curtain.

William pointed to the plates of steaming meat, "Mangez."

Kallín watched through the gap in the curtain as the young generals, half of them no older than he was, shouldered one another like hungry wolves around a kill. Then cutting the meat from the carcass with small finely-decorated knives that they produced from their belts, they used their fingers to unceremoniously stuff it into their maws and wolf it down.

There was no discussion during the eating of the food.

In the buttery, Brother Bernard hissed in a worried fuss, scolding Kallín, "Why were you paying so much attention to the map?"

Kallín replied, "It is of England."

Bernard held out his hands, "And what is that to you?"

Kallín told him, "I think they mean to invade."

Bernard put his hands over his ears, "I did not hear that," and repeated with more certainty, convincing himself, "I. Did. Not. Hear. That." Then he looked to Kallín, "Do you wish to lose your head?"

"I do not," Kallín told him. And then he moved to the curtain to listen.

Bernard was about to scold him again, but he wanted to hear the war council as much as Kallín did; like Wulfnoth's cat, neither could resist the nature to be nosy.

The council spoke in the Norman tongue. Kallín had learned it to some degree but not enough to understand the finer details of their discussion.

Thankfully, Bernard was happy to give him whispered translations, "Tostig will land in the north with the Norse King, Harald Hardrada, and his army." Bernard's eyes widened as he reported further, "They will sail three hundred ships up the great Humber and take York ... with ten thousand men."

It was an army beyond their imagination. Neither Kallín nor Bernard had ever seen more than a hundred men in the same place at the same time.

The Generals went on and argued with one another about tactics and numbers. Kallín watched from the curtain as William sat and listened, all the time staring at the map. But any time William raised his hand to speak, they fell silent. And listened. None of them dared to question anything he said. They simply moved the pieces of their army around the map as he instructed.

Bernard explained, "William will invade from the south at the same time as Tostig and Hardrada invade from the north, splitting the English forces in two directions."

Kallín then watched Tostig making an argument with William. William slammed his fist down onto the map and roared, "Pevensey!"

Tostig fell silent.

The plan for the invasion of England was finalised.

Bernard whispered, "They will land the Norman fleet at the port of Pevensey... That port once belonged to our holy order, as did all that land there."

Willian stood and walked out without a word.

The council of war was over.

Kallín watched the young generals eyeing each other in the silence. He realised that they were not brothers in arms, they were competitors in arms. Once they completed the task of taking England, they would be shouldering each other around the bounty of conquered land to make sure that they got their portion of the realm to call their own.

He understood that what held the Norman army together was a great hunger and that England was the great feast.

37

CHEVALERIE

The next morning Kallín pushed a cart containing two barrels of slops to feed to the hogs. It was his least favourite duty in the kitchen, and he was more than happy to leave the distribution of the slops into the various troughs to the hunchbacked Brother Lebbaeus who was big as a bull and just as strong as one.

Brother Lebbaeus came to the old monastery in Wessex as a foundling left on the steps of the abbey. The misshapen little infant was taken in to die, but it stayed alive and grew into a large misshapen man. When the Wessex monks were exiled from their abbey in Hastings and came to their brothers in Fécamp, they brought Lebbaeus with them. The huge hunchback was seldom seen beyond the boundaries of the sprawling hog village, and he never had much to say for himself. But he took a shine to Kallín, probably owing to the fact that Kallín was as ugly and unpleasant to look upon as he was himself, and he loved to listen to Kallín telling him stories of the Rohán.

He made his big lob-sided-broken smile when he saw the young monk pushing the slops cart towards him, and told him, "Bigbolloxed king boar is not too well today then."

Kallín let down the handles of the heavy cart that were cutting into his palms and took a look at his hog nemesis, Bigbollox: the foul tempered king boar that attacked him at every opportunity. But today Bigbollox made no effort to rise from his straw bed. The king boar was the only boar in the hog village of sows, gilts and barrows, and he was kept for only one reason: to service the sows. Any male offspring that the sows produced in their litter were castrated so as to make them barrows, and they were then quickly fattened up and sold for high value tender meat. Each week Bigbollox was moved from sow hut to sow hut to perform his duties and farrow. But he was getting old now and not farrowing up to the standard needed to keep the young sows producing. He was spending more time sleeping than he was farrowing, and he was getting so fat that he might actually kill the young sows by lying on them.

Lebbaeus explained, "Happens when they gets old. They gets a liking for staying in the bed and starts to ignore his duties. I'm goin to pick a new good strong one from next litter and leave the bollox on'im. Make'im a new king boar."

The hunchbacked monk then looked far off to a lone stone hut on the hill, "Keep him in solitude until he grows his bollox and gets bad tempered and horny." Lebbaeus punched Kallín playfully, but hard, in the arm and laughed, "When the new young buck gets among them sows you'll see some good farrowing then!"

Old King Bigbollox came up to the fence, snorting. He seemed to know that the two monks were plotting his downfall.

Lebbaeus smiled at Bigbollox, "That's right, old king boar, I'll be hiding the young Prince from you so that you can't kill'im."

The king boar gave a long angry roar.

Lebbaeus laughed out loud, "I swear t'god that old Bigbollox does know what I'm sayin to'im." And then he shouted back to the angry hog, "You'll be boiled down into candle tallow soon. Aye. And haven't you had a good time of it here then?"

Kallín had no interest in farrowing hogs or anything else to do with the foul-tempered beasts. But he liked to eat them, and he liked the company of Lebbaeus. He liked sitting up late in the night and telling the huge childish hunchback tales of the Rohán. It gave Kallín a comfort to hear himself talk about his people and helped him not to forget about who he was.

After the hogs were fed, the hunchback and the young monk sat on a fallen tree next to the vast cornfield that was upwind from the hog village. The hungry duo got stuck into a large two pound wheel of soft cheese, two loaves of warm bread, and a bottle of wine that Kallín had liberated from the Bishop's cellar. The young Rohán, once happy to live from the fruits of the forest, was succumbing to civilisation and had acquired a taste for the soft cheese. In the beginning he could not get past the reek of it, but he was curious and eventually he took a bite. In that moment a new desire was born in him and a new world of the finer things was revealed. Now, the stronger the smell of the cheese, the more he liked the taste. He was also taking to the mellow oaky wine and finding that he liked the darker heavier wine over the light rosy kind. Lebbaeus was delighted with the stolen treats that Kallín brought to their secret feasts. They drank from the bottle, passing it back and forth. The cornfield hummed before them in the hot daze of the noon sun. The industrious bees went from flower to flower. Birds trilled and fed on the abundant insects. For a moment the world was perfect. It struck Kallín that if there was a God who made this world and everything in it, then this is how he made it to be … and if God was anywhere in this world, then he was here in this field. He was in the birds and the bees and the wine.

Lebbaeus smiled and said in his soft voice, "I likes this field most of all."

"Why's that?" Kallín asked him.

"Because when it is like this, with the sun up high and the air full of sweet smells, the warm breezes coming and going, it reminds me of our wheatfield back home in Hastings." He pointed, "That way to the east would be the way to Winchelsea and London. See how the field rises up the hill just the same way, and that way to the west would be to Bexhill and after that Pevensey Bay … and there, look how the slope of the land falls away fast into a flatland and then into the marshes in the just the same way as in Hastings."

For a moment Kallín joined the soft-spoken hunchback imagining that they were both sitting in a quiet corner of England called Hastings.

The daydreaming was interrupted by vibrations in the earth that increased until they formed into the drumming of galloping horses coming ever closer to them. Then the burst of thundering hooves came from behind a cob of trees as four fast horsemen came bearing flagstaffs. Keeping up a flat-out gallop along the narrow turreted path, they thundered by the two dumbfounded monks in a great cloud of dust and entered the wheatfield, immediately splitting up and setting off to the four corners, slowing in places to stab their flagstaffs into the ground … marking out the ground with different colours.

The two monks were at a loss, but they became only further

dumbfounded when they saw a single file of heavily armed horsemen making their way at a trot along the same turret path and filing into the great wheatfield in a seemingly endless column.

Brother Bernard came panting and heaving himself up the hill from the hog village. It was seldom that the great fat monk was found this far away from his kitchen. He struggled to get his breath back as he looked on in horror at the horsemen, "What are they doing? They will destroy the crop."

Kallín didn't think that these horsemen cared too much about the crops.

Lebbaeus looked on with a kind of childish wonder, "There must be a thousand of them."

"More," Kallín told him. He was impressed at how precisely the horses moved and formed into ranks without any fuss, as if the horses were trained soldiers. Then he noticed the most amazing thing about these horses, "The beasts are blindfolded..."

Lebbaeus nodded his head, "They are warhorses."

Kallín had never heard of this, "warhorses?"

Lebbaeus explained, "These Normans are Chevalerie. They fight on horseback."

This seemed absurd to Kallín. In England, soldiers only used their horses to ride to the battlefield, but they then dismounted for the fight. These warhorses were not like any horses that he'd seen before. They were much bigger than English horses and seemed to have tempers in them that they were eager to release in battle.

On and on they entered the wheatfield, stomping in perfect order. The only sound was their great hooves thumping into the shuddering earth and shaking the whole world. After an hour, or so, around two thousand Chevalerie had entered the field, formed into ranks, and waited in total silence. After a time, maybe it was another hour, Duke William arrived on a horse that was bigger than all of the others, and white as snow with black flaring nostrils and jet black eyes. Six mounted generals arrived behind him. Tostig was not amongst the cohort. Then behind the generals followed two dozen riders; six of which had bugles, and six had drums fixed to either side of their horses. The remaining dozen carried an array of flags of various colours on long thin flagstaffs. They formed up into a line beside William and his generals. Again, everything came to a silent halt while William had a discussion with his generals. Then William nodded and waved his hand. One of the generals spoke to the group of riders with flags, drums and bugles.

The flagmen suddenly held up their flags.

The drummers began to beat out a simple beat in repetition, and the buglers blew a simple tune that repeated itself over and over.

Kallín watched in amazement as the ranks of two thousand Chevalerie moved in unison. Each time the flags, drums and bugles changed their colours, beat and tune, the horses moved in different directions, in a great dance of man and horse. The riders did not use their reins to steer the horse, they used their stirrups. Their hands lay empty and idle. The two thousand Chevalerie performed these dance routines over and over until the sun began to set. Then William raised his hand, turned and galloped away. His generals and his signalmen followed him. The dancing drill was over. The Chevalerie left the field as quietly, patiently and efficiently as they had entered it. By the fall of darkness, the great field was empty.

"The crop is destroyed," Brother Bernard looked at the harvest that had been danced into the earth.

Kallín had never seen anything so amazing as the dancing Chevalerie.

Night. A great chorus of snoring and nocturnal farting filled the air from the two thousand Chevalerie now stationed in the grounds of the monastery of Fécamp with their two thousand huge warhorses, and a small army of farriers and various servants. But the nocturnal racket was not what was keeping Kallín awake. The young Rohán could not sleep because he was possessed with a curiosity to see that war map again. He listened to Brother Quentin's slack breathing and checked that he was indeed asleep. Assured that his cellmate was fast in his sleep, he slipped out of his bed, crept carefully to the door, and spitting on the door hinges so as to make sure that they would not creak, he slid the door open and slipped himself out of the cell into the hallway.

Everywhere soldiers slept on every available inch of the floor. He toe-picked his way through the spiderweb of sprawling limbs. Here and there an eye or an ear was stirred in his direction, but no one took any threat from a monk creeping in a monastery. He could not enter the main hall from the front, as it was guarded. This only made him all the more curious. He made his way through the kitchen and then along the service hall to the buttery, and from the buttery he slipped through the heavy curtain to find himself standing in the great dining hall again. The great dining table was still covered in the map of England, illuminated by the moonlight coming through the window.

He moved to it and examined it up-close, following the fleet-markers across the channel to the coast.

But then what?

A voice spoke from the dark, "Perhaps you should light a candle."

The startled young Rohán looked around him, reaching for a sword on his hip that he did not have.

Tostig emerged from the darkness and smiled, "You again," and he shook his head, "What are you?"

Kallín quickly measured up the situation. Tostig was alone. He carried only a dagger that was still in its sheath. He could be on him and have him. All he needed to do was to encourage Tostig to come closer. He played meek, "My lord. I was cleaning..."

Tostig snorted a laugh, "Fuck me... Really? Do you think I'm fucking daft?"

Kallín stopped talking.

"Drop the fucking pretence, will you? It's tiresome."

Kallín shrugged, there was no playing him. He told him the truth, "I was curious of the coming battle."

Tostig came closer, "I don't know what you are. You're not a monk, Silvatici. But I know you are lucky. And I make a point of never crossing a lucky man while his luck is still with him. I know you are a Rohán…"

Kallín weighed that.

Tostig smiled, "So why haven't I had you killed?" He waited, "Well?"

Kallín told him, "I have no answer for that."

"Ot course you don't," Tostig laughed, then became serious, "I didn't kill your father … What Morcar told you was a lie."

Kallín examined Tostig's face in the moonlight. There was no fear in it. His eyes did not flitter — they were direct.

Tostig picked up a length of cane and he pointed it at a spot on the map, "Here. Come see."

Kallín moved from the south coast and along the east coast until he stood at the Humber estuary, and watched Tostig pointing at a place he knew, "York."

Tostig nodded, "You can read a map?"

"Some of it," Kallín told him.

Tostig smiled, "You'll soon read all of it." And then he pointed to a spot just south of York, "Here is Fulford. During the time of the battle, I was the Earl of Northumbria. Morcar brought an army to depose me.

Your people, the Rohán, were his mercenaries. I was outnumbered greatly. I retreated out onto the low ground. With the river to my left flank and the marsh to my right flank."

Kallín agreed, "Good move. You have no worry of being out flanked."

Tostig smiled, "You know it. Good. My English troops deserted me. It is true, I was not loved by them. I was left only with my mercenary Norsemen. Morcar had five hundred bowmen and two thousand spearmen as well as his agile Rohán mercenaries who would break my shield-wall. I came to an agreement of surrender to Morcar and stood my Norsemen down. But I was aware of some ancient blood oath between your father and the Norsemen. This oath had nothing to do with me. I left the field as agreed. And I left England. I heard some time later of the attack made by the Norse on your clan. But ... It was not my order. I was told that your Rohán killed five Norse for every one of them in the battle."

Kallín thought about that. Why would this man lie to him? Equally, why would he tell him the truth? But he did have one man who spoke in his favour, Kallín asked him, "What of Wulfnoth?"

Tostig took a step back. "So it is true... My poor mad brother spoke the truth. He ranted on about his 'Moine des Loups' in the dungeon."

Kallín smiled, "I am much grateful for the cake that he gave me ... Your cake."

Tostig smiled, "You and I are not enemies. We are two Englishmen who are much wronged by foreigners. Are we not natural brothers in arms?"

Kallín thought about it and looked at the map, looked at the Humber, looked at the great forest, and he said quietly, "I must return home."

Tostig smiled, "You and I both. Let us make a pact here in the Norman dog's camp. You and I are brothers. I will help you home and you will help me take back York."

Kallín saw his way home, "Agreed."

38

BROTHERHOOD OF JUDAS

The next morning Kallín was surprised to see Brother Tomas standing at the door to his cell, "What have you been up to?" It was a rhetorical question, "Actions have consequences ... You have been missioned ... Do you know what that means?"

"No."

"You are to be the clerical aid to Tostig Godwinson." Tomas then turned to Quentin who was sitting gobsmacked on the bed and told him, "Leave us, Brother."

Quentin moved like a sudden draft out of the cell. Tomas sat opposite Kallín explaining, "It is a serious role," he began, "you have not been trained for it, and you will have to use what wits God gave you to learn quickly. What you do say, and in a lot of cases, what you do not say, is imperative. How are you following me so far?"

"So far, Brother, I am lost."

Tomas nodded, "Well, honesty is a good starting point. There are a handful of simple rules to help you in your decision making. First, your allegiance is always to the brotherhood. You are a Benedictine first and foremost. Is that understood?"

"Yes."

"I am told you have been taught to some fair ability to read and write?"

"Some."

Tomas reached into the pocket of his habit and retrieved a small metal phial no bigger than a half finger in length. "Do you know what this is?"

"No."

Tomas carefully unscrewed the phial and opened it, then from inside of it he produced a tiny scroll of parchment, uncoiled it, and handed the parchment to Kallín. "Do you see now?"

Kallín looked at the small scroll and saw the tiny writing.

Tomas explained, "The carrier pigeon wears a harness on its back. This phial is carried in the harness. All of your pigeons will fly back here, to Fécamp. Can you read that?"

Kallín examined the writing, the words were few and simple. "Prince talks of London."

Tomas smiled, "Very good."

Kallín asked, "This is from Scotland?"

Tomas lost his smile, "How can you know that?"

"It speaks of Edgar, does it not?"

Tomas shook his head, "I see you have the skill of deducing. That is good. But you must learn the skill of keeping your council. You will leave here with Tostig in ten days and there is much to teach you..." Tomas got to his feet, "It was my suspicion that God kept you alive for a reason." He looked to Quentin's bed, "You will have a new brother sharing with you. His name is Brother John. Do not leave his side and listen carefully to everything he teaches you. I know not the secrets of his craft, but I know he will teach you how to stay alive in the dangerous world that you are about to enter. God bless you, Brother Osbald. Goodbye."

Brother Tomas left the cell and some moments later a tall monk, dressed in a snow-white habit and white gloved hands entered. He then removed his hood to reveal his completely bald head of the whitest skin and eyes that were as colourless as orbs of sea water. He put Kallín in mind of the statue in the church.

The white monk spoke in a deep voice, "I am Brother John. God has called you to his service. Do you wish to answer his call?"

Kallín was about to make another lie. He was willing to say anything that might get him closer to home. But he stopped himself. There was something about this white monk, about his presence, that made Kallín believe that he could see through any lies he might tell him. He stood motionless and waited some moments until Kallín finally told him, "I am not a real monk."

"Only God knows what you are ... He made you." John waited for a moment and then asked him, "But you say you are not a monk. What do you think you are?"

Kallín thought about that, "I am a Rohán..."

John nodded, "And a Rohán cannot be a monk?"

Kallín explained, "I am a warrior."

John smiled at that, "You think that a monk is not a warrior?"

Kallín answered, "They do not fight."

John shook his head, "You do not know enough about being a monk if you think that we do not fight. Yes, some brothers like Bernard do the cooking. Some like Lebbaeus tend to the hogs and the garden. Some like Quentin tend to the books and study the law. Each one does what God made him to do. But some of us fight. Some of us are warriors for God because that is what God made us for."

John let that settle with the young Rohán. Then went on, "You can leave here, travel back to England with Tostig, and return to your people in the forest ... Make your way as a sword, fighting the fights of men for coin and taking no interest in the reasons for the battles that you fight in. That is your Rohán way, is it not?"

"Yes."

"Or you can do what God made you to do and take his side in the eternal war."

"What war is that?" Kallín asked him.

"The one war, the never-ending war, the war between the evil of man and the good of God. These evils that men do, slaughtering your clan, slaving your people, and worse, are the ways that the world will be consumed. Our fight as brothers is not to fight the man, but to fight the evil that is within him and bring the world to the order that is God's plan. For that, God calls warriors into his ranks. He has called you."

Kallín examined the seawater eyes, and asked him, "Are you a warrior?"

"Yes."

Kallín wondered, "What of the Norsemen who killed my people ... What of my revenge on them?"

John explained, "You have not been listening to me ... You will deliver God's wrath unto the evil men. You will carry God's rod and staff, and you will fear no evil. But the power of God is not wielded to make revenge ... Revenge is a savage impulse. The power of God is to be used by the good shepherd so that the strong cannot oppress the weak. But the good shepherd must be able to protect the flock and kill the wolf ... And that is who you are in God's eyes. Not the savage Rohán seeking only revenge, not Bishop Ealdred's creation ... You are indeed 'Moine des Loups', the good shepherd who can kill the wolves. God is at war. What say you to God's call?"

Kallín became aware that this monk was a very powerful man and that his questions were not really questions. The only way he was going to see his home again was to answer, "Yes."

John drew a dagger from his sleeve, "Give me your right hand."

Kallín gave him his hand.

The white monk gently made a delicate incision over Kallín's palm, it was not deep enough to penetrate the skin, but enough to draw fine lines of blood to the surface in the shape of the cross. Then removing his white silk glove from his own right hand that already bore scars on its palm, he made a fresh incision, and clasping their bloody palms together, he recited, "This is the blood of Christ, the blood that is God's covenant, the unbroken apostolic chain of the holy blood that was given by Christ to his first apostles, passed from loyal Judas to make the first soldier of God. And so Christ's blood is passed in to you. This holy blood anoints you and bonds you into the Brotherhood of Judas. Amen." John held Kallín's hand for a moment longer in a silent prayer and then released him, and asked, "We are a secret order. Our work is not known, not even to our Benedictine brother's. Do you understand ?"

"Yes," Kallín assured him, and then asked, "Judas?"

John smiled, "You have studied the apostles?"

"Brother Quentin has been instructing me. But, did Judas not betray Jesus?"

John smiled, "Yes he did. This is your first secret of the Order. Judas was the closest brother to Jesus, and loyal. Jesus ordered Judas to betray him..."

"Why?"

John told him, "Perhaps tonight I will explain more to you." John stood and continued, "But now, I have much to teach you and very little time to do it. Let us get busy ... Your true work will begin after William conquers England."

Kallín stalled and asked, "How can you know that William will win the battle?"

John smiled at him, "Because the Holy Father has decreed that William should win. He has our council. Come see. Let me show you how Harold Godwinson will be defeated by William the Duke of

Normandy." As they opened the door to leave, John added, "From now on you will always wear your hood so as to conceal yourself. No one is to be allowed an opportunity to make a memory of your face."

Kallín and Brother John made their way out along the path, past the hog village and on to the great wheatfield.

Lebbaeus watched from a distance, in no hurry to get close to the white monk.

On the edge of the wheatfield, John explained, "I want you to watch this drill."

Kallín told him, "I watched it before, Brother."

John's thin lips smiled from under the hood, "No ... The drill you watched before was the drill for the horses. This is the full drill. You must learn the ways of the Chevalerie."

The ground suddenly shuddered under their feet.

"Look. See. They come..."

Kallín looked to the narrow road and waited.

The ground continued to shake in a fierce steady trotting rhythm. The rumble grew louder and louder until the magnificent and terrifying sight of the Chevalerie rounding the bend. Both man and horse were now covered in armour and colourful ensigns so that they combined to be one single magnificent creature of war. They thundered past at a great speed, two at a time, and quickly and precisely fell into the same ranks that Kallín had observed before. Suddenly all was silent. Not even the birds dared whistle as two thousand battle-ready Chevalerie stood motionless, holding great garishly coloured long thin poles in the upright position as one would hold a flagstaff.

Kallín asked John, "What are those poles they hold?"

John told him, "They are called 'Lances', you will soon see their terrible purpose."

William arrived in full armour, and this time Tostig was beside him. The Duke's eyes immediately found the white monk and made a nod of acknowledgement to him.

John equally nodded back to the Duke.

Then William's eyes examined Kallín for a moment. Kallín felt the malice.

The signalmen arrived, and the generals broke into chatter. All attention turned to the field. Each of the orders were played out in the same way as before with drum and bugle, and the Chevalerie went through their manoeuvres as before. But this time they did it all at speed, and as they charged from one end of the field to the other, they held their lances low in front of them. Kallín realised that these great weapons were for spearing men, and from the size and ferocity of them, they could easily skewer three men at a time. No shield-wall would withstand such an attack.

Also the horses behaved differently.

When the beasts came to a halt after the charge they stamped their huge hooves into the ground, a dance that would be made upon the bodies of the fallen enemy. The horses were trained to fight and to kill. It would be a slaughter. But that is not the part of the manoeuvres that caught Kallín's attention the most. His eye was drawn to movement within the centre of the Chevalerie ranks … they were at something secret. Amongst all of the armour and flags, Kallín made out a black cloaked and hooded rider who wore no armour, nor did he have a lance. Instead, he carried, what appeared to be a cross…

"Who is that?" Kallín asked.

John told him, "He is called Tireur d'Élite… The best bowman in Christendom."

"What is that he carries?"

John smiled, "That is the key to victory … It is his bow."

Kallín told him, "You are mistaken, Brother John. That is not a bow."

John explained, "It is called the 'Arbalète'. A new kind of bow, that looks like a cross. Watch up on the hill there."

Away up on the rise of the hill stood a scarecrow in full armour. The cohort of Chevalerie that surrounded the 'Tireur d'Élite' formed a protective testudo shell of shields around him, and moved closer to the base of the hill. There, they stopped. In their centre, the 'Tireur d'Élite' stood in his stirrups, rising head and shoulders out of the testudo, and then he shouldered the arbalète — and fired its bolt!

Kallín knew that arrows were useless against armour. But this bolt from the arbalète hit the helmet of the of the scarecrow and penetrated it with ease. The Tireur d'Élite fired three more times in quick succession. Each time he hit the target to devastating effect.

John explained, "The next time that the Tireur d'Élite shoots at the armour, it will have King Harold Godwinson inside of it. The battle will be over and England will be William's. You are looking into the future."

As the next weeks passed, Kallín spent both day and night with

Brother John who never ceased talking to him in his low steady tone, imparting as much of his wisdom as he could in the shortest amount of time possible. Then they were suddenly out of time. Tostig waited for his attaché monk to join him so that he could leave for the port.

John handed Kallín a leather satchel, "This contains your seal from Rome that confirms you as a Papal attaché, and this will identify you to other Brothers of Judas." John slipped a large golden ring onto Kallín's finger that showed a simple red coloured cross, that was like the bleeding cross that John made on his palm. "The Blood Cross is our symbol. Wear this always. If you see another like it, then join your right hand with his, palm to palm, feel for the scar of the cross."

"I understand," Kallín told him.

"Finally," John told him, "Pull up your left sleeve."

Kallín did so, and Brother John fixed a thin scabbard, upside-down, onto the inside of Kallín's forearm. He then slid a slender blade into the scabbard and explained, "It is called a dague. I do not imagine that I need tell you how to use it."

Kallín smiled, "It is beautiful. It puts me in mind of another such blade that I was parted from."

John nodded, "Well, become parted from this one only in death. It is made from the finest cauldron steel, and it will puncture armour. It is blessed by the Holy Father himself. Holy oaths may be sworn upon it. In fact, it is the blade that William swore upon and made his holy pledge to the Brothers of Wessex."

"What did he swear to them?"

"That he would take back their lands around Hastings, and build for them a magnificent new abbey."

A short time later Kallín was making his way on horseback with Tostig to the boat. In his train, he had a packhorse that carried his carrier pigeons in boxes and his other pieces of equipment and bedding.

Tostig smiled to him, "You have moved up quickly." And he nodded to the ring on Kallín's finger, and went on, "I know what the ring means."

Kallín looked to Tostig's hand. He did not wear such a ring, so he did not engage in any conversation about the Brotherhood of Judas. Instead, as instructed by John for such crossroads in conversation, he steered the inquisitive Duke in a different direction, "I hope that the crossing will be a swift one."

Tostig looked to the sky, immediately consumed with concerns of bad weather. "Well, with you in the boat we should have God on our side, should we not?"

"We should." Kallín told him and he added, "If God intends for us to make the journey that is."

Tostig read that, "Why would God not favour us?"

Kallín kept him in place, "I know not what God thinks. Nor would I presume to."

Tostig smiled at that, "You have been taught the cleric's wit. I like it."

39

HARDRADA

Grim Haven was a shithole at the best of times, but in the murky drizzle of the late September rains, it was the most miserable place on earth. Kallín and Tostig arrived by boat under an escort of forty Flemish mercenaries. Their Captain threatened and bullied two other smaller vessels out of the way so that they could dock. Any opportunistic thieves malingering about the immediate vicinity quickly got offside and stayed out of sight. Boats travelling under heavily armed guards were dangerous places for anyone suspected of being a threat to them, and the Flemish mercenaries were widely known to be the most bad-tempered and the quickest to cut off heads. Tostig disembarked with Kallín. They were immediately met by Gustard, Tostig's agent, on the dockside.

Gustard, a large uncomfortably obese man with a greasy complexion that reeked of something damp and rotten, grunted as he moved about. He put Kallín in mind of the old big bolloxed hog, and just like the big old king hog, Gustard didn't like the look of Kallín. Not one little bit.

"What you doin with a bleedin monk then?" he grunted at Tostig.

Tostig assured him, "You let me worry about the company I keep Have you gathered the swords I asked for?"

Gustard half laughed and half grunted, "No shortage of swords lookin for work if you have gold. D'you have it?"

"I have the gold," Tostig replied.

That answer brought a glint to Gustard's eye as he scanned the boat quickly and asked, "On the boat in them caskets, is it?"

Tostig offered, "You can open them to look and see, if you wish ... But I warn you, my Flemish are very protective."

Gustard rubbed a throbbing boil on the back of his greasy neck. He knew that he should have it drained of its puss, but he considered it to be a good weathervane for trouble and a kind of lucky charm. He pulled up a yawning smile and answered, "No need for that, me lord, I am your obedient servant in all matters." Then he nodded to the mercenary guard, "Them Flemish isn't going to be going about the town making murder, is they?"

Tostig smiled and replied, "Not if I don't tell them to. Where have the swords camped up?"

Gustard nodded in some vague direction behind him, "Out along the river by the forest, aways from the townsfolk. Five hundred or so of'em. Sheriff doesn't want'em anywhere near here."

Tostig checked, "Who's the King's sheriff now then?"

"Lord Morcar —" Gustard caught himself, "Forgive me for saying his name in your presence, me lord, he did appoint his cousin Eric..."

Tostig darkened, "A proper cunt if there ever was one. I look forward to gutting him myself."

Gustard smiled, "But he likes the coin ... So he is well bought and we have no worries of him."

Tostig nodded, adding, "We will see. But let it be known, if the new sheriff shows his ugly face in Grim Haven while I am here, then I will end him."

Gustard grimaced with some unidentified pain shifting itself in his guts, and asked Tostig, "When do your Norsemen get here then?"

Kallín's ears picked up on the mention of the Norsemen and he quickly looked to the ground to avoid Tostig's eye that was watching him to see his response.

Tostig told Gustard, "I expect them here tomorrow on the high tide."

Gustard heaved himself away and spoke in short breaths as he went, "Well. We don't need a fuckin Norse army hanging about neither. There's already too much a smell of war in the air as it is. Feels like the whole country is going to burn. Hopefully you'll be swiftly away again to your victory and we can be settled again before the winter comes to bite us in the arse."

Tostig told him, "We don't plan on malingering."

"Good so. Fast army is a victorious army. That's what they say, eh?

This way then. I've secured lodgings for you."

Tostig and his monk followed Gustard's remarkably quick hobbled walk as he brought them to the end of the dock and into the heaving market area. Kallín's eye was drawn to cages full of miserable wretches. On seeing a monk, a number of wretches came to the edge of their cages and reached out, pleading with him for help — or a blessing.

Kallín stopped walking and scanned the cages.

Gustard noticed his pause and pounced, "Looking to buy a slave, monk?"

Kallín asked him, "Where are they from?"

Gustard shrugged, "The wilderness of Wales? The wilds of Scotland?"

Kallín examined him, "They sound like Umbrians."

Gustard looked from Kallín to Tostig, "What's this then? All them slaves are legal bought to be sold. I've got me licence from the King."

Kallín kept his eye on Gustard, "Which King is that then?"

"The new one. Harold!" Then Gustard quickly apologised to Tostig, "Sorry for the mentioning of his name, my lord."

Tostig shrugged it off, "So tell me, how much does my brother King take in payment to allow you to buy and sell his people?"

Gustard moaned, "Well, I paid his bloody reever ten pounds of gold for the season's privilege. The reever of the old King only charged me five pounds a season," Gustard played the victim, "and the bloody trade is down this season on account of the rumours of war. Nobody wants to buy new slaves when there is talk of war comin, gives them slaves ideas, and gets the fighting into them. Look at them ... I can see it in'im. I'll have to sell them all cheap to foreigners. Meanwhile the wretched things are eating my stores out."

Kallín asked him, "Have you sold Rohán?"

Gustard stepped back and nodded to his half dozen bodyguard, "Fucking Rohán? Do you think me fucking daft? I've nowt to do with fucking Silvatici..."

Gustard's bodyguard moved closer.

Tostig was quick to advise Gustard, "You would do well to tell your guard to stand down ... or I'll murder every last cunting one you."

Gustard waved his guards away, "Fuckin useless bastards."

Tostig went on, "Tell him about the Rohán."

Gustard measured Tostig and his monk. He couldn't tell which of them was the most dangerous, but he knew that they would both kill him in a heartbeat. He answered, "It's nowt to do with me. But early in the year a Norse ship came down the river with slaves … When I saw them I knew they was Silvatici. Maybe Rohán. I didn't want them. I don't need that kind of trouble."

Kallín pressed him, "What did the Norse do with them?"

Gustard lowered his eyes, "Took them with them out to sea. Poor wretches. Bad enough to be a slave here in England, but to be the slave of a fuckin Norseman?"

Tostig nodded to Gustard, "Show us to our lodgings."

Gustard turned and limped away, groaning, "Worried for fuckin slaves. What fuckin next?"

Tostig moved along, joined Kallín and told him privately, "I did not know that the Norsemen took your people as slaves?"

Kallín told him, "It's a very careless king that allows the slaving of his people. You have to ask yourself, what is it to be an Englishman if you and yours can be taken from your home to be bought and sold like cattle? Then the King will ask the same Englishmen to make a fyrd and muster on the battlefield? A man should know what he is fighting for when he goes to war. No man fights to be a slave."

Tostig smiled and shook his head, "Well … I will remember that. Those Fécamp monks have taught you much. Perhaps when I have taken back York, I will ask Rome if I can retain you as my council?"

Kallín simply nodded.

Tostig tested him further, "Would you be happy to serve me in that way?"

Kallín had answers ready for almost anything that Tostig could ask him, "I serve God first. Where the Bishop places me is where his work is to be done to the best of my ability."

"I see," Tostig agreed, though he knew that was a double-edged answer, "What God gives, the Pope can take away."

Gustard stopped at a dwelling that was crammed in between all of the other ramshackle houses, stacked together. He banged on the door, "Woman of this house is a good cook and the daughters will keep you warm in the night." He went for a smile that just cut his face into a grimace.

The door was opened by a young girl who kept her eyes to the floor and spoke softly, "Enter please."

Gustard stayed where he stood and spoke to Tostig, "I'll not be stepping inside. I'll come in the morning when you're fed and watered, and we'll enlist your swords and then you can pay me and … Well, go and do what is it that you are going to do."

Tostig kept his eye on the young girl, but spoke to Gustard, "That is a good plan. Tomorrow then."

Gustard nodded, threw a look at the monk and warned him, "If you're goin about the town, you watch yourself and that fine gold ring on your finger. There's heathens a plenty around here who care not for your christian God or any of his monks."

Kallín smiled at him, "Thank you."

Gustard shook his head and moved off, moaning, "Fuckin monks... Pain in my fuckin hole."

Inside of the house the two guests were greeted by five more young girls who lined up at the table while their mother ladled out stew into two large bowls, "Welcome. I'm missus Smith and these are me daughters that have names I won't waste your time with. Here's a good meat stew for you both. Lamb it is, spring lamb that I cured and hung dry through the summer. Slow cooked for a whole day and a night it is. Come and eat it now, if you will."

Kallín smiled to her.

Tostig was eyeing the array of young girls as he slid into the chair at the table and explained to Missus Smith, "I fancy some of that bread that I can smell to dip into that stew."

Missus Smith kept her eyes locked on Kallín, and spoke to one of the girls, "Gretta, get the bread."

One of the girls, the smallest one who was no more than ten winters old, peeled away and started to wrestle a loaf of hot bread from the oven. All the time Missus Smith kept her eyes on Kallín, focusing on the scars on his face, "Forgive me for asking," She began, "but are you the Brother they call the Monk of the Wolves?"

Tostig slapped the table and laughed, "Damn it! Moine des Loups, you're famous!"

Kallín smiled to the old woman and told her, "Please, call me Brother Osbald."

Missus Smith raised her eyes, picking out his accent, "You're Umbrian?"

Kallín knew he was already giving away too much about himself to this woman, he admitted, "You have a good ear. I am from these parts, yes."

"Where?" Missus Smith asked, "What village do you hail from?"

Kallín told her, "That I do not know..." Then after a moment added, "For it was dark when I left."

The girls broke into a nervous fit of giggling.

Missus Smith apologised, "I am much sorry, Brother, I am too nosy." She placed the bowls of stew on the rough, but spotlessly clean, table, "I was so instantly filled with joy when I saw you. We'd heard rumours from others who come and go from Grim'aven to Normandy and they talked about the English 'Monk of the Wolves'. And now to learn that you are an Umbrian, one of us, well... What a blessing to have under my roof."

Tostig plunged his spoon into his stew with a rasp of childish jealousy and asked Missus Smith, "What of me? Am I not a blessing good woman?" He plopped his purse of gold coins onto the table, "I am the man who is paying you the coin."

Missus Smith wrung her red calloused hands in her apron, "Of course, my lord, I meant no disrespect to you. Forgive me."

Tostig's attention was instantly consumed by his mouthful of meat, "What the...? How? This is the most delicious meat I have ever tasted."

Missus Smith blushed a bright red, "My lord," and she stiffly made a little courtesy, "Thank you."

Her daughters giggled some more.

Tostig went on, "Your good husband is a very lucky man indeed."

All of the girls blessed themselves, and Missus Smith, looked down and blessed herself too.

Tostig realised, "Damn it. He's dead, isn't he?"

Missus Smith answered, "He is, my lord, and may he rest in peace."

Tostig shoved more meat into his mouth, "This is so good. So good."

Missus Smith watched Kallín eating. Waiting.

He was so lost in the deliciousness of the meal that it was a polite cough from Tostig that made him look up and remember to compliment the cook. "Sorry..." He explained to Missus Smith, "I was lost in the taste of it. If food can be divine, then this is truly 'manna from heaven'. It has surely brought me home again ... and put me in mind of my mother's cooking."

Missus Smith's eyes welled up with pride, "Thank you..." She was about to turn but stopped.

Kallín sensed she had a question, and he asked her, "Yes?"

Missus Smith composed herself for a moment, not sure if this was something that she should say and then explained to him, "My husband ... he weren't a good man, and he never had my daughters properly christened ... Would you christen them?"

The five girls immediately knelt.

Kallín took a moment. He'd had the ceremony performed on him. He knew the workings of it. He dare not refuse. He got to his feet and asked Missus Smith, "A bowl of water, please."

Tostig rolled his eyes. He would not be fucking any of these newly christened girls tonight.

The next day three hundred and some hired swords were signed up by Tostig. They were the most desperate collection of men that Kallín had ever laid eyes on; underfed, no real meat on any of them, the flotsam and jetsam of the world that had been washed into the corner of some shitty harbour. Some of them were wily old soldiers that had somehow survived on their wits to be too long in the tooth for the paid ranks of the army. It would be a foolish man who would trust these old foxes enough to make a stand and fight next to them. They had surely survived by finding crafty ways to slip away from the worst of the battle. Others were young, fresh faced, wide-eyed and untrained farmboys with no place in the world. All men being required to have their own weapons, they came armed with the pitchfork or the loy. Kallín doubted that they would make any kind of fight at all.

The payment arrangements were simple enough. Tostig issued each man a promissory soldier's note. The payment in gold was left with Gustard who would honour the note after the battle.

Kallín observed the hired swords and commented to Tostig, "There are no fighters of quality amongst them."

Tostig nodded in agreement, and explained, "That's because my brother, King Harold, has hired every man he can find in anticipation of William's invasion." He smiled and went on, "But William has held his forces in Normandy all summer, forcing Harold to stay ready for his invasion and empty his coffers on a standing army. Much of Harold's fyrd have returned to their farms for the harvest. The time is now ripe. William's fleet will strike from Normandy, defeat my brother and take London. We will take York and the north."

Kallín nodded and agreed, "William is a clever strategist to have pinned the English so."

Tostig snorted a laugh, "You think this plan is William's?"

Kallín asked, "Is it not?"

Tostig put a hand on Kallín's shoulder, "The hand that put you here to be my monk, is the same hand that has put me here to be the Lord of Northumbria, and it is the hand that will put William on the throne of

England. We are all small parts of a greater plan … Rome tells us that it is God's plan. But I don't think that you believe that any more than I do."

Kallín's head swam a little.

Tostig slapped him on the back, "And now … Let us see to our boats."

Kallín stood on the banks of the wide calm estuary where the setting sun washed the slack tide waters in crimson so that it appeared to be a great lake of fire. Then on the horizon a dark shadow emerged from the edge of the world and poured towards the shore; the vast estuary was filled with a huge fleet of magnificent warships.

"How many are there?" he asked Tostig.

Tostig smiled, "At least three hundred … And ten thousand of the fiercest Norse warriors onboard."

Kallín wondered, "Who could muster such an army?"

Tostig smiled, "The most famous warrior in the world, Harald Hardrada, King of the Norsemen."

40

FULFORD

Kallín stood on the deck of Harald Hardrada's great warship. Before him sat the great King of Norway: the living legend who was the general of Constantinople's elite Varangian Guard, the Emperor's greatest warrior. It was a strange feeling for Kallín to be this close to the Norsemen. In the back of his mind he wondered if any of them were part of the army that killed his father and slaved his mother. The hatred always smouldered in his stomach like coals buried in a blacksmith's forge, ready to be fanned back to life. He could never stand to think of where his mother might be now. As he stood in front of the great warrior King, he felt his himself being consumed with an urge to murder him, and he feared that his growing rage would overpower him and carry him into a charge like a crazed warhorse.

Hardrada looked over the face of the young monk in front of him and commented, "I have never met a man with more scars on his face than I have myself." Then he added, "And I have never met a monk with any scars at all … Is it true that these are from a wolf?"

"It is, my lord."

Hardrada nodded and asked, "Is it also true that you were a wild Silvatici?"

Kallín felt his blood pound in his ears, every part of him wanted to attack, "Yes, my lord."

Hardrada examined him, "I have heard much about your kind." But Hardrada had not made it this far in his life without having good wits.

He sensed the danger coming from this young monk the same way he would from a young wolf. He told him, "Remove your hood."

Kallín pulled his hood away from his head.

Hardrada raised his eyebrows, "Look at this. Another skin-headed monk." Then Kallín looked behind him as a young monk, who was also fully head-shaved, joined them. Kallín looked to the monk's left hand and saw the blood cross ring.

Hardrada went on, "My own monk is similarly bald-headed." Hardrada's eye went to Kallín's hand, "And wears an identical ring." He asked his monk, "Have you two met?"

Hardrada's monk answered in a heavy drawl of an accent that Kallín had never heard before, "We have not met before, my lord." And he held out his right hand in a greeting to Kallín, "I am Brother Otto from the Abbey at Novgorod."

Kallín took his hand and felt the scar of the cross on his palm, "I am Brother Osbald from the Abbey of Fécamp."

They then exchanged a kiss on the cheek. At the same time, Otto whispered in Kallín's ear, "Be at peace, Brother. You show too much of your heart."

Kallín heard the warning. He was doing what he had been trained by Brother John not to do.

Hardrada laughed and commented to Tostig, "You see how they bond to one another in an instant? One is a Rus who was once a wild Pecheneg and other an Englishman who was once a wild Silvatici. Now they are brothers. This is a mystery me." He told Kallín, "I need to know I have loyalty when a man stands this close to me." Hardrada examined Kallín's eyes for a moment, reading the danger in them, "You have a blood oath against Norsemen?"

Kallín knew there was no point in trying to deceive Hardrada. He had looked into him and saw his heart.

Kallín told him, "The Norsemen slaughtered my clan."

Hardrada kept his eyes on the young monk who was seething with deadly intent, and he dug into him further, "What else?"

"My mother." At the mention of her, Kallín felt himself fill to the threshold with tears and feared he would break and cry them all out in front of the Norsemen. But he pulled himself together, held that dam in place and answered, "She was slaved."

Hardrada thought for a moment and then told Kallín, "All men who serve under me have something to lose and something to win. We win or lose together. What was that name of your clan?"

"Rohán."

A murmur went around the boat. The Norsemen hated the Rohán just as much as the Rohán hated them.

Hardrada shook his head, "Rohán..." Then he held out his hand to Kallín, "If I win this battle, I will find your mother, and if she is alive, I will return her to you. What say you now?"

Kallín did not need to consider the offer, he lowered his head and pledged to Hardrada, "I am your man. Tell me what you need of me, my lord."

"You can read maps?" Hardrada asked.

"Yes."

Hardrada smiled, and nodded to one of his Captains, who immediately rolled out a map on the deck of the boat.

Kallín saw that the map was identical to the one that he had seen in William's war council.

Hardrada explained as he pointed at a spot on the map, "We are here, in this shit-pit that is Grim Haven." He moved his pointer along the great Humber and then up along its subsidiary of the Ouse, and traced along it until he came to a city. "And here is York. Do you know it?"

"Yes."

Hardrada went on, "Morcar and Edwin know full well that I mean to take York. I dare say that they know my movements since entering the river and my numbers." He smiled to himself, "War is about information and the man who knows the most will have the upper hand. I know that Morcar and Edwin plan to ambush me on my march to York - here."

Kallín nodded and agreed, "An army is at its weakest when it is moving in column formation."

Hardrada smiled, "You know something of tactics. Good." He moved his pointer along the river, "Their place of ambush will be here, at a place called Fulford where there is good high standing ground for them to make their shield wall along the ridge of the beck ... This is where Morcar and Edwin will meet me ..." Hardrada smiled then held out his hand and was handed a scroll by Brother Otto. He rolled it open to show a sketched map of a section of the River Ouse that ran north under a bridge, but the river was also fed by a beck on its west side. "This is a copy of their battle plan and an inventory of their numbers."

Kallín did not dare ask how Hardrada came by the information, but a look to Brother Otto confirmed his suspicions that the information had travelled by pigeons.

Hardrada then ran his finger along the north side of the beck, "Here along this high ridge is where they have pegged out. It is a good six feet higher than its south bank, and it gives them protection on their flanks with the Ouse on their left flank and the flood plains on their right. They expect us to be attacking them straight on from the weaker southern position... " He smiled, "and that's exactly what we will do." He read Kallín's expression with a glint in his eye, and asked him, "What do you think of that for a battle plan?"

Kallín nodded. He knew he was being tested. He told the great warrior, "You will spend a lot of your men attacking a shield wall on top of a beck … you may as well waste them in a charge at castle walls … but there is no plan that survives contact with the enemy."

Hardrada looked to Tostig, "I like this monk, more and more." He looked back to Kallín, "Here is where you come into my plan." He pointed back to the big map of the river and its surrounds, and explained, "Here … at this large bend, when my fleet is still out of their sight, at a place called Riccal, here, I will disembark with my men … Tostig will sail on with the fleet that will have his army of hired mercenaries but with the ships made to look full of thousands. You … will lead me, and my men, overland from Riccal to this place called Fulford so that we arrive at noon along the riverbank on Morcar's left flank. It must be on the noon ... with the tide." He looked to his monk, "Are you sure of the tide, Otto?"

Otto assured him, "The tidal flow of the river lowers the water there. At noon it fully drains the beck..."

Hardrada smiled to Kallín, "Drains the beck ... and reveals a way across to the opposite riverbank. This bank sits so low that my men will be out of the line of sight as they cross … Do you my plan now?"

Kallín nodded. He understood it, "I see it."

Hardrada smiled, "He understands." Then his face fell serious, and he asked Kallín, "Can you get me there?" He pointed to a place on the riverbank at Fulford and added, "From Riccal quickly and unseen?"

Kallín glanced over the map. The whole interior of the forest and the marshlands were simply painted green with no details of the ancient pathways that he knew to be in there, but he saw the path in his mind's eye, and told Hardrada, "Yes."

Hardrada asked, "How long will it take to get there?"

Kallín explained, "In full armour, six to seven hours of hard march.

The ground is not easy going. Parts are boggy, and a man under the burden of heavy armour will not do well in it."

Hardrada asked, "Without armour?"

"We can make it in half that time…"

Hardrada looked to his grim-faced Captains, "The men are battle ready. We won't need armour. Speed of foot and the element of surprise will be our best weapons."

The Captains nodded in silent agreement.

Otto raised his hand, and when Harald nodded to him, he spoke, "My lord ... I fear I may slow down your progress on a quick march through rough terrain."

Harald laughed, "I fear it too. You will stay with the boats."

The Captains laughed.

It was only then that Kallín looked at the feet of brother Otto and noticed that he had only one foot. The other was a peg-leg.

Under the cover of night, the fleet rowed its way out of Grim Haven along the estuary into the great Humber River. The moon climbed high. Kallín sat up on the bow. The warships moved swiftly in pulsating surges from the heartbeat of the boat that was set in perfect time by the unwavering rhythm of the oars. The men talked low amongst themselves, here and there came a smile, probably made by the thought of the gold, or the kiss of a sweetheart.

The longer he was on this river, the more he felt Rohán again. This water and the lands around it were stirring nameless deep feelings in him. But there was one deep pine in his heart that had a name: Luna.

He rolled himself up and covering his eyes with his hood, he slept in the rocking cradle of the warship.

As daybreak began its slow progress in the eastern sky they came to a great bend in the river at Riccal. Harald's best men disembarked. Some three thousand set up guard around the moored fleet, and some five thousand unpeeled their heavy armour and dressed for travelling light. They then followed their leader into the dense forest in one long single line that linked man-after-man in a great human chain, and at its head was their pathfinder: The Rohán monk.

Tostig went on up the river with the rest of the fleet, his men spread around to the gunwales so that the boats would appear full of warriors.

As Kallín made his way through the forest, he became aware that they were being stalked, but he was also aware that those eyes following his progress were not a danger to him. He pulled his hood down to reveal his face. A few moments later a wolf howled. The men close to Kallín felt their swords for comfort. But he knew it was her. He knew she was calling to him. Every part of him wanted to go to her. But he must save his mother. He felt that he was being ripped in two. He stuck to his task.

He pushed on to the edge of the forest. Ahead lay the treacherous marshlands between Hardrada's great army and Fulford. Kallín sent a warning back along the line, "Watch how you step and carry your boots in your hands if you do not wish to have them sucked away from you in the bog."

The men behind passed back the instruction. Hardrada took off his boots and joked to Kallín, "Do you plan to have us arrive naked for the battle?"

Kallín smiled, "The finest warriors ever to walk in the world fought naked."

As they moved on, barefoot, sinking their feet into the sucking bog, Hardrada became curious, "Tell me about these naked warriors."

Kallín told him, "They were the first of the Rohán. They knew no fear … so they had no need of armour."

After some distance Kallín stopped, "The beck at the place you called 'full ford' is on the other side of that embankment," he told Hardrada.

Hardrada moved with Kallín and a half dozen Captains. Lying flat on the top of the ridge on the embankment, they looked down onto the beck then along to the river to see the opposite bank. There they saw Morcar's men spanning the length of the high bank of the beck … waiting to make their ambush.

Hardrada ordered one of his Captains, "Form up here, stay low, stay silent."

Hand signals travelled along the line and the Norsemen moved quickly and quietly into ranks that formed up ten deep along the embankment.

They waited…

The sun climbed to its zenith, and the river waters swirled in the turning tide.

"The water drains quickly from the beck," Hardrada looked to the River Ouse, "Where is Tostig?"

Again they waited…

One cog of the plan cannot move without the other.

At last, Tostig arrived around the bend in the river with the fleet. Hardrada readied his men.

Kallín watched as Tostig quickly beached the boats on the south side of the beck where it met the Ouse and formed up his two thousand men that were a mix of Hardrada's men and Tostig's mercenaries. But it was the ragged mercenaries who made up the front line, and they did not present much of a threat. They began their progress to battle, getting their blood up, hurling insults and war-cries over the now empty beck that separated them from Morcar's line.

Morcar's men got worked up too, and chanted insults back over the beck, beating drums and shields.

Kallín could see that most of Morcar's forces, who numbered around seven thousand, were lightly armed fyrd. Only the front line of the shield wall, some two thousand men, were trained, properly armed and heavily armoured soldiers.

Both sides reached a fever pitch of chanting, and then Tostig ordered his men forward, down into the mud-bed of the beck. They then slogged across it, under waves of withering arrows, to the other side, and then they faced the climb up the steep slippery beck bank to face Morcar's shield wall. It was an impossible assault. They were made into fodder.

Kallín understood why soldiers didn't think about their orders. What man in his right senses would march from a place of safety into death. He looked back at Hardrada's best men formed along the bank, calm, no chanting, simply waiting. They needed no cheering nor speeches to make them keen for the fight. They all had sure cold eyes that looked into the coming battle without any fear or doubts about what they were about to do.

"Look now," Hardrada smiled, "Morcar makes his move. He has the upper hand on Tostig's line and comes down from the high ground to close on them. We go now." Hardrada simply waved his hand and his five thousand warriors rolled over the embankment like fog and swooped quietly down onto the hidden stretch of the beck, moving in a continuous unbroken wave of men, then splitting on the opposite bank, so that half went along to the riverbank and the other half climbed up onto the higher ground behind Morcar's position. Not a sound was made until they made contact with the rear of Morcar's line, and at that moment a great roar went up, five thousand Norsemen simultaneously attacked Morcar's exposed left flank and his rear.

Kallín was impressed at how the Norsemen fought in teams of four so that no man needed to watch his back or his flank. As one warrior went for the head, his fighting mate went for the enemy's legs. If the enemy grabbed the spear, the mate delivered a blow from his axe. Combined, they fought as a single beast with eight arms and legs, pushing hard into the English ranks, breaking their line, and happy to be surrounded by them in melee. Killing them on all sides.

Morcar's flank was now gone, his rear was in full retreat, and, crashing into his front ranks, his entire army collapsed into a disorganised rabble of desperate men. Within minutes the English were retreating in the only direction open to them, across the beck into the drained riverbed and on into the marshlands. The empty riverbed quickly filled with dead and Hardrada'a Norsemen ran easily over the compacted corpses to chase down the retreating English into the marshland that brought them almost to a halt. From that point on, it was butchery.

Hardrada's warriors were busy from noon to dusk, systematically carving their way through eight thousand English fyrd caught in the killing fields between the marshland and the River.

Kallín had not expected to see such determined slaughter. Hardrada made no calls to give the defeated any quarter. No response was made to the many who cried surrender.

Kallín had trained as a Rohán warrior to take life in battle but to give life when the battle was won. This battle at Fulford was long won but the Norsemen went on killing and killing. He began to understand that the Norsemen's killing was driven by a particular kind of hatred. The Norsemen's thirst for killing English men, women and children was a kind of madness. But the part of the battle that disturbed Kallín the most was the fact that Lord Morcar and his brother Edwin had been the first to run. They were safely back behind the walls of York while the peasants that they had marched into battle were slaughtered.

As the sun got low and gave its red flag, Hardrada's Captain came to him and asked, "Should we continue with the slaughter, my King?"

Hardrada looked out over the scene that was no longer a battle, and asked, "How many of them have we put to the sword?"

His Captain answered, "More than half of them … some four thousand. We are down to killing begging farmers and crying ploughboys."

Hardrada nodded, "We need some alive to work the land. Let the remainder live." Then a new thought came before him, and he told

Tostig, "Let us preserve York and offer Morcar a parley."

Tostig was not so forgiving, "I'd sooner march on the city and take it by force."

Hardrada nodded. "Yes. But I would not see it destroyed. We will simply have to carry the cost of rebuilding it ... You will have to rule there. Again. And this time you will rule with more authority."

Tostig understood the reprimand. He had lost York owing to a revolt. After today's lesson in slaughter, there would be no opposing Hardrada's Kingship of the north or the authority of his new Duke of York.

Hardrada added, "We will send them the monk as an emissary."

All eyes turned to Kallín.

41

REVENGE

The sun was low by the time Kallín walked to within sight of the great city of York. His eye was drawn to the bell-tower as six pigeons took flight. He watched them circle once to find their bearings then fly south with their news, making for London. King Harold Godwinson would know of the outcome of the battle at Fulford before dark. The London monks would then send relay pigeons at daybreak to Fécamp. William of Normandy would hear of the news over his breakfast. The Fécamp monks would in turn send relay pigeons to Rome. The Pope would learn of it before his supper tomorrow evening.

As he came closer, he glanced along the top of the York walls to see how many arrows were pointing at him from the crenels, but there were none, and no soldiers either. The great gates were laid wide open; he entered unchallenged.

Inside, there were no soldiers anywhere about the place, nor were there any people to be seen. The residents of York, he guessed, had either fled the city or stayed behind their barricaded doors.

On entering the main cobblestoned courtyard, he saw a face that he knew. Bishop Ealdred came forward, looked at him, and looked again. He recognised the young monk before him as they boy he had sent away as a decoy but also saw that he was now an entirely different creature.

"Brother Osbald."

Kallín approached the bishop and bowed his head, "My Lord

Bishop."

Ealdred placed a deft hand on his shoulder as a blessing and told him, "I am truly glad to see you…" And then as he shook the young monk's hand, he felt the scar of the cross on his palm, "I see you have met with Brother John."

The Bishop knew well of the secretive Brotherhood of Judas that existed within the ranks of the Benedictines, and the less he knew about their activities, the better for him.

Kallín reported, "King Harald Hardrada does not wish to sack York and instead sues for a peaceful surrender of the city."

Ealdred smiled, "I'm sure he does. Look around you … the city is already his. Please come in."

The Bishop's grand quarters seemed somewhat less splendid to Kallín now that he had seen Fécamp. As he entered the great room, he was not surprised to see the brothers Morcar and Edwin.

Morcar smiled, "You are indeed a charmed person."

Kallín responded by reminding him, "Not as charmed as one who leads an army of Englishmen to their slaughter and survives."

They took the slap of insult.

Morcar moved on, "Hardrada offers terms?"

Kallín reached into his habit, withdrew a scroll and handed it to Ealdred who quickly unfurled it and read aloud a quick summation of its contents, "He offers you both lands to the far west ... Tostig will be given the title of The Duke of York."

Morcar asked, "Does Hardrada mean to push on for London and take the crown of England?"

Ealdred rolled up the scroll, "That, it does not say."

The three men looked to Kallín.

"That I do not know," Kallín explained, "But if he should wish to to take London, he has the men to do it." He then told the Bishop, "I need to send a pigeon."

Morcar asked, "A pigeon for where?"

"London."

Morcar was at a loss, "London? Why are you messaging King Harold Godwinson if you are travelling with King Harald Hardrada?"

Kallín replied, "It is how I am instructed."

Morcar snapped, "Instructed by whom?"

Bishop Ealdred interrupted and told Morcar, "That is not a matter that we need to be involved with." He told Kallín, "I will have pigeons ready for you in the morning. It is too near night, and I fear they would roost in the trees, and that would be the end of them. But now, let us make you comfortable for the night."

Kallín answered, "I should return to Hardrada tonight with your answer."

Ealdred explained, "It would greatly aid us for you to wait until the morning. We too are awaiting pigeons."

Kallín nodded, "I will wait out the night."

Kallín woke, made his ablutions and went to the dining room where he ate a hearty breakfast with the Bishop. The doors opened and Brother John entered.

Bishop Ealdred stood without a word and left the room.

John smiled to Kallín and joined him, "How is it with you?"

Kallín smiled, "I am as you see me."

John told him, "Brother Otto tells me that you are bound to Hardrada by his promise to find your mother and return her to you?"

"Yes."

John nodded, "Know that we have found her … She is well."

Kallín filled with an uncontrollable tide of tears.

John went on, "She is in our Abbey in Novgorod. She knows you are alive, and we will bring her to you."

Kallín fell to his knees. Broken. He wept.

After some time, John lifted him back to his feet and told him, "You are no longer held to Hardrada. We have much work to do…"

An hour later Kallín had fully furnished Brother John with all of the relevant information regarding Hardrada's forces. He then accompanied him to the main hall where Brother John held council with Bishop Ealdred and Morcar. They listened as John explained, "Our King Harold marches to us with a great army."

Morcar punched the air.

John went on, "We need to set out our plans."

Morcar nodded, "We could hold behind the walls—"

John cut him off, "We would be overrun in a day. Get me the map."

Morcar rolled a map out onto the table.

John looked it over, "The King of Norway has landed a large portion of his boats at Riccal on the Ouse … We will agree to meet him at a point on the River Derwent to make our surrender. Thereby he will be forced to march overland and not be able to use his fleet."

Morcar followed the logic, "And he will leave a large force men at Riccal to protect his fleet."

John scanned the map for a perfect spot, "Tomorrow."

Morcar saw the flaw in the plan, "Forgive me, Brother, but we do not have the men to meet the Norse King in battle ... It is not enough time for our King Harold to reach us."

John assured him, "Our King will be here by nightfall."

"It's not possible." Morcar shook his head.

John smiled, "We are in the business of the impossible." He looked to Kallín, "Bring the King of Norway and his traitor Tostig to here for noon tomorrow." John pointed at the spot on the map that was eight miles from York, a spot where a bridge crossed the River Derwent at a place called Stamford.

42

STAMFORD BRIDGE

Kallín made the nine mile journey from York back to Riccal along the Roman road. About halfway along, where the road dipped into dead ground and was flanked on both sides by high reeds, in its lowest point where he could not see the way ahead, nor the way behind him, he became aware that hidden eyes were on him to his left and his right. At the same time a figure appeared ahead of him on the road: Luna.

"I had to see it with my own two eyes," Luna told him, "you live so."

"I do."

"You look different."

Kallín immediately went to her, and as he drew closer to her he saw her bump.

"You look much changed too."

She rubbed her stomach, "You put a child in me."

He stopped for a moment, regained his step and put his hand on the bump. "I've been working my way back to you."

She told him, "We've been tracking you."

"I know."

She asked, "Will you come with me now?"

Every fibre of his body wanted to disappear into the thick reeds with her and back to the forest. "Not yet," he told her.

"When so?"

"When I have taken my revenge on the Norsemen."

"When is that?"

"Tomorrow. Look here." He knelt, pulled his dagger and drew out a map showing the spot at Stamford on the river where they would meet and be caught in the trap of the English King. "This is where they will fall."

Luna shrugged, "Leave them to it and come now."

Kallín shook his head, "They will not go there without me."

Luna thought about it for a moment, "Tomorrow. We will wait here then." She marked the ground near them.

Kallín looked at Luna's large belly, "You are too full in the belly to be making battle. Go back to the safety of the cave, and I will follow. Please."

Without any thought, they found themselves embraced and kissing. After some time, a lookout whistled. She withdrew from him, "You have a shadow." She kissed him once more, "Come back to me." And she disappeared into the reeds. A moment after that, a rider appeared on the high ground on the road behind him, and stopped.

Kallín rubbed out the map in the dirt with his foot, and continued on his way.

It was unseasonably warm. The tide was low, causing the fleet tied up at Riccal to be mud-bound on the banks of the Ouse. Kallín was met by guards and taken to the centre of the great Norse camp, to the tent of Hardrada, who listened to his reply from Morcar. He liked the reply.

The Norse King then assembled two thousand of his best men to come with him to Stamford Bridge in order to accept the surrender of Morcar, and take possession of York.

Tostig was in high spirits and close-shaved his face and the back of his head, high up past his ears, in the fashion of a Norman. The morning air was already getting hot. They had a fifteen mile march ahead of them across broken terrain that would take four hours at a steady pace, and Hardrada decided that his men would not need to wear their heavy battle armour.

The men were happy to travel light.

Kallín was called again to the tent of King Hardrada who asked him, "You know the way to this place?"

Kallín told him, "Yes, my lord."

"Good. You will take us there."

Kallín lowered his head, "It will be my honour."

Most of all, Kallín was relishing the slaughter of the Norsemen. He did not love the English King Harold more or less than the Norse King Harald, but he did hate the Norsemen, and he knew how much they, in turn, hated Englishmen. There were many thousands of Norsemen here in Hardrada's army, and perhaps among them were the same men who had broken the treaty with his father, slaughtered his clan and slaved his mother. With his mother now in safe hands, it was indeed an honour and a privilege to lead them all to their slaughter.

Less than a half an hour later, they were on the march. Kallín travelled at the head of the convoy with King Hardrada and Tostig, leading two thousand men across the Yorkshire country. An hour into the journey the men became jovial and began to sing. Two hours in they began to grunt in the heat and curse it. By the third hour of marching, they settled into a grim determined rhythm.

The Derwent came into view, and they followed it until they came to the bridge. They had reached Stamford. It had nothing about it to make it remarkable. Its main feature was a narrow wooden bridge that spanned the river from east to west. It was a good place for a parley, the river separating the armies while the bridge offered a narrow place for them to meet. They stopped and waited in the wide field on the west side where the ground rose in a gentle slope northward. The breeze was cool but did little to fend off the heat of the sun as it climbed to its zenith and hit noon.

"They're late," Tostig grumbled.

Hardrada was clear, "If they are not here before the sun moves out of noon, we cross the bridge and march on York."

They watched the soft-sloped hills to the west of the river and began to see the haze of low-lying dark cloud that clung to the earth.

"Dust," Tostig said.

Hardrada knew from the size of the cloud, "Morcar has comes with an army…"

Tostig added, "Moving fast."

Hardrada weighed that, "So … they are not coming to make a peace." He looked to Kallín, "Well, monk. Did you know of this?"

Kallín shrugged, if he were to go home here and now, he would have the pleasure of telling his father that he had brought the Norsemen to their end, "Morcar is a prideful man. I didn't know of his plan … but I am not surprised by it."

Hardrada laughed, "Pride comes before the fall." He called out to his Captains and instructed them, "It seems they did not learn their lesson at Fulford. This time I will not be so forgiving. Make ready for battle. There will be no quarter given."

The Norsemen cheered.

But Hardrada was working his battle plan on the assumption that he was facing the remnants of the same army of Morcar that he had previously routed only the day before.

His men formed ranks and made ready to do battle.

Closer they came.

Tostig didn't like what he was beginning to see.

Hardrada also watched as it became clear to him that there were thousands of enemy shields glistening in the sun. He began to realise that he was greatly outnumbered, "Is that the King's banner?"

Tostig knew his brother's banner well, "Yes."

Hardrada realised that he was facing the forces of Harold Godwinson. He called two of his best runners and ordered them, "Go back to boats, bring up the reserves."

The runners set off on a journey that would take them an hour. It would then take the reserves, in full armour, more than three hours to arrive. Hardrada added up the hours, "We must hold them at the bridge for half the day."

He made a plan that would counter the advantage of greater numbers by reducing the battlefield to its smallest part: the bridge that was only wide enough for a cart to cross.

Kallín watched the great English army of King Harold Godwinson draw up in ranks on the opposite side of the bridge. Those who were on horses dismounted to prepare for battle. The King of England stayed on his horse so that his men could see him, and he sent his brother Gyrth forward with his monk to make a parley on the bridge.

Harald Hardrada then sent the Godwinsons their brother Tostig to parley. And Kallín, being their monk, was sent with him.

Tostig advised Kallín as they got near the bridge, "Listen well to what is said here and make a good report of it."

The two brothers, Gyrth and Tostig, came together on the bridge.

Kallín did as instructed and paid close attention to the discussion. He was aware that the other monk, who was also a Benedictine, did the same.

Tostig asked Gyrth, "How did you make it from London so quickly?"

Gyrth smiled and warned him, "We have God on our side."

Tostig looked left and right, "I don't see him. Where is he?"

Gyrth shook his head, "Blasphemy. Why am I not surprised? Look ...

Our brother has promised our mother that he will make an honest effort to bring you home. Come with me now, and he will give you an Earldom. He will forgive you."

Tostig was suspicious of the offer, and asked, "An Earldom? Where? On the shithole border with Wales or some such?"

Gyrth was already growing red around the neck from a rising temper, "If it were up to me..." He calmed himself down, and went on, "You will be well and kindly treated."

Tostig smiled, "And in his efforts for a peace, what will he give King Hardrada?"

Gyrth darkened and explained, "We did not march from London to make peace ... Hardrada will be given his allotted six feet of English earth." And then he added, "We have come here to make the same slaughter that Hardrada made on the fyrd at Fulford. There is to be no quarter given to the Norsemen."

Tostig had a decision to make.

Gyrth read the struggle in his brother and reminded him, "You owe this foreign invader no loyalty that is stronger than the blood bond to your brothers."

But Tostig had been too deeply wounded in the past, "The brothers that banished me? The brothers who leave our brother Wulfnoth to rot in a Norman dungeon? I see you have the superior numbers of men, but I don't think you have the superior quality of men. I will do battle on the side of the King of the Norsemen. And I will have York given back to me by him when we are victorious."

Gyrth warned him, "Do not expect quarter, Brother."

Tostig agreed, "And you should expect none either."

The two Godwinson brothers turned and parted company. The two monks gave each other a nod of recognition, then each of the men returned to their respective Kings.

Five minutes later the first wave of a thousand English infantry formed a block and marched on the west side of the bridge to face a similar number of Norsemen holding the east side. Both sides fired tremendous volleys of arrows, and both sides kept the main body of their armies out of the opposing archers' range while the selected combat units moved to the bridge under testudo. There they engaged each other with swords, cutting and slicing under the indiscriminate clouds of arrows that poured down upon them. English and Norse alike died side by side and turned the river beneath them red with their blood. Relentless, four abreast, the hacked corpses piled up, separating the living of the opposing armies with a wall of their dead. But it was the Norsemen who had come to Stamford Bridge in light armour, and they were suffering the highest losses against the well-prepared English who were fully dressed for battle in heavy body armour, chainmail and helmets.

The English infantry were surviving the relentless storm of arrows.

The Norse were not.

The Norsemen had committed the fundamental mistake of underestimating the English resolve. The English took full advantage of the Norsemen's folly.

Kallín observed the Norse frontline give ground.

And so did Harold Godwinson.

Gyrth urged his brother King, "Now."

The English King ordered a second legion of infantry, who were baying to join the fight, into the battle for Stamford Bridge.

On the bridge, the English soldiers at the back of the fighting, reversed their shields, so that they where now slung over their backs to protect their rear, and at the same time a thousand more Englishmen came crashing into them, locking with their countrymen shoulder to shoulder, creating a great scrum made of heavily armoured infantry.

The manoeuvre worked … and foot by bloody foot they heaved and regained twenty feet of England back from the Norsemen.

Hardrada knew he could not hold the English scrum at the bridge.

Kallín expected that the Norse King, with all of the facts clearly laid out in front of him, would order his men to make a good fast retreat to Riccal. They were light and the English were in full armour. They would have easily outrun them. But Kallín learned that sometimes a King will be his own worst enemy, that pride will easily overrule logic. Hardrada, instead of making the tactical retreat to a stronger position from where he would surely have won the day, ordered his men instead into the open plain to form a defensive circle and make a stand. To buy them some time to form the ranks, Hardrada sent twelve of his best men to delay the English advance on the bridge. It was a mission to their death, and Kallín could not understand how quickly and eagerly they marched off to a sure and bloody end. Among the twelve was a notorious giant old berserker that put the young Rohán in mind of the berserker that he killed with Ríona.

Hardrada told Kallín to watch carefully and take good note of what was about to occur. The Rohán monk watched as the twelve elite men took to the bridge, and the rest of the Norsemen fell back to form a huge compacted circle of a thousand shields that all surrounded their King.

They watched and cheered on the last man standing on the bridge, the great berserker, swinging two giant axes that cleaved Englishmen in half and held off their advance for what seemed like an eternity. His body filled with arrows, and still he would not fall, until a number of English spearmen made their way beneath the bridge and speared the great berserker from below.

Moments later the English were crossing the bridge at speed and forming into ranks on the east side of the river.

Hardrada shouted to his men, "If this is to be our last battle, then let us enjoy it! Let us die with our enemy's blood on our swords!"

Kallín, despite himself, was growing evermore impressed by these Norsemen who so wholeheartedly followed their King into death. And even Tostig, who was driven by an insult to his honour to stand with the losing side, was growing in his estimation. It occurred to him that he would most likely die here with the Norsemen.

The English began with volleys of arrows. The Norse shield-wall was expertly tight, and all of those fine arrows were simply being wasted, as was the time spent in firing them, time that that got Hardrada's reserves closer to him.

The English King, Harold Godwinson, was aware that he did not have Hardrada's full army in front of him. His scouts had informed him that at least half of Norsemen, some three thousand men, had stayed to guard the fleet at Riccal. Even a novice commander would understand that he had gotten lucky, and if he was to make good on it, he must use his superior numbers to win victory before Hardrada's reinforcements arrived. He must press his advantage.

Godwinson sent in his jacklers and skirmishers who worked the perimeter of the Norse defensive circle, searching for its weakest part. With no part of the wall being weaker or stronger than any other part, Godwinson knew he could not afford the time, and he ordered a costly full assault. A thousand English infantry formed up into a tight pack with their biggest and heaviest armoured men to the front. These front row men carried a shield in each hand and interlocked arms with the man on either side of them. Behind them, the second row carried spears. Behind them, the great body of swordsmen made ready to pour through the breach. The English attack-wall met the Norse shield-wall in a great heaving scrum— shield on shield — then both sides locked. The Norsemen held their ground with equal measure. Then on a timed drum-beat command, the English scrum pushed in a well drilled unison. Likewise, the Norse shield-wall pushed back. And that is how it was for a time, both sides pushing with all of their might, feet grinding the earth underfoot into muck. Then the second row of English spears began stabbing over the shoulders of the front row of shields into the eyes and necks of the lightly armoured Norsemen, blinding and wounding them. Norse arteries were opened and great gushes of blood went up to English cheers. The English scrum took heart, and soon worked out that they were better armoured than their opposition, and greater in number. Their spirits sang; great cheering began to come from the rear ranks, and formed into one word, shouted in unison, again and again: "England. England. England."

Then half a foot by half a foot the English scrum moved forward ... slowly, relentlessly, cutting, hacking, unstoppable. The English were in the ascension now.

Kallín watched as the Norse shield-wall collapsed. The English swordsmen poured in through the breach and began to put the Norsemen to the sword. Hardrada charged forward with his best men around him, and even though he was now an old man in his fifties, he fought, for a time, like the famed great warrior of legend. But his move forward put him in range of the English archers who released a snarling cloud of some thousand arrows at him, and while most of those arrows were absorbed by the men around the Norse King, one found its way into his neck and felled him. His close guard withdrew their fallen King from the fray and carried him to the centre of the great circle, and there they formed a testudo shell of shields around him. Kallín was called and entered into the sanctuary of the protective interior of the testudo.

Arrows now fell like rain outside and Hardrada spoke as best he could while the wound in his throat bled into his gullet and filled his lungs with blood ... slowly drowning him.

He gripped the monk's hand, "Keep a true account."

And on those last words his lungs could no longer take air. He lasted without breathing for as long as a man can hold his breath, and then his body convulsed, his eyes rolled, and he became still.

Kallín felt the King's grip fall away.

Outside the arrows fell heavier on the shield-shell, the English advance was running amok.

The Captain of the Kingsguard ordered his men back to the fight.

When Harald Hardrada's body was displayed to his men, his loss unleashed a new wave of ferocity in them, and they savagely started to take on the Englishmen with no care for their own lives. Many of them roared oaths to follow their King to Valhalla. And they did. But no matter the amount of rage unleashed for their dead King, there were just too many thousands of equally stout-hearted Englishmen, and they soon were slaughtering the Norsemen.

Kallín watched all around him as relentless fighting flowed like a great dam breaking its banks and flooding the fields. He had no idea why the warriors seemed not to see him. They moved around him as if he were a tree. For a time he imagined that he was not even there and that he was somehow in a dream. For how else could he be still alive amongst all of this carnage? Then across the battlefield he saw his opposite, the monk who travelled with the English King. He too was moving among the dead and dying in the middle of the fighting, and he made his way to Kallín and called to him, "Give comfort to them, Brother! No Christian will harm you."

Kallín realised that it was his monk's habit that protected him from attack.

Suddenly he felt a hand gripping his ankle and saw a bloodied soldier that he could not tell if he was Norse or English. He was just desperate and dying. The man cried out to him, "Bless me!"

Kallín knelt, he did not believe himself to be a true monk but he knew that in this moment it did not matter. He could help a man out of fear and help to send a soul on his way. Just as he had done with Ríona.

He dipped his thumb in the blood flowing from the dying man and he made the sign of the cross on his forehead and told him, "Go home..."

When the man expired, Kallín went to the next man who was dying, knelt and did the same. All around him the cleaving, hacking, stabbing and bludgeoning went on in a great rage of roaring and screaming, but he was looking and listening through all of that for the crying of the dying. He cared not who they were or on what side they decided to die. As he rubbed the head of man after man, he knew he would never forget the look in their eyes as they transformed from fear to a calm acceptance and left the world. He had no idea how long he had been going about the battlefield when he came across a bloody face he knew. "Tostig?"

Tostig had been cleaved and stabbed, and he was on his way out. He smiled to Kallín, and for a moment the cacophony of battle ran over them as if it were no more than the sound of waves crashing on the shore.

"Tell Wulfnoth..."

Kallín smiled at the name of the beautiful lunatic who had fed him cake and saved him.

Tostig smiled too, and continued, "Tell him how brave we were."

"I will tell him."

"He is truly without sin, is he not?"

Kallín told him, "Wulfnoth is a living saint."

Tostig smiled harder at that, "Relay to my King brother ... to bring him home. And pray for me."

Kallín brought his mouth close to Tostig's ear and whispered softly, "Go home, Tostig ... go to your father." He felt Tostig's life leave him in a sigh of relief.

The sun was setting as the killing came to a lull only to be rekindled by the arrival of more Norse warriors from Riccal. But having run the distance in full armour, they reached the fight exhausted, and they too were easily made fodder by the jubilant Englishmen who were winning the day.

The victorious King Harold Godwinson walked over the field looking for his brother and his eye was caught by the bloody monk going from corpse to corpse. He called out, "You there, monk, come here."

Kallín made his way to the victorious King , "My lord King."

"Where has my brother fallen?"

Kallín lead them to the body of Tostig, and told him, "He wished me to relay to you a message."

Harold was not sure if he wanted a message from the dead, but he knew he must hear it, "Tell me."

Kallín explained, "He wished you to bring Wulfnoth home."

Gyrth, who never left his King brother's side, turned away as if he had been wounded by the mention of Wulfnoth's name. And Kallín noticed that Harold's eyes filled up. But neither man said a word. They both simply nodded and then knelt by the corpse of their brother. The entirety of the English army, on seeing their King kneel, also knelt. Their own monk joined his King and lead them in prayers.

Kallín went back to his business of finding and comforting the dying.

As night fell, those that were victorious at the battle at Stamford Bridge entered into the natural euphoria that comes with having survived a battle, especially one that took so many thousands from the world. As the champion English King and his army entered York, the inhabitants turned out to welcome them with open arms and the great celebrations began. Kallín saw his opportunity for escape and return to Luna. He made his way to the stables.

"You deserve to go your own way, you have more than earned the privilege," a voice spoke to him from the darkness. He knew it was Brother John even before he stepped into the light to show himself, and he added, "And should you wish to leave now, I will not stop you. Your mother will be brought back to England and freed. She will not be a hostage."

Kallín was not for turning, he'd had enough of being a monk, "Thank you, Brother John. Then I will be on my way."

John nodded, "But go in the knowledge that a great war is coming that will engulf all of England in flames. It will find you and yours, even in the deepest forest."

Kallín reminded him, "The war was settled today at Stamford Bridge."

John smiled, "If only that were true, I would be out on the streets dancing with the rest of the people. Sadly, that was simply a precursor to the real fight. You know that William the Norman Duke will invade."

Kallín argued, "He has lost his opportunity. His fleet has dispersed. It will be next spring before he can make his invasion. By then, England will have grown stronger with an even bigger army to resist him."

John moved closer to him, "William's fleet merely relocated to the coast of Brittany so as to give Harold the comfort to come north and fight Hardrada. William now readies his fleet, and he will land at Pevensey in two days."

John watched Kallín struggle with that, "You have seen the Norman's war plan, and you have seen their training, their Chevalerie and their crossbow archers ... And you have seen how the English go about their battle work. Tell me now, do you doubt that William will win?"

Kallín did not answer that. It was clear to him that the Normans were a far superior fighting force, and that their Chevalerie would cut down the standing English ranks of infantry.

John smiled and told him, "Uneducated people think that knowledge is a gift. But you and I know that knowledge is a great burden, even a curse. We in the Brotherhood of Judas believe that God has turned his back on the world because it is the beginning of a new time, the time of Man. We have moved out of the time of God, and we are now living in the days when we are in control of our own destiny. We can steer our own course. With that knowledge, Brother, comes a great responsibility, not just to yourself, but to all of those you know and love, a responsibility to those who are strangers to you, who are blissfully ignorant of the truth. They are the flock who are ignorant of the actions of the good shepherd who protects them from the wolves."

Kallín sat on a barrel. He understood what John was saying to him, and he longed for the time when he would not have understood him. If he were to truly protect Luna and his child, and his clan, he had to be like Judas, and do what needed to be done. He asked John, "You wish me to go to King Harold and relay to him what I know of William's battle tactics?"

John sat beside him and produced a flask of port from his pocket, "No ... The outcome of the battle between William and Harold is a foregone conclusion even down to the time and place that William will win England. We cannot have any influence over that." John took a swig of his port and handed the flask to Kallín, and he went on, "Rome has decided that William will be King of England."

Kallín drank. The hot port felt good coursing through him, "What does Rome want of me so?"

John explained, "What Rome wants and what the Brotherhood wants are not married. England has a godgiven King in waiting."

"Edgar?"

"Yes..." John went on, "When Harold falls in battle, we must have the boy in London to be crowned. The Pope will not side with the Bastard Duke William against the legitimate blood King. And I feel that England will unite behind the boy. What do you think?"

43

HASTINGS

Brother John explained to Kallín what must be done. He was to travel to Riccal. On the way he would be met by a half dozen brothers. They would commandeer one of the boats from the abandoned Norse fleet and sail back down the Humber to the sea and then directly north along the coast to Scotland where they would collect Edgar and sail him south along the coast to the Thames and London.

King Harold's head pulsated with pain. There had been long celebrations in York for two days and nights, and now he was paying the piper for the merry tune. Gyrth came into his chamber to disturb him. Harold read his brother's face and knew he carried bad news, "What is it?"

Gyrth told him, "William has landed at Pevensey."

Harold thought about that for a moment, "What uncanny timing. And to choose Pevensey rather than sail straight up the Thames to London? What's he at?"

Harold peeled himself out of the bed, wobbled to a barrel of cold water and plunged his head into it, leaving it under the water to let the cold bite deeply into his skull. Only when he felt the rods of shock touch in the centre of his mind, did he pull his head out of the barrel and suck in the air. As he exhaled, he announced, "We march for London!"

Less than an hour later the convoy of the English army, made up of some ten thousand hungover men, marched behind their hungover

King. By noon most of the ill effects of their celebrations had been marched off and Harold discussed his tactics with his brother as they went along, "He will try for London before we get there."

Gyrth assured him, "We are told that he still does not have his full complement of men. He awaits his full force."

Harold was pleased to hear that. He didn't fancy having to take back London, and he would much rather be defending the City.

Gyrth added, "Leofwine has rallied the Londoners, and they are setting defences."

Harold shook his head, "I dread to think of our little brother anywhere near a battle."

Gyrth laughed, "Well, should things turn bad, he can always disguise himself as a maid, as we know he has great skills at that."

They both shared a laugh.

The sound of the King's laughter infused the men behind him with confidence. They began to sing a song about marching, and soon the seemingly endless convoy was in fine voice.

They stuck straight on the Roman Road so as to travel quickly the 190 miles from York to London, marching into the night and not stopping for twenty hours until they reached Lincoln the next day. Here, Harold let his exhausted army lay down in the road to be rested and watered for half a day.

Gyrth warned his brother, "A lot of the men will be going lame at this pace."

Harold bit back, "Better lame than dead. We will limp to London if we must."

In London Leofwine was busy organising what defensive forces he could find. It was not enough of a fighting force to stop an army, but he calculated that when William came to take the city, he would most likely come through the Southwark and over London Bridge. So he focused his attentions in the warren of the Southwark streets, blocking off some streets with false walls, and so directing oncoming foreign forces, who didn't know the lay of the land, in circles. It would not stop the Normans, but it would slow them down and hopefully make them easier targets for the London archers and spearmen. He poured over a scrawled map of the Southwark.

Edyth entered and told him, "Worry not, Leo ... our brothers have returned."

"So soon?"

The bells began to ring out, and the city erupted in cheering as

Harold's army returned through the north gate. By evening the army was billeted and eating.

Harold ate with his brothers and sister. He was troubled, "Why did William land at Pevensey?"

Gyrth offered, "It has a good Roman fort."

"For defence," Harold pointed out, "he's landed to invade ... not hold ground. And yet ... he has not marched on London."

Leofwine went over some of his reports, "He is raiding supplies and wasting farmland from the surrounding area ... Bexhill and Hastings."

"From our lands of Wessex — as an insult?" Gyrth asked.

They were for a moment at a loss as to the motives of William's actions, until Edyth spoke, "I am told that he carries the Papal banner..."

This brought a chill to the discussion.

Harold nodded, he understood the significance of it now, "Of course, Pevensey, Hastings... Lands confiscated by our father from the monks..." Harold thought and grew angry, "The church has been working against us ... I want all of the monks of the land imprisoned."

"We cannot," Edyth told him.

"I am King of England."

She reminded him, "But you are not King of heaven ... The monks are not answerable to any king."

Gyrth added, "Our sister is right, brother. Should you harm the monks, we will have the whole of Christendom invading our shores. Let us fight the battle that is in front of us."

Harold knew they were right, but it did not make it any easier to swallow. All he could do was set himself to making his defences.

A week later William had still not attacked London. Instead he continued to send out raids to provision his troops and began to waste Dover.

Gyrth worried, "He has an endless supply of food to raid, and winter comes. We have some fifteen thousand soldiers to feed and billet, and the Londoners grow tired of the military presence inside the walls. Does William mean to wait for a revolt and then lay siege on us?"

Leofwine paced. He was by no means a war general, but one thing became clear to him, "The longer you wait to take the battle to him, the more people become convinced that you fear him."

Harold turned on his brother, but stopped his hand before he struck him. His little brother spoke the truth. "You are right. I will keep the army behind the walls no longer. They are well rested and eager for battle. We will march to meet William in the morning. Make the preparations."

That night the smiths and armourers got busy making final repairs and adjustments to armour. The bright glow from their furnaces was a sure sign to Norman spies that the English army was making ready for battle. In the morning, those men who had an appetite ate. Those who thirsted drank. Most of the men saw to their weapons. Just before daybreak the gate opened, and the English army marched out of the city over London bridge and eagerly began the sixty mile march west along the coastal road. They made the most of the daylight, and when the early darkness fell, they made camp near Winchelsea some eight miles from William's positions at Hastings. The King of England was in high spirits as he looked over a battle map and shared the fire with his brothers, "Scouts tell me that he's left the high ground unsecured. We'll quick-march on Hastings at dawn and take the advantage."

Gyrth did not dampen his brother's enthusiasm, but he knew that if William had left them the high ground then there was a reason for it. But he could not figure out what that reason would be, so he did not raise his concerns.

The next morning William's scout returned to him and informed him that the English King had assembled his forces on the high ground, just as he had planned. The Captains of the Chevalerie were keen to hear William's plans and his reasoning for giving up the high ground to the English. William explained to them, "It is impossible to know your enemy's battle plan but now we know Harold's. He now has only one option: Defend the hill … It pins his army in place. And we can use the advantage of our Chevalerie to come and go at them, cutting them down freely."

The battle at Hastings began without a parley or any formalities. Firstly, the Norman Chevalerie tormented and bloodied the English shield-wall with thundering charges of deadly lances, coming and going at will. None of the English had met this tactic of fighting on a horse before. For a time they had nothing to offer. But Tostig then ordered the men to quickly begin spiking the ground with spears to deter the charging horses. The defensive worked and deterred a Norman charge on the English right flank, causing them to turn in a retreat. In the process some lamed horses threw some thirty riders, who then proceeded to run back to their lines, and Gyrth, seeing an opportunity, ordered his infantry to chase them down.

Harold watched in dread as his overly eager brother led his right flank in chasing a retreat that Harold feared was feigned.

As soon as Gyrth's infantry were far enough away from the safety of the shield-wall, the retreating Normans turned and faced the English and pinned them. Then two more waves of Chevalerie arrived at a fast gallop from both sides and swarmed Gyrth and his men, cutting them down, and killing Gyrth.

Harold had never considered being in a battle without the stouthearted Gyrth by his side, but here he was, in a field in Hastings with his right flank gone and his lines being devastated by damned Normans on horseback.

On the next Norman charge, when the Chevalerie made contact with the English shield wall, they held firm and engaged the English infantry in costly close quarter combat. Then unnoticed in the clouds of battle, the 'Trieur d'Élite' archer, hidden safely in their ranks, stood in his stirrups with a clear line of sight to his target. He shouldered his crossbow, took aim — and fired.

The aim was true and the bolt found the eye-slit of Harold Godwinson's helmet. The King of England was killed instantly.

Within minutes Englishmen began to lose their resolve, those furthest back broke ranks and retreated. The front ranks and the shield wall subsequently collapsed, and the Chevalerie poured in and made sport of the killing with their deadly lances.

Leofwine looked on. He had not come to the battle to be of any practical use. He never professed to be a fighter. He had ridden with his brothers to show that the Godwinsons were as one. Now he had watched his two brothers being killed in quick succession. Men came to him for orders. He knew this battle was lost, he ordered a retreat to London. However, had Leofwine taken any interest in military tactics he would have known that you cannot make an unguarded retreat. The English retreated from the field without a rearguard, and they were torn apart by pursuing Chevalerie.

Somewhere in the slaughter Leofwine was cut down so that all three Godwinson brothers were now dead in the same field.

The House Of Godwin had come to a bloody end.

When the battle was over, William ordered all the dead to be left for rotting . His army was to march immediately on to Dover. A thousand of his best Chevalerie were sent to take London and prepare it for his arrival into the city.

Unbeknownst to William, Edgar the Atheling had arrived into London by boat with his trusted monk that they called Moine des Loups.

Word came quickly to London of Harold's defeat.

The Witan met quickly and unanimously made Edgar King of England.

Edgar held a private council with Kallín and his trusted Huscarl Wulfstan. He shook his head, "I do not think I will be King very long. I have no army and the Normans approach in great numbers."

Kallín had found Leofwine's plans to defend the Southwark and told King Edgar, "This is a good plan." Showing him the map, he explained, "The Normans' strength is their ability to fight on horseback. But they need open ground to form lines of horses and make ferocious charges at standing infantry lines. But the Southwark is such a warren that there is no open ground. They will be forced to move through it in single file to make progress."

Edgar looked at the map, "Where they can be met one at a time."

Kallín added, "And blindsided."

Edgar looked to Wulfstan who was looking on, "What do you think?"

Wulfstan smiled, "I think the Normans will not cross London bridge, my King."

Edgar was delighted, "I will lead the attack and-"

Wulfstan cut him off, "My King, the sight of you being in reach will give more encouragement to the enemy than it will to your men. If I might suggest, it would be better for you to stay atop the wall, where all can see you but not reach you with arrows, and let us take the fight to them in the Southwark."

Edgar worried, "Do we have enough men?"

Wulfstan smiled, "We have around three hundred."

Edgar liked that and added, "A fortuitous number."

The thousand Chevalerie galloped onto the Southwark, expecting no resistance, but immediately found the main road barricaded. A flurry of arrows flew from unseen positions in the sprawl of shanty huts, and pinged harmlessly on the Norman armour. The Norman Captain split his men so that they went forward to either side of the barricade and entered the narrow winding walkways of the Southwark interior. They did not have far to venture before the 'hit and run' attacks began. The Huscarls brought the most ferocious of these attacks that left riderless horses galloping about in a panic, some dragging their dead rider along the ground, his foot pinned in the infamous Norman stirrup. Other men galloped without an arm, and there was even one Norman seen galloping on his horse without his head.

The Chevalerie soon realised that they were being lambs to the slaughter in the tight confines of the Southwark and they withdrew, but as they fled they set buildings alight. The Southwark burned all night long. In the morning it was ashes, but the Norman Chevalerie were nowhere in sight.

However, everyone feared that the Normans would be coming back.

William was furious when he heard of Edgar being crowned King, and he went into a blind rage when he was informed by his monk that Rome had sent word that he must now lower the Papal Banner.

"Am I to leave England?" he roared at the Emissary from Rome.

"No, my lord," the Emissary explained, "but from this point on, the Holy Father cannot take sides in this war. But … should you win, he will bless you as the King of England."

William reconsidered his position and realised that, if anything, breaking from the support of Rome was a fortuitous turn of events for it meant that he would not be held in check by the Bishops and monks who constantly shadowed his every move and were always petitioning him to show mercy and restraint.

"Now I can go at them as I wish to," he told his Captains.

The Papal powers that had kept William in check, had now released a demon upon England. The Normans began inflicting a circle of devastation around London, looting Dover, Canterbury and Winchester and burning everything that lay between them. Outside of London, there was nothing to stop William.

Brother John made his way to London and found Kallín, "You must get King Edgar to safety. I fear the Witan will hand him over to William."

Kallín knew the situation, William was closing in, Earls were bending the knee along the way. He asked John, "Where is safe for him?"

"York."

Kallín thought of the long treacherous journey, and they would not be able to sail out of the Thames, it was now full of Norman warships, nor would they be able to use the roads that were full of Norman patrols and checkpoints.

John added, "You are the only one who can find the way."

Kallín cautioned, "It is not an easy way through woods and marsh. Our young King might be better off in the custody of William."

The voice of Edgar interrupted them, "I would rather be dead."

Kallín nodded to the young King, "We will be weeks in the open, and winter is coming."

Edgar understood, "In case we do not make it. I want to perform one final act as King before we leave." Edgar looked to Wulfstan, "Give me your sword." Wulfstan handed over his weapon.

Edgar told Kallín, "Kneel before me."

Kallín knelt.

Edgar placed the tip of the sword on Kallín's shoulder, "In the witness of Brother John and Wulfstan, I make you Duke of York... What name will you be called?"

"Kallín."

"Kallín?"

"It is my Rohán name." He explained.

"So be it. Rise Sir Kallín of the Rohán, Duke of York."

Kallín stood.

Edgar hugged him, "We will leave London as equals."

Kallín smiled, "Thank you... My King."

John told them, "I shall have it written, and when we find a way to drive the Normans from England, and take back the realm, we will celebrate ... Until then, you must go and stay alive or we have no ground to fight on. As long as you are alive, there is hope for England."

Kallín decided, "We will travel to York — just us two."

Edgar was surprised, "Not with Wulfstan?"

"No. The Normans will be looking for you travelling with an escort. Two woodsmen can slip through towns and villages unnoticed."

"Woodsmen?" Edgar was confused, "Not monks..."

"No," Kallín explained, "If we are to survive the cold, we must dress in furs and hunt as we go. We will be woodsmen."

In the dead of night John and Wulfstan escorted them to the north gate. John blessed them on their journey, "Be brave in all things and know that God is on your side." And he turned to Kallín, "Do not forget the Brotherhood that you are sworn to, and the brothers who are sworn to you."

With that they set off into the darkness, and after some distance they left the road and made their way into the outland.

44

SILVATICI

The pair walked through the night hours without talking. The day began to break. Kallín told Edgar, "Should I be killed, you must keep on for York." He stopped and drew on the ground with his dagger, "You will know your way by keeping the coast on your right until you can go no further. That water will be the great Umber. Follow the river by Grim Haven until it splits away right to be the Ouse that flows from the north. This water brings you to York… "

Edgar insisted, "You will not be killed."

Kallín smiled, "I like how sure you are about that."

Edgar nodded, "I plan to make sure you stay alive."

Kallín smiled again, "But should your plans fail, please set this map to your memory and … when you are here." Kallín pointed to the part of his map that was across the river from Grim Haven, "You might meet Luna. You remember her?"

"Of course." Edgar laughed, "How could one forget her?"

Kallín agreed, "Yes. You might meet her. Tell her I was always working my way back to her "

The young King saw the seriousness in his companion's eyes and understood the nature of their journey. "On my word I will find her and tell her."

Kallín suddenly looked into the nearby field.

Edgar whispered, "What is it?"

Kallín whispered, "Rabbits."

Edgar was at a loss, "What rabbits?"

Kallín explained, "The ones we are to eat."

Then Kallín handed him a bow and an arrow, "Here."

Edgar made no effort to take it, "I cannot use it so well as you can."

Kallín wasn't buying it, "I know for a fact that you are tutored in archery."

Edgar explained, "Yes. Sending the arrow to a target. A rabbit is a different matter."

Kallín read him, "You have never hunted before?"

Edgar shrugged, "I have always been ... indoors. And many of the rabbits I knew were ... pets."

Kallín shook his head, "What is a pet?"

Edgar searched for the words, "Like a favoured hound."

Kallín's eyes popped wide with amazement, "A rabbit is not a hound. What good would it be for hunting?"

Edgar shrugged, "It gave me pleasure to pet them?"

"Pet them?" Kallín was still at a loss.

Edgar tapped Kallín upon his head, "Thus."

"What a strange practice. And did you then eat them, when you had petted them?"

Edgar sighed, "No. You don't eat a creature that you also pet."

Kallín was very lost, "What do you do with them?"

Edgar made one more attempt, "You just keep them. To pet them."

Kallín thought about that, then raised his arrow and found a rabbit. Then quickly found another.

A copse of trees made perfect cover for them to skin and cook their rabbits. Kallín did both the skinning and the cooking and Edgar rambled on about his life in the Royal Court of Hungary, "For so long there I would only wish to be out of it and in England. Now look at me. I am a wildman. And I am cold."

"This is not cold," Kallín assured him.

"No?" Edgar wondered, "How cold have you gotten?"

Kallín turned the rabbits on the spit, "I do not know because at a certain place in being cold, you lose all feeling in your body."

Edgar liked that, "That's not so bad then, is it? To feel nothing."

Kallín shrugged, "But you get all the pain when you are warming up again. Tenfold."

Edgar nodded, "That makes sense."

Kallín asked him, "Sense how?"

Silvatici 1066: The English Resistance

Edgar surmised, "If you have pain, it must go somewhere, and when you cannot feel it, you are saving it up as you would coins in a purse."

Kallín thought about that. There was truth in it, "And revenge ... is that the same then, you think?"

Edgar weighed that, "Yes. I would imagine that the longer you cure your revenge the more delicious it is when you serve it."

Kallín handed him a cooked rabbit on a stick, "Then in that case I am looking forward to putting the Bastard William on a spit."

"And I will eat the other half of that meal with you!"

They both laughed and got stuck in to the rabbit.

Kallín advised, "We should keep some meat for later in the day."

Edgar agreed. But neither of them saved any meat, and they were soon lying on their backs, sucking on bones and watching the clouds go by.

"I am too fat to walk," Edgar groaned.

"I am the same," Kallín agreed and added, "I missed eating rabbit on a stick."

"Hmm." Edgar asked him, "Have you ever had smokey rasher?"

Kallín told him, "I had it in York with the monks."

Edgar thought of other delicious things, "What about cream and strawberries."

"I had cream in Normandy... But not with berries," Kallín told him, "the best berries are in the bramble."

"What is that?"

"It is the place where the berries grow, and they are protected by thorns. It was our safe place to hide."

"What happened?"

"Norsemen burned it down."

"It wasn't a good safe place then, was it?"

"No." And Kallín reminded himself, "Nowhere is safe." He got up, "We need to move. But wait..."

Kallín pulled up fistfuls of long reads and high grass and wove it into their furs until they looked like two bushes, "Now we can walk in the open."

They left the cover of the trees and set off over the open ground keeping a view of the coast to their right but their eyes peeled to their left. If any danger was going to come their way it would come from the west. Should they see any movement the plan was simple, "Stand still like a bush."

Some days later William accepted the surrender of the Witan and the

Crown of England. But on taking the City of London, he was told that Edgar had vanished. The new King immediately ordered a search and then offered a great bounty on Edgar's head. As the letters of congratulations and recognition came pouring in from the various states of Europe, warnings also came from Hungary, The Holy Roman Empire and even Rome that William should take great care not to harm the deposed young King Edgar, and that if he should find him, he should be taken into safety. Unharmed.

William also saw the great danger of Edgar making his way into exile and being protected by a foreign power to once more await his opportunity to take the crown. He ordered his Captains, "Double the bounty. When you find him, kill all who are with him, so that he will be alone when he is brought to me."

The great bounty on Edgar's head made the word spread like wildfire across the land. But the people of the land did not see it as a bounty on a criminal, they saw it as a bounty on their rightful King. It gave all who heard the news that Edgar was still alive hope.

Kallín and Edgar once more found themselves in Grim Haven.

"We need to cross the Humber," but the tide was not fully out. Kallín knew the current of that wide expanse of the water was too strong to swim across, "We will slip away in a boat."

Edgar advised him, "We would do well to stay away from the Wolf's Head ... It's a place of ill repute and full of the worst types."

Kallín wondered, "How is it you know so much of such a place?"

Edgar shrugged, "I have heard soldiers speak of it…"

The dockside heaved with traders and seafarers and nobody took too much notice of two scruffy woodsmen mingling among them. Kallín knew what he was looking for, "We want a small skiff that two of us can row..." Then he wondered, "Have you rowed a boat before."

"I have not," Edgar told him, "but I have seen it done many times... It looks simple enough."

Kallín groaned, "Skilled hands have a way of making difficult tasks look easy..." Then he spotted the perfect craft for them, tied on a long rope and resting on the strand. "We wait for the night to steal that boat, and then we will cross under cover of darkness."

Edgar worried, "I fear we do not have the luxury of time to wait…"

"Why?" Kallín asked.

Edgar whispered, "We are being watched."

Kallín looked to the crowds that passed them by without a care, and saw that Edgar was right. One man stayed fixed on the spot at a stall, pretending to examine some wares there, but all the time shooting quick looks over his shoulder in their direction. Then further along the dock two more men were watching them.

Edgar admitted, "I may have come across them before..."

"In what way?"

Edgar explained, "I think I had an altercation with one of their companions in the Wolf's Head tavern."

"I see, what was the nature of the altercation."

"Well ... it ended with one of their company being decapitated ... and it most likely revealed my true identity and lead to the incident in the monastery, which you were part of."

"I see." Kallín needed to rapidly change their plan. He looked out onto the strand that spanned the great mile-wide estuary of the Humber at low tide.

"We have to run," Kallín told him.

"Run?" Edgar asked, "Where?"

"Out there..." Kallín nodded to the estuary.

In the next moment they were both running out onto the wet sands, splashing through the standing pools and rivulets.

A dozen men broke from the crowds and chased after them. Then other bounty hunters soon realised the great prize that was running free in the estuary, and in the next few moments some fifty or more men were chasing them.

"Don't look back!" Kallín warned Edgar, "Stay as straight as you can for the far bank."

They made good ground until they came to the wide fast flow of the river that sat deeply in the middle of the estuary.

"Strip!"

Edgar was not sure he heard right until he saw Kallín quickly peeling off his furs and getting naked. He looked back and got sight of what was coming after them, and then he also began to strip.

The two naked boys plunged into the ice cold water and the strong current immediately swept them along in the direction of the sea. They both swam hard and slowly made way against the pull of the current.

Behind them, hasty bounty hunters jumped into the water, clothed, and were quickly swallowed into the undertow and washed away. It looked like the rest might think better of it, but a number of fresh men arrived with small skiffs that they quickly filled with eager bounty hunters who began to row.

At last, Edgar and Kallín felt solid ground under their toes and they scrambled and crawled up the far bank and broke into a staggered run to the far shore, and the safety of the forest that lay just beyond it.

It was not long until men crossed the river and closed on them.

"I can't." Edgar fell to his knees.

"We are so close! Look!" Kallín implored him, "The trees."

Every part of Edgar wanted to make it to those trees, but he could not move.

The first of the men closed in to take his spoil but was suddenly brought down with a sure arrow into his head that killed him on his feet. His corpse wandered a few steps before slapping down into a puddle.

The hoard of bounty hunters stopped for a moment and turned to the trees. They shared looks, and moved as one, slowly, forward to the prize, only to be drenched in a cloud of arrows that took out half of their number dead on the spot and injured all those who remained.

One of the wounded men looked to the trees and saw a figure emerge from the darkness, her face painted green and her wild red hair woven with vines. He roared a warning, "Silvatici!"

All of those men who could turn and run away, did so. Those who could not run away, crawled away.

Kallín smiled to the apparition walking out from the forest: Luna

Aifi, Brun and Dawn came running out and scooped their arms under Edgar and helped him into the safety of the forest.

Kallín walked to Luna, and they kissed.

Then they too vanished into the interior of the trees.

Epilogue

EPILOGUE

King William of England listened to the reports from Grim Haven about the Silvatici rescuing Edgar and the 'Moine des Loups'. He ordered a thousand of his Chevalerie to go to the north and search the forest until they find Edgar and kill every last Silvatici.

Printed in Great Britain
by Amazon